Ascension

Matthew Johnson

Ascension

Published by Untold Stories

Riverside California

Copyright © 2016 Matthew Johnson

Cover design by Farrah Evers

All rights reserved.

ISBN: 0997084618

ISBN-13: 978-0997084610

Dedication

To all the hard-working artists. May your dreams come true. As always, to my darling Wendi.

Author's Note:

The following is a continuation of *Retribution* a novella found on my website for free at www.professorgrimdark.com, or in the appendicies at the end of this novel. Enjoy

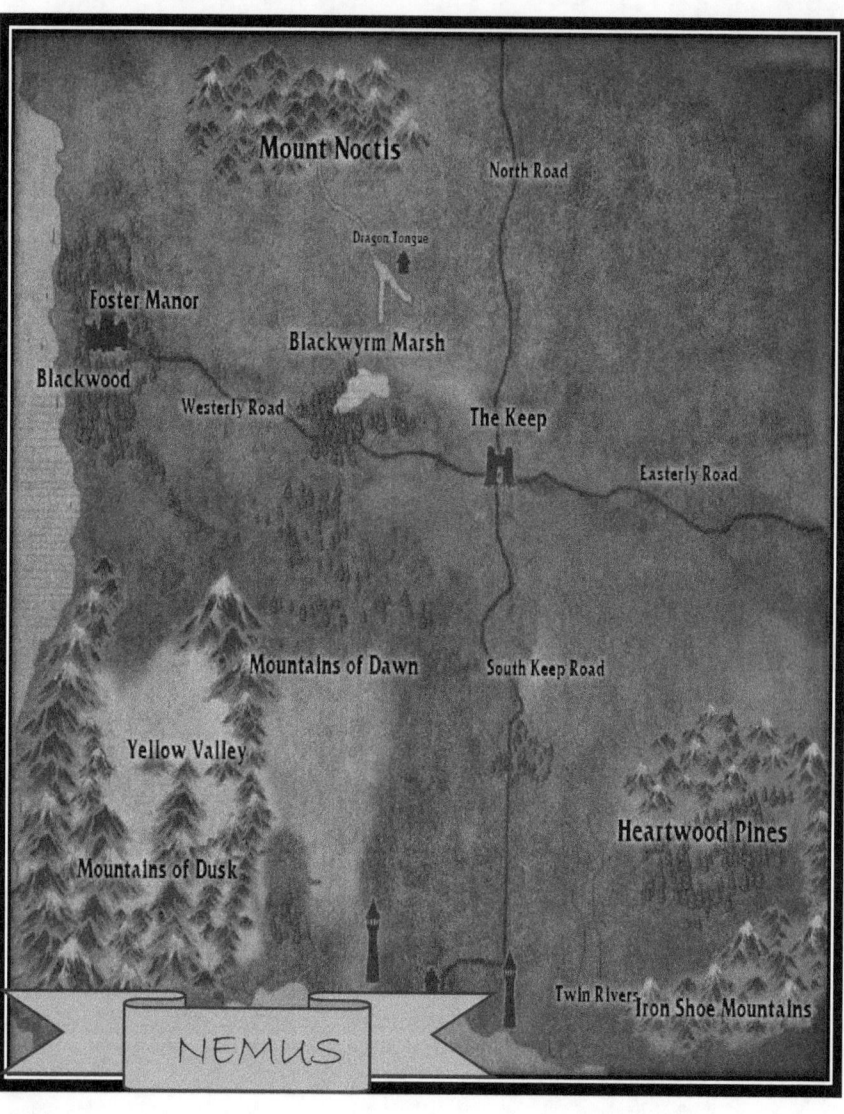

Table of contents

PROLOGUE: TIGHTENING THE YOKE

𝒫ale blue light radiated from the stone walls in the Grand Hall. White mist draped from the ceiling, carrying the scent of spiced cider and sweet pastries. In the far corner, an ancient aria played on the golden strings of Harmony's Harp. A long wooden table occupied the center of the room. Exotic fruits overflowed golden platters and mead shimmered in silver chalices, enough food and drink for three dozen men. At the head sat a woman, her ageless face contemplating Huron as he entered the hall. Cobalt eyes betrayed nothing of her intent.

"You sent for me, Mother." Huron removed his helm and held it against his right hip, above the hilt of a long sword. A second was scabbard on his left. Emblazoned swords crisscrossed the chest of his black scaled armor, an iconic insignia identifying him as the Blades Man.

"I did." Mother's long, graceful fingers pinched the stem of a silver chalice, swirling the mead around. "It seems your intrusion in the Struggle has created a storm of protest among your brothers and sisters."

She guarded her expression well, making it impossible to tell if she was pleased, or infuriated, by his actions. Leather bindings creaked as he rested a hand on the pommel of his left sword. "I merely intervened on behalf of a brave warrior who prayed for my assistance."

"Brave warrior." Mother smiled, setting the silver chalice on the table. Her white gown rustled against the wooden chair. The air carried her like a swirl of cloud, hair radiant as the sun. Although he towered over her, he was merely a shadow stretched out in his black armor, and like a shadow, he would be nothing without her light.

"Of all the warriors in the land of the Created, you have not chosen a champion in three centuries. Oh, don't scowl, I know *she* didn't meet your expectations." Mother gripped his forearm and removed his hand from the pommel. She slid her fingers along his bracer and gently squeezed his hand. "Still, I wonder about this farm boy you declare a warrior."

"He is pure of heart, unlike she-who-dwells-in-shadows." Huron turned his face away. The memory of the shameful events still stung.

"You once thought the same of her." She touched his cheek. Cool, gentle. Huron cringed and tried to pull further away from her touch. *I don't deserve her... pity.* Long fingers tilted his face so she could gaze into his eyes. He clenched his jaw, powerless to look away. "My sweet boy, love blinds us to their true nature and they are so very good at deceiving us. And themselves."

"Until it is time for Judgment." The smell of food cloying in his nose, he ached to escape this illusion of sanctity they had created.

"There will be no Judgment for the farm boy." She sat on the table edge and plucked a grape, rolling it around between her fingers. "He must ascend." She tossed the grape into the air, catching it in her mouth. She bit it and swallowed. "Or you will fall with him."

To know the pangs of death. He nodded, understanding the rules all too well. He could not bring himself to ruin over the girl, however, the boy—

"If I fail in this endeavor, then I dishonor you and all of the children." *Except the one.* He clenched his fist. *She I must destroy.* "I will become one of the Created and die."

"So honorable." Mother stood on her toes and kissed his cheek. She lingered a moment, her warm breath against his ear, as she whispered. "You are not alone in choosing a champion. Another has bestowed the gift. Once again, the Struggle continues, balanced on the edge of a blade."

Is it her? The question hung unspoken and unanswered between them.

"Perhaps it is best you leave mortal affairs to the mortals," she said, taking his hand in her own smaller, delicate one. She dropped an object in his fingers and folded them closed. Sharp edges poked his palm.

Mother withdrew, veiling her true intentions in a smile. Ambitious ears listened to every conversation, especially private ones. He read the response in her eyes. This *other* knew his weakness. Too many secrets he had mistakenly divulged. Honor led many a warrior to their doom.

Honor and love, as Mother would decry. The one hiding in shadows lacked scrupulous and must be destroyed before she caused more harm.

"If you excuse me, Mother," he said, bowing, eyes lowered on his black boots. "I have duties I must attend."

"You have my blessing, child." She turned her back on him and drained the cup of mead, blue light reflecting off the silver like she held the sun in the sky and drained it away.

A chill settled over him. He strapped his helm on his head and retreated down the hall. The object in his hand beckoned to be examined, but he turned it over in hand, testing its rough edges.

Turning the corner, he stopped short of running over a petite form. The moonlight goddess, Sin, glared at him, frowning in her smug knowing-all way. Her silver hair glistened in the light as she tossed it over her shoulder.

"Careful where you're walking," she sniped, baring tiny teeth. She looked him up and down. "Don't you have another suit of clothes? The black armor fashion went out last century. Unless, of course, there's a war going on I haven't heard about."

Then you haven't been paying very good attention.

"Pardon, sister," he said, giving a quick bow.

Sin flapped her hands at him in a shooing gesture.

"Go play castles or something." She moved past him and he heard her tight, irritated voice call out. "Mother, do you have a moment? I know you must since nothing ever gets done…"

The rest was lost as he moved away, heading down a series of passages leading to the lower levels of the Placid Palace. Mother was correct. The boy was not a fighter. During the battle at the tower, he had possessed the boy, working through his fleshy limbs to kill those men and save the lives of his friends. Dire need drew him to the boy the first time, creating the special bond. The same need drew them together again. Before the boy ended up dead. Left alone, Huron was as certain as the sun rising in the east, the boy would die.

Unless a sacrifice was made.

He looked down at the oblong crystal pendant Mother had gifted. It was warm and an ethereal blue light glowed from the center. None of the Ascended could enter the created world, except through dreams or possession.

Or a soul pendant.

Deep within the palace's heart resided the Pool of Reflection. Often gods and goddess would contemplate the Created at the water's edge. In the Pool's chamber, green vines crawled up the stone walls bearing white bulbous flowers, their core emitting a white light. The light resonated off the Pool's calm, cloudy surface. His footfalls echoed in the chamber as he approached the water's edge. He imaged what he desired to see and then touched the water's surface. Bubbles effervesced from the center, clearing away the cloudy foam as they radiated to the pool's edge and then dissipated, leaving behind a clear surface. He peered through the surface much like looking through a window. A window to the land of the Created.

The boy stood in the hill's shadow, striking the ground with a hoe. A small patch of furrowed ground formed where the boy worked out rocks and tore up grass, sweating beneath the hot sun.

Once a farm boy, always a farm boy. Huron smiled and latched the soul pendant around his neck. His body tingled, warmth spreading through his appendages. He gained a strange weight not felt in centuries. Leaning over the Pool's edge, the rough stone against his fingers, he peered at the world below. The boy raised his hoe, paused, and then looked up. Green eyes gazed at Huron without seeing. Huron took a step back. Bubbles fizzled and the water clouded over as the portal closed, hiding the boy from his sight.

Soon, my friend, you'll see me in the flesh. Huron closed his eyes again and imagined a forge deep within the ruins of a long-lost city. The thought of it brought sorrow, but also hope. The portal reopened onto a darkened land covered in dense trees and heavy brush. Beneath it all, he sensed the power of the fires sleeping in never dying embers. As far as he could tell, it had remained undisturbed since last he used it nearly three centuries ago in the body of a young girl who prayed for protection from a deceased race of men. The tools he required were buried in a ring surrounding the embers. The rest he would acquire from a nearby village.

When you do see me, you won't like what I have to do.

Huron, the god of war, worshiped by the Created naming him Blades Man, stepped into the Pool of Reflection. Water covered his boots and then he sank past his knees. As soon as it reached his chest, he slipped under the clear blue water and descended.

CHAPTER ONE

Life began when a void cried out to be filled.
We created them in our likeness, only they became unlike us.
So we struggle with how to interact. Do we guide them?
Answer all their prayers?
How can we, when we don't even answer our own?
— From "The Book of Creation"

"Jarrod." Hannah stood at the edge of the furrowed ground, holding a bucket of water and ladle. He heard wood thump against wood, the slosh of water teasing his thirst, but didn't turn around. In a frightened whisper she asked, "Is something coming?"

Something's here. He wanted to tell her. To have one more person know would be a relief. He glanced over his right shoulder, briefly, so he wouldn't miss whatever it was he sensed. Hannah shielded her eyes, chin tilted up in the direction he was looking. A breeze tugged at her pale blue dress and tossed tufts of blond hair in front of her face. She swiped it away.

The hoe slung against his left shoulder seemed weightless, a part of his body. Hairs stood up on his neck and he spun his head around, searching, seeking that which sought him. This wasn't the first time he sensed it. After surviving the Watch Tower, there seemed to be omnipotent eyes studying him.

In his mind he screamed, *"Leave us alone!"* Words fallen on deaf ears. It seemed a passing dream. A premonition of what may come. Beneath his tunic, just left of his spine, his scar itched, reminding him of reality. He resisted the urge to scratch it.

Every day spent in the Yellow Valley is one more away from family. Pah! Family! More like one more day waiting for soldiers to march through the wilderness and up the hillside to discover our camp. He shook the hoe at the sky. *Come get me yourself, coward!*

"Jarrod," Hannah repeated softer. "You're scaring me."

When the soldiers eventually arrived, Jarrod knew he couldn't save Hannah and the children like he'd rescued them from the Watch Tower half a season ago. He didn't possess the skills to fight. He had been possessed by a god. A god who all but promised war had not ended for Jarrod.

Yoked, hilt to blade.

"Jarrod, please."

Jarrod blinked and eased the hoe back down to the ground. How long had he been standing there? Did he really shout to the gods or was it all his mind?

"It's nothing," he said, giving a big smile and leaned on the hoe. He swiped an arm across his forehead, mopping the sweat off, and hoped his face didn't look as red as it felt. "The sun is getting to me."

"I thought a really bad storm approached by the way you were looking at those clouds," Hannah gave an uneasy titter, moving a strand of hair from her face. It wasn't what she thought, Jarrod noted, though they all had secrets. Her shoulders tightened, hands gripping the bucket with white knuckles. Hannah tilted her head in a coy manner, trying to cover her embarrassment and unease.

"Nope." Jarrod wrinkled his nose and tried to spit. His mouth was too dry. "No storm."

"Mother's blessings. I think when the rains do finally come, they will wash us all away." She set the bucket in the shade of a wispy willow. "Come here and rest." She patted a small patch of grass. "No need to get sun-stroke."

"Good idea," he said, glancing once more at the sky. Clouds. Nothing but clouds.

Jarrod set the hoe against the white spotted wisp's trunk. Hundreds of pink cone-shaped blossoms hung from spindly branches giving off a faint, bitter scent. His mother taught him to use the dried blossoms for brewing tea for settling an upset stomach and dispelling melancholy. He picked a couple and placed them in his pocket to dry for later. Taking the ladle from Hannah, he dipped it into the bucket and drank the temped water. It had a metallic taste from being boiled. Hannah, or one of the other children, collected water from the stream several hundred yards down the hill side. They heated the water over a fire in an iron pot to make it safe to drink.

"Do you think we will have a harvest before the snows come?" Hannah asked, light blue eyes surveying the broken ground. Just past fourteen name-days she possessed a scarred innocence. Dark circles under her eyes and worry lines grooved the corner of her mouth made her more adult than child. She wore her sandy blonde hair back in a braid, revealing a round face speckled with faded brown freckles. She was pretty now, but Jarrod imagined as she truly aged, Hannah would make a stunning woman.

"The seeds should germinate quickly. Everything depends on how long we need to stay here." *And when the war ends.* He wasn't sure if it had even started. No messenger brought word of events at home. If there was even a home left to return to… for all he knew Heartwood Pines was gone and everyone they loved dead. These fears he kept private. *Don't be a scared little rabbit! Gabriel is busy with war preparations and doesn't want anyone else to know where we are secreted away. We are fine on our own.* "We'll have bitter greens, butter leaves, blood fruit, quick beans and string beans and pole beans…"

Jarrod broke off his list. The abundance growing in the tiny plot of soil was an excitement he alone understood. Hannah seemed to be half-listening, though her eyes lingered on his until he looked away. "We have enough supplies to last until winter. Longer, if necessary, with our plantings here."

"That's good," Hannah said. "I don't like being cold *and* hungry."

"Ishmael is working on the cold while I am solving the hunger part." Ishmael, the eldest son of Gabriel, had started building them a more permanent structure than the tents they were currently staying in. Tents were fine for the warm season, but when it began to rain and snow, they would be swept away or buried. Although he slept alone, some nights Jarrod woke with Lily, Hannah's youngest sister, curled up beside him, especially after she'd had a nightmare— watching her mother and father get murdered, Jarrod empathized with her night terrors. He often dreamed of fire and screams and blood, waking up wide-eyed and sweaty.

Hannah giggled, putting her hand on his shoulder, giving it a soft squeeze. It lingered there for several heartbeats before she stirred the ladle around the bucket.

"A happy home is full of love," she said, absently. She looked at him with watery eyes and shrugged. "Something my mother used to say."

"I agree," Jarrod said, squirming uneasily. *She's been acting kind of odd. I wonder what worm is eating at that apple.* It wasn't his place to ask. She would tell him if she wanted him to know. "I guess we still like Ishmael even though he is grumpy."

Hannah nodded.

The dark circles seemed to fade a little since her captivity. Neither she, her sister Kellen, nor Ishmael's brother, Azriel, talked about their imprisonment, as brief as it had been. As a child among strangers who threatened your life, every moment would be terrifying. To top it off, they each had lost a parent or more. Azriel his mother, and Hannah and Kellen were both orphans. Smiles from Hannah were brief, a ghost upon her lips, and a rare vision.

"Everything will work out fine." He patted her hand. "We do our part to make sure we're safe. We have plenty of food and clean water."

Hannah took the ladle and scooped out water, pouring it onto a rag. She handed it to Jarrod. He thanked her, wiped away the sweat on his forehead and back of his neck. It was a temporary relief. He would sweat all midday until well into evening. The ground needed to be tilled so he could keep his promise of enough food. Without a proper plow, his father's hoe would have to suffice.

"Do you ever miss them?" Hannah asked.

"Who?" Jarrod paused, chin raised as he scrubbed the stubble growing on his cheek.

"Your parents."

He wrapped the rag around his neck, considering the question. Both of his parents died during the Ascension War nearly three years ago. Prince Thomas' soldiers attacked the family homes as a diversion, while the men were off fighting or training. Jarrod's mother was murdered in the attack, their house burned and her body found in the front yard, her dress torn and bloody. When he thought of his mother, the anger and sadness blurred the picture he had of her in his mind. He only had to peer into a looking glass to see her reflection— he was told he had her eyes and chin. Strangely, the scent of lye soap and fresh baked apple pie were stronger than any image he could conjure.

His father's hard, leathery face and stern green eyes often came to his thoughts. "You weren't meant to dole out death, son," his father had consoled him after every failed fight training at the Fox Den. He'd clean the blood from his son's lip and help him limp away, bruised and jeered by the other boys. "Some people are not soldiers and that's fine. It's how the gods made them. My advice is focus on living." He would take away the sword and hand Jarrod a hoe. Shortly after their home was destroyed, his father died at the Twin Rivers' battle.

Jarrod twisted the rag, water running down the sides of his face.

"Not a moment passes I don't think about them."

Hannah stared down at her dress, twirling the string around her finger. When she spoke, her voice was quiet and thick.

"Buttercup and Lily-pad sometimes cry for mother." She dabbed at her eyes and drew in a deep breath. Her body shivered and she released a pitiful sigh, almost a sob. "They talk about how father used to tell us stories of fairies bringing us sweet candies if we left out milk on the back stoop. Then he would kiss us on the forehead before mother said prayers with us. Now, I rock Buttercup and Lily to sleep, singing songs mother sang to us during thunder storms." A tear slipped down her cheek and she furiously scrubbed it away. "I can't cry. Once I start, I don't know if I can ever stop. My heart breaks and I have to hold the pieces together. I try praying but—"

Hannah noticed Jarrod watching her. Blushing, she jumped to her feet and wiped grass off her bottom.

"Sorry, I didn't mean—"

"No." Jarrod took her hand. It was warm and soft. She didn't resist as he gently pulled her back down next to him. His heart ached for her and blame flared up like a knife digging deep inside his innards. He looked into her teary, red eyes and held both of her hands. "You have a right to be sad... and if you need to cry, then do it. Don't cry in front of your sisters if you want to be strong for them. We carry enough burden in this world. Mourning loved ones is never a weakness."

Hannah's lips trembled as she tried to speak. She clung onto Jarrod, burying her face into his shirt as she wept, probably the first good cry she had since the night Fraster and the Manus Poena burned down her home.

You were there and did nothing to prevent it. Guilt demeaned.

I saved the girls. If I hadn't been there, they would be dead too. The sentiment, as justifiable as he wanted to make it, felt hollow and empty. He should've turned Fraster and the others in as soon as he heard of their plan for retribution. Anger and grief blinded him. All he wanted was revenge for the war. *Such a fool! I was easily duped by conniving men. Blessed Mother, we need an end to the violence.*

Jarrod held Hannah until she finished crying. Grief was like a dark cloud clinging to the edges of a sunny sky, ready to drop rain at any moment.

"Thank you," she said, rubbing her eyes.

Jarrod nodded. They sat together, his arm around her waist and she laid her head on his shoulder. Quietly they watched the clouds move across the sky and listened to the cicadas hum in the tall grass. The distant pounding of a hammer from Ishmael building their new temporary shelter, laughter and shouting from the girls came from the camp. Jarrod hadn't noticed them until now. So loud, so noisy. The stones called to him, the dirt demanded to be torn, ripping grass and roots, so he could sow new life. All this time they created too much noise. *Need to be more like bunnies in a warren and less like the screeching hawk.*

No, they are children, Jarrod reminded himself. *They deserve to run and shout and grow.* Keeping them hidden in silent fear would not be good for them. Besides, Ishmael wasn't forcing them to hide, so maybe they were fine after all. Jarrod looked down at Hannah who smiled at him. She slipped her hand into his and squeezed, then she kissed him on the cheek. Without saying a word, she gathered up the bucket and returned to camp.

Jarrod watched her disappear around a crag, the lingering warmth of her kiss glowed on his cheek. Grinning and shaking his head, he lifted the hoe. In the shadow of the Mountains of Dawn, the Yellow Valley's ground was rocky, but fertile. A variety of plant life thrived and he was certain they could live off the wild plants if they ran out of supplies, but he wanted to be sure they would eat well this winter.

As long as the gods don't interfere, we will be fine. He gazed up at the sky, certain once again that he was being watched. A hawk circled and swooped down into the tall grass. It then soared upward clutching a small creature in its talons. He turned away and thrust the blade into the ground.

Supper consisted of nut paste spread on hard wafers and a side of berries the girls had scavenged alongside the streambed. They ate around the campfire, silently watching the flames. A cool breeze swept up a cluster of cinders, carrying them into the dark where they flared like stars before burning out. Hannah sat cross-legged beside Jarrod, her right shoulder brushing against him. She smiled and casually placed a hand on his leg.

At least she is happy, for once. Jarrod stared at her hand, filling his mouth with dry wafer. He choked. Hannah sat up and handed him a cup of water. Jarrod drank it down.

"I'm fine," he said in a gravely tone as she refilled the cup with tepid water and brought it to him. He drank it anyway.

Lily, Hannah's youngest sibling, scrapped her plate clean and set it aside.

"Fix my hair, please." Lily said, dropping her head in Hannah's lap.

"Since you asked so politely." Hannah gathered up long strands of Lily's hair and began weaving them.

Across from them Kellen, the middle child, whispered to Ishmael's sister, Elly. They twisted long blades of grass around their ring fingers, held them out as though inspecting silver bands. Elly giggled and covered her mouth.

"Silly, aren't they," Hannah said.

"Their pretending to get married," Lily said. "Like you and— ow! That hurt!"

"Sorry, your hair is a mess."

"Whoosh!" Azriel, Elly's younger brother at six name-days, poked a stick in the flames. Embers sailed upwards and burnt out like little stars. "Look at them burn."

"Best be careful they don't catch your shirt," Jarrod said. "Then you'll be a bright star falling to the stream below."

"They won't get me," Azriel said, tumbling on the ground. "I'm too fast."

Jarrod laughed. It was a good night.

Then he looked over at Ismael.

Ishmael sat on his carved stump, head hung between slumped shoulders, eyes cast onto his empty plate. He was two name-days older than Jarrod, being nineteen and Jarrod seventeen. Ishmael hardly spoke, ruminating over some problem or other. Azriel bumped into his brother's leg, jostling him from his thought. Ishmael raised his head. Eyes distant and brow furrowed.

Azriel scurried back to Elly.

"Do you have to be so sour?" Elly asked.

"I was just thinking," Ishmael said.

"Brooding," Elly said. "You look like father did after the tree limb crashed through the barn roof and all the hay got wet and full of mold. He sulked for half a moon until moth—"

"Enough, Elly," Ishmael said, voice raised so Elly's mouth snapped closed. "I don't need you nagging me. I was thinking. Can't a person think?"

"About what?" she asked, softer.

"After this shelter's built, I'm going back to Heartwood," Ishmael pointed at the small shanty attached to the rock's face. The framework for a floor was in place, spanning three lengths back into a cleft. The cleft widened the further back it went under the foothill, providing secure space for walls and would make it difficult for their house to be noticed from afar. Ishmael had explored the cleft, clearing it of unwanted creatures and built a makeshift front wall complete with door frame before Jarrod arrived. A strong wind had knocked it down before it was secure, forcing him to start anew. "It should be enough to keep you warm and dry through the snows."

"You can't abandon us." Elly stood up and folded her arms. "Father wanted us to stay here."

"You will," Ishmael said. "Jarrod's going to watch over you."

"It's not right, Ishmael." Elly shook her head. "We need to stay together."

"I don't think leaving is a good idea," Jarrod added. "Travelling the roads alone is dangerous, and with an army prepared to march on Heartwood, that makes it twice as risky."

Ishmael glared at Jarrod. "I already lost Michael and my mother. I'm not about to lose my father, too."

"What about Azriel and me? Don't we count? We lost Michael and mother, too!" Elly said. Her lips trembled and she started to cry. Azriel hugged her legs. "You'll leave us without anyone."

Ishmael jumped up, arms waving around. "What are we doing out here anyway?"

Surviving, Jarrod frowned, saying instead: "Waiting for a messenger to tell us it's safe to return."

"Where are the other families?" Ishmael countered. "Where are the women and children from Heartwood? Why are we the only ones hiding out here? Alone." He paused, waiting for a reply, but everyone remained silent. "Like you said, Jarrod, an army's going to march on our homes. My father and the other families are protecting them, while we hide like animals cowering in bushes and hoping the hunter passes us by."

"Then we are all going back," Elly said.

"Yeah," Azriel said, taking Elly's hand. "We all go."

"No," Ishmael said, cutting his fingers across the air, silencing his siblings. "Just me. I am the only one who can fight."

"Jarrod fights, too," Hannah said, placing a hand on Jarrod's arm. "He saved me, Kellen, and Azriel from the tower. He killed eight men by himself."

"Then he'll be perfect to protect you from whatever bear or wild cat that comes sniffing around." Ishmael stalked toward the tents. "This is not open for any more discussion. I leave, alone, when I'm ready. Nothing will stop me from going or change my mind." He flung open the tent flap and went inside.

Elly trembled, tears shimmering in the firelight. Kellen wrapped her arms around her shoulder and Elly hugged her back. Soft sobs followed by Kellen's comforting words. Jarrod tried to stand up, only to be pushed back down. Lily climbed up into his lap. Her knees balanced on his thighs, small hands clinging to his arms. Pale blue eyes earnestly looked into his, as she said in a loud hushed tone.

"You can't let him leave us. It's making Elly and Azriel sad."

"Shush, Lily-Pad," Hannah said, taking her sister by the waist and lifted her up on her hip. Lily had grown and would soon be too big to carry. Hannah gave Jarrod an apologetic smile. "Ishmael is being a grumpy bear. Besides, Jarrod can take care of us all."

Jarrod gave his best affable grin.

"Is he really going to leave us?" Azriel asked, tugging on his sister's arm. "Like Mommy and Michael?"

Elly stroked his head, closing her eyes and taking a deep breath. Her shoulders sank as she replied: "I don't know." She looked to Jarrod, a desperate plea in her eyes.

Ishmael does what pleases him. Jarrod scratched his head. *Am I supposed to tie him up to prevent him from leaving?*

"I'm going," Jarrod said, backing away, pointing west, to where they corralled the horses. "Well, not leaving... just walking this way to the horses. They need me." He spun on his heels and began hurrying away, cursing how stupid he sounded.

"Let's pray Ishmael comes to his senses," Elly said. Jarrod could feel her eyes on his back as he slunk away. "Help me get the dishes cleaned up and you can sleep with us tonight."

"Alright," Azriel said. "You won't go away, will you, Elly?"

He was too far to hear her response, but he knew it nevertheless—she would make promises only the gods could keep. Guilt poked like a bur inside his boot. Ishmael blamed Jarrod for losing his mother and brother, especially since Jarrod was the one who'd brought the girls to their home. As a result, Thramel wanted them all dead for being traitors.

I should've stayed on my farm. Jarrod quickened his pace to the makeshift paddock where they kept four horses tethered. Happy wickers greeted him. He dragged a sack of alfalfa and oats out from its canvas cover. Digging a tin cup into the sack, he scooped out the grass and filled their feedbags. *On my farm I was oblivious to everything.* A deeper, darker side spoke up. *And died like your mother. Tool shaped by the gods! Ha! You are broken.*

"We are all broken," he said, setting a bag in front of each horse. A dappled grey nickered as he placed her bag down. She nuzzled his shoulder, tongue licking his neck. Then her head swayed away, her large, browns eyes rolled and she gave another soft nicker as if to say, *"Maybe you are, but as long as you keep feeding me, we can all get along."* "If only everything was this simple."

Around the camp fire, five silhouettes danced with the flames. How was he supposed to take care of them by himself? He hardly slept enough keeping watch half the night.

Ishmael should be grateful. I saved his little brother and stopped Thramel from slaughtering his father. Gods, what more can I do? He ran a brush down the grey's flank. *No amount of contrition or retribution would restore the dead back to the living.*

"I should have stayed on my farm." He tossed the brush into an empty bucket and returned to camp.

Dishes were cleaned, food sealed up and placed into the narrow crevice, removing temptation from wild bears, cats and other creatures of the Valley. All the children nestled into one tent. He heard Hannah talking, most likely telling a story. He wanted to listen, snuggled under warm blankets and pretend some higher power watched over them. Protected them.

I'm too old for stories. He set a blanket down on the hard ground to keep first watch.

Settling in next to the dying embers of the fire, Jarrod enjoyed the last remains of heat before the cool, dampness would intrude later in the evening. He held the hoe across his lap. He had more confidence in using it as a weapon than the sword tucked away in his tent. The hoe once belonged to his father. After the war began, his father put it down in favor of sword and spear. He never had the opportunity to pick it up again. The head was made of good metal, the blade still sharp and the handle came from a heavy, solid oak well-balanced for easy carving into the soil. Not only was it a good tool, but it served as a reminder of his true identity: Farmer, not a warrior as the gods desired to shape him.

Nightingales chirped from the valley below, mournful songs joined by crickets humming in the grasses. The rushing stream provided a soothing undertone to the night. A half-moon rose up in the clear sky, surrounded by countless pinprick stars. When the moon peeked overhead, he would wake Ishmael for his watch. Ishmael's tent was quiet. Jarrod imagined him asleep, dreaming of fighting for the glory of Heartwood. The only reason Ishmael built the wooden structure was to ease his conscious for when he eventually left them.

Not that he was really here. Jarrod dug a groove into the dirt with his heel. *How am I to watch all night and be awake to tend the children in the morning?*

Once the shanty was built, he figured there wouldn't be much need for nightly vigilance—not that he conceived of sleeping through the night anymore. Nightmares full of blood, destruction, and worse... the gods forging him into a weapon the way a master smith hammered molten steel, bending him in the shape of a blade, and honed the edges to hack off limbs... he woke from those dreams sweaty, heart racing well before the sun rose. The gods watched him. The Blades Man for certain, since he told Jarrod they were "Yoked hilt to blade." At other times, the eyes of heaven held enough malice to raise the hairs on his neck. They measured him, prodded for strength and weakness.

Something softly touched his shoulder. He squeaked and spun on the blanket, kneeling on one knee, the hoe clutched in both hands over his head to ward off an attack. Hannah leapt back, raising a hand to her mouth. She grinned beneath her fingers and gave a small giggle.

"What are you doing up?" Jarrod whispered, sounding sharper than he intended.

"It's kind of crowded in there and I couldn't sleep." She lowered her eyes, looking at her bare feet. "I didn't mean to startle you."

"You're lucky I didn't hit you with this." Jarrod held the hoe out before setting it on the ground. Hannah rolled her eyes and gave a curt "Ha!" Jarrod felt his face getting warm and a little sting at her scoff. Not like he was trying to impress her. *She's just a kid*, he reminded himself. "If you want, you can sleep in my tent tonight. I will take Ishmael's when he comes on watch."

"I want to stay up with you," Hannah said, changing her tone— the haughtiness replaced by a playful pout, arms behind her back as she swayed at her hips. Her lower lip stuck out a moment before becoming a grin. "Do you mind?"

"It's not that exciting." Jarrod stood up to adjust the twisted blanket. He gave it a quick snap to flatten it out. He sat cross-legged, looking up at the sky. "Most of my time is spent counting stars."

"How many are there?" She sat next to him, pulling her shift down to cover her feet.

"I counted twenty before being distracted by the thousands of others impossible to count." Jarrod pointed at a cluster south of the moon.

They formed three triangles, each decreasing in size. "Those I call the three sisters. The little one is Lily-pad, the next is Buttercup and the third—"

"Oh let me guess," she said. "The biggest and brightest is called Hannah."

"No." Jarrod laughed. Moonlight shined in her eyes as she cocked her head, raising her brow in expectation. "That one is called—"

A high-pitched scream shattered the night's serenity.

"What was that?" Hannah squeezed Jarrod's arm.

"Sounded like a person," Jarrod said. The scream brought back memory of the night Fraster burned down Hannah's home, a horrified mother clamoring from the flames, running, arms reaching for her children, never to reach them. He shook the image away and snatched the hoe. "Stay here."

Hannah got up and began to follow him.

"I mean it, Hannah." Jarrod held a hand out to stop her. "Wake up Ishmael. Stay with the children."

"Fine." She huffed and ran toward the darkened tents.

Jarrod watched her to be sure she wouldn't follow. He didn't often order her around like a child, especially since she didn't act like a child, but he couldn't have her endangered again. The scream could be nothing and may pass them by, which was what he hoped. *Hope is not an action,* his father said to him during the Ascension War, after they discovered their home burned and the body of his mother strewn in the scorched grass. *It's the delusion of a soft pillow beneath your head when a sword was at your throat.*

The scream came from east of their camp, carried over the stream bed. Enough moonlight shone for him to pick his path along the steep precipice where one slip would send him tumbling to the sharp rocks below. He reached the outcropping overlooking the streambed. A small grove of willow wisps occupied the other side of the stream. Jarrod crouched and watched the trees, seeking the source of the cry. He saw nothing.

Maybe it was a wild cat killing another creature, he thought. He'd heard a wild cat's warning shriek, although it sounded almost human, it wasn't. He kept searching, nearly believing the gods blessed him, and whoever it was continued east away from their sanctuary. A shout echoed from the willows below. Branches shivered and a woman tumbled from the cluster of willow wisps, sliding down a small ridge and landing in the stream. A small child fell after her. The woman yanked the child to her feet and gripped her arm as they scampered into the water. The stream grew deeper at the center, rising up to the woman's thighs. She stopped and lifted the child in her arms, then began trudging across.

Two men emerged from the trees. Chainmail rattled and dark cloaks trailed each of them as they stalked after the woman and child. They splashed into the water moving quicker than the child-encumbered woman.

They will catch her at the shallows. Jarrod stood and looked back to see if Ishmael was coming, but the path was empty. *I can't wait!* He hefted his hoe and slid down the embankment. Landing at the stream's bank, he ran into the water.

Blades Man guide my hand. He raised the hoe, blade twirling overhead.

The closest man looked up as Jarrod swung, wooden handle cracking against the side of his head. The man plummeted like a rock, splashing in the shallow stream. *That was easy.* He tried to sense the warrior god's presence taking control like before. The only presence he felt was his quickly beating heart.

Water sloshed to his right. He turned as a blade slashed at him. It scrapped along the hoe's wooden handle, carried away from his ribs. The vibration stung his hand and he nearly dropped the hoe. Planting his feet, Jarrod twisted his body and pivoted his arms, aiming the handle at the man's face. The man caught it on the sword guard. A quick upward thrust, the hoe flew from Jarrod's hands, spinning off into the night. It splashed somewhere further upstream. Jarrod leapt back escaping another swipe. The man cursed, slashing and jabbing. Jarrod retreated further into the stream. Water rolled over his boot tops. Slick stones under his soles made him dance. His arms dipped into the frigid water, fingers searching for the hoe or anything else he could use to defend himself and coming up empty. Moonlight glinted off the steel cutting down at him. Jarrod stepped on a rock, his ankle twisting. The rock slipped beneath his weight and he fell sideways into the water, the edge of the blade narrowly missing his nose.

"I don't know who you are," the man said, placing the blade against Jarrod's throat, "but you chose the wrong fight."

"Any time men threaten women, it's my fight," Jarrod said.

The man laughed.

"You have no idea what you're dealing with here. The sad part is, you forfeited your life for nothing." Lifting the sword, he prepared a backslash to end Jarrod's life. Jarrod watched the blade angled for his neck, knowing he wouldn't be quick enough to dodge the killing blow. *Mother forgive me and watch over Hannah.* He closed his eyes, waiting for the cut, a flash of pain, and then silence. The man grunted and water splashed Jarrod. He opened his eyes, catching sight of the man floating faced down, an arrow jutting from his temple.

Thank the gods!

Ishmael slid down the embankment, another arrow ready to draw.

"Who are these men?" He scanned the willows and the stream.

"I don't know." Jarrod stood up, water dripping from his soaked pantaloons and tunic sleeves. He sloshed his way to the stream bank. "They were pursuing *them*."

The woman set down the child, a little girl of Lily's age. She wrapped her arms around the shivering child, leaning over her in a possessive manner. Her chest heaved as blue eyes darted from Jarrod to Ishmael and back on Jarrod. His breath caught. The woman was wild and beautiful, as though cut from the night sky. Tangled hair hung over her face and bits of branch and leaf caught up in it, like a nymph in a story he once heard that stole the heart of the man before she devoured him. *Qetesh! What's this creature you lead here?* Jarrod's heartbeat quickened and his mouth felt dry.

"Are there any more?" Ishmael asked.

"No," the woman said, her teeth beginning to chatter.

"Don't stand there like a fool, Jarrod." Ishmael nudged him. "Go check on the bodies."

"Yes," Jarrod said, nodding like a simpleton. He turned away, desperately hiding his face from the woman who seemed to be staring at him. He felt her eyes on his back. *Cows show more grace, you stone!* He moved up stream, resisting the urge to look at the woman. A sharp edge struck his shin and he reached down, picking up his hoe. The wooden handle had a new nick, but it was still in one piece. Strangely enough, his prayer was ignored by the warrior god. *I guess it's on his terms now. Or he's busy with the hundreds of real warriors dying in battle further east.*

He checked the first man he struck. Breathing. Jarrod dragged him up on the embankment. As he flopped the man down, the moon shown a gold outline on the man's cloak.

"Ishmael, do you know this?" Jarrod pointed at the sigil on the back of the dark blue cloak: a golden star and half-crescent.

Ishmael shook his head.

Jarrod knelt next to the man. A welt grew above the right temple. *He'll have one terrible headache when he wakes up.*

"What are your names?" Ishmael stepped toward the woman and girl.

The woman put the girl behind her.

"We won't hurt you," Jarrod said, setting the hoe down and holding out his palms to show they were empty. "We want to help."

"Bekka," she said, nearly whispering the word. "My name is Bekka."

"Welcome to the Golden Valley, Bekka," Jarrod said. "Looks like you need a place to rest for the night."

Ishmael glared at him. He'd hear about it later, but there was no way he would turn away a woman and child in need.

"Thank you," Bekka said. "For the night."

CHAPTER TWO

She loved the darkness. The way moonlight
Shone on his soft, pale skin. Flesh she would
Never know as her own, caressed
Through a glove. Hair dark as night, shimmered
Moonbeams in her fingers. Their skin touched.
Desire a great candle in a dark room
His passion, melting wax pouring over her.
In the end, he drifted, leaving her
An ember choking on air, flaring brightly
A falling star lost in the night sky.
Cast in despair, alone and silent.
From this broken vessel her children were born.
　　　　　　— *From* Sin's children, *Book of Creation*

𝔇ark trees silhouetted against shifting phantom light. Gaps formed between thick, black trunks, then closed, blocking her escape. *This is a dream.* A distant thought. She stumbled over roots and fell against a tree trunk. Rough bark scraped her palms, stinging in the cold. Holding onto the tree as a guideline, she circled it. *There has to be another path.* Other trees grew too close, blocking her limited sight. Thick, gnarled roots caught her toes, her ankles, forcing her to step deliberately as though walking on broken egg shells. She stopped. Light shined in the distance as another small path opened. She lunged for it. Roots reached out, encircled her ankles and tugging her boot, tightening around it.

She slipped the boot before the root crushed her foot. She limped forward, one foot bare and the other still in a boot. Sharp stone teeth bit into her soft flesh every step she took. The ragged numb flesh leaving a bloody foot print behind. She pressed on, driven by the need to find him, to help him before—

"Shane!" she cried, her voice going no further than the nearest tree.

Darkness swallowed it up.

Trees shifted and the wall opened before her.

Screams, human and inhuman, echoed in the distance. She tried to slip through the gap, but something clutched her skirt's fringe. Growling, she twisted away. Cloth tore, knocking her backwards through a dark hole. Fingernails scraped against rough bark, catching for a moment, then tearing as she continued to fall. Teeth clicked together as she hit the ground. Instinctively, her hands touched her belly, the slight bulge near ripening. His love grew inside of her and she needed to protect it. Needed to protect him. *Flee*, Shane had told her, *survive for the both of us*. She wouldn't leave him to die alone in the woods. Gathering her legs, she wobbled upright and followed the battle sounds.

"Shane!" Blood and sour sweat permeated the air. Torch lights burned like souls of the dead, leading her astray. She squinted. Dark-winged shapes flitted around the torches, striking at writhing shapes of wolves and cats, slashing them apart. They died, screaming in fury. One form drew close to her, torch light bright as a fire ball ready to burn the entire woods. Bekka pressed against the trunk, holding her breath. The torch stopped on the other side. Heat radiated as though she sat exposed to the sun. Sweat rolled into her eyes, and she blinked it away, praying for the torch to move on.

Instead, the light grew closer, burning away the dark. Bekka covered her mouth, trapping the scream before it betrayed her. Bodies piled up at her feet, faces turned towards her. Fire blazed in glazed eyes, accusing her of bringing death to them. A chant began like a whisper in her head—*it's all your fault! It's all your fault!* Steadily it grew, becoming louder until it was a shout. *ALL YOUR FAULT!*

Bekka sat up, drawing a sharp intake of air, and held it. *A dream. Only a dream*, she reminded herself, slowly exhaling. It was dark and she didn't immediately recognize her surroundings. She reached out to the small form sleeping beside her, reassuring her frantic mind the girl was safe. Safe. Were they really safe? Three days of running at night and hiding during the light, safe wasn't a word she trusted. Especially in a camp full of strangers. They were given privacy in this tent, for the night, to recover from their flight. As far as she could tell no one stood watch. The two boys looked old enough to fight, and they fought well against the Manor guards, even if they did catch them by surprise. The children worried her. What were they doing out here in the middle of nowhere?

Sarrah groaned and rolled over.

"Hush little one," Bekka whispered, stroking Sarrah's black hair. "Go back to sleep."

"We're not leaving?" Sarrah yawned.

"No." Bekka turned on her side. She needed to rest. "Not tonight."

Very little cajoling was required. Sarrah's soft breathing told her the child was asleep. She deserved this break. So very brave, not making a sound while the guards pursued them. A night or two and then they would move on. South of Nemus, past the desert of Lost Souls, was Meritum. Shane spoke of a sanctuary for their kind in a village west of where the City of Light used to exist. Elysium he named it. He wanted to take her there, away from the danger of the Manor. "Somewhere safe," he had said.

When the boys first brought Bekka and Sarrah to their camp, she only got a cursory glance. The hillside hid them well from immediate view down below in the valley. At least the dark covered them from distant prying eyes. Their perceived safety could prove to be their downfall. Pressed against the rock, there wasn't much room for retreat except to go down into the valley.

Voices mumbled outside. She reached for the tent flap, her fingers brushing against a rough spun pack. Rummaging through the pack she discovered mostly clothes, then she touched a firm piece of leather. She gripped it, smiling, and removed the leather sheath, a knife secured in it. Untying the thong wrapped around the hilt, she loosened the blade and drew it out. The blade was as long as her hand. Returning the knife back to the sheath, she placed it under her pillow.

She found the tent flap and peeled it back enough to spy out. The camp was quiet. Then she heard crunching footsteps and the young men who'd rescued her appeared. They carried a slumped form between them. A cold ball formed in her stomach. *He* survived.

Mother, I hope they knocked him hard enough so he can't remember his own name.

The way the gods played against her, she knew her prayers fell on deaf ears. Lying back, she rubbed the bulge in her belly. Soon she wouldn't be able to run anymore.

We have to leave.

She looked at Sarrah, sleeping more peacefully than at any time in the last moon. Waking her would be too cruel and she didn't have the heart to disturb the girl. Bekka closed her eyes and tried to imagine the sanctuary Shane longingly spoke about: "We will be safe, Bekka. We will be free."

Jarrod helped carry the unconscious man into Ishmael's tent, holding him under the arms while Ishmael hefted his legs. They set the body down in the center of the tent, placing a waded up old tunic under his head. Jarrod's back cracked as he stretched his arms side to side. He winced at the sharp pinch from the scar. A double finger's length to the right and he would've been paralyzed by the knife blade. Strenuous tasks reminded him of the fact. Carrying a man uphill was as strenuous an activity in his recent memory.

It didn't help that the man was big. Even stripped of armor and weapons, he still strained Jarrod's arms like lifting a cart of stones. They bound his hands and feet with hemp rope, then tied a gag around his mouth so he wouldn't create any noise when he regained consciousness. They had had enough excitement for one night without bringing more unwanted attention to camp. The dead man's body was gone, swept down the stream and beyond their control. With any luck it would carry out to the Placid Sea.

"I will stay with him tonight," Ishmael said, piling up blankets against the side of the tent.

"Then what?" Jarrod handed Ishmael his bow and sword. "We can't keep him bound forever."

"We'll talk about what to do next in the morning." Ishmael laid his head back and closed his eyes. "For now, try to get some sleep."

"Are you sure you don't want me to stay with him?"

Ishmael waved him away.

"Shout for me if he wakes up and tries to kill you," Jarrod said and Ishmael grunted. Jarrod ducked under the flap and sealed it behind him. Outside, the air was crisp and the moon had slipped behind the Mountains of Destiny. Morning light wasn't far off. Again, he stretched his back, wincing at the pinch from the scar. Pink and raw, the itching and pinching reminded him that he was alive. Alive because the gods were not done using him yet.

I am done! Let them kill me in my sleep. At least then I can sleep like the dead. He shuffled to his bedding, looking over at his tent where Bekka slept with the child. Part of him wanted to check on them, to make sure she was real. He could make them tea from the blossoms he'd dried earlier. Tea required hot water and hot water required starting a fire. Fires weren't allowed after dark.

Let them sleep. It's a greater kindness.

Kicking off his boots, he dropped into the blankets, staring up at the sky and listened to the distant stream. Although he was bone tired, sleep evaded him. He kept waiting for another shout to break the solitude of night, or worse, the sound of footsteps climbing the hill to assault them. It reminded him too much of life in the camps during the Ascension Wars. Moments of restless peace, then losing half a night' sleep to guard duty. Constant vigilance and lack of sleep took a toll on people, made tempers flare and more than one man tried to desert his post, only to find himself strung up in a tree. Corpses swung, bloated and crow peeked, for several days as a reminder of the consequences for cowardice. All he'd wanted was to fall asleep each night and wake in the morning to discover it a bad dream.

Then came the surprise night attack. A startled, gruff face roused him out of a warm blanket and shoved a sword into his hand. Fire and sweat filled the air as men shouted or screamed, cut off, and some gurgling like men drowning, not in water, but in their own blood. He'd coward behind a supply cart, watching men fighting other men so mixed up he couldn't tell friend from foe. Bodies dropped around him and all he could do was shake, closing his eyes, and wait for the blade to end his life. At fourteen name-days, he was still a boy and not ready to become a man. Not that killing made anyone a man—he'd killed one man in that war, and only after his father's death. The act made him feel more like a child. One who threw a temper tantrum at being struck by a rock and then beating up the boy who did it. After the bloodshed and shattered bones, pain remained, doubled because he had killed the object of the hatred and fear, leaving only the deep well of grief.

I am still the object of grief. When will any of this end?

Two princes killed and one princess took their place. It seemed an endless cycle.

He couldn't figure out why those men pursued the woman and child. They were guards of sorts, but the Yellow Valley was far from any place of civilization, so they must've wanted her for a good reason. None that were obvious at a glance. Bekka and Sarrah merely possessed the ragged clothes they arrived in. No food. No water. No place to hide anything, except Jarrod knew they had a secret. The way the woman guarded the girl from them, refusing to let her out of sight...

Part of him hoped that when he wok they would be gone. Then he wouldn't have to worry about a retaliation from whatever faction wanted them. As it was, a troubling choice lay before them about what to do with the unconscious man. *I don't want to leave, again.* Jarrod watched the stars glistening overhead. He was beginning to like their little camp site. It was the longest he stayed at one place since the Ascension War.

Mother bless us, but she won't leave so soon. Not when they have a small moment to rest. He understood what it was like being pursued, the lack of sleep, and fear of being caught. Any respite would be a gods-send.

He thought about Bekka's brown eyes, the weariness he saw made his heart ache for her. She refused food and water, opting for rest instead. In the morning they would be starving. He would make sure they had plenty to eat. A wash, too. She was very pretty, even covered in the grime.

His eyes shut and sleep began enfolding him in her arms. *Is this what it would be like to have Bekka's arms around me?* He imagined her soft, delicate body pressed to his as he breathed in her scent.

A cough startled him and he opened his eyes. Too slow and groggy to react. A poor sentry he'd made this night. Let the enemy slip right—

Hannah stood over him.

"I didn't mean to wake you," she said, speaking softly. "I only wanted to know if you were dozing off so you wouldn't hit me with that." She pointed at the hoe within reach. At his quizzical expression, she replied: "I got the children back to sleep."

"Why aren't you with them?"

"I'm staying out here with you," she said, arms folded.

Jarrod opened his mouth to rebuke her, but closed it. *No use in arguing,* he yawned instead. *She would wait until I'm asleep and steal under the blankets anyway.* He nodded and pulled back a corner. Hannah slipped under the blanket, her cold feet touching his leg and freezing him. He groaned and shifted away. She scooted close, her hip against his thigh. Once more Jarrod slid over until he was outside the blanket. He sighed, laying on the cold ground.

"What are you doing?" Hannah asked.

"You stole all the covers."

"I was just trying to get warm." Hannah returned to her spot and then pulled the blankets back. "Get in here before you catch cold."

"Only if you stay on your side."

"Fine." He could hear the exasperation in her voice. "You have to make everything so awkward."

"You're the one making things awkward." Jarrod tucked the side of the blanket nearest Hannah under him, forming a protective layer. "Are you sure the girls and Azriel didn't kick you out for taking all the blankets?"

Hannah laughed, then smacked his shoulder.

"Go to sleep, silly."

Jarrod began to doze off when he was jolted awake by Hannah whispering his name.

"Hmm, whatever it is, tell them to go away," he mumbled. "They can try killing me in the morning."

"No one is going to kill you," she said.

"Good." He yawned and began to drift away.

"When this is all over," Hannah said and paused. He thought she had fallen asleep, and prepared to do the same, then she continued speaking. "Will you stay with me?"

"What do you mean?"

"Help me take care of Lily and Buttercup."

"Yes," Jarrod said. *As long as the gods let me live,* he thought. "We are family."

Smooth lips brushed his cheek and warm air caressed the skin, an instant there and then gone. Hannah rolled over onto her side.

"Good."

Before sleep claimed him, he heard distantly, "…love you."

Love is not always enough chased him into the empty abyss where dreams die.

CHAPTER THREE

Life springs forth love, tender young
A mewling child grown strong under
Gentle hands, watchful eye, and proud heart
Love strikes boldly, intemperate and virtuous
Casts forth a light best left in darkness
Birthing Shadow to blight the living
And brings forth death
—From "The Ruin Prophesy"
Tome of Essence

"Love is not always enough," Mother said, gazing down into the Pool of Reflection. She trailed her long fingers over the water. Blue tendrils crisscrossed over the starry sky pictured in the Pool. They branched out, creating an invisible web over Huron's chosen champion. She pinched her forefinger to her thumb and the web cinched together. The protective veil sealed him from the view of others. The farm boy was ignorant of his importance. He knew nothing about the care being taken to protect him. As it should be when gods watched over their creation.

Let him sleep in peace as long as he is able. Her hand caressed his watery visage. *Once the stars align against him and the Shadow has her way, he will never have peace.*

For now, anyone seeking the farm boy, either by using the Pool or through other reflective means would be blind, viewing only a dark veil. The veil wasn't permanent. It didn't prevent anyone by chance stumbling upon him physically. The veil should, however, protect the farm boy from secret divining long enough for Huron to find him and prepare him for the trials ahead. As long as Huron moved quickly and some other ill, unforeseen event didn't occur. There was only so much Mother could do. Any further assistance she provided increased the risk of her being discovered. Direct interference in the Struggle was forbidden.

It had to be enough.

Knowledge of her involvement in mortal affairs would sever the tenuous peace among the Children. She could sense them splitting into factions— those who desired non-interference with the Created and those who wanted to dominate them like vengeful gods of old, smiting the guilty or fraternizing with them as Sin had, creating hybrid creatures. Since Father's absence, the Children lacked an iron fisted ruler. Cowering, obsequious attention to the mildest command, fear and adoration of the Father... gone.

She was the only one preventing the Ascended from tearing each other apart. If she were seen to favor one side, that control would dissolve into war. A war to destroy all of Creation. A war to fulfill the Ruin Prophesy.

You, my boy, the Blades Man's chosen Champion, are what stands between ruin and life.

The Ruin Prophesy foretold the end of everything she and Father built: both above and below. Mother had spent much of her time studying the book of Prophesies, constantly reading and re-reading each line, trying to tease out their meaning. There were so many threads, so many possibilities, that not even the speaker of the visions understood their intent. *Love, Life, and Shadow.* These had to be representative of the Ascended and yet, she couldn't associate them to any of her children no matter how vigilant, scrutinizing every action they took.

Then Father disappeared. She spent less time reading and watching, and more energy dealing with quibbles and settling petty disputes. She had become lax, wearied by her new role as sole supreme, sitting alone on the Rose Throne. She hardly noticed when the first step in the Ruin Prophesy began.

It was the girl. Mother glared down at the young woman sleeping beside the farm boy. Love always seemed to be a distraction, but this girl had done nothing to earn her ire. Yet. Another girl, from a time long ago and forgotten by most, twisted her child's heart like a strand of Love' Lace around her finger. Huron refused to listen to her concerns. Mother knew the girl's heart was bent on vengeance disguised in sympathy.

I should have struck her down as she stood in the flesh.

Fear restrained Mother. Fear that her very own love would have turned Huron against her, thus fulfilling the first part of the Prophesy. Fear had a way of coiling around a person, squeezing like a giant snake until they could no longer breathe. Her own inaction triggered the trap.

Shadow stalked the land.

It's so very difficult doing all of this alone. Mother's fingertips touched the farm boy's watery cheek. A nudge to ignore the call of love. At least the farm boy would be happy.

She gave a weary sigh. Despite his misogyny and trysts with other goddesses, she missed Father. He would know what to do to prevent the Ruin Prophesy from becoming reality. Without him, all her actions were based off of blind guesses and hoping all worked for the best. Worse yet, the Disk of Darkness was missing. He had worn the amulet around his neck for safe-keeping. Father was gone, perhaps a victim of his misbehavior. Wherever he went, she knew in her very essence the disc was stolen. Mother was certain of who had done the deed, but not how. The Disk of Darkness contained the other half of the power for creation. Only Mother and Father knew how to harness such power, and without the Star of Creation, very little could be done with the disc.

Mother touched the pendant hanging around her nek. Like the farm boy, she would keep it safe and find a way to get the Disc of Darkness returned to her. Otherwise, the Ruin Prophesy would continue to build beyond her ability to end it. Everything she and Father had created would dissolve into dust blown through the cosmic winds.

Mother stiffened. Light footsteps, barely audible in the serene stillness, approached. She waved her hand above the water. Bubbles filled the pool as the portal to Creation closed, leaving her own worried reflection staring back at her. A tall goddess, thin with olive skin and ebony hair entered the vestibule. She wore a nearly transparent, form fitting robe with two strips latched at the back of her neck and gliding down over large breasts to form an X where they crossed over her midriff. A golden belt knotted around her waist as the material continued down her thighs, spilt on the sides and ended above her naked ankles. Vanilla and sandalwood preceded her appearance. When the goddess Qetesh saw Mother, she halted, eyes widening in surprise and hand covering her mouth.

Qetesh dropped her hand over the silver cup clutched to her chest.

"Mother," she said in a quiet, sweet voice. "What are you doing here?"

"Watching the sunrise, my dear," Mother said, sitting at the edge of the pool and trailing her fingers in the water. "Occasionally, I suffer from nostalgia. Looking at the sun reminds me at how such simple things are sometimes the most beautiful."

Qetesh blushed, casting her eyes to the side.

Mother smiled. *Flattery has always been this one's flaws.*

"What do you desire from the Pool?" Mother lifted her hand and let the water drip from her fingertips.

"I felt a sudden, strong pull from the Created, Mother," Qetesh said, avoiding her gaze. "I wanted to see who prayed to me so I may enter the devoted one's dreams."

"Why didn't you use your lotus cup?"

"I did," Qetesh said, glaring at the cup as though betrayed by it. "The image was empty. I burnt incense to cleanse the water, poured in lotus petals… I tried everything. It was as though a curtain was cast over it. I could feel the pull, yet not see the one calling out to me."

Mother's eyes narrowed.

"Interesting," she said. "Perhaps this love comes from one who seeks another's affection who cannot, or will not, return it."

"Perhaps," Qetesh said. She bit her soft, pink lips. Mother knew she was ruminating over this suggestion. Then Qetesh shook her head, dismissing the idea. "The pull is much too strong. That is why I need to use the Pool of Reflection. To seek out this devotee calling out to me."

Love is not the only thing you'll find blind. Mother smiled, looking down at the Pool. All these factions pulling at the poor farm boy. She envied his position less and less.

"I see that I should come back another time." Qetesh bowed her head and made to leave.

"Not at all, dear Child." Mother stood up and touched Qetesh's shoulder. "I hope you discover what you seek. Some things, I fear, you might have to leave well enough alone."

"I would, Mother," Qetesh said, and bit her lip again. Her fingers ran up and down the side of the cup, stroking its edges. "I wish I could. However, the call is so strong. Stronger than the Star-Crossed Lovers. I have to know before it tears me apart from longing."

Once more the love of a child may be our undoing, Mother closed her eyes to feign impatience. Making them believe she was disappointed was more effective than actually being so. Qetesh rocked nervously on her heels, as though she wanted to retreat and dive into the pool at the same time. The Lady of Love wouldn't let this go. She would chew her lip off in a nervous fit if Mother remained much longer. *Nothing else can be done about it tonight. This disturbance must be fleeting like a fire which burned too bright, consuming its fuel quickly before perishing. If not, then I'll have to break the farm boy's heart before his spirit gets broken.*

"Seek this desire," Mother said, walking away from the pool. She paused at the chamber's archway, casting her words over her shoulder so they echoed around the stone. "Just be wary of drowning in it."

Bernal woke up with a splitting headache. The room blurred and spun like the morning after a bender on cheap wine and cheaper girls. His tongue scrapped the roof of his mouth. *Dry as an old cleaning rag. What did I drink last night?* He tried raising his arm, discovering both hands bound behind his back. Groaning, he wrenched them back and forth, but they were knotted too tight. Looking down at his feet, he saw that they were also bound. That wasn't all that he noticed.

He wasn't alone.

A young man, barely out of boyhood, leaned against the side of the tent. His chin rested on his chest, rising and falling in shallow breaths of deep sleep. At the boy's side was an unstrung bow on his right and naked sword to the left. Bernal eyed the blade. It was so close, a few steps away, but in his current state it would be like sneaking into a wild cat's den to steal a kitten. *Janus' luck!* The two-faced goddess toyed with him, again, if she'd ever stopped. She may never end until he ended up dead. An opportunity, such as this, didn't come more than once. *Damn the gods!*

Bernal raised his knees to his chest and jerked them down, using the motion to scooch along the floor, like a worm caught out of the rain and trying to get back to the dirt before he withered on the rock. The tiniest motion sent a wave of nausea over him. He paused, knees drawn up and willed back the vomit. With his mouth sealed by the gag, retching would end his exploits, drowning him in his own stomach fluids. *Slow and easy*, he told himself, making each movement deliberate.

The rustling was loud in his ears. Loud enough, he feared, to wake the dead. He glanced at the boy. *Yes, stay asleep, nothing to worry about here. Rest is good for growing boys. Janus keep your dreams as sweet as honeysuckle.* Bernal wiggled closer. Judging he was near enough, Bernal flipped over, fingers blindly seeking the blade. His nails scraped against the steel, but couldn't find purchase. Hands sweating and head pounding, he tried again. This time he eased the tip up with his middle finger, working it to the pointer, almost enough to slip it between the rope.

"What are you doing?" The sword was ripped from his hand, slicing his index finger. A blunt blow to the small of his back turned him over, flattening him onto his stomach. Bernal grunted in frustration, the gag muffling his curses.

Rough hands grabbed his tunic and he was lifted up, spun around until he stared up into his captor's angry face. Red, blood shot eyes stared down into his. The sword point rested in the small of his throat as the young man yanked away the gag.

"Don't try anything," he said. Bernal coughed, spitting up fibers. He managed a nod. "Who are you and why were you trying to kill those girls last night?"

"Water." Voice raspy and tongue stuck to the roof of his mouth, tasting of boiled onion and horse shit. The boy dropped him and left. Bernal desperately searched for something else to cut his bonds. Tossed blankets, several packs, and the bow. *Aha!* He spotted an arrow carelessly cast outside the quiver. He squirmed closer to his target, nearly reaching it when the boy came back in.

Curse you Janus!

The boy dragged Bernal to the center of the tent, propping his head up on a bunched-up blanket. Water poured from a skin into his mouth. Bernal swallowed what he could while the rest ran over the sides of his mouth. Coughing, he choked up a thin stream, spilling it down his chin.

"Let's try this again," the boy said. "Who are you?"

Bernal chuckled. "Not very good at interrogating are you, boy?"

Water splashed his face, going up his nose so it burned as he coughed and closed his eyes. He shook his head, spraying water all around and laughed.

"That's the way you do it."

"Next time it won't be water on my tent floor." The blade touched his throat again. "Name."

"Bernal," he said, blowing out water, dripping from his head to his nose and mouth. "I come from Shadow Manor."

"I don't believe you." The point pressed to his skin, pricking him so blood trickled out in the water droplets.

"You know it as Foster's Manor," Bernal said.

Pressure eased and he swallowed.

"What do you want with the woman and her child?"

"They're here? In your camp?" The boy tried to guard his emotions, but the slight rocking on his feet and narrowing of his eyes was all the answer Bernal needed. "You're going to be one sorry son-of-a-whore when those two bitches turn on you."

Bernal laughed at the boy's confused expression.

"Oh, they didn't tell you. The little girl is a skin-changer and the woman has one in her belly. They killed thirty manor guards, big, strong men. Good men. Loyal to a fault. Each well-armed and armored. I would watch my back around them, wear some wolf's bane and alder berry around your neck."

"You're lying," the boy said.

"Why else would the Manor Commander give us a silver gorget to protect our throats? Check my armor, it should still be there." Bernal appraised the boy. Indecision and self-preservation hung on his face. "Cut my bonds and I'll take them off your hands. I swear by the Blades Man no harm will befall them. I'll take them back with me to the Manor for trial." He changed his inflection, trying to sound friendly, almost conspirator-like, adding: "No one will know of your little camp. Release me and it'll be like we never crossed paths."

"If I don't." The boy sounded churlish. *A step in the right direction.* Bernal thought, *just be patient. Give the boy more time to let the gravity of the situation sink in.* Manipulation had always been his weak point. His sword was quicker than his tongue. Disarmed, he needed the reverse side of the Janus' coin to pull off any form of verbal persuasion.

"Kill me now and toss my body off the highest cliff." Bernal laid his head down. It ached and he didn't care at the moment if it remained attached. "I really don't want to be food for the little one."

The boy shoved the gag back into his mouth and left the tent. Bernal closed his eyes. The time would come when he should struggle, but for now, he needed rest. *Janus bless me! I put the fear of the Shadow in that one. I just might persuade him to give Bekka and the little girl to me.* If not, when the chance arose, he would kill this band of children and then march back to the manor with his prize.

"They can't stay."

Jarrod squinted in the half-grey light of morning. A dull sheen blurred the figure so close yet far enough away to be a distant dream. He shut one eye and shielded the other with his cupped hand. Ishmael's stern face leaned over him. Dark circles sagged beneath his eyes. *He's sleep walking.*

"Go back to bed," Jarrod mumbled. Mere moments passed since he had fallen asleep, wrapped in a blanket next to the dead fire pit. "Sun's not all the way up, neither should you." He turned on his side away from Ishmael, pulling the blanket over his head.

"Get up." Ishmael shook him so his teeth clanked together. "We need to talk."

Jarrod waved him away.

Ishmael grabbed Jarrod's hand and pinched the flesh between thumb and forefinger.

"Ow! Alright, I'm up." Jarrod sat up, rubbing his hand. A small bruise started to form. He began to scold Ishmael when a weight shifted beside him. Blonde hair poked out from a cocoon of blankets where Hannah soundly slept. He peeled the blanket off, climbed out, and stumbled a few paces away. The air held a sharp chill and Jarrod crossed his arms over his chest trying to keep his body heat from escaping.

Ishmael followed Jarrod, jerking his thumb over his shoulder. "What's all this about?"

"Nothing." Jarrod yawned big, his jaw bone creaking. "She couldn't sleep in her tent and mine was occupied."

"Whatever this nothing is, keep it between you two. For now, I need you to listen carefully," Ishmael said, speaking slowly. "Bekka and the girl cannot stay here."

"You're not making sense." Jarrod stretched. His whole body ached from sleeping on the hard ground. The rush from last night's skirmish left him drained and his mind was fuzzy. "You want to send them away? Where are they going to go?"

"Back the way they came." Ishmael dangled the red cloak with a golden sun in front of Jarrod's face. Jarrod batted it away. "This belongs to a Shadow Manor guard. We killed a Manor guard last night!"

"Never heard of Shadow Manor," Jarrod said. "Why do they have a sun as the insignia?"

"This isn't the time to be esoteric, Jarrod. We have way more important issues on our hands than wondering at sigils." Ishmael began pacing. "Besides, Shadow Manor used to be Foster's Manor."

"It makes some sense. Foster's Manor isn't that far away." Jarrod's father had taught him the history of the Manors in case he ever got wanderlust and desired to explore Nemus. Four Manors spiraled off the Keep in each direction, designed to be strong holds to protect against invasions. However, they did nothing to prevent them from traitors within— Lord Desmond marched from the Northern Manor to kill King Reuban. At the Ascension War's end, the Eastern Manor was destroyed, the South abandoned, while lesser nobles occupied the North and West by the good will of the council that governed Nemus. *Well, used to govern before Joanne killed them all.* News from the Manors rarely reached Heartwood Pines, which was one reason they didn't know about Joanne's return until Thramel's betrayal.

"How did you know its name changed?" Jarrod scratched his head. His hand froze in his tangled hair. "Did the guy wake up? You spoke with him?"

"We had a brief conversation," Ishmael said.

Jarrod didn't ask what Ishmael did to get the guard to talk. His father excelled at extracting information in unusual ways. Jarrod could taste the bitterness on his tongue from the drugged tea. No doubt Ishmael picked up a few of those techniques.

"What else did he say?"

Ishmael hesitated, rubbing his neck and grimacing.

"Do I need to ask him myself?"

"No," Ishmael said, annoyed. "He's convinced that the girl with Bekka is a skin-changer. He said they killed thirty Manor Guard."

"I don't believe it." Jarrod recalled the little girl hiding behind Bekka's leg. She was more terrified of them than anything else. "If that little waif killed thirty grown men, why didn't she change and kill the two hounding them?"

Ishmael shrugged.

"That's reassuring," Jarrod said, stifling another yawn. "I think you should sleep out here while I take a turn watching him."

"Listen, Jarrod." Ishmael lowered his voice. "He promises not to give away our location if we let him go." Jarrod waited for Ishmael to finish the thought. There was no way the guard would graciously forget about them, especially not after they killed his partner. He gestured for Ishmael to complete the rest of the demand. Reluctantly, he did. "And we give him the woman and girl to take back for trial."

"You can't seriously consider these as options," Jarrod said, raising his voice. Hannah stirred and turned over. Jarrod put a hand on Ishmael's shoulder and leaned in. "You're not thinking about it are you?"

"If they hurt someone, they should stand trial," Ishmael said.

"Trial." Jarrod swallowed his laughter. "The way Bekka's belly bulged I'd wager my favorite plow horse that she's pregnant. There's no way I'm going to stand by and have this guy take them back to a biased and unfair trial. Pregnant or not, Bekka would swing at the end of a rope. The girl she protected would be sold off into servitude, or worse." Jarrod took a deep breath and let it slowly. "We saved them. They're our responsibility now."

"If that woman and child are so important, I don't think the Manor will forget about them. For all we know there could be a detachment of hundreds scouring the valley. What do you think they will do to us if they discover we killed one of their own and trussed up another?"

Ishmael asked. "I don't want to fight another battle when we already have a war."

"It's all one and the same," Jarrod said. "Sacrificing their wellbeing for our safety isn't the answer. Even if we defeat Joanne, what kind of people would we become? Would we be any better than Fraster or Thramel?"

Ishmael tossed up his hands.

"What do you want to do with the guard? We can't keep him bound and gagged forever?"

"Can't we blindfold him and dump him off deeper in the valley?"

"Might as well slit his throat. He'll have no food, or water." Ishmael pinched his nose and squeezed his eyes closed. "If he happens to live, he will just come back."

"Then we move," Jarrod said. "Go back home."

"You're not going back to Heartwood Pines with me," Ishmael said. "My father will kill us both."

"You can't leave me alone with all of this?"

"Why not?" Ishmael growled. "You had to play hero and save them instead of leaving well enough alone."

"You mean let them die so we stay safe?"

"Too many people died because of you." Ishmael clenched his jaw, biting back the next words Jarrod knew were in Ishmael's heart, even left unspoken.

"Go ahead, say it." Jarrod stood up, sticking his chin out. "Blame me for your brother and mother's deaths."

The blow came unexpectedly. Ishmael's hands lashed out, striking Jarrod in the chest hard enough to knock him to the ground. Jarrod tried to get up, but Ishmael shoved him back down. Straddling Jarrod, he gripped the front of his tunic and lifted his head up. Jarrod saw anger, hate, and worse in Ishmael's eyes, the anguish of failure. Failure to protect his family. Failure because he hadn't been there to save Michael or his mother as they were slain by Thramel's men.

"Not you!" Spittle flew from Ishmael's bared teeth, his face kissing distance from Jarrod. "Don't speak of them ever again! Not a word of their name from your lying, betraying lips! The only reason I don't beat you senseless is because I need you to atone for the blood on *your* hands." He shook Jarrod once to emphasize his point. "Don't speak their names again. Ever! Keep your gods-damned mouth shut."

Jarrod tore Ishmael's hands off his tunic. He tried to buck him off, but Ishmael outweighed him by three stones. When Ishmael tried to grab him again, Jarrod seized his wrists and twisted them. Giving a furious growl, Ishmael broke free and raised his fist, ready to strike.

Do it! Jarrod willed.

"Why are you making so much noise?" Hannah sat up, shoving hair from her face and glaring at them.

Ishmael relaxed his hand, lowering it to his side. He glowered at Jarrod for a moment, then got off him. Standing next to Jarrod's pile of belongings, he picked up the hoe and tossed it Jarrod's feet.

"Go play farmer," he said. "It's the only thing you're good at."

Jarrod grit his teeth, watching Ishmael stalk off down the hill. *Go play farmer! That's all I want to do!* He ached to shout. *All I ever wanted and no one will let me.* Jarrod scrubbed at his mouth in frustration.

"I never asked for any of this," he said, talking to himself.

"What was that all about?" Hannah asked, tossing off the blankets. She padded over to him, concern on her face. "Was he going to hit you?"

Jarrod nodded. She offered him her hands and he took them, standing up on shaky legs. His entire body felt tense, ready to snap. Hannah tried to catch his attention, but he stared at his feet, hands balled into fists.

"Why?"

"Nothing to worry about," Jarrod said, sounding curter than he intended. He dusted off his shirt and looked over at his tent. "I'm going to check on our guests."

"I'll join you."

"Fine," Jarrod said. He had his fill of arguing.

I'm surprised everyone isn't out here watching what's going on. The children usually woke up at first light to dress and get chores done. They probably heard him arguing with Ishmael and thought better of coming out. When his parents used to argue, Jarrod would go walk the fields, kicking up stones and chuck them at the crows. They would caw angrily and fly off to the highest branch out of stone chucking reach. Not that his aim was any good or his arm strong enough to throw very far.

He stopped next to his tent and took a deep breath, then exhaled it. He pushed Ishmael and crows from his mind. *Speak with compassion,* he reminded himself. *It's not their fault Ishmael's angry. They didn't cause the argument, either.*

The hard knot in his gut refused to go away.

"Hello." Jarrod tapped his fingers on the flap. "Are you awake?"

No reply.

"Maybe they're still sleeping?" Hannah suggested.

Jarrod rapped the tent pole. "Sorry if we were loud. I just want to see how you're doing and if we can get you anything. Breakfast or tea or whatever we're able."

"We should leave them alone," Hannah said after no reply came again. "They'll come out when they're ready."

"If they're still in there."

Jarrod resisted the urge to flip open the flap. A strange man walking in on a woman and child wouldn't be the best scenario he desired to create. The situation was tough enough without adding in that extra embarrassment. He raised his eyebrows at Hannah. She sighed and rolled her eyes.

"Fine, I'll go."

"Thank you."

She opened the flap and ducked inside. Jarrod looked around to see if Ishmael had returned. As expected, Ishmael was nowhere in sight. *Probably brooding along the stream until he's had enough grumbling,* Jarrod's belly rumbled, *or gets hungry.* It wasn't the first time Ishmael left angry, but it was their first real fight, mostly because Jarrod avoided conflict. *Father's truth and Mother's mercy, I'm not going to allow him send the woman and girl away.* Jarrod listened for Hannah to let him know it was proper for him to enter. A breeze picked up, rustling the quiet tent. *They're sure taking their time.*

From his limited experience with women, he learned one thing. If a woman could keep a man waiting, she did. Never once had one hurried up on his account.

"Hannah," he said, tapping the post again. "Everything alright in there?"

He waited a few heartbeats. No one responded.

"Hannah. I'm coming in."

He pulled back the tent flap.

"Hannah?"

CHAPTER FOUR

Torn asunder by doubt and greed
Mother, the blessed word becomes a curse
Upon the lips of children.
Gnashing teeth and venomous glare
Rise up, my children from the depth of
Shadow and despair. Strike down
Deceitful words.
Love was never enough
                    —*From "The Book of Prophesy"*

Hanse Tanner knew the man who entered his shop was different. It wasn't his black armor emblazoned with two swords, or the fact that he paid in silver bars— those raised a thick, black eyebrow as his green eyes lit up in amusement. The man smelled different. No sweat, nor dust from travelling. Clean, like a newborn babe freshly delivered into the world. Only one road led into and out of Elysium.

Many leagues of empty desert resided to the north, separating Nemus and Meritum. To the south was deep, dark forest before one met the rocky crags of the Placid Sea. Yet, not a speck of dirt on his shiny black armor. Also, any man in his right mind wouldn't travel with so much weight, unless he was expecting to go into battle. The dual long swords at his hip told Hanse the stranger just might be doing that.

Wouldn't surprise me if he just stepped out of Venustas Lux, Hanse licked the tip of the charcoal pencil, made a a few marks in his ledger, before closing it..

"How may I help you?" Hanse asked, giving a cordial smile. The kind that got people to purchase goods in his store, even if it's a copper for a honeysuckle stick to chew, and kept them coming back.

The stranger set a large pack on the counter. Something inside clanked heavily as the contents shifted. The stranger returned Hanse's smile, though his seemed out of place on such a grim face.

"I'm seeking to trade for a horse and a moon's worth of supplies." He had an odd accent that Hanse couldn't place. It sounded regional, but older, like how Hanse's grandfather spoke after he drank too much hard cider.

"We don't keep horses in back." Hanse laughed at his joke, but the stranger's smile faded. *Alright, he must've heard that one too often.* "What sort of supplies?"

The question surprised the stranger. He blinked, furrowing his brow as though trying to remember what he required.

"Food and drink," he said, listing them off on his fingers. "Tack and saddle for the horse, and a bedroll."

"For the horse?" Hanse asked, attempting another joke. He got a perplexed stare.

"No, for me."

Hanse nodded, marking down on his sheet everything the stranger requested. Beside it he wrote: sense of humor. Out of stock.

"It'll take a short time to gather some of this together. Enough for you to visit the stables." Hanse turned the yellow page over, charcoal pencil posed to record. "What kind of food do you eat?"

"Whatever you have available is fine."

Not a picky eater. He'll make some lucky woman happy, if he don't scare her away first. Hanse made some quick marks on the paper, estimating the cost of the order.

"To trade?" He spun the final number around for the stranger to see.

The stranger ignored it. He unlatched his pack and set out two bars of silver. Hanse's mouth wanted to drop open. Gritting his teeth to keep from looking like a slack-jawed fool, he took out a file from beneath the counter. A quick shave off the edge of the bar would tell if it were real silver, or plated lead. As he scored it, more shining silver shone beneath. It was real. Enough silver to purchase his entire store filled the stranger's bag.

"Is this sufficient?"

Hanse swallowed and nodded.

"Where can I find a horse?"

Huron left the general store and stopped on edge of the cobblestone road. A group of villagers gathered around, keeping at a distance. Solemn faces studied him in silence. Silent enough so he could hear the breeze rustle through the thatched roofs and the distant rattle of a cart rolling over the uneven stone. He counted twenty villagers in total, including one peering out the window of the seamstress shop across the way. The number had doubled since he first entered Elysium. Word of his presence had spread. Golden brown and iridescent green eyes kept watch like wary predators when a strange creature enters their territory.

He shifted the pack on his left shoulder, leaving his sword arm free, and hooked a thumb into his belt. Most of them stared at his black armor. *I think it would be wise to obtain inconspicuous traveling clothes.* Even stripped off his armor, he felt certain they would recognize his true nature. The Elysium villagers shunned the outside world for reasons Huron didn't know—unlike some of his brethren and sisters, he didn't pay attention to the created unless there was war or bloodshed when prayers for his guidance rose up like great waves in a sea. This part of the world remained quiet and peaceful as it had for centuries. These people were different, more perceptive, like they could smell his otherness. He would have to step lightly to prevent disturbing them anymore than he already had. Other ears may hear and then he would no longer hold the advantage of stealth.

"Which way to the stables?" he asked.

No one responded. Green and brown eyes all flecked with gold continued their wary vigilance. He was about to give up and walk in the direction given by Hanse, hoping to stumble on it. Then a man lifted an arm, pointing east.

"Thank you."

They spread apart as he approached. Some dispersed to go about their business, others continued the vigil. Huron pretended not to notice them. He followed the cobblestone road and some nodded to him, as if to say he was on the right path.

The stables were located at the far end of Elysium, isolated away from the villagers. Huron thought the stables would be in a more prominent location, or at least easier to access, since riding was the best mode of transportation to and from Elysium. He hadn't seen a single horse in the other parts of the village. Instead, men yoked to the shaft by their shoulders drew the carts. They walked with ease, pulling carts loaded with crates and barrels, or other items.

Impressive, he observed, but did not engage in further conversation. The display of prowess could be cultural, but he figured there were other underlying factors. Factors he didn't have time to puzzle through. Since the men pulled the carts, what need would they have for horses? *I might need to travel on foot.* It would be more than a mere inconvenience. Haste was needed to get to the boy.

A combination of fresh hay, wood chips, and horse sweat led him the rest of the way to the stables. It wasn't hard to find once he reached the edge of the village. No other buildings were built within two hundred yards of it. Three horses occupied the stalls, their long tails swishing away flies. They were smaller than he remembered. He estimated their height ranging between eleven and twelve hands. The last horse he rode was over seventeen hands. Lamgor was his name, meaning pile splitter. Strong back and thick legs powered him through the throng of battle. The sleek black destrier broke the pike and shield line, leading the point of the charge. Men fell to kicks or had their faces torn off by the destrier's teeth. Lamgor died the day Huron ascended. An axe split Lamgor's skull and he crashed on top of Huron, crushing his leg and hip as he lay helpless on the blood soaked dirt. The last thing Huron remembered was hammers and axes pummeling his black armor. Crumpling steel echoed in his ears as he screamed...

"Are you interested in trading or just admiring the view?" A burly man asked, lumbering around the side on the stable. Thick black beard covered his chin and curly black hair stuck out from beneath the brim of a woven straw hat. His nose was crooked like he broke it and never set right. He wore a brown vest over a sweat stained tunic. An apron tied around his waist held a small hammer and brush. His hands were clasped together close to the hammer.

"Not too many folks come out this way." He spat a green wad into the dirt. It had a smell of mint. "The horses get a bit peculiar around those who do."

"Why is that?"

He shrugged.

"Miles." He held out a large, calloused hand. He lowered it after not having the gesture returned.

"Which ones are for trade?"

"All of them." He went over to the first stall and led a dappled grey and brown horse out. "She's a well-dispositioned lass. Stronger than she looks. Won't be any good for a battle, if that's what you intend."

The mare snorted and nodded her head. Miles held up a slice of apple and she gobbled it down.

"The only thing is this one has a sweet tooth."

Huron examined her haunches and withers. The mare looked well-taken care of. She didn't shy away as he stroked her neck. Miles grunted at this. Huron set his bag of silver down as he lifted the leg to examine each hoof. They were shod with a sturdy shoe.

"How well will they hold up for travel?" They seemed pampered and he didn't want to get halfway to Nemus only to have them die in the middle of the desert.

"She and the other two were brought down from Seaptum." Miles patted her rump. "A travelling merchant stabled these beauties with me. Said he'd be back for them once he was finished trading his wares. He traded in Seaptum steel and fine metal workings, nothing we needed here, but he was stubborn and wouldn't hear differently. He had a pale and feverish look about him, too. After three days I got word he took ill. Sure enough, the next day he died of some fever caught out in the desert. I only think it fair to recoup my cost by trading these for fair value."

Huron inspected the other two horses. They were lean, but not gaunt. Coats groomed and they walked without a limp. Hooves were well-shod, no sign of cracks. They were young, easy tempered. No shying away as he approached. The merchant took good care of the horses. Almost better care than for himself.

"You have all their tack?"

"Sold it to Hanse at the general."

Huron nodded. At least what he traded for would fit.

"I will take these two." He indicated the dappled mare and a white gelding slightly taller. Opening his pack, he took out four silver bars, watching Miles' eyes widen and then narrow. "They are pure, just ask Hanse."

"I believe it," Miles said, nearly a whispering. His eyes widened and his voice hitched. "You are him...the Blades Man, aren't you?" He coughed and blinked, clasping his quivering hands together. "Of course, you are! No one else would be foolish enough to carry a pack of pure silver with him through the wilderness. Except, you didn't come from no wilderness... at least none we ever saw."

"If you know who I am, then count yourself blessed by my offering." He handed the four bars to Miles who took them absently.

"Forgive my irreverence." Miles bowed, dropping his eyes to the dirt. "I meant no disrespect."

"No offense was taken," Huron said. Unease began to overcome him. The idea of being worshipped in public wasn't appealing and A blind man could foresee this would catch the attention of the Shadow. "My apologizes. I must go... I have much to attend."

"Of course." Miles hurried to help him remove the gelding and brought the third along. Huron gave him a questioning look. "This is my offering. May he bring you many blessings."

"I will not forget your generosity." He placed a gloved hand on Miles' shoulder. The man bowed his head and knelt. "May you prosper in this life and the next."

Tears filled Miles' eyes as he rose, and he swiped them away. The Blades Man's blessing held no power in the current form, but he left Miles with a little wealth and a sense of well-being. Not every man can profess being touched by a god and live to tell the tale.

Taking the three horses, he led them back to the general store. They balked when any of the Elysium villagers got too close, but otherwise were easy to handle. Hanse had all the tack and supplies ready when he arrived. More solemn villagers watched him saddle the horses. He was happy to have the third since it made distributing the supplies easier.

He was about to mount the mare, when a small hand tapped his leg.

"Excuse me," one little girl asked. She wore a plain brown dress with a white bonnet covering thick folds of long brown hair. Golden brown eyes looked at him in earnest. "Are you a god?"

Huron crouched down to look into those strange colored eyes.

"I am as you are," he touched her shoulders and looked directly into the golden-brown eyes. He saw her innocence, a simple curiosity as she waited patiently for him to continue. "A child of Mother."

The girl smiled.

"Breanne, leave him alone." A woman broke from the onlookers and scooped up the girl. Her cheeks were red. She lowered her eyes, also brown but with green to match her dress. "She's a child and doesn't understand..."

"She understands enough," Huron said. "We are all children of Mother.

The woman hurried Breanne away. The child smiled over her mother's shoulder, revealing sharp canines, and waved. Huron waved back. A sense of relief filled him as he rode south. No more watchful gazes or the sense of being out of place. The Gods' Forge waited for him. He could do the job he came to do and return home. Not much time remained to train the farm boy into a warrior.

CHAPTER FIVE

We touch them, meld into their souls
Like fire hardening soft, rich fertile soil
Into clay, leaving behind tiny fragments
Pieces of ourselves.
We become one.
                    — *From "The Book of Creation"*

"Hannah?"

Jarrod poked his head inside the tent, half expecting to find a hole in the floor dropping down to gods-know-where? Dim-light shown through the opening, revealing empty, rumpled blankets at the center. The tent was large enough to hold four people comfortably, which suited Jarrod well since he liked to spread out—any smaller and the thrashing about in his sleep would bring the entire contraption down on his head, poles and all. Yet, it appeared empty. Like they had Ascended.

That's not possib—

Someone whimpered. A chill raised gooseflesh on his skin.

"Hannah?" Jarrod rolled the flap up to allow in more light. Sarrah quivered in the far corner. Big, round eyes widened and she threw her arms over her face.

"Where's your mother?" he asked, stepping inside. Sarrah shook her head and crumpled into a ball, arms crisscrossing in protection. The hairs on the back of Jarrod's neck stood up. *This is all wrong.* He looked to the left and his heart sank. Weariness bleed away, leaving him in an almost dream-like state. Hannah stood stiff in the corner, eyes wide and mouth covered. But not by her own hand. Like a silent specter, Bekka held Hannah's head against her belly, a blade to her throat.

"What's going on?" He took a step towards them, and Bekka pulled Hannah back, the knife drawing closer to her skin. Hannah squeaked, eyes pleading for him to do something.

This can't be happening. Jarrod's mind raced to puzzle out the situation that was too familiar, bringing back memories of the Watch Tower. *Where'd she get the knife?* He kicked his knapsack and it opened. Jarrod groaned at his stupidity. *I need to go back to sleep and restart this morning.*

"Stay there," Bekka said in a low growl. Her black hair was a tangled knot, giving her the appearance of a crazy woman. The sympathy Jarrod felt for her last night slid beneath a fog of fear. Determination glimmered in Bekka's blue eyes as she held his gaze. *She'll kill Hannah if I force her hand.*

"Alright, just don't..." Jarrod held his palms up. "Don't hurt her."

"Close the flap and then sit over there." She motioned to the back corner with a nod of her head. Jarrod didn't move. Closing the flap would seal them in and any opportunity of raising an alarm to Ishmael would be gone. "Do it." Her hand twitched and Hannah gasped.

The fear in Hannah's eyes brought out the helplessness again, like when Thramel put a sword in Jarrod's hand and placed the point on Hannah's breast. Jarrod loosened the tent flap and let it flop. Gloomy light filtered in, casting shadows around Bekka's face, and stole away her beauty, leaving a savage mask in its place.

Stay calm and maybe we can get out of this unscathed. He sat cross-legged, and awaited more instruction.

"Now, I'm going to remove my hand. Don't either of you make a sound unless I tell you. Nod if you understand."

Both he and Hannah nodded.

Bekka moved her hand away, dropping the arm around Hannah's midsection. She hugged Hannah, pinning the girl's arms to her sides. Hannah gave a startled cry and she looked at Jarrod. He tried not to let his own fear show, so he glanced up at Bekka.

"Who are you people?" Bekka demanded. "What are you doing out here?"

Jarrod swallowed hard, licking his dry lips.

"We are war orphans, tired of soldiers and civilization. We came out here to make a new home. Her parents were recently killed by soldiers. Mine died in the Ascension wars."

"Jarrod saved me and my two sisters," Hannah said, voice shaky.

Bekka eyed them suspiciously.

"If we wanted to harm you, I wouldn't have stopped those men from cutting you down last night," Jarrod said. "The only reason I came in here was to find out if you were hungry and what we can do to help."

"I heard you fighting with the other boy," Bekka said. "Didn't sound like you wanted to help us."

Jarrod clenched his jaw. *Ishmael, your big mouth has got us in trouble!*

"Sarrah and I will leave your camp," Bekka continued, "after you give us a horse and supplies."

"We don't have much—"

"More than what we have."

"Yeah, but we have five children here."

Bekka's mouth drew tight.

"Give us enough for a day or two," she said, "we'll manage on our own afterwards."

Stealing, more the like.

"Put the knife down and we'll talk about it," Jarrod said, but Bekka maintained her hold—the blade a simple flinch away from severing Hannah's throat. "I can't make you do anything, but if you hurt Hannah, you get nothing from us. We want to help... I want to help you, though right now, you aren't assuring us of our own safety." He realized he was babbling, but he had to keep talking so she wouldn't change her mind and harm Hannah. "How do we know the Manor Guard isn't right about you? Did we make a mistake? Will you hurt us or come back in the night and steal all our supplies?"

After a moment of consideration, a moment where Jarrod measured his chances in tackling the woman without Hannah getting cut and they weren't very good—he was bigger, but the knife was too close to Hannah—Bekka lowered the knife. She released Hannah and the girl threw herself across the tent. Jarrod caught her in a tight embrace.

"She didn't hurt you?" He lifted her chin and checked her neck for blood. Not so much as a scratch was visible.

Hannah trembled in his arms, shaking her head as her lips tried to form words. She swiped at her eyes and dropped down next to Jarrod, glaring at Bekka.

"We aren't thieves." Bekka tossed the knife into the pile of blankets. "Or murderers."

Skin-changers, Ishmael called you.

"I didn't think you were," Jarrod said, rubbing Hannah's back. "Nor would I allow Ishmael to send you away."

"Well, we're not anyone's responsibility, either."

"No, but your daughter needs somewhere to rest and recover from whatever nightmare you two escaped from," Jarrod said.

"She's not my daughter." Sorrow thickened her voice and she glanced at Sarrah. Sheepishly, Sarrah left her spot and hugged Bekka's leg. "She is my ward and I will protect her no matter the cost. I know you understand."

"Yes, I do." He put an arm around Hannah and squeezed. Hannah smiled gratefully at him. "Why don't you go out and start up a fire for breakfast. Rouse up the other children to help you. I want to talk with Bekka for a little bit longer."

"Will you be safe?" Hannah asked, indicating Bekka with a quick sidelong glance.

Jarrod smiled and nodded.

Hannah gave Bekka a dark look, scowling at her as she left the tent. Bekka either didn't take notice or ignored it.

"Is she your... betrothed?"

"Gods, no!" Jarrod said. "She's pretty and... and will make someone a fine bride one day... but not me. I mean..." His cheeks flushed. *Gods! I'm rambling.* "She's my ward."

Bekka smiled and nodded, not at all convinced.

"Hannah and her two sisters watched their parents get murdered," Jarrod said. "These men sought retribution from the last war for some imagined slight. I was there that night they burned her house. I stopped them before the men hurt the children. We've been running ever since."

"Forgive my presumption," Bekka said, "it's just the way she looked at you."

"I think that was relief," Jarrod said. "She is too young."

"How old is she?"

"Fourteen."

"Girls have been betrothed at a much younger age." A sense of knowing edged her voice as it dropped off at the end.

"Well, I'm not interested in a child bride," Jarrod said, scratching his head. The conversation travelled an awkward path. One he wished to divert from to a safer road... with less brambles. "Besides, they are like my sisters now. With their parents gone, I take care of them."

"Very noble," Bekka said.

Jarrod's cheeks flushed again. The compliment stirred more than pride in him. "Since we are on the topic of wards and betrothal." He shifted uncomfortably. "Where is the father to your child?"

Bekka touched her belly and frowned. "Dead."

"I'm sorry."

"That's why we are traveling to Meritum." She stroked Sarrah's hair. "There is a place for people like us."

People like us? Jarrod didn't voice the question. He doubted he'd get a true answer. *Skin-changers,* Ishmael's voice chimed in. Jarrod shook it away.

"Meritum is far away. You have to cross a desert just to get there."

"I know." Bekka sighed. "That's why we require a horse and supplies."

You need more than a horse a few days of supplies. Jarrod frowned, but didn't press the point. "I will talk with Ishmael and see what we can do." He had an idea that conversation wouldn't go very well. At least not without some sense of security. "Why were the manor guards trying to kill you?"

"Because we are different," Bekka said, sitting cross-legged. Sarrah pressed up against her, hiding her face in Bekka's bosom while Bekka studied Jarrod in uncomfortable silence. Then Bekka gave an uncomfortable smile, nodding her head as though making a decision. "Four moons back, those men attacked the people I lived with on the outskirts of Foster Manor. We were a small community residing peacefully in Blackwood. To those who didn't understand us, we were always considered different, outsiders. I guess a rumor spread to the Manor that someone was being held against her will. The strange people who lived in the forest kidnapped her. So they came at night, torches blazing and swords dripping blood. Men, women, and children were slaughtered. Only Sarrah and I survived."

"They wanted to take me away," Sarrah said, voice muffled by Bekka's arm.

"I would never let that happen." Bekka wiped strands of hair from her forehead and kissed her. Looking Jarrod firmly in the eyes, she added: "No one will ever take you away from me."

I have enough children to take care of, I don't need another, he wanted to say, but held his tongue. She was afraid and determined to survive. The veiled threats were more than empty promises. Especially after four long night and days on the run from men trying to kill them. He understood perfectly well the lengths Bekka would go to protect her unborn child and the girl.

"I will do my best to get you what you need. You are welcome to rest and regain your strength for as long as you require." Jarrod's stomach grumbled. "Now, I'm going out to get something to eat. Join us for breakfast when you are ready."

"Thank you," Bekka said. "It's been a long time since we had a meal."

"I'm so very hungry," Sarrah said.

"I guess we will join you now," Bekka said.

Jarrod stood and opened the tent flap. Bekka and Sarrah went out first. He ducked under and followed them.

Children busied themselves around camp. Azriel carried a sack of groats while Lily scooped several spoonsful into metal bowls, then added cold water from a bucket of boiled water from the stream that had cooled. Kellen helped Hannah at the cook fire, adding kindling to the build up enough heat to boil water. Jarrod yawned, tired from last night's adventure with little sleep. *Gruel for breakfast, again,* he grimaced at the thought. They had over a dozen sacks of groats, enough for a hundred breakfasts if required. He'd happily give one or two sacks to Bekka just so he didn't have to eat the same mush every morning. Activity stopped as all eyes moved to newcomers. Sarrah clung to Bekka's hand, keeping a step behind, wide eyes taking in her surroundings.

"Where's Elly?" Jarrod asked.

"Tending to the horses," Hannah said, dumping water into a black metal pot pitted over a small fire. She set the bucket back down and turned her back to Bekka. After she fed more wood to the flames, she gave a cold look over her shoulder, lips pursed together.

Jarrod scratched his head. *I hope this blows over soon. I don't need to be in the middle of another battle.* "Do we have any dried berries left to add into the gruel?"

"Of course," Hannah said, sounding cheery. "Lily get the berries when you finish up, please."

"Is there anything Sarrah and I can do?" Bekka asked. "As gratitude for saving our lives."

Hannah harrumphed.

"No," Jarrod said. "You can clean up at the stream."

"I can show them," Kellen said.

"No," Hannah snapped.

"Why not?" Kellen folded her arms and pouted.

"Because you are helping me." Hannah glared at her younger sister, silencing anymore protest. She held out a long, wooden spoon. Kellen hung her head and took it from her sister. "Stir it until I tell you to stop."

The others avoided making eye contact to prevent themselves from being the next target of Hannah's scolding tongue.

Jarrod sighed.

"Follow me." He slipped on his boots and took up his hoe.

Part way down the hill and out of ear shot of the camp, Bekka stepped close to Jarrod. He could smell her sweat, and noticed the strands of hair sticking out. *One of the girls might have a brush... if Hannah allows them to lend it to Bekka.* He suddenly felt awkward thinking about Bekka's disheveled hair. His mind raced for something to say, to break the silence. All he could think about was how beautiful her skin on the back of her neck looked in the sunlight.

She turned back and smiled at him, as though reading his thoughts. Dirt streaked her face like war paint added to, rather than took away the beauty of it.

"I have made an enemy it seems," Bekka said.

You did put a blade to her throat. He nodded, then realized what he was doing, quickly shook his head. Bekka laughed, a small but mirthful sound. He felt his face flush. *Even without talking, I make a grand fool!*

"She will forgive you," he said trying to make up for his first blunder. The doubt on her face made him add quickly, tripping over his own tongue, "in time."

"I hope so," Bekka said. "I didn't know what to expect from you all. Sarrah and I were on the run for so long. I didn't know what else to do."

They reached the stream and Jarrod stood several yards back while Bekka and Sarrah took off their worn shoes and waded in. Without warning, they began stripping down to their small clothes. Jarrod spun away, looking up at the sky while trying not to blush. He heard splashing and a cry from Sarrah that it was too cold. He scanned the rock cliffs, wondering where Ishmael went off to this time. That was very much like him. Wandering off when something didn't go his way. Never around until trouble started, which was why he's so upset at Jarrod. Trouble seemed to find its way to Ishmael, the way a dog sniffed out a ham bone. Jarrod gave a wry chuckle. *Ishmael doesn't want to be here. His heart and mind are set on returning to Heartwood Pines.*

A breeze picked, blowing back his hair. *Where are you?* He heard his thoughts echo back, almost like a whisper in his ear. The wind blew again, stronger. Invisible fingers poked and prodded blindly. Only they didn't touch his clothes or body, but his mind. *Champion! Where are you?* Fingers tore at a dark shroud in his mind's eye. He could hear them scraping, nails gouging deep indentations. *Where are you, Champion?* The nails scraped again and again. There was a brief tearing noise. *Ahhhh! I see you!* Jarrod shielded his eyes, crying out as dark claws reached for him. He dropped to the ground, head filled with anguish. *I'm coming for you. When I find you, I will break your blade and shred your flesh from bone.* Something pried at his arms, trying to break them apart. No matter how hard he fought, needles pricked his flesh and his arms were forced down, pinned to his side. Glowing indigo eyes flashed at him. *I'm coming for you! Champion!* A loud, painful shriek filled his ears and he felt his arms released. Jarrod cried out again. Pain flared in his head and he pressed his hands into his ears, trying to blot out the noise.

"Mother save me," he whimpered, thrashing around on the ground. Mother couldn't save him. He was a tool for the gods. One mortal man against all the higher powers and they would destroy him, break him as certain as a thick stone shattered the plow. He beat his hands against his head, forcing the thoughts to end, willing the deep emptiness of unconsciousness to come take him away. "Leave me alone! Leave me alone! Leave me—"

Soft, cool hands touched his face. They closed over his hands, stopping them from battering his skull. Then they lifted his head up and cradled it in a damp cloth. The visions retreated and he opened his eyes. Bekka looked down at him with concern. She stroked his hair, making hushing sounds. The dampness he realized was her wet shift. It clung to her wet body, outlining her breasts and the slight bulge in her belly. The sky spun overhead and he closed his eyes again, willing everything to settle. Waves of nausea struck and he moaned, trying to turn his head to vomit, but Bekka held him, rubbing his temples. Her touch steadied the swirling world and calmed his stomach. He began to shake. A sudden coldness spread over his arms, numbing his fingertips. Bekka stroked his shoulders, fingers tapping lightly up to his neck. Warmth spread across his skin.

"I saw…" He swallowed, taking a breath. He tried to recall the vision, but came up against a dark mesh that he couldn't penetrate. "Darkness. A voice… a malicious voice coming for me." He sat up. "It's gone."

"Was this the first time you had this vision?" Bekka asked.

"Yes," Jarrod said. Bekka leaned forward, searching his eyes. He felt more warmth at how exposed she was, sitting in her wet shift. Instead of looking away, he was compelled by some familiarity shared between them. The sense that they both have similar experience with visions. She knew what it was who stalked them. "Don't tell anyone at camp what happened."

"Get me a horse and supplies and no one will know a thing."

"No," Ishmael said, brow furrowing. He sat on a tree stump, cold bowl of half-eaten gruel in his lap. His boots scuffed the dirt, turning it in circles as he listened to Jarrod ask for horse and sack of grouts. He stomped his foot, startling a cry from Sarrah. "Absolutely not."

"It will get them far away from us like you wanted," Jarrod said, holding back the building frustration. Ishmael was being stubborn out of spite. He returned to camp as they were finishing eating, quietly took up a bowl of gruel and ate it, all without giving Jarrod a single look. Jarrod didn't care for the stubborn attitude and would be happy to ignore Ishmael all the rest of the day. That wasn't possible. He had to get Bekka and Sarrah away to safety, before tempers flared up worse. "We won't miss a single sack of grouts."

Ishmael refused to speak to him, eyeing his bowl instead.

"Mother always told us to help those in need," Elly said, taking up the empty wooden bowls and putting them in a bucket to be washed. Lily and Kellen helped, glancing at Ishmael and Jarrod.

"Look where it got us," Ishmael mumbled and glared at Jarrod.

"As long as we remain here, we pose a danger to you," Bekka said. She handed her empty bowl to Lily. Jarrod noticed it was scraped clean.

"How do we know you won't be a threat if we release you?" Ishmael countered, folding his arms. "You could ride back into camp and take everything, leaving us to starve."

"Sarrah and I just want to go to Elysium."

"Shadow damn it all! It's not about what you want." Ishmael narrowed his eyes. Elly flinched at the curse. She opened her mouth to scold him, when Ishmael leaned forward, raising his hand to silence her protest. "What about the manor guard? What do we do with him?"

"Whatever you see fit." Bekka matched him stubborn look for stubborn look.

"You would like it if we just killed him." Ishmael said, baring his teeth. "That way his secret would die with him."

"Ishamael—" Elly tried to protest.

"He told me about you and Sarrah," Ishmael said and gave her a smug grin.

Bekka instinctively reached for Sarrah. Then folded her legs beneath her and rested her hands over her belly. The stress couldn't be good for the unborn child, Jarrod thought.

"Believe whatever stories you want." The contention had left her voice and she looked off to the side.

"What secret?" Hannah asked Jarrod. "What did he say?"

Jarrod patted her hand. "I'll tell you later."

She gripped his fingers and squeezed them, leaning against him for a response.

"Later," Jarrod hissed and yanked his hand away.

"He'll still come after you if we release him." Ishmael said, voice softening a little. "Or worse! He'll bring back more men to take their revenge on us."

"Sarrah and I are leaving," Bekka said. "No matter what you decide."

"Not without a guarantee of our safety." Ishmael stood up and dumped water into his bowl. "You may be good people as you proclaim, or killers, as the guard said. I don't know who to believe at the moment."

The bucket clattered to the ground, dumping out the bowls as three sets of eyes turned to Jarrod, seeking the validity of the accusation. Jarrod felt like strangling Ishmael in that moment. Bekka flushed and Sarrah began to cry in her lap. Hannah got up and began picking the items off the ground, sending Kellen and Lily off to wash them at the stream. Elly refused to go.

"Either way, we have to protect our own." Ishmael stopped Kellen and placed his own bowl into the bucket. He smiled at her, moving a piece of loose hair out her face before patting her on the shoulder, signaling for her to continue on down to the stream. Kellen looked back, confused at Ishmael's behavior. "We love our children as much as you love your own. If you were in our situation, what would you do?"

"We have nothing to give you." Bekka spread her hands out. Frustration shown on her face and in her voice. "Otherwise, I would just trade it all for a horse and a small supply of food."

"I could ride with her to see her safely away from camp." Jarrod offered.

Hannah pinched his arm and slid her hand through the crook of his elbow, pulling him down to her level. She whispered: "You know what she can do. You can't go alone."

Ishmael laughed before Jarrod could respond.

"She'd slit your throat as you slept." He returned to the stump. "Then come back and kill us all."

"You're acting like a child," Elly said. "She's done nothing to hurt us. All you have is the word of a man, a man who wanted to hurt them. He's probably working for Joanne. I don't think it's a good idea to give that evil woman anything she wants."

"You may be right, Elly," Ishmael said, rubbing the corner of his mouth. "I just don't like the idea of letting them go and finding out that you are wrong. Jarrod isn't capable of doing things right, unless it's playing in the dirt. Even if she finds her way to the desert, he would just get lost and bring a pack of soldiers to our camp."

"Fine," Jarrod said, trying not to get upset over Ishmael's jabs. The earlier accusations still stung his pride. If war taught him one thing, pride killed more men than it saved. "You ride with her. We all know how badly you want to go back to Heartwood. So just go, leave. Take the manor guard with you. Maybe your father can get more information out of him about Joanne."

Bekka glanced at Jarrod, but she remained quiet. Ishmael looked off to the east, contemplating the choices. Jarrod expected him to continue arguing. Instead, he nodded and turned to Jarrod.

"Smartest idea I heard from you, yet," Ishmael said. "That's the way it has to be."

"You're leaving us," Elly said, fists balled up at her sides.

"We're going, too," Azriel said. "I miss daddy."

Ishmael knelt in front of Azriel, touching both shoulders and holding him at arm's length. "I'll be gone only a short time, getting more supplies for winter. As soon as I can, I'll come back for you." Jarrod heard the hollowness in the words. Azriel didn't believe Ishmael either. He shook his head, trying to wiggle free.

"Listen, little man." Ishmael's touch changed into a grip and he gave Azriel a quick shake. Azriel squeaked and began crying. "It's too dangerous for you and Elly. Besides, someone has to stay here and help protect your sister."

"Leave him alone," Elly said, prying Azriel away from Ishmael. "Go away if you want, but don't pretend it's for our good. Don't lie to him."

Ishmael stood up, reaching out to his sister. "Elly—"

"No, Ishmael, no." She backed away, holding Azriel's hand. "Ever since mom and Michael died, you have been acting selfish. We miss home, too. We miss dad. We miss our family."

"Please—"

"Don't you get it?" Tears stood out in her eyes. "We don't want to miss you too."

Ishmael stood quietly.

Elly threw up her hands, gave an exasperated growl. She spun on her toes and stomped off to the tents.

"Why don't you want us anymore?" Azriel asked, then followed after his sister.

Hannah shot an accusatory look at Bekka before heading to comfort Elly and Azriel.

"It's the only way." Ishmael picked up the cold bowl of gruel and carried it to his tent. "If you think of something better, then let me know." He disappeared inside his tent, leaving Jarrod alone with Bekka and Sarrah.

"Are they always like this?" Bekka asked.

Jarrod shrugged. "It's not *always* this exciting." He scratched his head, wishing he could sleep for the next two days. Sleep, he feared, would be in short supply over the next couple of nights.

"When are we leaving?" Bekka asked, taking Sarrah's hand.

Not soon enough. Jarrod flopped on his bed roll. Although it was early, he felt like he could sleep all day. "Go get more rest, we can figure out the details once everyone has calmed down."

CHAPTER SIX

They stalked the battlefields, silent terrors with steel claws ripping entrails, red ichor dripping off metallic snarls. In packs they drove us through the blood-soaked field, slashing holes in our lines, clambering over the piles of dead to hunt those left alive. Our blades were switches breaking against their hide and our armor mere sack cloth shredded like a spider's web in a furious storm.

After each kill, they gave a howl that thinned blood, weakened knees, and turned the sternest spine into brittle wax. Many brave men fled at the onslaught brought about by the Death Howlers. Some swore we fought Demons, not men the day the Grime's field turned red.

— From "The Killing Field"
Fraster K'gnowin

Thramel strode down the corridor, footfalls echoing off the stone walls. On either side marched armed guards bearing the half-moon insignia on their breast plates. Dark cloaks billowed behind them with each stride, boots clanking in a rhythmic beat. Steel helms shaped like wolf heads hid their identity. They carried poleaxes, dual fighting swords sheathed at their hips. *Mors Faunis.* Death Howlers. Joanna's personal guard. Their tongues were cut out so they could speak of nothing they heard or witnessed in her chamber. The only sound they made were grunts, growls, and howls as they sliced their way through the enemy ranks. Watching them fight was much like watching a pack of wolves take down an elk. Harrying it from all sides. Bloodying teeth and claws, until the poor creature weakens. Then their jaws tear out its throat.

At least she thinks I'm still important. Thramel smiled, staring at the wolf heads. Best not to display fear when surrounded by the enemy. The moment he showed up at the Keep, he figured he had forfeited his life. After the Watch Tower, he didn't have anywhere else to go, except for hiding in the desert and living off sand and rock.

If Joanne wanted me dead, I would be a rotting corpse tossed out into the wild to be feasted on by carrion eaters, instead of being escorted to her chamber. This is another late-night pompous display of power, dragging me from my cold cell down the cold corridor to her cold stare. She's trying to dominate me like a dog humping my leg.

"She couldn't sleep, either," he said, giving them a huge grin, and winked at them. "Needed someone to warm her bed."

A wolf's head turned in his direction, metallic teeth bared in a snarl and dark, empty eye-sockets silently staring. A lesser man's bowels would have loosened, but Thramel didn't flinch. He had killed one of the *Mors Faunis* in the Battle of Twin Rivers in Heartwood Pines. Put a sword through its throat and, like any other man, red bleed out. *Explains why they're so eager to take off my head with their axes.*

Another silent *Mors Faunis* guarded the wooden door at the end of the hall. As they approached, he rapped on the door and waited. Thramel grinned at the metal wolf's head. They were all alike, hiding the identity of the creature that once was a soldier. He didn't know how Joanne chose, or bred, men for the *Mors Faunis*, but he knew once they joined the rank, they were no longer human.

"She must've changed her mind," Thramel said, stifling a yawn. "Unless this is a new form of sleep deprivation. I don't mind running with the wolves all night, as long as I get to sleep in at dawn."

Empty eye sockets and wicked snarls focused on him. Silently standing still, patient as predators lurking in the night for their prey. Thramel returned their stare, looking into the dark abyss where gods knew what eyes lay beneath. He didn't know what they saw, or if they even had thoughts beyond the bestial command of their alpha.

I wouldn't mind skinning a few more of you. His hand reflexively went to his hip, but his sword was secured in his room. Joanne forbade him to carry it in the Keep. Just another little annoyance, being told where and how he could travel around the Keep like a boy scolded for clomping around in muddy boots on a newly scrubbed floor.

The *Mors Faunis* closest to the door tilted his head as though listening to an inaudible signal. Then he opened the door, standing aside as Thramel's first escort entered, followed by Thramel, and then the second Death Howler.

Candles half-lit the room in a solemn glow meant for prayers to the gods, or seduction. A sharp scent of cinnamon spices permeated the air and a small fire crackled at the hearth where Joanne stood, her back to him. Long brown hair hung loose to her shoulder blades. Her head tilted up at the painting of Lord Desmond the Usurper hung over the mantle. Thramel was surprised it still existed after the peasants ransacked the castle villa and slaughtered Desmond's son, Alfred, in this very room of the Keep, the blood stain covered by a gold-braided rug. Thramel admired Joanne's form beneath the white shift she wore. The way it hugged her round, bare backside, shaped like a plump apple. He imagined biting into it and smiled. Sheathed knives belted at her narrow hips deterred him from trying.

Either she sleeps with those knives, or this isn't a formal visit. He frowned. *Bad news doesn't bode well for me.*

"Good evening, your Highness." Thramel bent his knee, noticing her bare feet. She must have just awakened or didn't sleep at all. Thramel smiled at the idea she had lost sleep over him. "Or is it morning? I can never tell locked away without fresh air or moonlight."

"Enough of your prattle." She sounded tired and frustrated. Shoulders pulled tightly back, she gripped a crystal goblet full of red wine in her right hand and turned it at the stem on the mantel. The wine swirled like blood. "I should have your tongue removed and make you a Howler."

He knew better than to tempt her temper, but couldn't resist. Pride got the better of a man and down he tumbled.

"I'd serve you better with my tongue in place, than as your lapdog."

She spun, throwing the wine into his face.

"You serve when and how I declare it." Blue eyes flared and her mouth twisted in disgust. The crystal goblet pointed at his heart and he knew he pushed too far. Fortunately, it was a cup instead of a knife in her hand or the blade would be plunged hilt deep into his chest. "Your failure to pacify Heartwood Pines created our problem."

Your problem. Thramel kept his mouth shut. Another provocation and he would find his tongue cut out, or worse. *My head on a pike.* He couldn't care less for the dung swamp and its inbred farmers. Heartwood Pines was just another piece of timber that could burn up in a puff of smoke and it wouldn't change his life. Gold talked. The only reason he fought against Thomas was to preserve his wealth. The usurpers purchased iron ore from Thramel for steel and armor. Thomas declared the ore mines sovereign territory and when Thramel refused to hand it over, Thomas marched upon Heartwood Pines— to his demise. With the brothers both deceased, Joanne made up for their err and began paying him for the ore, and extra coin to create dissention among the leaders of Heartwood, so she could march in and annex the territory, taking its fertile farm lands, leaving his ore mines alone.

Sour wine dripped from his nose and chin. The very thought that his mines would remain exempt seemed dubious. He kept his eyes lowered to her bare feet, staring at her toes painted a bright red. Teeth grinding, he swallowed back his retort. *I may have lost a battle, but what is upsetting you about the war outcome?*

"Sometimes I wonder if you forget which side you serve," Joanne said, turning away, her feet pattering once again towards the hearth. Crystal clinked on wood as she set the empty goblet on the mantel. "You are fortunate I find your skills useful. I have a task for you to again prove to me why I keep you around."

"Yes, your Highness," Thramel said, the words like splinters piercing his lips.

"Rise, so I can see the fire in your eyes instead of hearing it in your voice," she said. Thramel stood up, her blue eyes engaging his. Anger blazed so he felt the heat in his belly, rousing a bitter passion in him. Thoughts of her nude form writhing beneath him like a snake coiling its victim excited him. She spoke, shattering the image.

"You think I'm cruel."

"No, your Highness," he lied in a steady voice. She smirked, seeing through his words. *I think you are a dark hearted she-devil, forked tongue and frigid womb.*

"You could've been a great man despite your failings." Joanne said running a hand through his hair and down the side of his face. "You could've had much, much more than the dark hole in the ground full of little, black stones."

She pressed a finger to his lips.

"First, you need to learn humility." She twisted his lower lips between two fingers. Thramel refused to cry out or pull away. He stared into her sadistic eyes, watching the pleasure she got from the pain she imagined she inflicted. "You run your mouth because nothing has ever been denied you, greedy little man."

"Until now." She yanked and let the flesh slip through her fingers. "If you want to earn my favor once again, you must succeed in this one task."

"As you will," he said, curling his lip. It tingled and he must have looked like a flesh version of the wolf's head, teeth barred and ready to bit. Not yet. He had to bide his time, then tear this she-bitch's throat out. For now, he'd pretend to be her lapdog.

"Good, you're learning new tricks. You're not as daft as I feared." She patted his head and tried not to cringe. "A small manor of mine has experienced a problem. The guard has decided to gallivant off into some woods to kill a small band of rebels. They have not returned." Joanne held out a leather tube. "Here is a map to the manor, it is easy to find on the West Road. However, the road has been in ill-repair so you might have to detour around rough patches. I have horses and supplies ready for your journey. You will go at once and investigate the area. I have word that several of these rebels survived the attack. You must hunt them down and bring them to me. Alive. I am sending two of my guard, as well as a tracker, with you. I expect word of your success within a moon phase. Otherwise, I shall assume you are dead and seize hold of all your land and mines."

Thramel looked over the map. By his calculations it would take two and a half days to ride to Foster Manor. Twenty-six remained to seek out and capture remaining survivors. "That's not enough time," he said. "It could take that long just to discover the rebel numbers. Who knows how long it could take to find a trail, assuming there is a trail to follow."

"You will be briefed on the important matters during your journey," Joanne said, waving away his concerns. "I suggest you make haste."

"My lady—"

"Don't say another word." She glared at him. "I've heard enough of your excuses. I want results or I will take everything from you. Everything."

"As you wish." Thramel stood up, the *Mors Faunis* at his side, hands on sword hilts.

She waved him off.

Thramel bowed and exited the chamber. He returned unaccompanied to his cell, fuming over her demands. *Might as well shave my beard, slap a satchel on me and a half-moon on back! An errand boy! That's what she makes of me! Mother damn the woman and Shadow Walker slit her throat before I do.*

They housed him in a single windowless cell that stank of sweat and mold. A bed and a trunk were is only furnishings. In the corner stood a washstand full of water and a clean rag set out by the maid. Slapping the cold wet cloth on his face, he scrubbed wine from his face, turning the water and cloth a deep, purplish red. On his way out of the chamber, he grabbed his sword belt and shield—a hand crushing a snake emblazoned black on a yellow square. For the first time in nearly two seasons, the door to the outside was left unguarded. Thramel walked out, squinting his eyes against the grey morning light, feeling like a wraith escaping the tomb he'd been locked away in for centuries. In the courtyard, eight horses waited. Supplies loaded down four of them, two *Mors Faunis* mounted on the wings and a short man dressed in a green and brown tunic, sat in the middle, nose sniffing the air.

"Sweet River red," he said, smiling at Thramel, teeth crooked and his tongue lapped at his lips.

"What?" Thramel asked.

"The wine on your tunic," the man said. "It originates from Sweet River, which happens to flow past her Highness' homeland. The grape has a delicate bruised colored skin—"

"Shut your mouth before I give you a delicate bruise," Thramel said, strapping his shield on an unencumbered mare. The man's smile dropped and he glared at Thramel, eyes droopy and red rimmed. *This must be Joanne's tracking dog.* Thramel laughed. *Less hound and more rat-catcher yipping at my heels. I'm amazed the wolves haven't eaten him yet.*

"What's so funny?" the rat-catcher asked, peevish and sullen.

"Nothing you would understand." Thramel mounted the mare. At least this creature was sturdy. He turned in the saddle to face the rat-catcher. "What are you called?"

"Snout," he sniffed, turning his nose away in contempt.

Well won't this be a pleasant journey.

"Light's burning, Snout," Thramel said, pulling on the reins and squeezing his knees to get the mare into a canter. "Time to put your nose to work."

He didn't know which was worse, the scorching sun or the biting gnats. Locked away in the Keep for two seasons, Thramel forgot about the annoying humming in his ears and swatting the buggers before they pricked him. The sweat gluing his tunic stuck to chest and back attracted biters like starving dogs to an unattended feast. Squinting, he shielded his eyes until his hand grew tired.

This is how a bear must feel after waking up from hibernating in its cave. He smacked a bitter on his ear, leaving behind a hollow ringing. He gritted his teeth, growling in frustration. *Furious with the mad world and ready to eat anything that annoyed it.*

Snout whistled through his teeth—a spike driven through Thramel's throbbing head. "Look at that beautiful blue sky. Not a cloud in sight." Snout leaned across his saddle horn and nodded at Thramel. "Perfect day to color up your face. You, sir, are as pale as a ghost."

"Another comment like that and I'll make you into one." Snout grinned at Thramel, and took out a dark leathery strip from his saddlebag. He bit off a piece, chewing away wet and noisy. Thramel tore a rag from a shirt in the saddle bag and poured water from the bladder onto it. He tied the rag around his forehead, already feeling crispier than spitted mutton too close to the fire. He noticed how the gnats and biters didn't bother Snout. "Why aren't you covered in flies? I smelled rotting corpse less ripe than you."

"Honey draws more than vinegar." Snout stared at him through droopy eyes. Thramel couldn't tell if they held malice or boredom. The tracker's nostrils flared and he snorted, nose wrinkling as he touched the tip. "Smells more of piss than vinegar."

"Flies land on all sorts of shit, not just honey." Thramel scattered a black cloud of the little bitters. They split apart long enough for his hand to clear through and reformed a moment later. They didn't bother landing on the mare but circled him, nipping at any exposed skin. Tiny, red bumps formed on his neck and back of his hand. The bites itched so he alternated from swatting the buggers to scratching so much he nearly peeled his skin off.

"Aye they do." Snout grinned. "They do."

Thramel tore more strips off the shirt and wrapped it around his face, leaving enough room for his eyes—even then he covered them to narrow slits, since the bastards kept diving at him. *I'm either going to go mad or blind.* He slipped on his gloves and suffered in the sticky heat. Sweat dripped from his skin and dampened the cloth. That seemed to send the bitters into a frenzy. They could smell the tasty morsel hidden beneath so they buzzed around and around in a quickening black cloud, seeking an opening. Thramel could feel them crawling over the cloth as they sucked up his sweat. He smacked them as they crawled towards his eyes. That only served to make the bitters even more irritated and desperate in their onslaught. He gave in and covered his eyes to even smaller slits, allowing his horse free reign to keep pace with the others.

The Death Howlers flanked him at the furthest edges of the road. How they weren't cooking inside their metal wolf helms and armor was a gods-blessed miracle. *Don't they ever take those things off?* Maybe it was part of the transformation. They no longer felt discomforts of an average person. Without a tongue, they couldn't voice their complaint. Thramel had never seen them eat or piss or do any other natural thing. *Did she remove their manhood?* The idea sent a cold shiver down to his root. Not that he pitied them. Pity someone that wanted to rip out your guts, well that would take a better man than him. He'd much rather see them strung up and skinned like a wolf trapped after attacking a farmer's herd.

The *Mors Faunis* remained silent, following orders, probably not giving him a second thought. Unless he tried to leave. Then he'd have their attention as sure as startled rabbit raises the hound's dander. The chase would be brief and most likely messy for him, not that Thramel would forfeit life and lands so easily.

"When do we stop for a rest?" Thramel asked. The fact he had to ask permission twisted his gut. *I've grown soft in captivity. After only three leagues of riding my legs stiff and my back is sore!*

A snarling wolf head turned and stared at him.

"Yeah, I'm talking to you wolfie. My arse has welts and I got a bladder near ready to burst." He cringed at the whining in his voice, sounding like a spoiled girl—the kind he wanted to smack to give a reason to cry.

The *Mors Faunis* raised a hand from the pommel and Thramel flinched back ready to be struck. Instead, the Death Howler flashed a signal. The one opposite Thramel responded with rapid hand movements.

"What are they doing?" Thramel asked Snout.

Snout shrugged.

The *Mors Faunis* on his right drew his horse close and snatched the reins from Thramel. They slowed to a halt and he led the horse to the side of the road. The *Mors Faunis* pointed at Thramel, then at the brush. Dense bramble weeds and stubby Whitewood trees went on endlessly.

"You're not going to hold my hand as I cross over?" Thramel asked, dismounting and taking his sword scabbard, belting it around his waist. "I might get lost."

He felt a presence come up behind him. The second *Mors Faunis* waited, arms crossed. As sure as his shadow, the Death Howler followed him as he entered the brush. Thramel used his blade to push aside thorny bramble, picking his way to a taller Whitewood that reached shoulder height.

"So are you going to grip the shaft? Or waggle it dry?"

The metal wolf's snarl silently watched him.

Back on the road, Snout had dismounted and was scenting around the bushes. Thramel was about to ask him what he was doing, when Snout hushed him, finger to his lips. Crouching down on all fours, he crept forward, waited, and then leapt in between two brambles. Branches rattled like a battle took place in the brush. A terrified screech shot out and was quickly severed.

Snout emerged, dangling a dead jackrabbit by the ears. A dopey hound dog grin covered his face. Leaves stuck to his jerkin and twigs poked from his mass of black, curly hair. His brown eyes lit up in excitement.

"Look at what we got here," Snout said, stroking the rabbit's dust-colored fur. He sniffed it from tail to long ears. "Dinner."

"Good boy," Thramel said, clapping his hands. "Now bring it here. Bring it here, boy."

"Piss off," Snout said and dumped the rabbit in his saddle bag.

"Who'd want it after it's been in your dirty paws." Thramel muttered under his breath and mounted his horse.

Once again, the *Mors Faunis* flanked him and Snout took up the rear. As the sun dragged on overhead, the biters returned in a small cloud hovering above him. As far as he could tell, not a single biter flew over the Howlers or Snout. He slowed his mount so Snout drew close and the cloud seemed to arch away from the tracker's direction, repelled by some invisible hand.

"Shadow take me! They act like I'm a bloated corpse ripe for their little teeth."

Snout just smiled to himself and dropped back.

Night brought no relief. The little biters were replaced by bigger bloodsuckers, loudly singing past his ear. The group moved off into the thicket, whitewood trees grew denser here, and set up camp in a small glade. As Thramel sat by the fire, Snout's rabbit roasting nicely on a spit, he followed the smoke hoping to get clear of the creatures. *Choke on it, you little bastards!* Soon he was the one coughing, eyes burning and watering. He sat away from the smoke, miserably huddled to give them less flesh to target.

Snout snorted, licking grease off his fingers and tossing the bones into the brambles.

"I give up! What spell did you cast to keep the biters and bloodsuckers off of you?" Thramel smacked the back of his neck, fragile body exploding into a wet smear. Tiny welts rose up on his skin.

"No spell," Snout said, taking a swig from a wine skin.

"Tell me before I gut you and wear your innards."

"That won't work, either." Snout eyed him, measuring him. He spat into the dirt. "For a man about to lose everything, you sure don't know how to form alliances very good. You'd think I was your best friend… Mother! Your only friend left in the entire world. I can save your sorry arse from being locked away with nothing. Yet here you go treating me like a dog that just piddled on your braded carpet and afterwards humped your wife's leg."

Thramel gritted his teeth. He'd knocked out soldiers for less insubordination. This lowly dog, lower than even the rock shifter in his mines, ranked higher than Thramel. The worst part about it, he was right. Thramel had nothing left and was at his mercy. He gave up everything, his home, his mines, his family and friends, when he agreed to Joanne's conditions. Only agreed was not the right word, coerced was more like it. Work for me now or I march my army down your throat doesn't leave room for much negotiation. Another war was not winnable, not with the size of her army. He couldn't muster the people of Heartwood Pines to fight, not after the Ascension War. They would have been slaughtered like chickens asleep in a coop.

"I'm…" Thramel chewed on the word souring in his mouth. "Sorry."

"What's that? Sounded like you are sucking on stones."

"I'm sorry." He tried not to growl and ended up whining like a sulky child. He looked away, clenching his fists. If the little rat-catcher gloated even a little, he would rip his throat out and bathe in the blood. Maybe that would feed the creatures for a little while.

Snout didn't gloat. He nodded and tossed him a small leather bag. Thramel unlaced it, wrinkling his nose at the astringent odor mixed with garlic. He dipped his finger in, a ground black powder stuck to the tips. "Mix with water and dab it behind the ears and under your pits."

"That's all?"

"Unless you want to eat it." Snout snorted. "It tastes worse than it smells."

Thramel took a dab, sprinkled it in his hand and poured water in the palm. He let it soak, turning into a brown mush. The blood-suckers flew a wide circle away from the stuff. Thramel laughed, putting it behind his ears and under pits.

"No more free supper for you, bloody bastards."

He tucked the rest of the bag away into his belt.

"How long does it last?"

"A day or two." Snout set up his bedroll next to the fire. "Depending on how often you bathe."

So it must last you a moon, Thramel thought, but kept his word. He laughed manically as he dabbed the brown grit around the points Snout stated. After a while, he got used to the smell, and Mother bless him, nothing so much as landed on him.

That night Thramel slept uneasily. The bloodsuckers quit their insane humming— he scratched at a few bumps on his neck and arms until they bled. Snout snored under his blankets, a wretched noise that Thramel was certain would draw a night predator or two to their camp. *Good thing we brought our own creatures,* he thought, staring up at the wide dark sky. When the moon went up, the *Mors Faunis* disappeared into the night. With them prowling around, Thramel figured Snout and he were safe to sleep the night and not need to keep watch.

His thoughts prevented him from sleeping. *Stupid farm boy*. It was his fault that Thramel was here, suffering under the angry fist of Joanne. The idea that such a simpleton, who didn't even know how to hold a sword right, somehow fooled Thramel. Not only fooled him, but killed eight trained soldiers in the tower. He had trusted the boy for some odd reason and Jarrod let him down. *Couldn't even kill a simple little girl!* Often, he dreamed of that moment, taking the sword from Jarrod's grip and cutting off the traitor's daughter's head. Before the horrified expression could leave Jarrod's face, he would plunge the sword into the bitch's whelp's gut, carving out his innards and using them to hang the farm boy's body outside the Watch Tower's window. He still hadn't given up on that dream.

Manus Poenas, the hand of fate, had a long reach. He may yet find the boy and girl. Thramel grinned, fantasizing on what he would do to them. Traitors to the cause, one and all. Those who resisted Joanne in Heartwood Pines would feel the heavy hand of fate close on them, crushing their bones and breaking their spirits. Thramel would lead the way and gain favor from her. He knew she liked him. All he had to do was complete this menial task, use his charms to seduce the girl....

Then I will kill Joanne and take it all for myself. He laid awake awhile, smiling and plotting until sleep claimed him, dreaming of bloody swords and weeping women.

The boy was god-touched. Bekka didn't require Shane's keen nose to smell it on Jarrod. Collapsing into a seizure proved as much. From the way he begged for Mother's mercy, it wasn't a benevolent god, either. *Was there such a thing as benevolent gods when children suffered and died by the swords of evil men?* Bekka gave up praying the night her brother and lover were slain. There had to be some purpose— they had to be more than just little markers moved along a game board for the delight of some higher power. She couldn't see the purpose of it all.

Shane had explained to her why their kind clustered in Blackwood and Elysium.

"There is power here," he said, as she lay with her head in his lap. He stroked her hair while she drowsily listened. "Our mother, the true mother who bore the first of our kind, planted an Ash tree in each land as a sign, a promise of sanctuary wherever we choose to travel."

"Who is the true mother?" Bekka asked. As far as she understood, Mother and Father were the only gods capable of creation.

"Sin," Shane said. "The moon came down in human form and lay with our father, Volksing, a powerful war lord who ruled the lands up north. She gave birth to twins, a boy named Volfhearth and a girl, Silver. The children were marked by their golden eyes and the people feared them. Volksing died in a battle and his people cast out Sin, along with her children."

"That is such as sad story."

"Many stories that involve the gods have sad endings."

Shane was nearly prophetic. Not long after that lovely night, he was dead. She heard his voice sometimes. He beckoned her to take up the roll as the new Sin and be the new mother to their kind. "Come north, my love," it said. "Go to the City of the Rising Sun and bear my son. Together, Sarrah and he will become the new tribe of Moon Walkers." As sweet the voice sounded, it couldn't be trusted. Shane was dead, killed by her brother's knife. When he was alive, Elysium, in the south, was all he spoke about. She never heard of this City of Rising Sun. It didn't even sound like a place her kind would want to live. So, she ignored the plea and concentrated on getting her and Sarrah safely to Elysium.

Sitting in Jarrod's tent, Bekka tried to get a restless Sarrah to fall asleep. She sang a little love ballad her mother would sing to her as a child. A song she still enjoyed because it reminded her of Shane.

> *"He found me there on a moonlit night, scared and all affright*
> *Lost, lost, I'd wandered far from home*
> *He came to me dressed in lace, he came and by my side took his place*
> *There he comforted me with soft words of hope, that I was not alone*
> *Lost, lost I'd wandered far from home*
> *He took me to his castle upon a hill, there gave me jewels and gowns of silk*
> *At dawn I was made his bride, and forever he stood at my side*
> *Lost, lost I found a new home."*

"Do we have to leave?" Sarrah asked after the song had ended. She yawned and stretched her arms from beneath the bedroll. "Couldn't we stay with them?"

"What about the place in Shane's stories?" Bekka touched Sarrah's cheek. "Don't you wish to go there?"

"It sounds nice, but I like Elly and Lily and Kellen," Sarrah said, screwing her face into a soured look. "Even Azriel, though he *is* a boy."

Bekka laughed and stroked Sarrah's black hair. In Blackwood there was a boy named Sampson who would tug Sarrah's braid and run away. Sarrah would chase him around the hovels, catch him and punch him in the arm. Sampson would tackle her and they'd wrestle until an elder broke them apart. Then the manor guards arrived and everyone in Blackwood had been slain. The thought that Sampson would never pull Sarrah's hair again ended Bekka's mirth.

"There will be other children in Elysium," Bekka said, solemnly. *Children like you..*

"Not the same," Sarrah groaned. "I like it here."

"Trust me, sweet one, we will be safer," Bekka said. "Elly and the rest, they will be safer once we are gone. They are not from our world, and we need to hide from theirs."

"They're so nice."

"Because they're young and don't understand, like you, little pup." Bekka kissed her forehead. "Get some sleep."

"Yes, mama." Sarrah turned over. Mama, a word that mixed fear and joy together stinging Bekka at the same instance it filled her heart. Sarrah hadn't called her that word before and Bekka didn't want to spoil the moment. She pulled the blanket over Sarrah's shoulders. Before she closed her eyes, Sarrah asked one more question. "Can we stay just a little longer?"

Bekka felt a tight ball form in her throat. They couldn't wait. The more time she spent with Elly, Lily and Kellen, the harder it would be to say goodbye. Part of her wanted to whisk Sarrah away this very night. Steal a horse and some food, then take off for the desert. She couldn't force herself to act so unkind, at least not yet.

"We shall see."

Sin watch over us, Bekka prayed. *Let me make the right decisions.*

Bekka leaned over to kiss Sarrah's forehead again. She was fast asleep.

Yearning throbbed within the pit of her being— if she had a soul, it would've burnt to cinders in the blaze. The cup showed her nothing and the pool was no better. An impenetrable black shroud clung over where the girl should be. Qetesh could sense her love, infuriatingly close, much like a moth beating its wings against a shuttered lamp. Blindly she sought the source until her head ached from the effort. *Does she even exist?* Qetesh wondered. The yearning replied with a strong tug on her very being, dragging her through hot coals, and filling her chest with burning embers, the weight of which, making it hard to catch her breath.

I am being driven mad by need. She flopped back on her bed, burying her head into the pillow. Part of her wanted to cry and throw a fit, but who could she complain to? Mother made it clear she wanted nothing to do with this problem. Probably because she still mourned the loss of her love. No other god or goddess would understand, Qetesh, lost in their own pitiful squabbles. She suffered alone, quivering under the waves of desire that struck her, each more powerful than the last.

I can't fight this anymore! She tossed over onto her back, touching her breast beneath the sheer dress. Her heart pounded and she closed her eyes, allowing the need to carry her off, following its flow like sinking into a warm bath. Her back arched and fell. She sighed, the pulse thrumming along her resting body.

When she opened her eyes, the world seemed dimmer. The bright sheen wore off, dulled by smoke and fire. Wood crackled, the flames warm on her flush skin. Small conversations carried on around her, but she remained silent, staring into the blue eyes of the boy she loved so deeply. These were not her eyes, or limbs. The hands trembling to touch him were small and delicate. The fingers splayed out on the firm dirt as she leaned in close to the boy, smelling his earthiness. *Look at me*, she willed.

"Hannah?" He spoke her name—no, the girl's name—confused, a stupid look that she found endearing at the same instance. He slid away from her, prickling her. Her soft lips puckered in annoyance.

Stupid boy, Qetesh thought, retreating into the girl. *Can't he sense her love and adoration? It should be as obvious as a log hitting him over the head.* She felt the girl's cheeks blush, a warm spread from the very roots of her hair. The girl turned away, the sting of rejection and her own conflicted thoughts and emotions storming inside. Desire tugged at Qetesh like a distant rope tethering her to a rock slowly sinking into great depths, ready to drown her.

Too much! She gasped inside the girl's head. *Too much!*

Qetesh relinquished her hold and slipped back into her body. Her eyes snapped opened and she beamed. *I touched a mortal*, she giggled and covered her mouth. *I was inside one of the created for the very first time.* Her body shook from the lingering experience. All those sensations: acrid smoke, hot fire, cool earth, and the smell of sweat. She had forgotten the smooth touch of skin since the ascension transformed them from mortal to immortal. She wanted to use the hand to touch the boy, to feel the texture of his skin beneath her fingertips, but he acted like a frightened bunny confronted by a snake. *Should have grabbed him by the ears and leaned in, kissing...*

A shadow loomed over her.

"You look shaken, my dear," Dandulain, the Mistress of Shadows said. She looked huge, drawn up like someone twenty feet tall. It was an illusion, Qetesh knew, a trick of the light. No less frightening. Dandulain approached her bed, face cloaked and voice low, bordering menacing. "Bad dream?"

Qetesh narrowed her eyes. "What are you doing here?"

"Checking on you, love," Dandulain said and pulled back her hood to reveal raven black hair, pale skin and piercing eyes that lacked the concern displayed in her voice. "I have heard that you are suffering from a disorder. A vision impairment, perhaps, or another sort of blockage."

"What do you mean?" Qetesh shrank back into her bed, sliding under the covers. The Mistress of Shadows had a dark mind. Qetesh had heard the rumors like all the other gods. The appearance of this shadow cloaked assassin didn't bode well. She noted the twin daggers at her belt. The same that were said to have killed Father. She didn't understand how a god could kill another. Nor did she want firsthand tutelage.

"No need to play coy with me." A dangerous hint of annoyance in her voice. "Anyone with eyes can see how you pine away for some mysterious love. It isn't one of us." Dandulain examined her. Gooseflesh raised on her arms and back of her neck. The predatorily eyes seemed to measure her, calculating when to end the play and begin the meal. "You could have any god or goddess you desired. All you need is to bat your pretty eyes at them and they'd fall into your arms like rose petals floating on water. Therefore, it must be one of the created."

"I don't—" Qetesh tried to protest, but Dandulain sat on the bed and placed a black gloved hand on her covered leg. She tried to recoil, but the Mistress of Shadows squeezed her.

"You wouldn't be the first to have a dalliance with lesser creatures." Dandulain grinned. "Sin did it, birthing her abominations."

"It's not about me at all," she said.

"Who is it about, my dear?"

About the girl. Her love for a naïve boy who doesn't understand how she burns for him, a flame kept under wrap so it smothers.

"No one," Qetesh said, blushing.

"That's a lie." She pinched Qetesh's leg. "I understand your trepidation to speak about these emotions warring inside you." She bared her teeth, emphasizing the next words, "but don't lie to me again."

"Mother will—"

"Mother will do nothing, just like she did nothing when father disappeared." Her tone changed, dropping the threatening demeanor and turning smooth, silky. "Oh, sweet one, no need to tremble like a little bird. I believe we seek the same worm."

"Why should I trust you?"

"Because, I know what is causing your misery," Dandulain said. "I know how to end it."

CHAPTER SEVEN

A strange heat radiated from the soil where
Nothing green ever grew. Faber dug the bones
Of the earth and laid the foundation for his forge.
Stone melted and iron bent under the fierce heat.
Faber's own skin blistered and scarred. Through
Unknown arts, he completed the ever wakened forge
No water could extinguish the fire. The forge was
Always awake. Always burning.
The tools and weapons forged in those fire
Remained ever sharp, rust refused to mare metal
And they were nearly indestructible.
Faber remained in the city for less than a season
Then he was gone and none could master the
Fires of the Gods' Forge.
  — "Origins of the Gods' Forge"
    From Tales of Venustas Lux

Silver from the gods.

Hanse Tanner gripped the bar in his hand, turning it over, examining it for any imperfection. A nick, a dent, something to prove that mortal hands had touched it before his own. As far as he could tell, nothing marred its perfection. The scale told him the weight was dead on. Not an ounce more or less. Of course, the second bar he scored for purity, but he assumed it would otherwise prove exactly the same.

The problem remained on what to do with the silver bars?

Silver wasn't common currency like the gold doublins and copper pennies. He supposed he could melt the silver down or wait for another merchant to travel through and trade it.

I might just keep them. He pulled the bar off the scale and held it up to the lantern light. *A family heirloom granted by the gods, literally handed to me by the God of War, Huron, the Blades Man.* He set the silver on the counter. *Except no one will believe me. Like a two-penny salesman driving up the price with a tall tale.*

"Hanse?" A woman's voice called from the stairway leading to the rooms above. "Are you coming to put Jarl to bed?"

"Just a moment," he replied. "Finishing up the ledgers and I'll be there."

"Don't be too long, he is washed up and changing."

The door shut. Hanse sighed. *I'll decide what to do with them later.*

Lifting the silver bars off the counter, he carried them to a barrel and wrapped them up in a piece of oil cloth. The barrel was heavy, full of iron nails, and he tilted it on his hip and rolled it to the side. Then he felt along the floorboard until he found the false board. In the crack he pressed the lever that unlocked the boards, and then laid them aside. A concrete lined hole, two hand spans deep and four wide, resided beneath the boards. Hanse pushed aside several coin purses full of gold doublins and set the silver bars inside. He stroked the oil cloths delicately before replacing the boards and sliding the barrel full of iron nails back into place.

Doesn't seem real. Hanse scratched his head, staring at the barrel. He wanted to move it aside and look at the silver again to make sure he didn't imagine the encounter. Marta had the patience of a boiling kettle. Once she started steaming, he had to get out of the fire or be scolded.

Hanse climbed the stairs to the second story rooms. Living above his shop wasn't ideal, but it made for an easier, affordable living situation. Turning the handle on the door, he cracked it open, and was greeted by the lingering smell of venison stew. Marta glared at him, forehead wrinkled as she furiously wiped the supper table. She threw the rag atop two bowls in a metal tub and began to pour hot water over them. A lone bowl sat at his spot at the table

"He's in bed, waiting for you," Marta said, scowling. "If he hasn't fallen asleep already."

"Thank you," Hanse said. "The soup smells delicious."

Marta harrumphed and went about scouring the bowls.

I'll do better tomorrow. He kissed her cheek and walked down a short hallway to the door at the end. He opened it without knocking.

Jarl wasn't asleep. He sat up on his pillow, lamp burning bright, a book opened in his lap and mouthed the words. Bright yellow eyes wide in delight as he read *"Adventures of Kiltrum the Stormbearer."* At six name-days, Jarl was a away full season from working in the shop, learning basic arithmetic and stocking inventory.

"What trouble has Kiltrum found himself?" Hanse asked.

"He's about to steal the emerald egg from the giant tree spiders," Jarl said, excitement rose in his voice and his yellow eyes glowing in the lamp light, caught in the fantasy land. A place of wild possibility rather than stock and goods and numbers. "Dad, are there tree spiders in our woods?"

"I'm certain there are," Hanse said, sitting the edge of the bed and ruffling Jarl's reddish mane of hair. "I don't think they're as big as most men, but I haven't gone to the heart of the woods to find them."

"When I'm older, we can explore them." His yellow eyes sparkled with the thought of adventure. "Stephen went hunting with his dad last moon and he's two name-days older than me."

Stephen's dad is a better hunter than me. Hanse didn't want to admit it out loud, but the truth remained. Hanse expertise lie in numbers and bargaining. It's very difficult to bargain with a boar not to skewer you with its tusks.

"We'll see what your mother says," Hanse said, taking the book from Jarl and sitting on the edge of the bed.

Jarl groaned.

"Mom never lets me do anything fun."

"Where should I be—"

A loud crash sounded below.

"Marta?" Hanse asked. *Why would she be in the shop?*

Feet thudded up the stairs and he knew it wasn't his wife. Thieves. Thieves looking for the silver given to him by the gods. Hanse put a hand on Jarl's shoulder. "Stay here and put the covers over your head."

Jarl nodded.

Hanse moved quickly to the dining area. Marta stood by the door, bolting it and pressing an ear.

"Stand back, Marta," Hanse said. The hairs on his neck began to rise and his skin prickled, the first signs of transformation.

Marta shushed him, leaping back as the handle jiggled. The door shuddered once, twice, before bursting open. A man wearing silver chain mail burst into the room, sword drawn. Marta hissed, leaping at him as her fingers formed into claws. A sword point took her under the chest and she gasped, coughing up blood. Hanse took several steps back as he watched his wife die.

No! I was going to do better! Tears stung his eyes as disbelief overcame him, slowing his mind as though moving in molasses. More armored men entered the room, breaking his paralysis.

Jarl! Have to get Jarl out!

He ran to his son's room. Jarl remained hidden under the blankets. A single window at the back wall dropped two-stories below to cobblestone. *If Jarl shifts, he might survive the fall.* He reached his son's bed as two soldiers entered the doorway. Tearing the blanket off his shaking child, he tossed it at the guards, hoping to delay them enough for Jarl to escape.

"Change!" Hanse shouted. "Now!"

Jarl stared up at his father, tears shimmering in his terrified eyes. *He's only a boy. He hasn't had his first hunt yet.* The thought sent a wave of rage through him. Hanse turned on the soldiers as they freed themselves from the blanket. His skin rippled and crawled as fur sprouted over his body. Canines grew, elongating into sharp razors as his mouth widened, and nose formed a snout. The first soldier was close enough that Hanse batted away the blade and sank his teeth into the man's face. A satisfying crack sounded under the pressure. Blood filled his mouth as he tore flesh off of cheek, exposing white bone. The man screamed.

Hanse outweighed the soldier by at least ten stones and they collapsed onto the floor. Head jerking back and forth, he shook the man's face until he heard a snap and the screams ended.

A sharp pain tore through his back. Hanse released the dead soldier, but couldn't turn around. His hind legs went numb, no longer obeying his command. *Paralyzed,* Hanse thought, snapping at another soldier's leg. A boot caught the side of his face and he yipped, black butterflies fluttering across his vision.

Small snarls snapped him back to the room. Jarl growled, biting at his attackers. Hanse watched helplessly as a noose dropped over his son's head. Jarl shrieked. *Bastards are using wolf bane!* Hanse struggled to pull himself forward, his back legs useless. The soldier holding the rope yanked it so the boy fell face first onto the bed. Two more soldiers bound his son's hands and lifted him from the bed, careful not to get too close to his teeth, despite the fact Jarl could no longer shift with wolf bane around his neck.

"What do we do with this one?" a soldier asked, placing a sword point at the base of Hanse's skull.

"Put 'im down."

"No!" Hanse growled, dead legs flopping as he tried to twist away. A boot stomped on his head, flattening his face to the floor. He watched them carry his son out of the room, kicking and snarling.

"Daddy!" Jarl called in a high-pitched animalistic screech before disappearing. A sharp pinch burned at the base of his skull.

"Jarl!" Hanse whispered. Bone snapped and he felt nothing more.

Where are you, Champion? The malicious voice echoed in Jarrod's head like metal grinding against stone. Jarrod stared up at the blue sky. Dark clouds thickened until a pin-prick of light hovered over his head. The light, a deep red, sank down like a fire bug burning through the darkness. *I will break your blade and shred your flesh from bone.*

Who are you? Jarrod shouted, raising the hoe and swatted at the light.

The light shifted, angling to create a shadow, his shadow, red spread across the dark grass, like a puddle of blood. Jarrod tried to move, but the darkness folded in on him. Black fingers pressed through the darkness, bending it like a gloved hand reaching for insect and pinning him in place. They began to close over him and he shrank.

Leave me alone! Jarrod thrust the hoe at the darkness, swiping the angled blade back and forth. *I'm a farmer, not a fighter!*

Where are you?

Something gripped the metal edge, tore it from his hands. Jarrod blindly reached for it. He grasped the wooden grip, only it wasn't wood. It was soft leather. Lowering his arm, the light reflected off a different blade. A sword thrummed in his grip. The steel glowed red, heat wafting across his face drawing sweat from his pores.

Yoked hilt to blade!

Laughter, deep and cruel echoed from the darkness. The blade began to bend inward against his will, point aimed at his heart. Jarrod threw the sword down. It transformed into a large wyrm, black and squirming at his feet. Fangs struck, sinking into his boot and he rocked back and his feet, falling, falling...

His head jerked up and he sucked in a deep breath. It was dark, the fire light waning. *Camp!* He panted. *Yellow Valley.* Wiping spittle from his mouth he looked around at the familiar surroundings. *Asleep, a dream. Nothing more.*

A cup of cold tea sat on a flat, circular rock. He'd knocked it over and the burning wood hissed. Jarrod blinked.

Lily stood beside him, silent in her white nightshift.

"What are you doing out here alone?" Jarrod reset the empty cup. Pungent weeper blossom lingered. He remembered drinking half of it, hoping to catch a quick nap before his long watch. Ishmael hadn't emerged from his tent since the argument and their two guests, Bekka and Sarrah, took over Jarrod's tent, making the stars his canopy once again. "Where's your sister?"

"Why's 'Annah acting weird?" Lily put her hands on her hips and frowned, resembling her eldest sister so much Jarrod had to stifle a grin.

"What do you mean by weird?"

"She's told us a sad story and it's your fault."

"My fault?"

"You made her feel bad."

I didn't do anything. Jarrod blinked. A brief image from earlier. Hannah had leaned in awkwardly close, sniffing him like he was a new flower she'd discovered. When he looked into her eyes, it was as though someone else was there. He had an uncomfortable idea that she, or the other in her, wanted to kiss him. *That was part of the dream, wasn't it?*

"Did she say I made her feel bad?"

"No," Lily said, giving him a look like he was dull. "She didn't have to."

"How do you know it was me?"

"Because she likes you."

Not this again! Jarrod felt like rolling his eyes.

"Of course, she does. We're friends," Jarrod said. "You and I are friends, too, right?"

"Of course," Lily said.

"Let me tell you happy a story then."

Lily plunked down in his lap, leaning back into him, and playing with his fingers. His scar twinged. She had grown this past season, filling his lap with an uncomfortable weight. He bit his lip and waited for the pain to quiet.

"Are you alright?" she asked over her shoulder.

"Right as rain," Jarrod said, took a breath and began the story. "There once was a special little girl who had a very special power. She was all alone without any sisters or brothers to play with—"

"I thought this was a happy story," Lily said, giving him an earnest expression. "How can she be happy if she's lonely?"

"Sometimes happy stories don't always start out happy," Jarrod said. "It's how they end that matters."

"Will we have a happy ending?" Lily asked, innocent eyes shiny in the fire.

Jarrod knew the answer she wanted to hear. An answer all children desired even as their homes burned and soldiers marched away with their parents, or even sometimes them. They needed the simple comfort of knowing there was a happy ending waiting at the edge of sorrow. *I'm still waiting for mine, Lily-pad.*

Jarrod smiled and nodded.

"Yes," he said. *Mother, don't make into a liar.*

Lily reached up and hugged his neck tight so he couldn't breathe. Jarrod wrapped one arm around her and used the other to loosen her grip.

"I miss my mom and dad," Lily whispered in his ear. "I'm happy to have you."

"Always, kiddo." Jarrod's heart ached. *Mother, make it so… for a little longer at least.* "How about the rest of the story?"

Lily pulled back, her small fingers still laced at the base of his neck. In a very serious tone she asked, "Does she find a friend?"

"Yes," Jarrod said and laughed. "In fact, she can talk to animals and has a fox for a friend."

"Really?" Lily's eyes grew big.

"I told you she was special," Jarrod said. "She can talk to animals."

Lily sat back down, nestling her head into Jarrod's stomach as he told her the story. About half-way through, he heard her breathing softly. Her eyes were closed and she was fast asleep. He lifted her up and laid her on the blanket. Flickering red embers remained of the fire and a chill settled in the air. He covered her up, knowing he would be up for the rest of the night.

Jarrod looked back at the tents where the others should be asleep. Hannah crept out of the dark and looked down at her sister.

"I wondered where Lily had run off to," she said, sitting beside Jarrod. "I was trying to console Elly and Azriel about Ishmael leaving. Lily slipped out for a cup of water and didn't come back. I figured she came to you. Still, I'll have a talk with her in the morning on the dangers of worrying big sister."

"She wanted a different type of bedtime story," Jarrod said.

"We all want a different story than the one we are given," Hannah said quietly. "Is it true?"

"What?" Jarrod asked.

"Are they killers?"

"Do they look like killers?" Jarrod retorted. "Sarrah is the same age as this little one here." Jarrod rubbed Lily's back. She snorted and shifted to her right side. "Could you imagine Lily hurting anyone?"

"You know what I mean." Hannah gave him an incredulous look. "Bekka could have killed one, or more of those manor guards. Somehow convinced Sarrah to help."

"Why run from the two men chasing them?" Jarrod asked. "Why not kill those as well?"

"I don't know." Hannah lowered her eyes. She looked at Lily. "I don't have the heart to wake her or carry her back to the tent." Lifting up the corner of one blanket, she tucked her legs under and settled in. "We'll have to sleep here tonight."

"What's wrong with your tent?"

"Nothing." Hannah smiled. "Someone has to protect you from her."

"Maybe Kellen, Elly, and Azriel will come out tomorrow night and want to sleep under the stars. Then I can get a tent to myself," Jarrod muttered, sitting on the blanket and began his long watch.

Miles startled awake. He always slept with the window slightly cracked even in the coldest, snowy nights so he could keep an ear on the horses in the barn. Sometimes a snake would curl up in the hay to get warm and he would have to fish it out with a pitchfork, the thing hissing and dangling like a worm at the end of the tine. Other times the horses would complain about rats or other larger rodents in their feed. Miles would get up and chase the buggers off like a father pursuing monsters under his children's bed, except these monsters bit for real and carried nasty diseases.

The scream that woke him sounded terrified. Miles sniffed the air, realizing why.

Smoke! Barn's burning! Miles threw the blankets off and jumped into a pair of trousers. He was halfway to the door when he remembered— all three of the horses were sold. *Who's screaming? And why?* He yanked open the door and listened for more sounds.

A strong breeze carried burning wood smoke from the west. Miles lived alone on the outside of town since the horses didn't care for the residents very much. In the dark night he saw buildings silhouetted against bright orange flames.

Elysium was on fire.

There should be a bucket chain drawing from the well closet to the village square. To prevent the fire from spreading to consume the rest the village, every hand was needed. He ran down the cobblestone street, tightening his cloak against the chill. As he drew closer, disordered shouts from men turned into screams. High-pitched howls stopped him in his tracks.

The villagers in Elysium were *different*. This he understood. He also understood to lock his doors and shutter the windows at night when the howls began.

Blades Man, give me courage. Miles swallowed hard, watching as the fire grew. He could feel the heat beading sweat on his skin. If he didn't do something to help, there would be only burnt-out shells where the village homes once stood. He swiped at his sweaty forehead, forcing his feet to move forward. *I am blessed by the gods.* The mantra gave him strength, evoking courage from the blessing given earlier by one-who-walked-among-them.

A group of men marched from the village square. Boots clacking on cobblestone. They held torches and tossed buckets of water on the thatch roofs. The perimeter guard, soaking the other shops and buildings to contain the fire. Miles didn't recognize any of the men. One of them tossed a torch on the General Store. Fire blazed and spread quickly.

They're not dousing the buildings in water. Miles realized in growing horror. *It's pitch!*

Someone noticed him standing in the street and pointed. Three men broke from the group. Miles watched them draw swords and begin a quick walk towards him.

Oh gods! Soldiers! Miles spun on his heels and ran back up the cobblestone. He could hear their boots pounding and metal jangling as they gave chase. His lungs burned and a stitch formed in his right side. He grabbed it, feeling bile rise up in his throat. *Don't vomit! Stop to vomit and they'll kill you.* He swallowed the hot bile down.

His feet pounded the stones in rhythm to the throbbing in his side. It ached like a pitchfork jabbing his ribs. He began to slow. His house was close, just up the next block. A horrific idea occurred: even if he did reach his house, what *could* he do next?

The back gate. I could—

His foot caught the edge of a stone and he toppled forward, throwing his hands out to catch himself. He heard bone snap before the pain flared in his left wrist.

Damned useless. He clenched his teeth against the pain. *Don't scream. Get up and go!*

Rolling over onto his back, he watched the soldiers close in. Swords drawn, they approached him. A dark shape leapt out from the alley between the buildings, knocking one soldier to the ground and causing the other two to halt. The creature growled, teeth chomping on metal, its heard twisting violently from side to side. The soldier screamed. A tearing noise resounded over the screams and his arm came loose in the jowls of the beast. His companions hacked at the creature.

Miles dragged himself up. He limped, clutching his shattered wrist to his chest and hid in the shadows of an alley between the granary and carpenter shop. Without looking back, he circled around the buildings.

The sound of fighting grew distant. Smoke thickened, burning his eyes and throat. He stifled a cough as more shapes scurried past. By dawn, Elysium would be nothing but charred remains. He needed to leave before he become part of the ash. His stables were close by. Past those was the east gate.

Peeking around the corners, he studied the shadows. Nothing moved. He scurried from his hiding place like a frightened mouse in a room full of cats. About a hundred yards separated him from freedom. *Mother protect me, Blades Man give me courage, Father give me strength*, he prayed as he made the long walk in open space. He flinched at the scraping of his boots, certain a cry would rise up and he would be cut down where he stood. He kept going. *Mother protect me, Blades Man give me courage, Father give me strength.*

Miles reached the back gate which was barred and unguarded. Beside it was a watchman's door. A thick metal bar secured it on the inside and the scraping of metal sounded like a loud signal in his ears. A quick glance showed he was alone.

"May I prosper in this life," he whispered the Blades Man's blessing. The door opened and he felt the life drain from his face. Several dozen soldiers waited on the other side.

A grim face grinned at him, and said, "Thanks, fella," before plunging a blade into his gut.

"Gods be damned," Miles said. He stumbled backwards, wetness spreading between fingers that covered the wound. He dropped to his knees, watching soldiers flow through the back gate like wildfire. *Gods be—*

The rest of Mile's thoughts were lost to the eternal sleep.

Shadows flitted through the village of Elysium like bats circling insects. Fires consumed the buildings, aided by pitch the soldiers used to coat roofs and doorways, turning them into flaming suns. As the flames flickered, twisted shadows writhed on stone walls, stretching the bodies of soldiers raising giant black sword or spear to strike snarling beasts, jaws gapped open to devour men. Blood sprayed against the wall as man and beast fell.

A shadow shaped in a woman's figure peeled away from the firelight, hiding against the dark edges. She touched the circular disk that hung from a silver lace around her neck. Concentrating on its dark energies, she felt her body take form, to gain substance in the world of the created. The substance was an illusion. A bright flare up intruded on her dark corner and the place where the light touched her disappeared. She felt no pain. One moment there and the next, a lighted hole on the wall. She backed away, deeper into the shadows. As the fires continued to burn, there would be no place for her to hide in Elysium.

A soldier ran past, sword in hand. She stared at him, reaching out to his mind.

Bring me the children. Alive!

The soldier paused, head tilted as though listening to a distant voice. "Yes, Mistress," he said and continued on to his destination.

She had met with the leaders of the army before their attack. In the chaos of battle, orders sometimes were not always carried out as demanded. Moving from shadow to shadow in Elysium, she found clusters of battles, relaying the message to every soldier she encountered. Several times she delayed a sword stroke that saved the life of a young male. Instead of slaying the creatures, the soldiers subdued them with clubs and nets, carrying the unconscious forms to awaiting carts outside the burning walls.

Fools would slaughter everything. They truly are children breaking toys in a frenzy. She would rather kill the men, but required their servitude first.

At the south part of the village, she sensed something odd, something familiar. It was like walking into a room and smelling the sweet, rosy nosegay, recognizing the man who carried it in his pocket. Only this was freshly oiled armor. The smell came from within one building where fire birthed on the thatch roof. She hurried inside, following the scent. It led to a barrel. She tore the lid off and stepped back.

Nails! She lifted a small metal spike up and sniffed it. Dropping it back inside the barrel, she looked at the floor. What she sensed was beneath the barrel. She gripped the barrel's edge and sent it sprawling, hundreds of metal nails tinkling on the wooden floor.

Some of the boards, she noticed, didn't match up with the rest. She felt along the surface for a catch or a seam in which to separate the boards. Her fingers found a latch. She touched it and a catch released. Setting the boards, she knelt and peered inside. Her eyes narrowed on coin purses tucked around larger objects wrapped in oil cloth. She unwrapped the cloth.

You were here. She stroked the smooth silver bars. She frowned, realizing where he would go and what he intended. Letting the silver bars clank back inside their hole, she stood up. *I need to stop him.*

It would be daylight soon. Daylight both created and destroyed shadow. She was too weak to remain here in her current form. She needed to find another, one more permanent and easier to manipulate. First, she had to obtain one particular item. Exiting the burning store, the Mistress of Shadows listened to the sounds of battle din. Satisfied that the soldiers would do her biding without further supervision, she touched the black disk. Concentrating on the dark well of power, she released her hold on it. Creation faded away like morning mist.

Venustas Lux, City of Light and Beauty, was once home to artisans who sculptured statues made in the images of the gods, painted murals chronicling stories Father and Mother creating the universe, composed songs and poetry about love and struggle and peace, and crafted tools for creating, not killing. Dead for three centuries.

Giant redwoods and thorny mulberry shrubs grew from its bones. Thick, woody vines suffocated those, leaving skeletal branches poking out from beneath corded rope. Lush fan-leaves formed a canopy to enclose the shattered remains of the once thriving city. Creeping vines clung to crumbling walls, draping out empty windows of grand buildings that used to rise beyond the trees tops to create the largest, most expansive city the Created ever achieved.

Spider webs shimmered in the light slicing through the shadows on the canopy overhead. They clung freely to the trees, catching gnats and blow fly that inhabited the sea of green. Bird songs reverberated overhead in competing cacophony, full of squawks and beating wings. A lizard scurried away, jouncing across the vine in front of the Huron. Vines rustled loudly against his black boots, sending waves through the green sea of leaves. A hot, sticky wetness filled the air, like a soaked towel wrapped around him with the cloying undertone of rotting vegetation. These sensations were strange to the Huron. He had forgotten what it was like being part of the Created. All these assailing sensations, how did it not drive them mad? Or maybe it explained why they acted as strangely as they did.

We were merely tapers believing ourselves to be the sun, burning and slashing in our Struggle. If only they could open their eyes to the misery inflicted on themselves and others. There's no destroying that which waits patiently. Life finds a way. I must guide him *to find the way.*

Huron touched the soul pendant around his neck. Once again, part of the Created. He marveled at the idea. Flesh and blood, centuries erased by simply returning a soul to his ascended form. Like the Created, he was vulnerable to the trappings of life and death. Not even Mother could protect him here. All he had was his sword, armor, and wits. They had to be sufficient, and hopefully his intrusion into the struggle went unnoticed by the others. Just long enough to accomplish these few tasks.

A careful study of the ground showed that the vines grew in a spiral, rippling out from an epicenter at the heart of the ruins. Power coursed over the thick cords, using them as conduits to dissipate the strength before it could consume the whole surrounding area. The ground grew warmer the closer he got to the epicenter where the Forge of Gods slept. It sensed his presence, sleeping embers stoking to life.

I am here, he sent out soothing thoughts.

Leaves smoldered, curled over and turned black. A pungent odor superseded decomposing vegetation. Roots, vine, and leaves burned away revealing a stone pit, cherry red embers blazing. Huron's gloved hand swept off the dead creepers, uncovering a rotted wooden chest. The lid collapsed at his touch, tearing away from rusted hinges that groaned and snapped in a puff of red dust. Inside he discovered the anvil and hammer he had locked away so long ago using delicate hands made strong by his essence.

Huron lifted the hammer. A surge of delight brought a smile to his stern face. He'd missed its weight even after all this time. It felt good to hold, not as a vector in another's body, but with his own hands. Shifting the hammer from hand to hand, he examined it. The handle was still smooth, no sign of rust on its galvanized steel head. He placed it on the anvil, then looked down into the forge. Heat radiated as its fires lapped hungrily at the stone containing it.

Huron set the pack full of silver bars beside the forge and stripped off his armor and sword belt. He stood in tight black pantaloons and long sleeve jerkin to protect him from the sparks from shaping the sword for his Champion. He dug out a leather apron from the side pocket of his pack and tied it on. Then he took the metal tongs sitting on top of the silver bars. Using the tongs, he lifted the first silver bar, ready to feed it to the fires.

He stopped.

A ripple quivered through the vines like a fly disturbing a web. Placing the tongs on the forge's edge, he reached for his sword belt and loosened the sword in the scabbard.

"I know you are here," he said.

The vines went still.

"You would be wise not to interrupt." He glanced around at the sea of green. She had found him. Anger coursed through his body, tightening his limbs like a coil ready to spring. Wings flapped and a large black bird perched on a dead branch. The branch creaked under the bird's weight. It cawed, sounding like derisive laughter.

"The fool speaks of wisdom as a child calls the moon a sun," the black bird said, speaking clearly in a voice he knew all too well. "Not so long ago you possessed me and I stood before the forge, sweating and hammering away at steel until my hands blistered. At that time, I didn't understand the power that surged through the earth's veins. When my daggers were complete, I knew full well what I could do."

"A lesson I regret teaching," Huron said.

"Now you do the same for the boy," the black bird continued. "What will you make him? Armor, shield, a sword?"

Huron refused to be baited into banter. A warrior chose his battlefield carefully and banter put him at the base of a steep hill. He gripped the sword's hilt, waiting for her attack. She knew he was vulnerable in this form. She also knew he retained his fighting skills, giving him the advantage in combat. Always the shrewd one, she was diverting his attention. From what, though?

"I do admire your efforts, futile as they are," the black bird cawed. "He will fail. With his failure, comes your demise. A pity. You loved me once. Do you love the boy?"

Huron frowned, the familiar pain squeezing his heart. *She is trying to distract you with old emotions*, he reminded himself. He centered his thoughts on the steel ready to be drawn.

"Would you cry to Mother if I pecked his eyes out?"

"Come down off that branch and I will demonstrate what will happen to you."

What I should have done centuries ago.

"Soon, my love, when shadows meet, you will know the bit of my blade. I'm sure Mother told you I have chosen a Champion. She always spoils the surprises." The black bird cackled. "Mine is not some peasant boy fresh from some farm, but a true warrior. You used to know what those were."

"I was blind to many things." He took a cautious step away from the forge, checking his peripherals for an ambush. Nothing moved and the vines were still.

"Truer words were never spoken." The black bird lifted a round silver bead clutched in her talon, transferring it to her beak. Then she launched from the branch, darting toward Huron. He drew his sword out of the scabbard, slashing at the black bird. Black tips of feathers floated where the bird had flown, shifting course to sail over the Gods' Forge. The sliver bead dropped from its beak and into the fire. Steam rose up from the forge and it hissed and crackled.

The bird struck a tree trunk and fell dead in the vines. Her essence had abandoned the poor creature. Unlike man, animals couldn't ascend making them neat little vessels for the Ascended to use and shuffle off, leaving a dead husk behind.

White steam hissed from the forge and then dissipated. Huron sheathed his sword and ran to the forge. He leaned over the stone, now cool to his touch. Lifting his head, he growled and gave a loud, frustrated scream.

"What have you done?" He stared down at the grey ash. Knuckles white as he gripped the stone, as though he could tear it from its roots and toss it to the heavens. "What have you done?"

For the first time in over three hundred centuries, the embers no longer glowed red.

The Gods' Forge was dead.

CHAPTER EIGHT

They crawled from the mire on scaled bellies black as night. Fire blazed on their tongues, swallowed from the bowels of Creation, regurgitated, consuming all in flame. Their claws rendering flesh from bone and teeth gnashing as they devoured all to cross their path. Such a creature could not last. Such careless death and destruction, intolerable. Such a creature hunted to near extinction. Wyrm of the gods, writhing back into its dark depths. Never to be seen, except by the dead.
— From "All the Gods Creatures"
Master Huntsman Claudius Gladstone

"What's that stench?" Snout wrinkled his nose and grimaced. They had traveled less than four leagues before the tracker stopped, sniffed the air and turned his face away like a child forced to eat a vegetable he didn't like. "Smells worse than a carrion cart ripe with bloated corpses."

"That, my friend, is Black Wyrm." Thramel took a deep breath and caught scent of horse sweat and the garlic tincture he'd rubbed on to keep the biters away. The tincture stayed true. Not a single creature buzzed near him, starting the morning off in a more pleasant manner. "You have an impressive nose. We aren't even close to see its mark upon the land. The swamp's dark blemish is more like a pox scar on a lady's smooth cheek. Black Wyrm's three leagues of thick black tar bubbling up in stagnate waters. Dead, black trees and a muggy heat that feels like a moist cloud wrapped around you. If the road is passable, it won't take but half a day through to the other side."

"This is close enough," Snout said. He pulled out a cloth and small bottle. Removing the stopper, he dabbed the oil, rose and clover by the smell of it, on the cloth and covered his mouth. "My nose burns. We should turn south and take the valley strait."

"Gods no!" Thramel shook his head. "It'll take a day just to find the strait and another to cross it. I don't want to lose my properties because you're afraid of a little swamp. Besides, there's nothing like it you will ever see in this life. The water catches fire, burns as bright as the sun, and then sizzles out."

"How does water burn?" The question came muffled from the cloth.

"Swimming in its depths is a giant, black wyrm."

"How big can a worm get?" Snout squinted his eyes.

"This isn't the little birdie catches the worm. This is a big bugger. Spanning at least five men from nose to tail." Thramel spread his arms wide as he could reach. "Rumor from the roads say its nose smolders and it coughs flame. This is what sets the water on fire."

"A fire breathing worm." He lowered the cloth, grimaced, and spit before covering his mouth again. "Why the gods would we go within ten leagues of such a thing?"

"Never seen one personally," Thramel said. "Not that I've gone searching for it."

"I don't believe a single word," Snout said. "Sounds like ale-muddling."

Thramel smiled. "True. Ale creates a great many fantasies. You don't mind a short trip through a smelly swamp, to save us time."

Snout considered the option.

"Fine, but if my nose falls off from the stench, you're on your own."

If it falls off, it won't be from the swamp stench.

"We'll find you another. I'm sure there are any number of villagers willing to trade their dog for the good grace of their new mistress, the mighty Joanne," Thramel said and heeled his horse into a canter.

He could feel Snout glaring at him, droopy eyes boring into his back. Coming from Seaptum, Snout's ignorance of Nemus showed. The Black Wyrm was well documented by any who dared venture into the marsh. It didn't always make an appearance, but when it did, those who survived didn't stay around and make study of the beast. As far as he knew, no one had seen it in a generation.

Mother's blessing, neither will we.

Whitewood trees grew denser, encroaching on the Westerly Road and narrowing it by half. As they drew closer to the Marsh, the trees became stunted. Those whose roots drank of the water no longer had white bark, but a strange grey fungus stole over the tree and they bent over like crooked-backed men, as though trying to escape the sulfurous stench. What leaves budded on the east side were sparse and brown, their branches withered into decrepit hands curled over with brittle bone. Grass and thickets browned, thinning out until only strange, tall cattails with black fuzzy spikes growing at the tips sprouted from the murky marsh.

At the trailhead limp dark vine draped from dead branches overhanging the entrance. A worn wooden sign leaned to the side, partially covered by black vine. Scorched into the wood was a warning— Be Wary: Black Marshes. Black Wyrm Ahead.

"Not too late to turn 'round," Snout said in a thick voice. His eyes were red and weeping.

"Let's take a vote." Thramel took off his glove and dabbed more garlic tincture under his nose. It masked the sulfur stench belching from the ground. "All in favor of taking the straits south, say 'ay.'"

"Aye," Snout said.

The *Mors Faunis* remained silent.

"Seems like you are out voted." Thramel heeled his mare. She balked, whinnying and shaking her head.

"Seems like you forgot to take in consideration the silent voters." Snout laughed.

"Bloody beast, what demon has gotten into you?" Thramel squeezed his knees into the mare's ribs and pulled back on the reins. The mare refused to move forward. She chomped on the bit, white froth bubbling up over the wood. She tried to turn, but Thramel fought her.

"It's the smell," Snout said, sniffing and hawking back in his throat. He lifted the cloth and spat into the dirt. "Are you sure you don't want to recant? Think of them as your canary in the mines. If they don't want to go, maybe we shouldn't either."

"There's no time," Thramel growled, tightening the reins to keep the mare from bolting. "We can get through the marsh and be at Foster's Manor by nightfall."

Eyes droopy and watery, Snout watched him fight for control while his own mare remained calm, tail flicking and skin quivering. The *Mors Faunis* sat on their mounts, statuesque, wolf heads turned and snarling mouths twisted like toothy grins.

Thramel cursed them all.

After a moment of deliberating, Snout puffed up his cheeks and shook his head, grumbling something about regretting the decision. He rode up to the struggling mare and dismounted. The mare jerked sideways, nearly knocking him over.

"Whoa, girl," Snout said, catching the reins and began stroking the mare's nose. "I don't like it none neither." Taking out a glass vile from his pouch, he held it up. Blue liquid, like ink, shone in it.

"What's that?" Thramel asked.

Snout ignored his question. Twisting the cork off, he rubbed a dab of blue ink into his hands before re-sealing and putting it way. Then he continued stroking her nose, working the liquid beneath her flared nostrils. She puffed twice, then her ears perked up and she quit pulling on the reign.

"Let's be quick about it," Snout said. "She's spooked real good. I don't know how long this will last."

They entered Black Wyrm Marsh, riding single file. Thramel took the lead followed by Snout, the supply mounts, and the *Mors Faunis* at the rear. The air was warm, as sticky as tack gluing hair and cloth to skin. A thick fog clung to the ground making it seem like the horses walked on clouds. Sickly yellow light cut through the branches. Twisted trees reared up from the muck to form a corridor made of black vines and yellowing leaves. A sulfurous stench mixed with spoiled eggs and fermented yeast, thickening as they moved further inside. Thramel coughed, gagging. He gave in and covered his face with a wine-soaked cloth to cut the stench. His mare no longer bulked, but her tail flicked continuously and her skin quivered. He was becoming more and more grateful for the little rat-catcher.

Little guy's proving to be more valuable than a lap dog. Thramel watched the overgrown road. *Perhaps I won't put a knife between the bugger's ribs after all is done. Unless he bites the hand that feeds him. No, he is too loyal to her. The pack must die to preserve the flock.*

The horses' hooves squished in the soft dirt, slowing their progress. Where the fog thinned, Thramel saw brown water encroach on the path. After the rains, it would be impassable as the marsh would swell and swallow it up. A creature began screeching deeper within the trees. Horses perked their ears, whickering softly. The screech continued, sounding worse than a cat with its tail trapped in a door. It escalated into a high-pitched wail, and abruptly ceased. Soon after the hums and croaks started in musical cacophony.

"How much further?" Snout asked, voice muffled by the rag covering his mouth.

"We are about midway," Thramel replied, watching the black trees. *I think we are.* Distance was hard to judge. The road seemed to go on with no end in sight. Hairs on his arms and neck stood on end. The stench of death and decay was stronger here. He thought he heard a noise off to his left and swung around to look. *Nothing.*

Nothing was the problem. He tilted his head to the side, listening. No croaks. No humming. The marsh became eerily silent. *Canaries in a cave.* Something moved in the water off to his left. Ripples spread toward the road, broken by the stunted trunks of black gum sticking up like rotted teeth. The mare whickered, side-stepping to the right. Water sloshed and Thramel caught sight of a black scaly tail, as long as the horse, rise up and slip under the brown water.

Thramel turned back to see if Snout had witnessed the event. His head was tilted, and eyes scanning the water. If Snout had a tail, Thramel was certain it would be standing at alert.

"Let's pick up the pace," Thramel said, tugging the reins. The mare didn't need further motivation to increase her trot into a gallop. Ripples spread along the road's edge, picking up speed.

"Hiya!" Thramel shouted and wiped the reins, glancing briefly at the water. The ripples were about to surpass them. "Faster before we're wyrm food."

The mare whinnied and made a sharp right turn, legs slipping in the hidden muck. Thramel braced his knees and hugged her neck to keep from being tossed.

Brown water bubbled, then exploded. A giant form leapt up from the muck, splitting a black gum tree, its trunk snapping in half as the creature crashed through and landed at the edge of the road.

Shadow take me! He tugged on the reins. The mare whinnied, eyes bulging as she splashed through the brown muck. A long, reptilian head, black scales and yellow-eyed, snaked forward, its teeth snapping at the mare's legs. She leapt in a spray of mud and water as the teeth closed on empty air.

Thramel heard Snout curse and glanced back as his mare narrowly avoid the beast's maw. The next horse in line, carrying half their supplies, wasn't so fortunate. The wyrm snatched the mare in its jaws, crushing its forelegs and dragging her towards the waters. The horse screamed and bite the dark scales to no avail. She disappeared, spreading a pink foam across the brown water.

"Ride! Shadow take you!" Thramel lashed the reins and leaned forward, ducking beneath branches. The water bubbled again, rushing along the edge of the road. He didn't know if it was the same creature or another. As far as he knew, only one black wyrm resided in the marsh.

Gods! Don't let it have a mate.

Hooves thundered close behind. A rider-less pack horse jostled past, spraying muck back on Thramel. Black-leaved thicket clogged the path ahead, narrowing it into a gap big enough for one horse to pass. The panicked pack horse slipped through. As Thramel's mare approached, another large body collided with his mare, nearly crushing his right leg. He caught a flash of brown and a streamer tail as the second rider-less pack horse sprinted past.

Then the world tilted sideways.

Thramel threw himself from the saddle. Thorns tore his clothes and scratched his face as he crashed through the thicket, landing on his shoulder. He tucked his chin into his chest and rolled, branches snapping as he crashed through them. His foot struck a gum tree's black trunk. He spun around, flipping his over on his back, warm water soaking his clothes. A foul taste filled his mouth: salt and grit and blood. Thramel turned over onto hands and knees, coughing up brown water until strands of red spittle clung to his lips. He'd bit his tongue and it stung. He stared at the water. Ripples moved toward him again.

Shadow take 'em all! Pain radiated up his left leg as he clambered to his feet. His armor, sword, and shield were all attached to the saddle on the mare. The poor creature screamed, legs kicking and head bobbing, trying to extricate herself from the brambles. He saw Snout's horse sprinting down the road. Thramel waved and shouted, but Snout flew past without a single glance in his direction. *Bastard left me!* Thramel looked back to the dark form surging towards him.

He hobbled through the thicket, half-dragging his injured leg. He ducked under the terrified creature's flailing legs, looking for his sword. It was there out of reach in the scabbard tied to the saddle. Shield and armor were nowhere in sight. Water spouted behind him. He didn't waste time looking at what he knew to be coming. The Black Wyrm whetted its appetite and wanted its main course.

Thramel dove over the prone mare, cracking his knee on her thrashing legs. He scrambled over her heaving flank, clawing along heaving ribs until he reached the scabbard. A great rumbling vibrated up his bones and he gripped the sword hilt, ripping it free from the scabbard. The mare gave a terrified scream, kicking hard enough to send him tumbling over into the bramble. Covering his face with one arm, he held the sword away from his body with the other. Thorns shredded what remained of his sleeve, gouging out flesh as he flipped over. He landed hard, the small of his back striking flat wood, not the gnarled root he had expected. Sitting up, he felt his shield beneath him.

Mother bless me. He patted the metal and laughed. *Maybe I have a chance.*

The moment of hope was short lived. The brambles shook with a terrible force and the mare gave one last terrified screech as it was plucked up in horribly sharp teeth. Thramel slipped his forearm through the shield buckle and turned to see the mare's back legs kicking, her head in the gullet of the large, black-scaled wyrm. Powerful jaws snapped down, crushing bone and shredding flesh. Limp legs bounced in the creature's mouth while it chewed, coal black eyes leering down at Thramel. The wyrm jerked its head aside, tossing the carcass over Thramel's head. Blood and gore rained down on him.

Swinging his blade, Thramel cut a small path through the brambles in the opposite direction of the Black Wyrm. He stumbled into thigh deep water. *I'll be stuck like a horse in mud.* He turned, watching as the wyrm dove under water. As quick as a serpent, it twisted around the trunks of black gum trees, heading back his way. *It thinks I'm stuck.* Thramel spun and sloshed his way towards the road. His feet hit solid ground when a sheet of smelly, warm water cascaded over him.

Not going to be an easy meal. Thramel turned and faced the black wyrm. It stood three times taller than him, head shaped like a lizard and coal black eyes that stared hungrily at him.

"Come on, you greedy bastard!" he shouted, blade clanging on shield. He embellished the extent of his injury by appearing to stumble back as he planted his injured foot. The ankle and knee ached, but he could walk on it, possibly even run, though running would end with him down the wyrm's gullet. He hoped it was enough to fool the creature.

The black wyrm lunged, mouth open and breathe smelling of blood and raw meat. Thramel leapt to the side, bringing his blade down to strike at its eye. The sword glanced off its great brow, blade tremoring in his grip. A small gash bled red. The wyrm growled, snaking its jaws at Thramel's legs. Thramel slammed his shield on the beast's snout. Its head jerked up, throwing him backwards. He crashed in the middle of easterly road, a jolt running up his backside. The wyrm pawed its snout and gave a deep, growl shuddering across the water.

Yellow eyes gleamed, glaring at its prone prey. Then it lunged once more. Thramel jammed his shield into the open maw. With a great twist, the buckle strap snapped, yanking it off his arm and the powerful jowls clamped over the steel enforced wood, shattering it into splinters.

This is it. Thramel held his sword point at the massive creature—it would be no better than a thin needle pressed into hard leather. *Gods judge me kindly.*

Howls shouted from the mist and two wolf-like creatures bounded at the wyrm, tearing at it before it could reach Thramel. *Mors Faunis* struck quickly, their blade scarring the wyrm's hide. It hissed and snapped its giant maw, missing the leaping Death Howlers. Their blows fell quickly as they struck and deftly avoided its teeth. The Black Wyrm shook its head and retreated further back into the marsh. Scores of red wounds blossomed on its tough hide and it screeched. The *Mors Faunis* clawed at it with their blades until it slipped under the water.

"That's right! Run away, cowardly lizard!" Thramel yelled, picking himself up, carefully testing his weight on his injured leg. It was sore, but held him. "Find an easier meal."

One *Mors Faunis* sheathed his blades and disappeared back into the mist, while the other kept watch. Thramel limped over to the mare to see what he could salvage. Her head was torn from her neck. *Poor thing never had a chance.* He stroked her blood matted flank. *It's my fault for leading you in here. May you ride the green pastures of the gods.* He found his armor bundled up a few yards from the carcass. It was scuffed and dinged, but still wearable. He dragged it back onto the road as the *Mors Faunis* returned with their two horses.

Thramel rode behind as they left Black Wyrm Marsh. They found Snout half a league away, sitting in the road chewing a piece of grass. Two of the three pack horses were tethered to a tree along with his horse.

As soon as he saw Snout, Thramel clambered off the horse and limped toward the little rat-catcher. Snout spat the grass out and stood up, wiping his hands on dirty trousers. He seemed about to speak when Thramel punched him in the mouth, teeth scrapping his knuckles. Snout's head rocked back. Then Thramel grabbed him by the rough spun tunic and shook him.

"Why did you leave me?"

Snout went limp and Thramel pulled him in close enough to smell the garlic on the rat-catcher's breath.

"I told you we should've found another way around," Snout said, wiping blood on the back of his hand. "Either you were dead or you would fight your way out. I would be a fool to get in the way."

"Shadow take you," Thramel said and tossed Snout. Thramel drew his sword. "You're nothing but a cowardly cur. I should cut you in half now and save myself trouble later on."

Snout didn't flinch or cower as Thramel had expected, infuriating him even more.

"Do it and you'll never find those rebels," Snout said, smiling through mashed lips. "You'll lose everything. Joanne will never forgive you and you will have nowhere to run."

Thramel slowly lowered his sword.

"You better find them," Thramel said. "Or I'll gut you and leave you for the Black Wyrm."

Thramel spat on him, and then moved under the trees and sat down to inspect his leg. A dark purple bruise marked his calf and his ankle swelled. He touched it gingerly, wincing at the burning pain. If he broke it, he wouldn't be walking, he figured, and wrapped the ankle before putting his foot back in the boot. He then went to a supply horse, dumping baggage to lighten the load. He stripped his soaked, putrid smelling tunic and breeches down to his small clothes, and tossed them into a bag. He threw on an extra set of clothing, before loosening the reins and leading the mare onto the road. Without a word, he left the others, wanting to get far beyond the reach of the marsh before dark.

"It's still not right," Elly said, walking back from feeding the horses. Kellen walked beside her, silently listening and nodding. Azriel followed close at her heels. *Her little shadow.* Jarrod dragged on his boots, his mind frazzled from oversleeping. An urgent need to plant seeds in the tilled soil before the sun made it unbearable to work nagged him, yet he wanted nothing more than to just sit there and be a passive observer of events. "Da sent us all out here to keep us from the fighting. A soldier shows up and now he's going to leave us."

He sympathized, guilt once again weighing around his neck. His fault for telling Ishmael to take Sarrah and Bekka away. *I need to learn to keep my mouth shut.*

"Ishmael don't want to be with us," Azriel said.

"It's 'doesn't'," Elly corrected. "Ishmael doesn't want to be with us, but that's not true. He'd rather be fighting bad men, like most boys when they grow up. Wooden swords are not good enough anymore and playing dead is for keeps."

"I'm going to be a warrior when I grow up." Azriel picked up a stick and pretended to charge invisible enemies. "I'll protect you."

"No, you won't," Elly said, plucking the stick from her brother's hand. "You're going to be a gentleman farmer, like Da." She scrubbed at dirty speck on Azriel's cheek. "First, we're going to wash up and then get some breakfast."

Azriel's shoulders slunk as Elly plucked his sleeve and began leading him down to the stream.

"There's nothing you can say to him to keep him from going," Hannah said, shaking the loose dirt from the blankets. She handed a corner to Lily and folded her edge over on it. "I know you're thinking about it, the way your eyebrows squeeze together like two caterpillars kissing." Jarrod touched his forehead and sure enough, his brow was tight-knit together. Hannah and Lily giggled as he wiggled his eyebrows. Then Hannah's expression became serious and she looked at Jarrod's tent. "Besides, we'll be safer once *they're* gone."

"It won't be this day," Jarrod said, slapping the dirt from his bottom. "Or the next."

Hannah gave him a questioning look.

"That's not finished." Jarrod nodded at the bare bones of the wooden structure. "He'll work on it until it's ready for you to sleep in, maybe not enough to keep the rain or snow out, but just enough to keep the rain from sweeping everyone off the cliff. Once he leaves, despite any number of promises, he's not coming back."

"What do we do about them?" Hannah pointed at his tent.

"Be nice," Jarrod said. "Remember being pursued by men who wanted to hurt you? The fear and uncertainty?"

"Yes," Hannah said quietly, "but we had you to protect us."

"And they have no one." Jarrod picked up his hoe. "Until now."

Hannah pursed her lips together, giving Lily the blanket and told her to take it to their tent. The children knew better than question her Hannah when she was in this mood and Lily was no different. She hefted the blankets in both arms, carrying them away.

"That woman put a knife to my throat," Hannah said, miming the action. "I doubt she cares if we are here to help or not. She's going to do whatever she wants to survive."

Don't we all. Jarrod nodded his understanding. Nothing he could say would change her opinion. Ishmael being angry at him was enough, he didn't need Hannah upset at him as well. *It's like we're being torn apart, dirt sliced by the edge of a plow blade. I'm the stone turned over in the dirt. Stumbled on, buried deeper.*

"Well, I'm off to the fields." He set his hoe down and stretched his stiff back, wincing at the pinch from the scar. He still had to find the seeds buried in the pack somewhere in the half-built structure.

"What about breakfast?" Hannah sounded disappointed.

As he thought up an excuse, the tent flap opened and Sarrah hesitantly walked out, looking around like a wary sparrow searching for the hawk to swoop down on her. Raven black hair was brushed and neatly braided. She wore a blue dress that Lily had outgrown. Sarrah gave Jarrod a shy smile, waiting next to the tent flap. Bekka emerged, wild, tangled hair tamed in a simple braid reaching down to the small of her back. She wore a pair of his breeches, the cuffs rolled up to reveal her bare ankles and one of his shirts, cinched at the middle with a belt, hung loose, hiding the bulge in her belly and the swell of her cleavage visible by over the sagging neck line.

Jarrod's mouth droped.

"You wear those better than me."

Bekka blushed.

"I couldn't find anything else to wear." She looked at Jarrod, eyebrows raised and her mouth pinched at the corner, waiting for a scolding. "I hope you don't mind."

"No, no. Not at all."

He turned to Hannah who glared at her, arms folded.

"I guess we'll have breakfast."

Hannah gave an angry, *Humpf!* She spun and gathered up the buckets to fill at the stream. Lily returned from dropping the blankets off, grinning at Sarrah.

"Oh, you look so pretty," she said and Sarrah's face lit up.

"Lily, come help me," Hannah said.

"Can Sarrah come?" Lily asked.

"If she wants."

Sarrah gave Bekka a sheepish look.

"Go on." Bekka patted her shoulder.

Lily took Sarrah's hand and gave her a small bucket while she took another. Together they followed Hannah down to the stream. After they were gone, Jarrod was alone with Bekka. His ears burned as his mind went blank on what to say. His feet felt rooted as Bekka approached him.

"Planting a garden?"

"Yes," he said, staring dumbly at the hoe. "Well, sort of. It's mostly done."

"I'm not very good with plants," Bekka said. "Too often the things I touch end up dead."

"I'm doing fine," Jarrod said and gave an awkward laugh.

Bekka smiled and nodded as though saying, *for now.*

"Is there anything I can do to help?"

"Most everything is being tended to already." He shrugged. "I guess we could fetch some bowls and bring the sack of wheat. Hannah's in charge of the meals, mostly, but I don't think she'll mind some help."

"As long as we don't make a big deal out of it," Bekka said. "I know what it's like interfering in another woman's duty."

Jarrod nodded, unsure as to laugh, or be stoic.

"Where do you keep it?"

"What?" Jarrod asked.

"The wheat and bowls."

Mother! Did you create such a bigger fool!

"Oh, yes. Over here," he led her to the half-built structure. They carried a sack and ten bowls out to the fire pit, two extra, in case Ishmael woke up and decided to feed the prisoner and himself. Ishmael remained in the tent too often. He'd neglected working on the shelter, refusing to allow Jarrod watch over the manor guard. Jarrod figured Ishmael didn't trust him. Somehow Jarrod would allow the man to walk free from camp, especially if Ishmael took an eye off him.

Let him handle this problem.

Jarrod set the sack of wheat down and then showed Bekka where the fire wood was stored. Bekka didn't speak. When Jarrod asked if carrying an armful of wood was too much for her condition, she just smiled and shook her head, the braid swaying side to side. *Better to shut my mouth and let her think me a fool, than open it and prove it so.* One of his father's proverbs. Their hands touched as they reached for the same piece of wood. Jarrod recoiled as though as spider crawled on him. Bekka laughed and Jarrod knew his list of proof grew by the moment.

The children returned, carrying three buckets full of water. Lily and Sarrah held each on opposite sides of one bucket so as not to slosh too much of it before they got to the top of the hill. Azriel and Elly had the second and Kellen and Hannah the third. They filled the pot and Jarrod started a fire to heat the water.

"I thought you were going to work in the field?" Hannah asked, nearly accusing.

"I needed a bucket to fill up with water for the plants," Jarrod hooked his thumbs into the side of his breeches. "You took them all, so I put myself to good use."

"Mhmm," Hannah said. She glanced quickly between Jarrod and Bekka, then frowned. She turned her back on them and prepared her specialty. Gruel, extra pasty.

"I'm going now," Jarrod said, snatching up an empty bucket. He half-expected Hannah to tag along, but as he marched down the switchbacks, he discovered he was alone. Bekka watched him a moment and as he looked over his shoulder, she waved to him once and moved away from the edge. A mild trepidation gripped his chest and he looked up at the sky. Clear, blue. No voice. No hands reaching from darkness, like in his dreams. Alone. Yet, he couldn't shake the sensation of being watched.

It's your imagination. He sighed. *Like last night, when you thought that other stared out of Hannah's eyes. Fear of what will come. They will come for me, sure as the sun rises in the east.* He knew he would be the one that would be forced to leave, for the good of everyone. Mother bless them, it won't be until the children were properly watched over.

The cold stream shocked his bare arms, sleeves rolled up so as not to get soaked. He let the bucket bob in the water as it rippled around the rim, and then submerged it, creating a void the water filled in quickly as he lifted it up. The bucket took on weight and he used too hands to carry it up the hill, sloshing his trousers. Wet spots spread against his thighs. As he reached the top, he heard Ishmael's angry voice.

"Where's Jarrod?"

What'd I do now?

Jarrod reached the rim. Dark hair disheveled, face pale with red blotches, Ishmael turned an angry eye on him. He stalked toward Jarrod, fists balled like he was going to hit him again.

"Where were you?"

"Getting water," Jarrod said, indicating the bucket.

"You left the children alone with *her*," Ishmael threw a finger in Bekka's direction and smacked the bucket in Jarrod's hand, "to get water when the caldron is full?"

"They were all together," Jarrod said, avoiding the response of needing water for his seeds. He set the bucket down, ready to defend against another shoving match like the previous day. "Did you think she would run off with them?"

"You should've awakened me," Ishmael said. "Or at the very least, sent one of the other children to fetch more water we don't need."

"I didn't think you wanted to be woken" *Because I knew you would be an ill-tempered bull, ready to plant his horns in the nearest victim, like me.* "Besides, you already agreed to take them. They don't need to steal what is already provided."

Ishmael chuckled, shaking his head and smirking.

"That's your trouble, Jarrod. You don't think. Which is why we're all here instead of with our families."

"Not this again," Jarrod said, tossing his arms up.

"If you boys are done arguing," Hannah interjected. "Breakfast is ready. Come fill your mouths full of gruel and not angry words you'll regret later."

Ishmael shot an irritated look at Hannah who held the spoon in one hand, like a drill master ready to smack the heads of trainees. Ishmael looked away, mumbling about how he regrets nothing.

"Can we please eat together," Hannah said, scooping up gruel and dumping it a bowl so it nearly jumped from her fingertips. "In peace?"

"Fine. Eat up," Ishmael said. "Afterwards I want three horses saddled."

"For what?" Elly demanded. "You don't mean to leave now."

"Exactly what I mean to do."

"You haven't finished building that thing." Elly was becoming frantic. "You can't leave us without a roof over our heads."

"Not yet, Ishy," Azriel said. "We're not ready."

"There's enough planks cut and shaved to finish it," Ishmael glanced at Jarrod, "even a simple farm boy could piece it together. Easy as hitting the hammer on the nails and avoiding the thumb."

"Why not finish it for us so Jarrod can get the garden done," Elly said.

"Mother's blessing! You're acting like I won't be coming back."

They know you better. Jarrod kept his mouth quiet and helped Hannah pass out bowls of gruel to Sarrah and Lily. Nobody ate, but watched the angry display.

"You won't," Azriel said and began to cry. "You'll abandon us like Michael."

"Shut your mouth," Ishmael said. "Michael did no such thing. He died trying to help us get to safety."

Azriel cringed behind Elly.

"You don't have to rush on our account," Bekka said. "Sarrah and I could use another day or two to rest. This gives you enough time to gather up supplies and make a plan of action. We aren't going anywhere without you."

"Fine," Ishmael said, scrubbing a hand through his disheveled hair. "Two days. Then we leave sunrise on the third."

"That's too soon," Elly replied. "Can't you wait until Da sends a messenger?"

"We've been through this argument," Jarrod said. He glanced at Bekka. "This is the best course of action."

"He's not your brother," Elly said. "You're not the one losing more family."

"Always the diplomatic one," Ishmael said, turning to go. "I've lost my appetite."

"Gods! Can't we have one day of peace?" Jarrod threw his hands up in frustration.

"In three," Hannah said, putting a bowl in his hands. "Eat up before it gets cold."

Bernal tried to grin behind the gag in his mouth. His cracked lips ached, rising at the corners before falling back tight ghoulish snarl. He heard them shouting, again—the little ones crying for their brother. They were arguing a great deal and each time the boy, Ishmael he heard them name the boy, flung the tent flap open and stormed in. Bernal caught sight of the boy's red face. *How much longer will it be before the boy simplified the argument and slit my throat?* That's what he would do in the boy's boots. A simple cut from ear to ear and half the situation was resolved.

Instead, the boy stood sullen, nearly pouting. The arguing became more frequent. Bernal had lost count in the haze of sleeping and waking. All he knew was his body ached from being trussed up and he smelled worse than a dead horse. He figured two days had passed, maybe even three since his capture.

Twice, according to his most recent memory, the boy brought him food. Bernal refused the first bowl. Gruel, it smelled like, but he wasn't taking any chances in case they added something extra to it. The second offering, his stomach betrayed him. He gobbled down dried fruit and lentil soup. He remembered saying something about using the privy or pissing himself. The boy wrinkled his nose and told him to piss himself. Bernal had laughed until his bladder burned. *That explains the urine and sour sweat stench.*

He watched the boy pace back and forth. Hands clenched and unclenched, as he muttered under his breath. Then he stopped and glared at Bernal. Bernal stared back at the boy. *Not going to die a coward's death!* A moment comes when everyone makes a difficult choice he has been putting off. A certain light of finality, damning the gods and the outcome. That light appeared in the boy's eyes. *The gods frowned and weighed his heart, judging the good and evil.* The piece of judgment book flashed through his head as the boy lunged at him. Bernal snapped his head back hard enough to see stars as he struck the hard dirt. Rough hands tore the gag off his mouth and he could taste as well as smell the sour stench he laid in.

"I'm going to untie your legs and take you for a little walk. I can't stand the stench of you anymore," the boy said. "Try running and I will hamstring you…then dump you into the willows for the wild cats."

"Such sweet words," Bernal said, his voice croaking. "Bring me flowers next time you come courting."

"I've had enough noise from you." The boy grabbed the gag and was ready to place it back over his mouth. Bernal twisted his head away.

"Wait! I'll shut my trap." He'd rather have his teeth broken then suck on the dry rag again. He held still as the boy loosened the ropes around his legs and slid them off. Had he been in better condition he would have snapped the boy's neck and slaughtered the rest of the camp. His calves tingled up his thighs and down to his feet. The boy told him to get up, but he couldn't move any more than a worm writing under the hot sun could escape the rock.

The boy dragged Bernal to his feet, holding him by the shoulders as he wobbled like a tipsy girl two cups into spiced wine. Bernal turned to ask what next when he noticed the drawn sword pointed at his back. He motioned Bernal towards the tent flap, held it aside with his free hand and waited for Bernal to exit first. Bernal ducked under the flap, managing a few shuffling steps on shaky legs. The pins and needles turned into a steady burn as he walked more steadily. Not enough to run, especially with his hands tied behind his back. Gods knew that this was an opportunity, he just had to figure out how to exploit it.

He squinted as the sunlight stung his eyes. Several small blurry figures ran around the camp, giggling and screeching. Then he saw her. Sitting cross-legged and laughing as the children danced around her playing pluck-the-daisies. She clapped her hands together. When she stopped, four children scrambled to be the first to touch her shoulder. As the children tumbled on the ground, she looked up at him and the merriment died as her eyes narrowed and her smile turned down into a frown.

Bernal gave her the biggest grin and puckered his lips at her.

"Get moving," the boy said and shoved him.

Soon my love. Bernal shuffled his feet quickly to keep from falling. *Soon I will have you.*

"I heard you arguing about me," Bernal said as they got further away from camp. The sound of running water in the distance and he noticed the grove of willows he'd stumbled through with his fellow guardsman, Donald. He should have listened to Donald and returned back to the Manor. "I'm flattered to be the topic of such passionate conversation. Reminds me of my parents the time I got caught kissing the blacksmith's daughter and rolling her in the hay. They had me thinking my head would be an anvil that rang with his hammer."

Bernal laughed, but the boy didn't respond.

"As you can see, he didn't kill me. Instead, he betrothed her to me and we were to be wed until the whore ran off with a merchant's son. Probably knee deep in squalling whelps by now. My point is it would be simple just to kill me. I think you would have done that by now, were that your intentions." *Or are take me out of sight of the children, then slice my throat like a pig.* He waited for a reply. The boy was being stubborn, a downright obstinate mule in his silence. *Got to loosen his tongue.* "Let me go and I will see to it you are rewarded by her Greatness. Give me the woman and girl and we could both be wealthy men. Titles and land...and women. As many as you like and your brothers and sisters could grow up as lords of the land."

The boy laughed. "You have no power to bargain."

"Maybe you're into other boys, you can have whatever you like." The stream was getting closer. Killing him at the stream would make the cleanup easier. As far as he knew, they got their water from along here so polluting it with a dead body would be counterproductive. Unless they intended to move on.

"Let me go and I will keep your secret safe." He stopped and faced the boy. The boy shoved him forward again. He nearly fell head over heels into sharp thicket. "You could tell them I out ran you, or that you finished me off and cast my body into the trees as you promised so often."

"Get walking," the boy said. "Don't make me hit you over the head and drag you down there. Bad enough I had to carry you once. A second time and you might not make it back—"

A meaty thump cut the boy's words off and he collapsed. *Mother bless me! Who is my savior?*

Bernal turned and looked Bekka in the face.

"Killing you is a mercy," Bekka said, holding up the dagger. "Especially after what you put Sarrah through."

Bernal laughed at that irony. The boy wasn't going to kill him. But this bitch would.

"Do you think she's pretty?"

Jarrod dropped a seed into the neat little hole. It was a green leaf seed, one that would sprout thick, crispy leaves by the next moon. He looked over his shoulder at Hannah. She held the bucket of water, her hands fidgeting on the handle. Her eyes searched his face, waiting to judge his response. His cheeks warmed, and not because of the sun. He turned back, patting the dirt over the seed and burrowed another hole, two hands spaces wide, his finger punching through damp soil to his second knuckle.

"You like her, don't you." Not a question, but an accusation.

"Why do you care?" He tried to keep his voice steady, clearing his throat to cover the hitch in it.

"It's fine if you do like her," Hannah said, by her sharp tone, she wasn't fine one bit, "but I wouldn't trust her. She must have done something to get the manor guards on her trail."

"Now you sound like Ishmael."

"Water the seeds yourself." She dropped the bucket and stormed off.

Jarrod sighed and shrugged. *I don't think I'll ever understand them.* As his father told him once: the gods created man in their image and then created women to keep men guessing at the mysteries. Bekka was pretty and mysterious. She intrigued him like a fire must intrigue a moth. He had to keep his distance, which would be easier once she left. Part of him longed to hear her entire story, to dig into the deep misery the way his fingers burrowed into the ground and planted the seed. Her soil was sacred, possibly even tainted. She would have to remain a mystery.

As for Hannah, he didn't know what to think or feel around her. This reaction solidified the fact he was as clueless with her as to why the sun burned in the sky. Plants were easy to understand. Life was bottled into a tiny seed, waiting for the right conditions to break open, grow roots, and dig deeper into the soil. All they required was water and sunshine.

Perhaps that explains love. Jarrod shook his head and laughed at the silly idea.

Planting the garden might seem a waste of time, especially since they could be gone before the plants fruited. Mights and maybes were for children to pretend in make believe games. Jarrod had to be prepared for the worse. Ishmael may never come back for them, leaving Jarrod to find a way to feed five children and himself. They couldn't live on gruel forever.

He finished off the row and tipped the bucket, gently allowing water to soak into the soil. Too much and the seeds would be washed away. Nearing the end of the row, he heard his name shouted.

"Jarrod!" Hannah ran back around the rock outcropping, a look of concern on her flushed face.

"What's wrong?" He set the empty bucket down.

"She's gone."

"Who?"

"Bekka."

Bekka was enjoying the game of pluck-the-daises. Especially watching Sarrah play with the other children, running and screaming in delight, rather than terror. After a tense morning, Elly apologized for her outburst. She and the other children acted friendly and included Sarrah in their games. Sarrah was no longer shy, hiding behind Bekka. She grinned and screeched joyously, holding Elly's hand as they chased Lily around the circle. All three girls crashed into Bekka, sprawling on top of her, laughing and giggling. Bekka clapped her hands and laughing as the girls helped her sit back up. The afternoon was a great improvement over the morning argument.

Until she saw Bernal.

Watching Ishmael led Bernal out of the tent at sword point, all delight had washed away. Bernal had the gall to smile and blow her a kiss. Bekka shuddered, flesh crawling like he had touched her with fingers prodding fresh cut meat. Ishmael didn't pay them any attention, intent on herding his prisoner down the hill.

What's he planning on doing with him? She sat stiff while the children went back to their semi-circle, this time with Elly playing the role of florist. Bekka continued watching Ishmael prod Bernal down the hill. After she judged they were a good distance, she spoke to Elly.

"I need to step away for a moment," Bekka said, touching her belly. "Do you mind keeping an eye on Sarrah for me?"

"Not at all." Elly smiled and they moved on to a new game.

Bekka went to her tent first and found what she wanted. Then she circled around and followed the path down the hill. Their backs were to her and the wind blew down the hillside. She walked on the balls of her bare feet to keep as quiet as a cat stalking a mouse. Neither looked back, and, as she got closer, she could hear parts of the conversation.

"...lords of the land."

Bekka shuddered, sensing blinding rage struggling to break free. *How dare he use Sarrah and me to bargain for his release!* She drew the dagger from its sheath. The blade surprisingly remained steady in her hands despite her racing heart. This man couldn't be free. Not so long as she had life in her body. *I will take Sarrah to Elysium. We will be safe from people like him.*

She wished she could see Ishmael's face, to gauge his reaction. Would he betray Sarrah and her for the safety of the group? He balked at giving them horse and supplies, and here was a way he could get out of it. Bekka's mind raced. She didn't want to kill Ishmael, only because she knew it would hurt Jarrod. Whatever disagreement they had together, Jarrod relied on Ishmael to help protect the children. In order to protect her child, Bernal had to die.

Wish I knew what you were doing with him out here. Bekka crept behind them. Suddenly they stopped. Bekka froze, close enough to smell Bernal's foul stench. Bernal's head turned and she crouched in the grass before he could see her. Ishmael shoved him forward.

Too close. She gripped the dagger high up on the hilt right before the sharp edge of the blade began. She tread a dangerous path and wouldn't leave it to chance to ruin everything. Rising from the grass, she walked briskly. Heart pounding and her eyes fixed on Ishmael, she raised the dagger, blade out and cracked him upside the head with the hilt.

Ishmael collapsed, a thin line of blood trickling over his right ear. Trapped by horror and regret, she looked down at him, wondering if she killed him after all. She almost knelt, but then Bernal turned around. The surprised look made him seem stupid, a dull child wondering at the beating from his father.

Bekka said the first thing that came to her mind.

"Killing you is a mercy." She raised the dagger to her breast, blade pointing at Bernal's gut. "Especially after what you put Sarrah through."

Bernal stood, unmoved by her threats, and grinned.

"That bitch's whelp?" Bernal said, chuckling. Her hand shook and she nearly lost her grip on the dagger, letting it slip through slick fingers. "She's a monster. Just like the thing growing in your belly. Fraylin was a fool to think we could save you. We should have burned the entire Blackwood and killed you like vermin."

"They didn't do anything wrong," Bekka said. "We never harmed you or anyone at the manor."

Bernal continued, ignoring what she said. "What's worse is you betrayed your own kind. You killed your brother for them." He spat at her feet. "The gods don't forgive fratricide."

"Lies," she said, her throat closing so the word came out hushed.

"You think killing me will end the suffering." He shook his head and gave a sadistic laugh. "The suffering is just beginning for you. Shadow Manor will not forget about us for long. Once they discover what happened, there isn't a rock you can hide under. They will find you and when they do, you better hope the beast growing in your body is still-born, because they will pluck it apart limb from limb."

"Enough!"

She lifted the dagger and plunged it down. The sharp point caught his tunic, tearing a ragged gash from neck to chest. Bernal stumbled over his feet, falling. Bekka yanked the blade back, before it was torn from her hands. She watched Bernal roll back on his shoulders, knees pulled in tight to his chest as he tried looping his bound hands under his feet. They caught on his heel.

Bekka growled, slashing at his exposed legs. He tightened into a small ball and rolled backwards heels-over-head. The blade swiped air. He sucked in his gut, drawing his legs up just enough to slip his hands under his feet. He sprawled onto his belly to stop his roll downhill.

No! He won't escape! Bekka chased after him.

Bernal scrambled to his feet as Bekka closed in.

"This is for Shane!" She lunged and he put up his hands defensively. Her eyes widened as the unexpected happened. The blade caught between his wrists. Grinning, he twisted the dagger so the edge sliced through the rope, and then grabbed Bekka's wrist. She slipped from his grip, losing the dagger as it wheeled around through the clear air and fell into a cluster of grass.

"There is your second mistake," he said, rubbing life back into his hands. He straightened up, standing a full-head taller than her.

Bekka turned to run, but he caught the back of her dress, tearing it at the seams under her arms. Strong hands nearly yanked her from her feet, dragging her into an embrace, her back against his front. A hand covered her throat, squeezing enough to make breathing difficult, but not entirely cut off. The other he stroked down over her breasts, belly, and between her legs.

"I'm going to kill the demon spawn in you. Even if I have to rip it out with my own hands," he said, breath smelling of old rotted onions. She tried to turn away from the stench, but he laughed, tugging up the front of her dress.

Bekka wiggled, hoping to loosen his grip. His arms were as strong as a vice clamp, pinning her arms to her side as he groped her. She dug her heel into his shin. He raised his knee so it struck her bottom, fingers tightening around her throat. Dark spots floated in front of her eyes. The light brightened and then dimmed. The world swam, blurry and her mind fought to keep conscious. If she passed out now, he would drag her away from Sarrah. Sarrah would be left all alone.

Shouts bellowed down the hill and two blurred forms ran toward them. One held a staff with a metal hooked end. Not a staff, but a hoe. It had to be her imagination. It couldn't be—

"I should snap your thin little neck," he growled, spinning her around to face him. "Shadow's luck! It won't be this day. Don't you worry, love, I will return for you."

He kissed her mouth, crushing her lips to his and leaving bruise marks on her forearms arms where he gripped her. The ground rushed at her as he threw her down. Her teeth clicked together as her bottom hit and she tilted onto her hands and knees, gasping heavily, air burning her throat. Tall grass whisked around her and Jarrod knelt, his hands running over her head.

"Are you alright?"

His voice sounded distant although he stood in front of her. Bekka nodded.

"Shadow take us! What did you do?" Jarrod asked. "Why'd you let him go?"

"I didn't." She coughed, then spat. "I was going to kill him."

"Why didn't he kill you?" Jarrod asked.

Bekka leaned on his shoulder and whispered into his ear.

"Because I am his betrothed."

CHAPTER NINE

Bringer of life and justice
Firm hand and stout heart
You braved the Void of our
Destruction, once more solidifying
Our home among the stars
A home we had created
Blessed are we to know you
Sorrowful is absence
Cold heart, cold hands
Oh Father!
We carry on.
We must carry on.
— From "Eulogy to Father"
Sin

Mother hunched over the Tome of Essence, full goblet of honey wine ignored at the corner of her desk. Blue orbs floated around the room, lighting the strange characters impressed on sativa pages. The hand writing consisted of looping swirls and harsh lines using permanent ink made from lampblack and black gum that prevented the strange characters from fading over the centuries. Stiff pages crinkled as she turned them, recounting for the hundredth time the history of the First Men.

The First lived much longer lives than the Created. Millenniums longer. Throughout their long-life span, they mastered lost arts of alchemy, astroplaning, and prophecy.

Words on the pages brought back memories of their triumph over death. Mother had contributed to the First's knowledge by revealing the secret to binding their souls to a plane outside of the normal sphere of planets and stars, infusing their essence in the space between. No one questioned whether they should change the nature of existence. No one ever questioned what they saw as a great advancement and improvement to their already utopic lifestyle. The ritual was performed and, as one, the First ascended, becoming immortal.

If we had only known the consequences. A deep longing filled her heart as Mother stroked the yellowed sativa pages. This rare book was all that remained from that world. After they'd attained the higher plane of existence, the cost was revealed—complete destruction of the world they once knew.

Stars winked out one by one, like forge fires extinguished, leaving the sky dark and empty. Their sun collapsed, emitting a blast of flames that burned away the rest of the planets and moons. Mother had watched the bright flames consume her home, leaving behind ash and molten rock. After the flames consumed everything, they too starved and died, and darkness rolled up the remnants like an old carpet to be discarded, leaving nothing. A great void.

Their own plane began to crumble. An illusion unraveling at the edges like a dream when the dreamer wakes and forgets what she has envisioned. Several of the First slipped away, disappearing into the unknown. Desperate to keep the rest from becoming a great mystery, Mother joined with Father, using the star of creation and disk of darkness. Together they formed another universe where theirs had once existed. They populated this new Creation with everything familiar: suns, stars, and planets. They also created beings in their likeness, infusing them with eternal souls. Souls which could be Ascended, no longer the created, but the creators. The First, or gods as they now made themselves into, could not walk among their new world, could not enjoy its splendor as they had in the old days, not without impressing their essence upon a Created's soul. This marked the Created as one who must ascend, or when the marked one died, the god fell and died as well. Together they winked out, stars imploding, leaving a void as they became part of the unknown.

Mother read these stories recorded in the Tome of Essence's opening pages. Beyond those were the secrets to ascension, transcendence, and prophecies. The Created grew beyond their control. No longer the shadows of a world once known, they took on a life completely their own. With this new life came new prophecies. The Ruin Prophesy interested Mother the most. Persephone, one of the Created and a priestess of Mother, was the first to have the ruin vision. Her vision foretold the First's fall from Ascension, return to their former lives, and the destruction of the Created. On her ascension, Persephone became Menrva, patron goddess to prophets and healers. She wrote all she saw in the Tome of Essence.

The visions didn't cease once Menrva ascended. Hundreds more followed and she recorded them all in the Tome. Mother read each and every one, once the ink dried. A little time before Father disappeared, she discovered the other prophecy. One that paralleled Ruin. This new prophecy focused on a specific Created who will ascend and transcend beyond the gods. Essentially, answering: Who created the creators? This prophecy Menrva called Transcendence.

Mother skimmed through the pages. Both had common elements, sharing similar ideas such as love creating a riff among the Ascended. She found the line and read it silently: *"Unfortuitous love breaks the hard façade casting dark wings over the eternal light."*

Mother flipped back several pages to Ruin Prophesy line: *"Shadow born of love."*

The language of both prophecies mirrored each other in how they were triggered. The difference being, which path were they on? How far along have they travelled?

"I really don't understand how you can favor him over any other," a dark, goading voice spoke from the shadows. Mother sat up, slowly closing the Tome of Essence. The ominous presence snuck up on her caught unaware like a cold breeze frosting the air. *She is growing stronger.* Mother calmed her rapid heart, casually leaned back and picked up her crystal goblet of wine and listened, taking in the cadence. "He is weak minded. I've seen drunken half-wits shit their pants and question the source of the stench make better decisions than this Champion of gods and men. Just look at who this *Champion* has chosen as his Champion."

"You whine like a jilted lover," Mother said, sipping from her goblet.

A misty fog secreted from the shadow, extinguishing one blue orb and casting half the room into darkness. The goblet frosted over, chilling in her hand and biting her skin. Mother dropped the goblet. It shattered into icicle shards on the floor. She slid the book into a desk drawer, preserving it from the moisture beading on the desk like gooseflesh, warping the ghost wood. Three taps on the drawer sealed the book safely inside where only she could access it.

"Yes, love is a curious thing." The frigidness in the Mistress of Shadow's voice made Mother wonder if this creature had ever known love, or was even capable of it. "It tricks our minds into believing that our actions are benevolent, wise even. Oh, but you and I know very well love is a mask for desire. A lie justifying our actions no matter how they harm others around us." The darkness crept towards Mother, a black glove reaching out to rest slender fingers on the desk's edge. "Sometimes, love is so strong it shines through the folds that blind us."

"That's far enough," Mother said, rising from her chair. Warm blue light shone in her hand. "I will not be threatened in my own room."

Derisive laughter echoed from the shadows.

"You share the same possessive, ill-conceived notions when it comes to the Created as he does. I can sense your touch on their world, a world in which I used to belong until he brought me here for a higher purpose." Silence consumed the room. The last word swiftly melted away. Mother felt her approach closer, the click of boot heels barely audible on the floor. "I'm not alone, either. For it seems love does have a purpose."

Qetesh! Worry gnawed away at Mother. This fiend must've found the farm boy. *Is she here to gloat?*

"Whispers about how Mother is interfering with the Struggle fall from your children's mouths." She made *tsk-tsk-tsk* clicks with her tongue as though scolding a disobedient juvenile. "Mendacities from she-who-made-all shall divide the house of Ascended. Havoc and chaos ravage the heavens, casting out all from the immortal planes. They shall fall and end creation."

"Quoting prophecy doesn't frighten me," Mother said. "Neither does your little trick of shadows."

Mother thrust out her right hand and swiped it across the mist and shadows like parting curtains to allow the sun to shine through the darkness. The veil evaporated, leaving a black cloaked woman standing in the blue light, hood obscuring her face. She wore form fitting leather vest and breeches. Two ebony hilted daggers hung on her hips, black sheathe and belt. The Mistress of Shadows, Dandulain, folded her arms under her breasts.

"Now that you have removed my veil, I have nothing left to hide," Dandulain said. "Do the same for the farm boy."

Ah, so she doesn't know.

"The boy is none of your concern." Mother stared into deep hatred, finding her inner calm. One didn't create worlds without darkness. "He is your old master's charge."

"How much longer do you believe you can intrude on the Struggle?" She hooked her thumbs through the belt beside the daggers. "I know you hide him from me on behalf of my old master. Just as I know my old master has become one of Created, most likely through your arts. Either give me the boy, or I will take away what you desire most."

"What I desire most is for you to return to that dark hole from which you climbed." Mother unclasped her hands, warmth spreading between her palms. *Threatening me is akin to a tantrum, but threaten my child!* "Since I know how willing you are to comply with my desires, I order you to leave before I am compelled to disperse you myself."

"All glory rained down on the heads of the Created." Dandulain reached for her daggers. A malicious smile playing on her lips. "Mother's tears weep as her children fall—the first shall be her greatest love!"

Mother threw the blue ball of light. A white streak, glaring like a comet's tail, struck Dandulain's chest. Blue sparks sprayed across her form and a blinding white light consumed the room. Mother shielded her eyes against the glare, listening to the deafening silence. From it came a chuckle. Mother opened her eyes. *It can't be!* She clenched her jaw to contain her surprise.

"Your power grows weaker, Mother." The Mistress of Shadow drew one ebony dagger. The black steel absorbed the light. "You can no longer banish me. I command the darkness and it protects me from your touch."

"What have you done?" Mother gasped, touching the hollow of her neck. The star of creation hung on the silver chain. It felt cooler, as though the warmth was leeching out.

Dandulain laughed.

"Not everything is recorded in your little book." She slammed the point of one dagger into the sealed drawer and shoved down on the hilt. The ghost wood frame splintered and the drawer slid open. *How?* Mother stared, dumbfounded by the broken seal, one she created and only she could unlock... at least until now. The Mistress of Shadows sheathed her daggers and removed the Tome of Essence.

"It won't do you any good. You cannot read the language."

"There are more than one way to comprehend the stories." She held the book out, taunting Mother with it. "Remove the veil and I will give this back to you."

Millenniums of stories and hundreds of prophecies bound in that one book. Her heart ached for it, but she could not give in to this creature's demands. It would be the end of everything, Created and Ascended.

"I'd rather see it burn than give you what you want."

The book disappeared beneath Dandulain's cloak.

"I will find the boy," the Mistress of Shadows said. "Both he and his master will die. I'll make certain that neither Ascend. Then all your ploys will be revealed and the Heavens will fall, their light extinguishing, casting a shroud over all Creation."

"No!" Mother lunged for the dagger.

Dandulain reacted quicker, lashing out with the back of her gloved hand. Pain exploded in the right side of Mother's face. The room spun and she collapsed to the floor. She looked up to see Dandulain remove her hood. Raven black hair flowed over her shoulder and neck. A pale, beautiful face with black shaded lips grinned at her. Mother's eyes widened as she noticed a single pedant on a gold chain circular with a round hole at the center against her throat.

"I could destroy you here and now." Dandulain loomed over her. Mother cried out as a black boot kicked her thigh. "Oh, but instead, I will make you watch helplessly as everything you created dies. I will take it all away, beginning first with this."

She reached for the star of creation. Mother raised her arm, fending her off. Dandulain grabbed Mother's wrist, and twisted. Sharp pain surprised her, forcing another cry. Swinging her free hand around, Mother pressed it against Dandulain's forearm, releasing a heat wave hot enough to melt metal. The Mistress of Shadows hissed, dragging Mother to her feet and flung her against the desk. Mother struck the edge. The air rushed out of her lungs and she collapsed to the floor, doubled over.

"Fight me all you want." Dandulain rubbed her arm. "I have grown beyond you."

Mother tapped the drawer in front of her. A click resounded. The drawer slid open enough for her to reach inside. As soon as her hand grasped the object, her head was yanked backwards by her hair. In her peripheral, she noticed a black, gloved hand snaking around to steal the star of creation. Mother squeezed the object in her hand, feeling it break and cut her palm. A fine powder stung as it mingled with her blood. Closing her eyes, Mother threw the powder overhead. Her head snapped forward as the Mistress of Shadows released her hair, and shrieked. A bright white light shone through Mother's eye lids and warmth spread throughout the room. When the light had dimmed, she opened her eyes. The room was empty.

"I guess you are not as strong as star dust," Mother said, touching her neck. Her fingers froze on her skin. "No, no, no, no." She shook her dress and searched the floor frantically. After a moment of not finding it, she knew it was gone.

The Mistress of Shadows took the star of creation.

Now she has both. Mother's knees weakened and she leaned against her broken desk. *She has the star of creation and the disk of darkness.*

Her head dropped to her hands and she wept.

Joanne meditated on the portrait of her father. The subtle strokes of black, brown, and gold focused her eyes on his face. Very much life like, she could almost reach out and touch the oil on canvas transforming into leathery skin immaculately shaved. The pink slashes on sun browned cheek and square jaw line, scars from battles won. He glowered at Joanne, head tilted slightly upward displaying his regality, his inhumanity. Sharp blue eyes stared at her, viewing her inadequacies, her failings. Even worse, they bent her to his will beyond the confines of death.

She felt very small, a little girl in a blue dress, picking a bouquet of flowers in the gardens. Lord Desmond had called her over, and placed a finger beneath her chin, forcing her to look into his hard blue eyes. The storm she had witnessed frightened her, sending her heart racing every time the sky grew cloudy and darkened. With a tenderness that floated from his lips, lost before it reached the swirling storm, he had said: "You will marry a prince one day, my little one."

"Yes, father," she had responded with the expected reply. Anything else resulted in a severe beating and she didn't desire being the focal point of the storm's fury. He patted her cheek and smiled, one that never went past his lips. Gladly she retreated back to her flowers, forgetting, as children often do, the promise and responsibility far off in the unknown future.

The prince her father had arranged for her betrothal turned out to be Fraum, the eldest, pox marked son of King Dryd of Seaptum. Not only was Fraum scarred from his childhood bout with scarlet rubella, or swine pox—named after the pink patches marring the skin, like a pig's hide, the disease left him stunted, blue eyes rheumy, and his throat gave a high-pitched squeak every time he exhaled. Thin black hair covered his flaky scalp and he sneezed so often, she wondered how the boy, six name-days older than her, still had a nose.

Joanne was thirteen names day old when her father told her of the match. On her fourteenth name day, she met the boy and immediately fled back to her room, horrified at her future spouse. Lord Desmond had found her weeping on her bed.

"So you decline this match?" Lord Desmond had asked calmly, standing in the doorway. She knew that tone. Although he sounded in control, reasonable, it was a warning, a flash of lightening before the thunderous downpour.

"I can't marry him, father," she had said, swiping away her tears. "He's a monster."

She hadn't been far off from her description as she would later discover. Fraum had a fierce temper and enjoyed using a horse crop to express his frustration. No one was immune from his disapproving crack on the legs, arms, and rear, anywhere that didn't mar their beauty.

"What the gods take away in physical nature they make up for in other ways." He had entered the room and stood before her bed.

King Dryd had enough wealth to purchase Nemus five times over. He also had a well-trained military and an eye for Nemus' rich resources. This prompted Lord Desmond to negotiate a peace treaty, offering his only daughter.

"Please Father, no."

His hand was swift. Joanne's head rocked back and she collapsed on the bed.

"I'll mark you so you're ugly, too." Lord Desmond took out his belt knife and pinned his prostate daughter on the mattress. The sting of his words and hand upon her cheek. Watching the blade's tip hover over her eye, her bladder loosened. A flick of the wrist would slice her flesh cheek to jaw as simple as tearing a petal from a rose. "Then you will be the right match for him. A pair of godsforsaken beasts rutting together to produce more vile creatures."

Joanne closed her eyes, crying for her father to stop. She promised to marry Fraum and satisfy his every desire, no matter how perverse, until the day he died. Joanne followed through on her promise, no matter how disgusted she became, hiding it in the deep regions of her heart for six long years. Then Fraum mysteriously died— physics blamed his weak heart. She gained his fortune and inherited an army that now roamed Nemus, nearly unifying it once again.

Just a few more pieces remained.

"I will have your legacy, Father," she said to the portrait, taking a knife from her belt and tracing the tip over his scars, carefully not to tear the canvas. At least, not yet. "People will tremble before me just as they once feared you."

"Not as much as they fear the gods," a woman said, hidden in the shadows of Joanne's room. The *Mors Faunis* standing at the opposite drew their swords. Joanne held up a hand to stay their attack.

"No man or woman commands the awe that the gods deserve," Joanne said and knelt. She placed her weapon in front of her, then flattened her palms on the stone floor.

"Rise, child," the woman said.

Joanne sheathed the dagger, then ran her hands down her white shift, smoothing out imaginary wrinkles.

"What does my Mistress desire?"

The woman emerged from the shadows, trailing darkness like a cloak. She wore black banded armor, form fitting to reveal the tight curve of her hips and breasts. She made no sound while walking. Long, raven black hair streamed over her shoulders. Stone grey eyes stared at

Joanne from the pale face. Bright red lips smiled at Joanne as she placed a black gloved finger on her shoulder and trailed it up her neck walking around Joanne. A warm tingling began at the base of her neck, running down her spine and around her breasts. Gooseflesh prickled her skin and she blushed.

"You know my desire."

"Yes, Mistress." Joanne said, eyes watching the bright red lips. "The woman and the girl. I have dispatched my best tracker and personal guard to hunt them."

"This I know also."

Of course, she did. Joanne blushed, again. *She is a goddess after all.*

"You disapprove?"

"No, child." The click of her tongue told Joanne otherwise.

"Was it my choice of sending Thramel?" Joanne waited for a response, then hurried to explain her reason. "He is very competent when properly encouraged."

"He is not of us." The Mistress of Shadows frowned. Joanne felt her disappointment like a slap that burned deep to her core. "Was it wise to send this outsider, this rebel turned traitor, on such an important task?"

"Yes." She cringed at the doubt in her voice. No man or woman could make her second guess herself, but the Mistress' cold stare weakened her belly.

"I hope for his success," The Mistress of Shadows said, taking off her glove and placing a pale hand on Joanne's cheek. The pain was so intense it made what Fraum did to her seem like a lover's caress. Joanne dropped to her knees, but couldn't escape the goddess' touch. Warm, wetness spread over her crotch and trickled down her leg. The Mistress of Shadows took her hand away and slipped the glove back on. "For your sake."

"Will you bless their journey?" Joanne asked, panting and trembling.

"I have other matters to attend." The goddess stepped closer to the shadows. The darkness bent towards her, creating a cloak. "Have your soldiers ready to press Heartwood Pines in a full moon. Send two squads to scour the Yellow Valley between the Mountains of Dawn and Destiny."

"Yes, Mistress," Joanne said, bowing.

"Kill anyone they find."

When Joanne looked up, the Mistress of Shadows was gone.

The heat had radiated for centuries alone and untouched, a dragon sleeping deep with its dark cavern awaiting its moment to awaken and rage with fire, was extinguished like a single tear drop on a lighted taper nearing the end of its wick. He had worked his frail body to near exhaustion trying to revive the embers. Tinder and torches and flaming oils all died out as soon as they touched the ashes.

Dragon's oil generated enough heat to burn water, evaporating it in mere moments and continued to burn through what lay beneath the water's surface. It was wild and uncontrollable, capable of turning the entire forest into a blazing sun. Huron dipped the tip of a stick into the small vile of dragon's oil. He was desperate. All other attempts to ignite the Gods' Forge had failed. He touched the tip to the small fire he kept. The oil flared immediately, consuming the dry wood at a rapid pace. He dropped it over the edge of the stone and into the dead ash. As soon as it touched, the fire sizzled out. He repeated the process one last time, emptying the entire vial of Dragon's oil into the Gods' Forge.

He released the stick and jumped back, expecting a massive fiery column to rise up to the treetops. Once again, nothing happened. His stomach grew heavy at the realization of his fears. *She dropped in a Pearl of the Pool!* He had denied the idea that she had knowledge of such a thing, let alone would use it against him. The ash would not dry out for another century and nothing else he could do would light the forge. *I play the part of the fool again!*

He grabbed the hammer and flung into the sea of green. Lifting the bag of useless silver bars, he spun it around until the fabric tore from his fingers and sailed off into the trees, scattering silver bars as it struck a tree trunk. Then he collapsed onto the ground, wrapping his arms around his head.

Mother weep! I should've known she would anticipate my coming here. A century ago, he had forged knives using her hands, ignorant to the idea that she would betray him not too long after her death.

Will the boy be strong enough to defeat her and her champion? Dandulain held the advantage. She knew who he chose to be his next, but he didn't know her chosen. They would be fighting blind. Dandulain would have studied the boy and discovered that he was no fighter, at least not yet. Huron had wanted to forge a sword for the boy, one that would hold the light of a dawn star and slice through the fugue of shadow, to counter the assassin's knives. With the Gods' Forge extinguished, that task was impossible.

She will carve him up. Another death on his head, except that this death would lead to Huron's demise. No one would be left to protect Mother and the Children. Dandulain would win and Creation would fall. The Struggle ends. Shadow spreads over creation, fulfilling the Prophecy of Ruin while he sat here, mourning his forge like a child losing his favorite toy. He touched the soul pendant. How easy it would be to smash it and return as a spectator to the fight, possibly a deciding factor by possessing the boy and fighting for the battle for him. Except he would lose. Only the mortal flesh can defeat the god and drive back the Shadow. He would have to force her to wager it all like he had on the fight to come.

Here I sit, wailing like a peevish boy because his milk soured. Have I gone soft? Have I forgotten the glories of victory?

He gathered his legs and tracked down the bag of silver. Dragging it from the tangle of vines, he slung it over his shoulders. He left the abandoned remains, going to where he left the horses. When he arrived, they were gone. Frayed ropes dangled off branch like something chewed through them. *Rats!* Plump, gray bodies lay scattered around the tree trunk, beady eyes glazed over and tiny needle teeth bared.

"Mother bless me, I'm going to make her pay for all this suffering." He adjusted his pack and began the journey on foot.

Sweltering heat made oppressive by clouds swimming in the shallows of blue soup overhead, ignited Huron's fury. Clothes clung to his skin, black armor clanking beside the pack filled with silver bars. He'd traveled countless leagues on foot, thoughts bent on how he would revenge himself on Dandulain for not only extinguishing the Gods' Forge, but spooking his horses. All of his provisions, including food and water, ran off with the horses. He had one water gourd for when he began the hot, tiresome work at the forge. He finished off the last of the water over night. The gourd tied to his waist hung empty.

Tired, hungry, and thirsty, he stumbled along the road west of *Venustas Lux,* back to Elysium where he purchased the horse and supplies. *Maybe they went home.* That idea of going home was very tempting. His hand brushed the soul pendant. Despite the heat, the crystal was cool against his skin. Breaking the soul pendant would release him from Creation, release him from this miserable burden men endured. How could they stand the conditions of the body? The need to eat, drink, sweat and all these tugging on his emotion, like a knife scraping bone. Worse was the need to sleep. Sleep felt like a preview of death, except for the dreams. Dreams of walking in the City of Light and Beauty, of touching the warm stone of the forge before he fed it the first meal of the new dawn, of fire raving in the city and people screaming and blood and death. Father lifting his frail, broken form from beneath his horse on a bloody battlefield. Spoken words of comfort: "Don't be afraid, my son. Your service here is over. You are now ascended."

Father now gone, betrayed because of him.

He couldn't leave this world yet.

Running water caught his ear and he hurried up the path to a small grove of Blood Berries. He dropped his pack and armor beside a shallow creek. He dipped the gourd into the clear water, the cool water shocking to his hot arms that he nearly released it. He poured the water into his mouth, sucking the sweetness down before refilling. The next fill he dumped over his head, heart skipping a beat as the water shocked him again. Face dripping, he looked at the bright red fruit dangling from the trees. They were nearly the size of his little finger and he remembered the Blood Berries had a tangy flavor and he hoped they hadn't changed in the centuries, remaining edible and not toxic. Plucking a cluster from a low branch, he stripped the berry from the stem and chewed. A sweet, tangy juice filled his mouth. Tiny, hard seeds scraped against his teeth. He spat those out, trailing red spittle that looked like blood. He grabbed handfuls of the berries, eating so many his tongue burned from their juices. He took out an empty bag from his pack and piled in as many blood berries as he could.

Grabbing another bunch, he squashed them in his hand. The red juice dripped from between his fingers and into the soil. "Mother's blessing." He washed the sticky remains off his hands and continued his journey.

The sun peaked overhead at midday. Very few clouds floated along to cover the sun, leaving him exposed. He was half a league from the village of Elysium when he noticed a column of smoke rise to the clear sky. Small animals migrated towards him. First it was rabbits and a deer followed by a fox. They gave him a wide berth, running towards the east and hiding in some shrubs.

Wildfire? Huron shielded his eyes and looked to the west. A rider-less horse galloped along the road, teeth bared and ears pinned back. Huron leapt out of the horse's path just moments before it trampled past. He watched the horse continue sprinting away, not recognizing it as one he had purchased.

This is not a natural wildfire. He dusted his clothes. The horse had a saddle and as far as he knew, he had taken the last horses in Elysium. He studied the smoke. Too much volume for a camp fire and not enough for a wildfire. He had seen many villages burn during war. The way the smoke seemed contained reminded him of fires with the walls of a city, or village.

Huron felt unease creep over him. It was no coincidence this fire and Dandulain's presence at the Gods' Forge. Why would she attack the village? Did she have an army he didn't know about? Were other Children helping her? She had a hand in it, that's all he knew in his heart.

Whatever the cause, he needed to help those people. Huron strapped on his armor and jogged at a steady pace to the village.

White smoke billowed up from the wooden walls. Ash fluttered down like a light snow. An acrid stench filled the air. Nothing living moved this close to the east gate. The gate was open and he saw the crumbled remains beyond. Brown smoke drifted from portions of the wooden wall. A light wind could ignite a fire to finish off the remnants of Elysium. Huron walked up to the gate and examined it. *No signs of forced entry. It had to have been opened from inside.* South of the gate, a body lay near an opened watch door. Thick black beard and curly black hair identified the man who sold him the horses. Coagulated blood marked where he had fallen from a gut wound.

Miles. He shook my hand and named himself as Miles. Mother! I blessed this man and look at where it got him. He looked at the open door. Either Miles was part of the ploy to sack the village and was betrayed, or he was trying to find a way out only to get a sword in the belly. *He wouldn't have given away his last horse if he planned on escaping a burning village.* Anger rose up, lending strength to his previous need. *Whoever did this, I will find them and give these people retribution.*

Several houses and shops smoldered along the cobblestones. A once peaceful center of life, reduced to nothing but cinders and ash. He found another body belonging to an elderly man. Wispy grey hair wreathed his ears. He was face down in a smear of blood and entrails, stripped naked. A chunk of flesh hung from his teeth, his mouth a red smear of dried blood.

More bodies littered the road. Men and women. Blood painted mouths and fingers bent into claws. All were nude.

What went on here? Huron moved carefully around to avoid stepping in pools of blood. *Too early for scavengers to steal from the dead. Carrion birds haven't even arrived.* The smoke was too thick yet for them to swoop in and dine. Other carrion eaters, like the fox, ran the opposite direction. The fear of fire, or something else, deterred them.

Further west, Huron found a body still clothed. A soldier's body leaned against a collapsed foundation, paled faced and right arm torn off. His clothes smoked, singed at the edges. Huron knelt down, searching for any signifier, an insignia or emblem to match a potential house. Footfalls on the cobblestone caught his attention. Huron stood up, crossing his arms with a hand on a sword pommel watching three soldiers circle around from the burnt husk of a building. They stopped, giving each other dumbfounded looks

"What do we have here?" The middle soldier asked, a wet rag covered his mouth and nose. Grey ash clung to the outside, sprinkling his brown hair. He was shorter than the other two. Dark rings under his eyes told of a hard night's work. All three wore the same dark blue uniforms and silver gorgets matching the corpse. "Looks like we missed one."

"He's not like the others," The soldier on his right commented. "He's not changing."

"Doesn't matter," the shorter one said, drawing his sword. "Orders are to kill every adult." The other two spread out, covering the escape points so he had the smoldering building at his back.

Huron calmly observed the way they walked, the handling of the sword, their head and eye motions. The first attacked his right flank, as predicted by their proximity. Huron stepped away from the blade, grabbed the man's sword arm and kicked him in the ribs. He spun the soldier around, shoving him into the next attacker. They collided and fell to the cobblestones. The shorter soldier struck and Huron drew his long sword, knocking aside the thrust.

The man retreated to his companions.

"What did you do to these people?" Huron took up *Ox Guard*. "They didn't deserve this."

"People!" The shorter soldier replied, spitting out the "P's." "They're abominations of the gods, not people. They need to be destroyed."

Once more the soldiers spread out, forcing his back to the blacked remains of a burnt-out building. Quickly his pose changed to *Three Wonders* with middle point, gripping the hilt in his right hand and extending the left to grip the blade. He thrust at the first soldier's head, who leapt backwards and cut towards the second, the blade slicing through chainmail and scarring flesh. Sliding to the side he grabbed the first soldier's arm and slammed his pommel into the crook of the elbow. The soldier grunted and dropped his sword.

"This isn't a fight you can win," Huron said, standing at the crux, forcing their backs against the smoldering remains. "Yield or you force me to kill you."

The wounded soldier made an overhead cut, throwing his body in a desperate attempt to overpower Huron. *Crown of Thorns* caught the arching blade. Sweaty, dirt-streaked face grimaced, teeth clenched as he tried to break the hold, Huron thrust the blade up and he kicked the exposed soldier in the gut. The soldier doubled over, head bowed. Huron clanged him on the helm with the pommel, dropping him to the ground. Then he stomped on the back of the soldier's neck, snapping bone and tendon.

He deflected a swipe at his thigh and swung the sword around to defend his right. The shorter guard shifted offensive poses to drive Huon back, allowing his companion to retrieve his weapon. Falling back into *Three Wonders*, Huron parried the cut and responded with *Falling Star*. The soldier defended, but was thrown off balance. Huron's thrust found the weakness under the soldier's left arm and the point of his blade ruptured the soldier's heart. The man screamed, words drowned in bubbling blood gushing over his lips and fell over. Huron ripped his sword clear, deflecting a cut intended for his leg. Spinning with fluid motion, the flat side of his blade smacked the guard in the back of his head, sending him sprawling face first into the cobblestone. Stepping on his sword arm, Huron kicked the blade away.

"Yield." Huron held the point under the soldier's chin.

The soldier batted it away, yanked down his kerchief and spat.

"Go wank off, you'll get nothing from me." He put out his neck. "Finish me so I can tell the Shadow where to find you."

That's not how things work. Huron pressed the point against the soldier's stubble covered throat. No remorse was in his eyes.

"For the murder of innocents, I condemn your soul to be weighed and cast into oblivion." Huron thrust the tip under the man's chin, slicing sinew and grating against bone. The tip of the blade, slick with gore and grey matter, protruded through the top the man's head. He yanked the blade free. The body flopped, lifeless, to the stone. Wiping the blood on the dead soldier's trousers, he sheathed the clean blade. The one he had knocked unconscious still breathed. Huron stripped him of his armor, tossing them into the embers. Using a knife from the soldier's belt, he carved a message into the man's chest and abdomen.

Blood flowed free and strips of flesh splayed out to read: "I live by mercy of the gods."

He took a cloak from the dead soldier and covered him so the bright orange insignia showed: a star with a lightning bolt slashing diagonally through it. As the blood soaked through the material, he tried to recall where he had last seen that sigil. So many houses rose and fell over the centuries, each with various stars, suns, moons, and lightning bolts, none matching what he saw here. He picked up his pack and made his way through Elysium, searching for survivors to seek answers or soldiers to exact retribution.

At the charred remains of the general store, he discovered a long, smeared trail of blood. He followed the bloody trail to where it ended under a villager on his back, empty eyes staring up at the sky. Red ichor painted the mouth of a man as though he gorged on some Blood Berries, face frozen in death in a snarl. Bits of flesh stuck on his teeth as though he bit one of his attackers.

Such strange business.

A child screeched. He ran towards the source, squatting beside a stone wall and observed around the side. Two soldiers lifted a girl under the arms as she kicked at them. Huron recognized Breanne, the little girl who approached him in the streets. A third soldier grabbed Breanne's left leg and tied a rope around it. She kicked him in the ribs. The soldier dropped her and she landed on her hip. He then backhanded her hard enough so the smack carried to Huron. Breanne rolled over, covering her face, and sobbed. The soldier grabbed her hands and bound her before tossing her in a wagon full of more crying children.

Another soldier rode up on a horseback. He wore a gold hilted sword and a gold star with lightening slash brooch pinned on his cloak. The other soldiers saluted him with a clenched fist drawn to the center of the chest under the chin.

"Quit playing around and get these children loaded up." The commanding officer scowled at them, turning his horse to view the cart. His back was to Huron, but he could tell the commanding officer was counting the children. He swung his horse back and asked, "Anymore boys?"

"No, sir," one soldier responded. "We have men searching the surrounding areas for remaining refugees."

"This will have to be enough." He moved up the side of the wagon. "Move them out."

Mother! Huron counted the soldiers escorting the wagon. A squad of twenty surrounded the wagon, not counting the commanding officer. *"Are you a god?"* Breanne's innocent question rang in his heart. His reply: *"I'm as you are... a child of Mother."* Everyone he had interacted with in Elysium were dead as though his presence was a plague on them. *I have to help those children!*

Jarrod needs my help. Dandulain will murder him unless I am there to protect him. Then all things are done for nothing.

A direct assault wouldn't fare well for him. The sheer numbers would be his undoing. The wagon moved further away the longer he waited. Soon it would be out of sight.

Those village children also require aid, part of him demanded. *Who knows what those soldiers will do to them?*

He did know one thing for certain. Those soldiers had horses. He needed the horses to cross the desert. By helping the children, he would in turn aid his own cause. Huron emptied his pack of silver bars, leaving only the water gourd and bag of Blood Berries. *Mother if you can hear my prayer, watch over the farm boy until I get to him.* He left a small fortune behind in the burnt-out ruins of Elysium. Dead weight he no longer required. *You were right, Mother, I do have a soft spot for those unable to fight battles bigger than themselves. Let's hope it doesn't become my undoing!*

Slinging his nearly empty pack over his shoulders, he trailed after the cart.

CHAPTER TEN

The stars faded. Worlds swept away in a great wind of undoing. Nikko's hand stretched out, fingers splayed. But I could not save him. He slipped away in the consuming unknown triggered by our actions. To attain salvation, I knew we had to re-create. A stable world. One where we would rule above. Judges, condemner of souls. When it was over, who would judge us? Where would be condemned?
—From "Creators and Created"

Dark clouds gripped the eastern sky, promising an abatement to the heat, but like the clouds, the promise was empty. *An homage to this day's events.* Thramel licked his dry lips. Most of the extra water skins were lost in Black Wyrm when its serpentine resident tore up the supply horse. He'd rather jab a rusted nail under his eyelid than go back to that dank, smelly marsh to search for lost food and water. The last remaining skin he'd finished off half a league back. *What I would give for a splash of wine!*

Behind him, Snout sucked on his water skin. Water sloshed and he glared at Thramel with abused hound dog eyes. *Still hasn't forgiven me for nearly throttling him.* An angry bruise shined on his cheek. Thramel smiled, though the rage threatened to rekindle. It didn't matter he forced them to go through the vile inhabited marsh. *The bastard left me like some mangy cur after the handouts were gone.*

Snout lifted his nose to the air, making exaggerated sniffing noises. Thramel cringed and gripped the reins until he was white knuckled. His

ankle throbbed in his boot and he could feel his leg stiffen. His entire
body felt like he'd been hit by a pile of rocks. He wanted a drink and a
long nap.

"Smells like rain," Snout said after he finished snorting the air. "A
sprinkler to tease the parched soil"

"Can you really tell that much from smelling the air?" Thramel asked.
Like a godsdamn snake! "Or are you making it up to keep your place?"

Snout tucked the water skin into the saddle bag.

"Smells are distinct. Not just weather, or flowers, or horses, but
everything has a smell. Even people and their emotions carry a scent."

"So, if I were to ride off to some far away woods, you would still be
able to smell me?"

"Not you exactly," Snout said. "Your trail, rightly so. All I have to
do is follow the pungent garlic mix I gave you. I can track the garlic
anywhere now you got it in your system. Also, I can smell emotions. I
know you're angry. A bitter, sour stench mixed with copper filings. I
can almost taste the bile crawling up your craw. That is how you
smelled when we first met, well that and the sweet river wine our
Reverent Queen tossed in your face."

"I take it as more of a blessing for my long journey ahead." Thramel
pointed at the *Mors Faunis*. "What do those things smell like?"

Snout went quiet for a moment. Thramel didn't expect a reply. When
it came, he shivered.

"Like metal and death," Snout said. "Always... metal and death."

They reached the border of Shadow Manor and came upon the first
sign of civilization. A small farm house, no better than a lean-to hovel
built from whitewood and straw. Its thatched roof stuck out against
the sparse landscape. Cleared fields surrounded the hovel. Small dust
clouds blew out in the southern field closest to the road where a sun-
darkened man trudged along, attention focused on the field. He leaned
on a plow dragged by a team of two horses, large-brimmed hat flopping
over his ears.

Thramel stopped at the edge of the field flanked by the *Mors Faunis*.
Snout rode up beside him, droopy eyes staring the man in the field.

"What do you want from here?" Snout spat and continued chawing
on some brown goo that had a hint of mint.

"Resupply." Thramel shook his empty water skin.

Snout nodded, slouching in the saddle.

Dust settled as the man halted the train. He limped to the front of the plow's blade, favoring his right leg. Thramel sympathized, his own foot dully throbbing. Despite the pain, the man lifted a stone the size of a melon from the path, thin arms straining to loosen it from the ground. As he hunched over, stone sagging between his arms, his hat fell off. Setting the stone aside, he snatched his hat and clutched it to his chest as he caught Thramel's eye. For a moment, Thramel noticed a flash of fear, like a man watching a rockslide. He thought the man would run, as any wise man would flee the crushing torrent of stone, but this old man continued to stare, eyes narrowing.

Thramel held up his water skin and turned it over to show it was empty.

The man adjusted his hat, patted the first horse, and whispered into its ear. Shoving his hands in the pockets of his dusty breeches, he shuffled along in a slow wobble.

"What can I do, by the Mother, to assist you gentlemen?" he asked in clumsy, thick words as though he had woken up from a drunken stupor. Blotchy wrinkled skin and dark circles around his brown eyes told the effects of working outdoors most of the day. Clothes hung loosely and he had a slight tremor. The old man's eyes darted from the *Mors Faunis* to Snout and stayed on Thramel.

"Water," Thramel said, tossing the skin at him. It struck the man's thin chest and fell on his tattered, dusty shoes. The man stared stupidly at it. Thramel rolled his eyes. "It's not a snake. It won't bite you. Go ahead. Pick it up."

"Who honors me with such a menial task?" The bite in the old man's voice was like a toothless dog gumming a bone. When no one replied, he bent, winced, and grabbed his lower back. "Forgive me for being slow. My back isn't what it used to be several seasons ago. I pray patience while I get your water so you can be on your way, may it please you."

The old man began to shuffle away.

"What food do you have in your larder?"

The man froze, shoulders sinking as though he carried the weight of the world and no longer could support it. Hands hanging listlessly at his side, he turned and looked at Thramel from beneath the sagging hat brim. His entire face pled the way a petulant child would put on a pitiful countenance to escape a beating.

"A paltry stock, good sirs," the man said, a tremble in his voice. "Enough for one man to get by until the harvest."

"You won't mind if I inspect it for myself?" Thramel stepped down from the horse, wincing at the pressure on his sore foot. "'Feed a traveler, for you never know when a god walks among us,' isn't that the adage? For all you know, I could be Donn to weigh the value of your soul."

The look the man gave him said Thramel was more demon than god. *If he only knew.* Thramel took a couple of steps closer to the house.

"No!" The old man choked back the shout and become sullen again. "By Mother's light, I would give you anything you want, but I have none to spare."

Thramel saw a face in the window peek out and quickly disappear. *So he is hiding something. Or someone.*

"You're alone?"

"Yes."

"He lies," Snout said. "I smell the fear on him."

"Who's in the house?"

"No one."

Thramel drew his sword and limped to the hovel. The old man stepped in his path, putting up his hands as though he could hold him back. Thramel shoved him out of the way simpler than tipping a drunk off a bar stool. The man continued to beg from the ground and Thramel kicked him in the ribs, hearing the man's grunt and pleas change to groans. Two silent forms flanked Thramel. He pointed for one to go around the house to cover any escape through a back door or window. The *Mors Faunis* slipped away.

Following orders? Thramel raised a brow. *I guess standing my ground and almost being devoured by the wyrm improved my status in the pack.*

The second followed him to the front door. Thramel wrapped his knuckles on the frame.

"Drop any weapons you have and come on out," he said. No one responded. He tried the door knob. It wouldn't turn, either. "Who do you have in there, old man?"

"No one." The man groveled on the ground, crawling towards them. "Please leave."

Thramel reared back on his injured ankle, nearly toppling over from the pain. With the flat of his boot, he kicked the door open. Out of instinct he ducked. Instinct served him well as an arrow thrummed by his ear. The hovel was dark, smelled of old dirt, and radiated heat. Movement caught his eye and he swung his head behind the edge of the door frame as another arrow thumped against the inside wall. He held up two fingers. The *Mors Faunis* nodded, then leapt inside.

Crashing and screams ensued. Thramel crouched, making himself a smaller target, and entered. Moments passed as his eyes adjusted to the gloom. A small table was overturned and a body lay on the floor, blood seeping from a gash in his throat. Metal clanked together in an adjoining room. The *Mors Faunis* deflected a sword, driving the attacker back. The boy tripped over a chair and fell on his backside.

"Stop!" Thramel growled before the *Mors Faunis* could run the boy through. The Death Howler placed the blade on the boy's throat.

"I yield," the boy said, dropping his weapon.

"Bring him closer to the light," Thramel said. "Let me get a good look at him."

The *Mors Faunis* lifted the boy by the collar of his cuir bouilli, shoving him backwards out of the hovel. Thramel grabbed the boy's dark black hair and tilted his head up so he could see his face in the fading light. He looked at the old man crawling around on the ground like a slug.

Thramel grunted. *I should've guessed.*

"Is that your brother inside there?" Thramel asked.

The boy nodded. He couldn't be no more than seventeen name-days, though the dark circles under his eyes aged him some.

"You boys abandoned your post at the Manor?"

"No, sir." The boy squinted. "We were run out."

"By who?"

"The she-bitch who usurped our land," the boy said.

Thramel smacked the boy hard enough for his head to snap to the side. A red bruise formed on the boy's cheek and he could almost sympathize with him. The boy glared at Thramel through a swelling eye. Thramel resisted shaking the defiance out of him.

"You will speak well of your new queen," Thramel said. More the idea of abandoning fellow soldiers than insulting Joanne that angered him.

"She's no queen of mine."

"Brave." Thramel smiled and shook his head. "One thing you should learn in life is that brave words are just salt poured in your water. Drink a little and you're fine, but over time, you'll die of thirst just the same. Snout!"

Snout leaned over his saddle and shouted back: "Yes!"

Thramel waved for him to come closer. Snout took his time, ambling over on horseback.

"This one doesn't suffer from the need to be brave, or be in haste," Thramel said and nodded at Snout. The horse stopped at the edge of the hovel. Snout leaned lazily over the saddle once more, chewing on something. "These the rebels Joanne was talking about?"

Snout squinted at the boy and took in a long draw of air.

"Nope."

"Take him to that tree and string him up." Thramel pointed at a tall whitewood. The *Mors Faunis* began to drag the boy.

"No!" the boy's father shouted, falling to his knees. "Please. Take me instead."

"We will." The second *Mors Faunis* grabbed the father by the arms. "For harboring a traitor, we'll hang you first so your son can watch. After he's knocking at Donn's door, hang the boy."

The Death Howlers dragged father and son off. The old man wept and the son resisted. Thramel turned his back on them. He had seen his share of hangings in the Bloodline Wars and didn't need to watch anymore. They all ended the same.

"Why didn't you tell me there were still Foster sympathizers remaining?" He went to Snout, ready to cuff the cur. He relaxed his fist. A beating wouldn't get him what he wanted.

"You never asked." Snout spat green goop.

"What else are you not telling me?"

Snout shrugged.

"Tell me everything I need to know about Foster Manor."

"That will take a while."

"Good, we have all night here." He gave Snout the water skin. "Go fill it up while I find out what else the old man was hiding."

Thramel dragged the second son's corpse outside and placed it under the tree where his father and brother swung from the end of hemp ropes, legs occasionally twitching and eye balls bulged. Inside the hot hovel, he set up the table and chairs, then dug through the larder. The old farmer hadn't lied to him after all. Canned fruits, dried beans, pickled cabbages and few sacks of flour and potatoes, enough to last one man until the sowing. With two boys hiding out, they would have been forced to steal supplies or starve.

Did them a favor. Opening up a jar of sweet nectarines, he plucked out a piece and slurped it down, sticky juice running over his chin. *The old man would've starved trying to save his sons and they would've got themselves killed over food.*

He grabbed a couple more jars and carried them out to the table. Leaning back in the chair, he propped his legs up, kicked his boots off and continued eating the nectarines.

Those guards at the Manor need an awakening. He sucked the juice off his fingers. *How many other former Foster troops did they miss?*

Snout thumped into the hovel, water skin in hand and nose lifted to the air.

"Early bloom golden nectarines," he said, staring longingly at the empty jar in on the table. "Are there any more?"

"I have another full jar right here." Thramel held it up, pulling it back as Snout reached for it. "It's yours... after you tell me everything I need to know about Foster Manor."

Snout's shoulders sagged and he gave Thramel a dopey hound dog stare. The kind that makes you wonder if he's going to lick your hand or bite off a few fingers. After a moment, Snout stepped around the drying blood and scooted into a chair. He rubbed his chin, then nodded.

"Deal," he said, holding out his right hand. Thramel looked at it, the deep grooves crusted with dirt as though the man hadn't washed in a moon. Then Thramel grabbed it, his own swallowing up Snout's smaller paw, and gave it a hard, vigorous shake.

"First things first; it's no longer called Foster's Manor," Snout said, rubbing his right hand with the left. "Her Highness has renamed it to Shadow Manor in honor of her new patroness god."

"I'm so glad that misconception is cleared up," Thramel said and slapped the table. "I'd give two hard lumps of shit what god or goddess she worships, but at the moment I'm all out. Get to the important information. How many Foster Guards have gone missing? What troops does Joanne have stationed at Shadow Manor? Who exactly are the rebels we're hunting? Names, gender, a brief description, not of their bloody smells, either. And why, by the Shadow, did the whole unit of guards go after two rebels?"

Snout blinked at the onslaught of questions. Thramel prepared to ask them again, slower, like training a puppy. He held up the glass jar of nectarines and shook it. Snout snapped out of his stupor and began rambling off information.

"Joanne sent one thousand Seaptum light infantry, five hundred long bow Seaptum stingers led by twenty *Mors Faunis* to pacify the Manor." Snout took a breath, eyeing the jar of nectarines. Thramel set it down, hand covering the lid while his fingers drummed the rounded glass side. Snout licked his lips before proceeding. "Ledgers captured after Joanne's soldiers occupied the manor recorded the number of soldiers in the Manor and outposts. Around four hundred Foster men garrisoned at the Manor itself, while another fifty occupied each of the three strongholds at the outer points, for a total of five hundred and fifty soldiers. During a three-day battle, four hundred and sixty three of those were killed. Another thirty were captured and executed by the time I received the urgent letter from Joanne reassigning me from Shadow Manor to the Keep. From the Keep—"

"Wait a moment!" Thramel's feet thumped onto the floor as he stood. "You were already there? At Foster's—"

"Shadow," Snout corrected.

"Shadow Manor?" Thramel said, growling at the annoying correction. "Why didn't you track the rebels?"

"I did." Snout blinked. "I just didn't follow them into the Yellow Valley."

"Why not?"

"I was under orders from the Commander at the time to kill all rebels, save for one."

"Who was the one?"

"The Commander's sister."

"Sister?" Thramel rubbed his temples. "The rebels we're looking for aren't soldiers?"

"No."

"What are they?"

"Skin-changers."

Thramel let out a loud laugh. Seeing as how Snout took it seriously, furrowing his brow and head tilted to the side, Thramel sat back down and motioned for the tracker to continue.

Snout explained how he'd joined Commander Fraylin and thirty other Shadow Guard as part of an expedition into Blackwood. They were hunting skin-changers, or so Fraylin urged them to believe.

"We thought Fraylin was pulling our leg about skin changers. They are children's tales after all and we thought he was half-mad from grief. For nearly a year after Fraylin's sister was reported to be killed by a mountain lion, the Commander talked about nothing more than finding the furry bastard who run off with his sister. 'It was a man, I tell you,' he'd say, staring us in the eyes, challenging anyone to doubt him. We were smart enough to hold our peace, so he would go on. 'A man who had the skin of a cat, but a man by the gods, who stole off with my sister. I'm going to find him and his den of abominations. Kill every last one.' No one had the guts to speak contrary to his face, but behind his back the men laughed and called him 'Fraidy Fraylin', saying, 'the Pussyman stole his sister. She must be eaten by now.'"

Snout shook his head and pointed out the window, and Thramel saw the bodies swaying from the branches.

"I told them, 'Making jokes of the dead always had ill-tidings.'" He took a long drink from the water skin. Some dribbled down the edge of his mouth and he wiped it away with the back of his hand. "At first, we thought we would tramp around Blackwood and find nothing, maybe kill a mountain lion and he would be satisfied. We weren't prepared for what happened next."

His droopy eyes got a distant look and he stared past Thramel, mouth falling, slack-jawed. Thramel snapped his fingers.

"Wake up!" Snout blinked. "What happened? What'd you find in Blackwood?"

"Skin-changers, like I said."

Thramel burst out laughing again. Skin changers! Mothers told their children stories about them so they'd not play in the woods at night where real dangers lurked. His mother had him convinced that Fraster's father changed into a dog once a moon phase to kill the neighbor's chickens because they produced more eggs than his own. Thramel wouldn't go near the farm until Fraster showed him the real skin of the creature killing the chickens—an old, grey bandit 'coon.

"You're funny, Snout," Thramel said, pulling the jar away as Snout reached for it. "I gave you a chance and you spin me a coal-digger's tale."

"Fraylin killed one," Snout persisted. "A large black puma and we all watched it change back into a man."

"Not a man wearing the skins of a puma?"

"You will see for yourself." Snout went quiet and sullen.

"What happened to Fraylin?"

"He died, killed by his own sister."

"So, she's the one we are tracking." *What do you want with a dead Commander's sister, you crazy inbred land snatcher?* Thramel rubbed his chin. *Why send me?*

"Is this sister a skin changer, too?"

"No," Snout said. "The child she travels with is one."

Oh, Joanne, you are just looking for another exotic pet.

"How will we find them?"

Snout tapped his nose.

"I've seen their kind. I've scented them. They will not get far."

Thramel slid the jar of sweet nectarines across to Snout. He twisted the lid off, sniffed them greedily, and smiled.

I think I have my new bargaining chip.

Thramel put his feet up on the table and watched Snout devour the nectarines one by one.

Donn held the heart up to his nose. Drawing a deep breath, eyes closed, he pictured the man's life. He was old, but old age didn't end his life. This man died in fear. Donn smelled the composite of bitter tears and sour regret. The heart itself was shriveled. That didn't mean he was a bad man—some of the most corrupted men and women have hearts as health red as a rose blush. It wasn't rare for children, pristine as fresh fallen snow, to have hearts in various degrees of decay, their flesh so acidic the tongue curled and the juices scour the sensitive palate. Conscience and emotions colored the heart.

This man recently lost something near and dear to him. Donn considered the covered silver-platter next in line. There always seemed an endless supply of hearts. Human frailty never ceased to amaze him, so he was surprised there were any Created left alive. The heart that waited beneath the next tarnished dome most likely held the cause for the old man's sorrow.

"A wife," Donn guessed. He licked the shriveled heart, tasting despair. "No, not a wife. Ah ha! A son. Such a pity to lose the very thing meant to replace you at the end of your life."

Donn set the heart on the empty platter, picked up a fork and knife. He sliced through the right ventricle and began to chew. Old hearts were the toughest to eat. So many memories flashed in Donn's mind: Smiling face of a mother, the rough hand of a father, the first time he killed a bird, sorrow and regret, joy at learning how to plant a field, to mend a broken fence. He sliced off the left ventricle and as he chewed it; witnessed a pretty face, so young, so fresh as morning dew, holding her hand and dancing at a festival ball, a gentle albeit awkward kiss, the binding of hands and laying down on the girl as he grunted, followed by sweet release. Donn swallowed the pleasant thoughts and cut the atriums in half. Teeth cut into the memory of a child, a boy birthed, teaching him the same lessons passed along to him by his father. A second boy born, working the land, thriving and growing like sun flowers. Pride in the uniform his boys wore.

Donn stabbed the remaining bits of the heart. He lifted it up on the fork tines. He hated eating this part. It almost always choked him, sticking in his craw like rotten meat all spindly with green webs. Judgement was needed. A man awaited verdict. Donn shoved it into his mouth. As soon as it touched his tongue, sorrowful juices were released. He watched the young girl, age and die, a silent baby in her arms, two graves dug for mother and child. A son returned, fearful and dejected. Men with swords and metal wolves dragging the corpse of the older boy from the house and a rope tied around the youngest son's neck. Tears and pleas as he watched his son die and he was hauled up on the same tree but on a different branch, staring at his son's bloated face as he slid away into darkness.

Setting the utensils aside, Donn picked up a napkin and wiped at a tear in the corner of his eye. The hard part was over. He had made his choice.

"Moko," Donn called. No one replied. "Where is that dumb brute?"

His cavernous chamber was empty, silent except for the harsh thrum of his own voice. Donn grumbled and the shouted once more. "Moko! Come hither, boy."

"What do you want?" A tall, broad-shouldered mountain of a god ambled into Donn's dining chamber. He had dark skin, cracked and pitted. His eyes were as hard as stone, red like clay. He always wore a hard expression, hardly ever smiling.

"Take this message to Seraphim," Donn said, scribbling a note on a small parchment. "Tell her, the man is released to her care and be gentle with this one. I have it written down in case you forget like that one time."

Moko rolled his eyes.

"It wasn't my fault. I'm no errand boy like Agni."

Moko, earth shaker and mountain mover, wasn't the best choice as messenger, especially since his last mess up sent the soul of a young, naïve woman who didn't know enough to shake the bushes for snakes and died a slow, painful death alone in the woods paralyzed from venom, to the darker torments. Donn had to personally reach into the pit, which was like covering a hand in honey and sticking it into an ant hill, and pull out her lacerated soul. Poor thing oozed despair dripping off her in red clumps. He spent countless days cleaning her up instead of judging a growing list of souls.

"Agni is not available right now." Donn tried to sound patient. It was very difficult when dealing with the inane. "So do as I ask."

Moko snatched the note and stomped away. Donn dragged the next platter closer. He reached for the heart, a fine, delicate piece, and stopped. A figure stood in the doorway.

"Seraphim," Donn said, observing the feminine figure. "I just sent Moko to you."

"Good help is hard to find," the figure said, stepping into the pale light.

Donn stood up, reaching for the silver knife.

"What do you want?"

"No need to get defensive." Dandulain, the Mistress of Shadows, sauntered to the edge of his lonely table. Her hips moved in such a provocative way Donn nearly forgot how dangerous this creature was that entered his chambers. "I only wish to speak."

"I'm not sure I will like hearing what you have to say." Donn set the knife down next to the platter. "I forget my manners. Would you like a taste?"

"Not for the life of me," she said and laughed at her own joke. "I have more pressing matters at hand. One that concerns all my siblings."

"Say what's on your mind."

"I prefer to show you, that's if you would care to join me?"

"I do not care."

The Mistress of Shadows pouted. "I thought you liked me."

Donn shrugged.

"No more or less than any other bitter heart."

"Join me and a few of our Brothers and Sisters at the Pool of Reflection later this evening." She turned her back and began to leave. Glancing over her shoulder, she grinned. "You will be enlightened."

Curiosity brought Donn from the depths of the palace. He climbed the silver stairway holding a metal ring, one key scraping along a loop. Yellow fire burned in glass orbs atop sconces on either side of the stairway. Near the top, Donn tilted one down, revealing a key hole. He placed the key in and turned. Above him stone scraped. A slab slid opened, dousing the dark in shimmering white light.

Donn shielded his eyes, stepping onto marble flooring. A high ceiling cascaded the illuminous white light from dozens of fire discs suspended overhead. *How can they stand so much light?* He squinted at white walls covered in silver tapestries reflecting the blinding glare.

"The Weigher of Souls rises." He jumped at the unexpected voice. Lowering his hand, he saw Sin smirking. She flipped her braided silver hair over her shoulder. Age lines around her mouth and eyes deepened in her mirth. "The Shadow's intrigue draws you from your den. I never thought I'd see the day you leave that dark hole"

"It must be good gossip to bring you down from your perch, yapping away like a manic whip-poor-will." Donn looked around the room. It was vacant except for the two of them.

"Good to see you," Sin said, leaning in and kissing his cheek. His pale-skin glowed in the shape of two crescent moons. "When the

Shadow sent me to wait for you, I believed she wanted me in the dark regarding matters. Now the dark rises up. This young one does have strong powers to unite both of us in one room."

"Where is she?" Donn asked, growing bored of the interaction.

"Follow me."

They walked down a long hallway, light pulsing from the stone, causing Donn's head to throb like a sore tooth. Sin made several quick turns down barren halls and they descended a set of stairs. He began to worry that it was some sort of set up and wished he brought Moko. Donn took no part in the quibbles among his brothers and sisters, but he didn't exactly trust them, either. They would turn on each other like dogs fighting for the last scrap of meat. All for what? To lick the boot heels of Mother.

"This better not take too long," he said, scrubbing his face. It was warmer than his cold tomb-like chambers. He was sweating on top of having a headache. "I have souls waiting for me."

"I would love to shine some light on the mystery," Sin said. "She has kept us all in the dark."

"All?" Donn said. "Who else does she have there?"

"A surprise."

"I don't like surprises."

At the bottom of the stairs the light dimmed, making it almost tolerable. The air grew warmer, humid. Sin stopped outside an open chamber. She held a hand up for him to wait. An uneasy feeling weighed on Donn and he nearly left. The problem was he didn't know his way back. The last time he visited the palace was for Father's memorial—one heart he never would taste. He had slunk back to his under-chambers from the crypt, a burning question that no one knew the answer. Where do gods go when they die?

Here I wait at beckon call for his killer.

No, it didn't feel right at all.

"Come in," Sin said.

"Take me back," Donn demanded. "I don't feel well."

"It's all those diseased hearts you eat," she said. "Besides, it's too late to back out."

Donn hesitated. A lethal, insidious meaning lurked in her tone. Sin stared at him, silver eyes piercing his depths. Donn nodded and motioned for her to proceed. Then he entered the chamber. The heat and humidity nearly bowled him over. Vines crept over the walls and at the center of the room was a giant pool, a yellow radiance glowing off it. Five figures spread out around the pool.

Hacawit dressed in red armor, curved blades tucked into a baldric stood closest to the door. Next to him was green-eyed Sierna wearing a gold trimmed blue dress with white lace foaming up at the collar. Red, curly hair accentuated the anger glare, her arms folded under a large bosom. Webbed fingers peeping from her elbows. The way she glowered at him, indicated that she was still angry over fact that the Created she fell in love, an evil, murderous pirate, Donn sent to the deepest, darkest regions of oblivion. After he died from a very serious misfortune, of course. Qetesh in her nearly see-through robe, gold bangles jangling on her wrists, as she sat on the pool's edge, knee bouncing up and down. She shied away from Moko who leered at her prodigious cleavage.

No wonder I couldn't find the brute.

"Who invited the soul thief?" Sierna asked.

"Don't be jealous that his judgment of men is better than your own," Sin said.

Sierna turned her glare on Sin. "You have nothing to speak about, old hag. Your offspring are unnatural, changeling beasts!"

"They may changeling beasts, but at least they don't kill women and copulate with their corpses."

"Quit your bickering." On the opposite side stood a black hole in the space of light, the Mistress of Shadow. Her back was turned to them. "You are not children, although you are called so by a false mother."

"What is this all about?" Hacawit said. "What game are you playing, bringing us all here?"

"Mother would be displeased," Donn said. "If she knew we spoke with you. We would all find out the true power of her wrath."

"Are you going to run and tattle on us?" Sirena asked.

"I will cut your tongue out before you uttered a single word." Hacawit said, drawing a cutlass.

Dandulain spun and her cloak billowed. A dark fog spread outward, consuming the room. Everyone went silent. When the mist dissipated, Dandulain stood next to Hacawit, holding one of his cutlasses. Hacawit went to draw his second, but she placed the blade against his throat. He eased his hand away.

"You are spoiled, lazy children, grown soft and weak because you think Mother protects you." She handed the cutlass back to Hacawit. "You forget the greatness that allowed you to survive the Ascension. You fight petty battles, squabbling like infants over trinkets."

Donn nodded in agreement.

"Once, you struck fear and awe in the Created. Once, they prayed for your mercy, made sacrifice to you." She looked around at each of them. No one dare made eye contact with her, except for Donn. "What happened to you all?"

Again, no response. The Mistress of Shadows held Doon's gaze a moment. He caught a glimpse of her smile, before she stepped beside the Pool of Reflection. She removed a black glove and dipped her long fingers in the water, swirling them.

"I give you a gift," she said, as the water began to bubble up and spread apart. "Knowledge."

Donn leaned in to see what was revealed. His shoulder rubbed against Sirena's. She hissed and he took a step sideways. Clear blue water was replaced by darkness.

"Is this some kind of joke?" Hacawit asked.

"Explain to them what they are seeing, Qetesh," Dandulain commanded.

"This is what I see when I look for a girl crying out for love," Qetesh said, wrapping her arms around herself and shuddering. "I feel her pain like a knife stripping skin from my back. It's a yearning like no other felt."

"Why can't we see her?" Sin asked.

"Because there is a veil placed over her."

"Who would do this?" Sirena asked, sounding appalled.

"Mother," Dandulain said.

"Why should we believe you?" Sin asked. "We all know you killed Father and took the disc of darkness. For all we know, you could have cast a veil over her to blame Mother."

Dandulain laughed.

"You see through me so well, Sin. Like a blind woman gazing into the sun."

She swirled her hand over the image. The water frothed, closing and then re-opening on another scene. A man dressed in black armor walked among the trees. He looked tired, yet determined.

Sin gasped, covering her mouth.

"Is that—?" Sirena asked, swallowing her anger and was unable to finish her thought.

"Huron," Donn whispered.

"It can't be," Hacawit said rising up. "How could he be walking the lands of the Created?"

Dandulain spread her fingers and the image enlarged, centering in on the man's face and chest. The twin blades crisscrossed on his armor was tell-tale enough to identify Huron, the Blades Man. His scowl and rugged face, covered in sweat confirmed it. A silver chain hung around his neck.

"He is Mother's favorite, is he not?" Dandulain asked. "She interferes in the Struggle. She allows this god to walk among the Created. She bestowed the favor on him, not for any of you." Dandulain looked up, focusing on each of them. "Sirena, when the storm blew and you begged Mother to save your love, did she bestow this gift on you?"

"No!" Sirena said, hands balling into fists. Her eyes remained on Huron moving through the woods, the image enlarged on the silver chain around his neck. "She conjured the storm to drown him."

"Sin, did Mother allow the husband of your children to ascend?"

Sin shook her head, a tear in her eye. Donn understood her pain. He judged his soul and knew that he loved her very much.

"You, Donn. You she harms the most." Dandulain narrowed her eyes. "One of the First Men, wisest and most powerful, forced to sit in judgement over lesser beings. To eat their bitter hearts and pass them on to a place better than you can imagine. Where is it that gods go when they die?"

"I know not," Donn said, feeling resentment rise up like an undigested meal.

"Nowhere," Dandulain said. "Mother never thought any of us would die, yet she made the Created so frail that is all they ever do. They give birth and then they die. Make war and die. Starve the weak, bring great sorrow, suffer disease... and die. All caused by her. All allowed by her. All suffer, because you, the greater beings allow her to do so. We are as culpable in this greatest of evils, no, more so, because we do nothing to prevent it."

"What about him?" Hacawit pointed at the water.

"He is a symptom of a greater problem." Her voice grew darker. "I will deal with him."

"We can't kill Mother, can we?"

"Won't it tear this existence apart?"

Donn remembered the bending of time and space. The screams of brothers and sisters torn apart. He didn't ever want to experience that pain again.

"There is another way," he said.

The sound of pounding hammers and sawing wood echoed down the hilltop where Shadow Manor's gate stood. Grey, lichen covered its stone and the wall flowed with the contours of the land, rising and falling, for nearly a league, the western section lost in trees. Half a steel banded wooden door stood shut in the gatehouse. Thramel noted the scorch marks on the wood and stone. A gap occupied the left side of Shadow Gate where rusted hinges hung empty.

"What happened?" Thramel asked, watching the flurry of activity. Like a beehive that had been kicked, dozens of men scurried about. Some carried tools and others hefted large pieces of damaged wood. A new gate was being fashioned off the side of the road. Ropes and pulleys held the piece up while men sealed the spacing between the slates and others attached long planks.

"Not sure," Snout said. "The gate was still attached when I left."

Five guards halted a line of carts, detaining the distraught farmers and merchants while the soldiers pawed through sacks and barrels. Thramel spotted another five archers up on the battlement. All wore chainmail and had dark blue cloaks over their shoulders. The sun emblem shone bright yellow on their cloaks. Two of the five guardsmen were armed with pikes, curved into a hook at end, just right for yanking people off of horses. Each soldier had a long sword at their hip and silver gorgets covered their throats.

A young, dark-skinned guard with short cropped black hair and a white sash tied around his belt, conducted the inspection of goods. He directed men and boys to step off the wagon where waiting guards patted them down. Women and girls were allowed to remain seated.

Thramel knew they were looking for rebel soldiers by the thoroughness of the search. *Not thorough enough.* Thramel watched the flurry of activity. *I would foster sympathy from the surrounding villages and have the women conceal weapons for me. More than their tongues can hold a sting. That's how I would fight this battle.* Soldiers pried off lids and sifted around each container in the cart. Some carts had five or more crates and countless sacks that were untied, inspected and re-tied.

"Who is overseeing this clogged shit-fest?" Thramel asked, tapping his fingers on the saddle horn and not drawing his sword to cut a path like he wanted. Daylight burned and he counted at least six carts before he reached the gate. *Shadow take them! They move like a bunch of slow-witted ninnies.*

"Corporal Nef," Snout said, a hint of distaste in his voice, almost like a mix of a growl and whimper. "He's not the guy you want."

"Was he with you chasing wild cats in Blackwood?" Thramel hoped he could find someone who could lend credence to Snout's tale. According to Snout's retelling of events, thirty-six manor guard, including Snout, entered Blackwood, and only six left it alive. Two of those six were off hunting the woman and girl. That left three witnesses for Thramel to question, to illuminate the blind spots in the story. Getting answers from Snout was like chasing rabbits.

"Nope." Snout leaned lazily over his saddle and scrubbed his chin. "Else he'd be dead, more-than-like."

"Who do we want?" Thramel stopped tapping and squeezed the saddle horn, knuckles turning white. The soldiers finally waved the first cart through the gate. At the rate they were searching, it would be midday before Thramel entered the Manor.

"That would be Constable Cinder." Snout gave a sharp whistle. "You don't want to be on Cinder's bad side. He'll make you dig a latrine with your bare hands, then piss on you afterwards."

"Not any relation to Joanne, is he?" He gave a hard smile.

"Distant cousin, I think."

"Figures."

Thramel rubbed his temples where a headache throbbed dully. Sleep was hard to come by last night at the farm house. His body ached, all the way up from stiff leg and sore ribs, jolting him awake at the slightest shift in body. Bruises darkened the skin up his sides and his left foot was swollen. The longer he remained on horseback, the more his body seized up like a rusty spring. He kneed his horse forward and went around the carts, earning scowls and a few grumbles about waiting their turn. One glance at the *Mors Faunis* and the grumblers turned their attentions on more important matters.

Corporal Nef held up his right hand while setting the left on his sword hilt. "State your name and purpose."

"Neither is more important than your head still attached on your neck," Thramel said and spat on the Corporal's boots. Corporal Nef lifted his chin, planted his legs and he loosened his sword in its scabbard. The *Mors Faunis* flanked Thramel in a defensive position, metal wolf heads snarling. "Don't think about baring that steel. My wolves will tear you in half before you pull loose that pig sticker."

The Corporal released his scabbard and held up his hands.

"Wise choice. I'm here on urgent business for her Highness, the most puissant Joanne. These two vouch for me." Thramel jerked his thumb over his shoulder. "So does the one who actually speaks."

"Corporal Nef." Snout tipped his cap as he passed him by. "Told you I'd be back."

Corporal Nef glared at them.

"Let them pass." He called back to the pike men. "They're the Constable's problem."

Pikes lifted and Corporal Nef waved them through, grimacing as though letting rodents escape the trap.

"What'd you do to get on his bad side?" Thramel asked. "Eat his favorite cat?"

"Something like that," Snout said.

The road cut through a large parade ground, now empty of foot traffic. Shirtless men sparred with wooden swords and staves. Slapping wood blended in with the construction noise. Another small wall separated the parade ground from the Manor proper. Across from the gatehouse were the stables. Thirty stalls lined each side, most were unoccupied. A young boy pitched hay from one stall, tossing it into an overflowing handcart.

Thramel dismounted and called the boy over while Snout wandered off to speak with the soldiers at the guardhouse. The stable boy shoved his pitch fork into the cart and ran over. He was small, maybe ten name-days, and wore a dirty tunic, red hair sticking out in tufts from beneath his cap.

"Are you the one in charge of the stables?" Thramel asked.

"That would be Master Givens, sir," the boy said, rubbing his nose on a dirty sleeve.

"Is Master Givens around?"

"Not presently," the boy said. "I can fetch him from his workshop."

"No," Thramel said. Waiting around wasn't on his list of accomplishments, even though it seemed the gods tried to press that virtue upon him. "Don't disturb the good Master. Here, I'll give you a copper pence to stable our horses. If you do well by them, another four copper pence will be your final payment."

The boy smiled, revealing a gap between his teeth. The coin promised to him was more than he'd see over a full Season. He counted the horses, eyes widening on the *Mors Faunis,* their snarling, metal wolf teeth ready to eat little boys who got too close. He took a step back.

Thramel caught his shoulder.

"Don't worry about finding a kennel for them." Thramel placed the coin into the boy's hand. "These wolves are with me."

The boy began leading the horses to the stable, taking a wide berth around the *Mors Faunis.*

"Don't you ever take those things off?" Thramel asked. "Or do you enjoy watching children piss their trousers?"

He walked to the guardhouse, knowing they would come to heel better than any trained hound. Only difference being, these wolves were more likely tear his hand off than lick it. They were more like his wardens, and Thramel their prisoner.

Snout handed a small leather bag to one of the guards. The guard stuffed it into his jerkin and clasped Snout's hand, talking so no one else could understand them. Snout nodded and laughed. Thramel raised an eyebrow as Snout came to him.

"What's the news?"

"Constable Cinder is at the Manor house," Snout said. "He's in a temper because the repairs are going slow and supplies are not coming in quick enough from the countryside. Some hold-overs from the Foster's guard keep raiding the carts. Seems they can't spare extra men to guard all the farms or supply carts."

"What about those inspecting the carts coming in?"

"Two full seasons back, someone disguised themselves as farmers and hid weapons in barrels and crates. They started fires, which explains why half the door is missing," Snout said. "They also killed four Shadow Guard before escaping."

"Because you weren't here to sniff them out."

"More-the-like," Snout said and frowned. "Don't go reminding Cinder of the fact. No need to make efforts more difficult for us."

Single story buildings lined the road. Narrow passages separated them and bustled with life. Children battled with sticks for swords, others carried baskets full of linens, women harassing them to hurry along. A few carts rolled monotonously up the road to a granary. Three more carts were being offloaded by four burly men prying open lids and examining the content. One argued visibly with a sun-darkened farmer, a sack of grain sliced open and its contents spilling out into the dirt. Soldiers approached to survey the situation.

"Weevils," Snout said, nose twitching. "Looks like he dipped into his stores."

A growing crowd of spectators ringed around them. The farmer bent to pick the sack up, but the inspecting man shoved him back. Using a long blade, he cut open another sack on the wagon. He quickly turned his face away as a cloud of black bugs shot out. He leapt from the wagon, coughing and covering his face.

"Close the granary doors" he shouted between coughs. "Close the damn doors, Shadow take you!"

Two men scurried to close the door before the swarm of weevils could fly in and taint the rest of the store. Glaring red-eyed at the farmer, he slammed him up against the wagon.

"Take him to the hold."

"It's not my fault," the farmer pled as a soldier grabbed him under the arms. "The rebels tainted it. They soured my land!"

They dragged him away, kicking and screaming.

"Burn it!" The soldier shouted, using his cloak to wave away the last of the weevils.

Thramel shook his head. "Pitiful."

On the opposite side of the road, the blacksmith's clanking rang throughout as they passed. Messengers ran in and out of the workshop marking impressions on wax tablets. With all the construction being done on the front gate, Thramel wouldn't want to be the one wielding the hammer. More shops lined the way from tannery to linen to cobbler. The buildings showed a few signs of battle. Broken windows covered with sheets that flapped in the breeze, scorch marks on posts, new wood on the doors not yet weathered. Stockades held a man and woman smeared in dirt. Thramel could smell them as they wallowed in their own waste. The woman's dress was torn and her bloomers were pulled down to reveal her fleshy backside, red and stained. Neither spoke a word, but stared with glassy eyes as they passed. A single rope hung from the gallows, empty for now, reminding the people to follow the new order or they would swing for the black birds.

The land rose upward forming another hill. The road went with it. In the valley below the hill more houses sprawled out and behind them giant trees rose up over the fortifications.

"That's Blackwood?" Thramel asked.

Snout nodded and scratched his nose.

At the top of the hill sat a three-story house made entirely of dragon-stone, black and glossy rock mined from the Mountain of Destiny where a large fire wyrm once resided centuries ago. Thramel only knew of the rock's existence because a trader in precious metals tried to sell him a lease on the stone. If it wasn't for the distance and difficulty of mining dragon-stone, he would've taken him up on the deal.

"Are all the Manors made of dragon-stone?"

"Just the ones still standing," Snout said.

"What about the mines?" He scratched his chin, calculating the stone's value. "Are any still operational?"

Snout narrowed his eyes and wrinkled his lip. "Do I look like a stone dog to you?"

"No, but you know more about the area than I do."

"Maybe you and I should go into business once this war nonsense is ended," Snout said. "I'll sniff out the good prices and you put down the coin. If you're still alive."

Snout made panting noises that Thramel guessed was laughter. He just grinned, thinking: *We'll do a body count later.*

Walkways and palisades circled the upper second and third stories of the Manor. Four archers patrolled the walkways, but they could easily hold a hundred or more men. Messengers in dark blue livery and a bright yellow sun of the left breast entered and exited the ornate wooden door. Two more soldiers observed the processions, halting them and asked their business.

"Emissaries from her Highness," Snout said, holding out a piece of parchment sealed with the same yellow star as appeared on the guards' cloaks.

The guards made them remove their weapons.

"No way are we allowing those things in here," one said, gesturing at the *Mors Faunis*. "They can wait right there."

Thramel handed the *Mors Faunis* his sword belt and shield. Snout gave over a belt knife.

"Sorry, boys, maybe next time," Thramel said. He got as much reaction as from a tree stump, albeit a tree stump with a scary face carved into it, but a tree stump nonetheless. Then he entered with Snout at his heels. White marble clicked beneath his boots as he marched through the foyer. Gold candelabras hung from low ceilings and more sconces lined the walls. None were lit since the sun's light cascaded through large windows secured with metal bars. There was an old, musty smell of paper and ink. A cold draft blew through despite the heat outside. Thramel followed the sound of talking—one voice in particular stood out, loud and gruffly speaking—until he reached a back office.

A man with brown hair peppered grey, sat behind a large desk. Frown lines marred his eyes and mouth. His forehead creased as he explained something to a young boy dressed in messenger livery. The boy nodded, took the paper and spun on his heels. Thramel saw the pale, worried expression as the boy circled around him in such a hurry, he nearly bounced off Thramel's leg.

More troubles. Thramel scoffed.

The desk was immaculate. Neatly stacked papers occupied one corner while an empty plate and a cup full of light greenish-brown liquid next to it.

"What now?" Constable Cinder sipped from the cup, grimaced and set it back neatly next to the plate. "Damn things gone cold. Can't even get a moments peace to drink my tea. Everybody needs me to do their thinking for them."

"Here's a small relief for you," Thramel said and handed him the sealed scroll.

Constable Cinder examined the wax seal and broke it. His brown eyes scanned the parchment and he grunted.

"I don't have one man to spare on this…" He tossed the paper onto the desk. "This fool's errand. It's bad enough I lost thirty good men, and the services of my best tracker." His eyes flicked to Snout, disapprovingly. "Not while Foster's men keep harassing us. I cannot spare one more, not a one… who are you soldier?"

"Thramel," he said, "First Commander of the Fools. I think I have enough to suit my needs."

"I never heard of a Commander Thramel." Constable Cinder tapped his chin. "Unless you mean the one who fought with the resistance at Heartwood Pines, preventing her Highness's brothers from ascending the throne. Now he would be intriguing to have in my presence. Yes, him I would like to ask how he defeated a well-trained army with ragtag farmers and rock diggers."

Thramel clicked his tongue. *Should I feel flattered or frightened?*

"Perhaps, Constable, you may meet this Thramel you speak of at another time," Snout said, twisting his cap. "For now, all we ask is a simple restock of supplies and fresh mounts."

Constable Cinder thought for a moment.

"Answer me this," he said. "What is so important about these outcasts that her Highness finds so desirable? Don't take it as a questioning of orders, but more of a professional curiosity."

"Even if we had the answer to that question, I don't think we'd be able to tell you." Thramel reached for the orders, but Constable Cinders snatched them off his desk, rolled them up and placed them in a drawer.

"Take what you need. I'll have my supply clerk make note of them." Constable Cinders pulled out a clean piece of parchment and scratched a note using a quill pen which he dabbed fastidiously in a jar of ink. "I expect a full report on your return, with or without the prisoners."

"Aren't you so kind," Thramel said, taking the note and reading it over. "I'll make sure to let her Highness know how accommodating you were to us."

"Like I stated before," Constable Cinder leaned forward, hands folded on the desk. He stared directly at Thramel, taking careful measure of him as though marking his face for later. "Under differing circumstances, you would have the entire garrison at your disposal. We would have *all* the treasonous fools bound and ready for the hangman's noose."

"Your ineptitude is not my problem," Thramel said. "Perhaps if you were not fighting from behind a desk, there would be no traitors left to cause you trouble."

"Be careful, Thramel, Commander of fools." Constable Cinders grinned. "The path you tread is dark and full of peril. I lost thirty men in the wild. One more corpse wouldn't matter in the eyes of the gods."

"Thank you for the fair warning, Constable." Thramel turned and stalked out of the room.

He slammed open the wooden door, starling the guards. He took his sword belt back from the *Mors Faunis*. Strapping on the sword belt, he headed down the hill, mumbling about doing everything himself. Snout caught up to him.

"Smart as poking a sleeping bear," Snout said. "He wants to string you up as it is without you handing him the rope."

"Shadow take him," Thramel said. "He's got some bug up his rear against Joanne and now I got to deal with this family squabble. If he can't handle a bunch of rebels, then why, by the Father, is he commanding a Manor? I would've sent the squads knocking on every door and slashing down every tree from here to Seaptum."

"An unencumbered man has many opinions about the weight another shoulders," Snout said.

Thramel rounded on him.

"What does that mean?"

"Something my father used to say." Snout sniffed.

"Your father can dine with the Heart-eater for all his empty words," Thramel said. "Shadow take you as well." Snout's eyes widened and his mouth twitched. *He's going to blubber like a baby who lost his mother's teat!* "Ah Father flay me, just show me where the bloody supplies are kept."

A large man, broad in chest and shoulders held a clipboard and watched what Thramel took from the shelves in the supply room. He marked everything, from dried fruits to nuts, in meticulously hand writing. They even had skins of wine that Snout sniffed, proclaiming them from the Southern regions by the coast.

"You can't have those," Petrive, the supply clerk, said. "Those are for officers only."

"I am an officer in her Highness's most prestigious army. Why else would I travel with Howlers as bodyguard and her best tracker?"

Thramel gave him friendly smile. "I believe the note from the Constable directs that you fill our needs."

"Needs, not wants," Petrive said, taking the wine skin from Snout. "We have a limited supply to keep our officers happy. With the rebels raiding our supply shipments, I don't know when more wine will come to replace what you take. Besides, you got enough for a squad of a dozen men to last you two moons in the field. I won't have you wasting what is needed here."

"It won't go to waste." Thramel hefted another skin from the shelves. It sloshed in his hands, so tempting to pull the cork with his teeth and drain it in front of the supply clerk. He pulled out a small coin purse and bounced in his hands, weighing both objects under the clerk's nose. "What do you say? Do we have a deal?"

Petrive took the coin purse and slipped it inside a pouch. He turned his back on Thramel, scoring a wax tablet in the corner. Taking the cue, Thramel slid the skin into his pack.

"Pleasure doing business with you."

The man grunted.

At the stables, Thramel dug out the wine skin and took a swallow. Bitter, tasting of char mixed with hardtack. He wiped his mouth on the back of his hand. It was an officer's drink, heavy on the taste buds, going straight from lips to head.

The boy, holding a grooming brush, tapped him on the shoulder.

"Back so soon, sir? I just fed and watered your horses."

"How fast can you get fresh mounts saddled?" When the boy balked, Thramel held up another small coin bag. More than likely, he wouldn't be able to read the note from Cinder, but coin was a universal language. Thramel was certain the boy's Master could read, and to save the boy a lashing, Thramel gave him the note and instructed him to hand it to Master Givens.

The boy nodded and hurried off. Not much time passed when he brought out five well-rested horses to Thramel. He tossed the coin bag and the boy caught it, grinning as he tucked it away inside his trousers.

They rode through the Manor and exited out a back gate guarded by another half-dozen soldiers. Large wooden gates rattled open, after they passed, sealed with a resounding thud sounded as the plank fell into place. The easterly road continued, winding down the slope and stopped at Blackwood. Thick trunks and woody thickets stacked tightly together. Heavy branches covered in star-shaped leaves loomed over them. *Like looking into a burial mound of unmarked graves.* Thramel shuddered. He didn't want to be caught in Blackwood past sundown.

"Any way into this place?" Thramel asked.

"Be best if we rounded south and entered there," Snout said. "There's more gaps for us."

Skirting the perimeter. The plan brought on a boding sense of wrongness. The feeling that he was intruding, an unwelcomed interloper into some solemn, sacred ground, grew stronger the nearer he drew to the trees. His mare whinnied, keeping away from them as far as he would allow her. It felt as though hundreds of eyes watched him from the gloomy darkness where light refused to go. A strange cackling noise, deadened by the thick leaves, rose up as a blackbird soared from the tree tops and flew over their heads.

Snout retched, doubled over the side of his horse. Thin strands of spittle hung from his lips as he looked at the dark trees. A sticky breeze blew from Blackwood, bringing with it a stench more putrid than Black Wyrm. Thramel covered his nose and mouth, using a wine-soaked cloth. Cloying decay penetrated the burnt vinegar odor of the wine.

The mare balked at entering Blackwood. He tugged back on the reins until her mouth frothed, turning red, and squeezed his knees into her flank. She circled once and then acquiesced. Less than a quarter of a league inside, the first bodies were found scattered on the forest floor. Crows picked at flesh, tearing it off in strips. They lifted their black wings and cawed at the group of riders that approached. Flies buzzed around in and out of gapping eye sockets, mouths with jaws hanging by scraps of flesh, or holes that once were ears.

Snout paled and his gullet heaved beneath the rag. *At least he didn't vomit again.* Thramel had smelled worse on fresh battlefields. This one was seven complete seasons old at the very least. The carnage would bring the carrion beasts for some time. The *Mors Faunis* sat straight backed on their mounts. *These wolves must be licking their lips inside their metal helmets.*

A verbal jest seemed almost sacrilegious, encouraging the wrath of Vanth as she courted the souls to their place of judgment. Thramel kept his mouth shut and pushed deeper into Blackwood. Signs of battle and slaughter scattered on the ground. Several nude, bloated objects that might once have been human—*or skin-changers, as Snout declared*—

lay curled up in death throes, some with swords thrust through their chest while their slayer lay not too far off. Legs and arms torn off. The dark blue cloaks stiff with dried blood. The further they progressed, Thramel noticed more nude bodies, only these became clear, predominately women and children.

"Good Father, who desecrated the bodies?" Thramel asked. A tiny part of him felt disgust. Soldiers raped woman. That was a part of the spoils of war. He had ordered the death of dozens of children in Heartwood, but he would string up a man by his sack if he found out the soldier raped the child first.

"None," Snout said. "We're the first to enter the Blackwood since the night of the assault."

Thramel grunted. Someone had to have stripped these rebels. Where else did their clothing go?

"Here he is!" Snout shouted. He clambered off his mount and stood over a nearly decapitated body. Flesh hung in ragged strips down his cheeks. White bone glistening through.

"Who?" Gold strips on the paladins marked his rank as an officer.

"The poor bastard who led this godsdamned mission." Snout spat on the body. "Fraylin the Obsessed."

"Who's that next to him?" Thramel pointed at the nude body to the side of Fraylin.

"His sister's captor, or so we were told. Captor, pisha! Lovers more-the-like and brother didn't want his family name disgraced. Poor fool got a blade to his chest for all his troubles. Should've left well enough alone and let Qetesh sort it out." Snout shook his head. "The girl has run off with a changer baby in her belly."

Joanne wants that woman and baby for some reason, Thramel scratched his chin. *If she wants them, then I must have them.*

"Use that nose of yours," Thramel said. "Let's find this woman and child before someone else does."

CHAPTER ELEVEN

Love is difficult.
A mother loves her disobedient child spitting foul words of pain
to cut her womb. The boy sat across the fence, or as close to the
fire flames hot, sweat beading, and he ignores your very
existence.
Or he is an outsider, castaway by civil communities to
reside in wild, passionate throes of nature away, so far away.
Love is difficult.
                    — From "The Book of Qetesh"

A leaf caught in a wind storm. Jarrod sat cross-legged in the dirt. The sun beat down on him, but he didn't dare move from his post although a shadier area was nearby. Sweat tickled his neck and a fly buzzed around his ear. He waved at it absently, watching the lip of the hillside. Ishmael would eventually appear in a rage fueled flurry to cut Bekka up into pieces. That's what the savage look in his eye told when he regained his senses after Bekka thumped him on the head. A welt had risen over his right temple and blood trickled behind his ear. Jarrod would be furious as well, but he couldn't allow Ishmael to harm Bekka.

Naked sword resting in his lap, the bared steel gave the semblance that Jarrod would defend, however poorly, the pregnant woman. *Might as well be a twig. Maybe the sight of the blade would give Ishmael pause, to think instead of just reacting.* This was wishful thinking, like praying to the gods to cease a wildfire while choking on the smoke. He chewed the side of his thumb and waited.

"She's a traitor!" Ishmael's high-pitched screech echoed below. Jarrod cringed at the sound, imagined it alerting whoever happened to be in earshot by at least a league. "She has to go... now! No horse! No food! Just what the gods gave her!"

Soft, caring mummers followed the outburst.

Mother bless you, Elly. When everyone else retreated from Ishmael's blazing temper, Elly tried to sooth it. *Sooth him like rubbing stinging nettle into an open cut. Might as well talk down a bear from eating you.* It was more than anyone else would due, including Jarrod. *I should have taken the knife away from Bekka, especially after she had pulled it on Hannah. This whole mess could've been avoided.*

"She didn't mean to hurt you," Elly said. Her tiny voice of reason grew louder, closer. "Bekka was just frightened—"

"She hit me and let the bastard escape!" Ishmael shouted. "Mother protected me that she didn't use the blade instead of the hilt."

"You didn't give her much option," Elly said, following close behind..

"We promised her a horse and food... gods, I was going to ride with her to the border of the desert!"

"As her warden, not a protector."

A long pause ensued.

Blessed Mother, did she talk sense into him?

"Either they go," Ishmael said, dashing his hopes for a peaceful resolution. "Or I go."

A hand touched Jarrod on the shoulder, startling him.

"I think he's right," Bekka said. Her voice was thick as though she had been crying or was on the verge of tears. "Sarrah and I should leave here. We.... I have caused nothing but trouble since arriving."

"No," Jarrod said. "Not while *he's* out there looking for you."

"You can't protect me forever, Jarrod." Her voice went low to nearly a whisper. "No one can."

"I don't need forever," Jarrod said, cringing at how silly the comment sounded. "What I mean is, be patient. All this rash talk and action hasn't done anyone a bit of good. Let's just think this through carefully. Without emotions clouding critical thoughts."

Hannah stomped over to Jarrod, petulance in her eyes.

Mother, what now!

"We need to talk," she said, giving Bekka a sideways glance. "In private."

"I can't go now," he said, marking the movement on the hillside. Elly retreated while Ishmael stalked up the hill, ready to focus his rage against Bekka. "Can it wait?"

"No." She took his hand and tried to pull him to his feet.

Jarrod yanked his hand away. "I'm not some mule you need to coax out of some fields."

"You're sure being stubborn like one," she retorted.

"Whatever you have to say, do it here. No more secret talks." Jarrod stuck the sword point into the ground. "We got to start talking things out together rather than act like squabbling children."

"Fine," Hannah said, folding her arms under her breasts. "Tell me about this big secret with Bekka. Who is she? What's she really doing here? Why'd she hit Ishmael and let that man go free?"

"She's right here and can speak for herself."

Bekka no longer stood next to him. She groaned and sat down, clutching her belly. Her face went pale, mouth puckering as she sucked in air and pushed it out. Jarrod knelt beside her. She grabbed his hand, squeezing it until he felt the bones grind.

"Get me some water," Jarrod said. When Hannah stood there, wide-eyed, he shouted: "Go! Now!" She ran off leaving him alone with Bekka. His hand throbbed in her grip. "Don't talk Just move you head in reply."

Bekka nodded, whimpering. She clenched her teeth and pinched her eyes closed.

"Are you birthing?" *Gods, please say she isn't giving birth now.*

Bekka shook her head. Beads of sweat appeared on her skin. She puffed her cheeks as she bent forward, chin tucked to the top of her cleavage.

Gods! What would they do? A newborn baby in arm, squalling all night to alert beast and man alike to their position. Jarrod rubbed her back, looking around for Hannah and the water bucket. He'd never seen a baby born, didn't know what to look for or what to do if it got stuck. *Mother, don't let us get stuck!*

Bekka gave one, final squeeze. Jarrod bit his lip to hold back a cry, sure she would tear his hand from his wrist. She inhaled sharply, eyes widening as she barked out a cough. Then she released his hand, leaving behind red fingermarks in his skin.

"I'm fine," she said, trying to stand up. Her legs quivered and she fell back down. Jarrod caught her to keep her from going over backwards. "It's passing."

Hannah returned with the bucket, ladling out water and offering it to Bekka. She pushed it aside. Sweat rolled down her forehead, forcing her to blink it away. After a few more breathes she drank from the ladle.

"Baby shakes is what my mother always called them." Hannah said, and swallowed hard. "Used to call them. Well, Lily shook her up plenty. She would get the sweats and belly cramps so bad she couldn't leave her bed, sometimes not for two or three days during the hard shakes. Father would swear she was giving birth to look at her and had to resist the urge to fetch Mildred Woodsworth." Hannah stopped talking. She straightened up, regaining her serious demeanor. "How far along are you?"

"A little over four moons." Bekka got to her feet. Jarrod helped steady her. "I just need to rest."

"Let go of me!" the angry command was followed by a squeak.

Jarrod noticed Ishmael shove his sister. Elly landed on her backside, and nearly tumbled down the hill. She stared up at Ishmael, eyes wet. "You hurt me."

"It has nothing to do with you." Ishmael spun away from her and looked from Hannah to Jarrod and glared at Bekka, anger twisting his face. His hands balled up and he moved towards them, shoulders up and leaning forward like he'd bowl through them to get to Bekka. Hannah moved to Bekka's side and Jarrod stepped in front of them both, sword raised. Ishmael stopped within a few yards. Dark circles under his eyes reminded Jarrod that none of them had slept well the past two nights.

"Stop, Ishmael," Elly cried.

Ishmael opened his mouth and closed it. He focused on the sword in Jarrod's hand.

"That's mine," he said. "Give it back."

"I will," Jarrod said, shuffling his feet. "After you calm down."

"Calm down!" Ishmael shouted, his face turning red. "I am calm, now give me back my godsdamn sword."

"You are being rash—"

"Rash?" Ishmael laughed. "You mean like when she hit me across the head and almost got herself killed for some Shadow-cursed reason?" Ishmael closed his eyes and pinched the bridge of his nose, as though he fought off a headache. He sighed and opened his eyes. Determination replaced the anger. "Blades Man knows I could pluck the sword from your hands and gut you before you fingers felt empty, Jarrod. You don't have the gall to strike me, so give me the sword before you hurt—"

Bekka groaned.

"You're making it worse, Ishmael," Hannah said, holding up the ladle and pointing it at his chest. "What would your mother think of you bullying a pregnant woman?"

Ishmael tossed up his arms.

"Am I missing something? Let me explain it again. Slower. I was hit in the head. With a dagger. By her." He touched the side of his head and winced. "So, I'm the bad guy, the bully of pregnant women. She helped the man, a man I rescued her from, escape, yet I am the one to be shamed."

"I won't let you hurt her," Jarrod said.

"Once again, *she* hit *me*." Ishmael gave a humorless smirk. "I just want to know why she did it."

"You're absolutely right." Bekka said, struggling to stand up. Hannah offered her a hand and she took it, leaning on her in obvious pain. "I deserve all the shame. I apologize for hitting you. After everything Sarrah and I have been through, I couldn't risk—"

"Giving him a bath?" Ishmael asked. "He stank and I didn't want my tent smelling like piss anymore."

Bekka blushed.

"You didn't want him talking to me anymore," Ishmael continued. "You're afraid he was going to tell us stories. Stories that would make us not trust you. Well, you wanted our help and now you don't get it." Ishmael jabbed his finger at her emphasizing the last three words. "Now he's free, running around while you're still here. We're in danger because of you. We have to move our camp. Because. Of. You."

"Sarrah and I will leave now." Bekka said, tears welling in her eyes.

"How? You cannot ride," Jarrod said. "Not without harming the child."

"Oh no! You don't get one of our horses," Ishmael said. "You get to stay with us, to help us watch for him and whatever godsdamn militia he brings to the Yellow Valley! Just to make sure of it, you will stay with me in my tent while Elly watches over Sarrah."

"You can't do that," Elly said. "She's not a prisoner."

"I can and will." Ishmael said. "She can start by cleaning up the foul area where the bastard slept. We pull up our tents in the morning."

"Where are we going?" Hannah asked.

"Back to Heartwood Pines." Ishmael stalked away. Elly gave Bekka an apologetic look and followed her brother.

"You need to talk to him." Hannah took Jarrod's hand and began wringing it. "We can't leave now. Here we're safe. This is our home."

Jarrod didn't know how to respond. He didn't want to leave any more than the rest of them. Nothing remained back at Heartwood for him. The farm was dead and so was everyone he had loved. Besides Hannah, Kellen, and Lily, there really wasn't much of a life for him. Looking at Hannah's pleading, fragile face, he knew what he had to do.

"Fine," he said. "Go boil some water and crush up the dried willow blossoms and steep them for Bekka. It should alleviate her pain without harming the baby."

"Take Sarrah with you, please," Bekka added. "I don't want her seeing me in such discomfort."

Hannah agreed, coaxing Sarrah out with a promise to show her another pretty dress that might fit her. Sarrah had only one outfit, dirty and thread worn due to hardships of their flight from the guards, and the small flower dress Lily gave her. After the girls had left, Bekka put a hand on Jarrod's arm.

"You didn't tell him." She clung to his arm.

"It doesn't matter if you were betrothed or married to the man," Jarrod said. "The fact that he tried to choke you to death makes him dangerous, and not a very good husband material. I think you can do better."

Bekka gave a weak smile.

"Thank you." She kissed his cheek.

His face grew hot and he nodded, not trusting his tongue to find the right words.

Bekka handed Jarrod the empty cup. *Still warm from her hands.* He watched her settle into the bedroll. Her breathing grew soft. Her face relaxed, lips partial open as she closed her eyes. *So very beautiful.* Part of him wanted to kiss her eye lids, to whisper sweet words to her until she fell asleep. He turned away, fighting the impulse to make a fool of himself. *Besides, she doesn't want to be here with us. She has her own place with people like her and Sarrah. I have the eyes of the gods upon me. Not exactly a match.*

"Shane," Bekka said drowsily and turned over on her side.

Another anchor around his burdened heart.

Jarrod quietly left the tent.

Ishmael sat by the smoldering fire pit. A cup of hot tea in his hands. He looked up as Jarrod approached.

"I'm not in the mood for an argument." Jarrod picked up his hoe and leaned on it, looking north. The Yellow Valley was aptly named. Beyond the green grasses and groves of weepers, yellow broom grass grew up from sandy soil all the way to the foot hills of Mountains of Dawn. So many places for Bernal to hide.

"I have none to give." He could feel Ishmael's eyes studying him. The tension seemed to cool like dying embers of a fire. Jarrod didn't feel much like rekindling the flames and nearly walked off to his fields when Ishmael spoke again. "You remember what it was like during the Ascension War." It was a statement, not a question, since he knew Jarrod couldn't forget the terrible time impressed on his young mind. "We were just boys, fresh from our farms. They took away our pitchforks and hoes and replaced them with swords."

"I could barely hold a sword," Jarrod said, cringing at the ridicule he endured.

"Still can't." Ishmael chuckled and shook his head. "I don't want to go back to those times. I don't want to watch anymore of my friends die fighting strangers."

Yoked, hilt to blade. Jarrod shivered at how no matter how he tried to hide, he was being drawn ever towards conflict. The gods' nets were drawing around him. It was a matter of time before they wielded him against his will, like a blade in the dark.

"Me either," Jarrod said. "Not since I lost my entire family."

"I don't understand how you can accept people and try to do what's right by them." Ishmael sipped his tea. Jarrod noticed a tremor in his hands. "Ever since Michael and Mother were killed, I don't know what to think or do. I feel hollow, like someone drilled a hole in my chest and scraped out everything except for rage. I want to fight something or someone all the time. It doesn't seem fair that we lose everything while those above us take whatever they want or kill us if we resist. We are all the same, made as the gods created us. I hate fighting over such petty things, or as my mother used to say: 'things of men to be torn asunder by the gods.'" Jarrod recognized the verse from the *Book of Life and Death*, a scripture popular in the Paternal Temple, destroyed by Thomas before the Ascension Wars. "Sometimes I imagine Azriel growing and fighting the same battles in a never-ending war. He's so young, but so was Michael. It's like the gods don't care about us anymore."

Or care too much about some of us.

"That's why I don't give up hope," Jarrod replied. "Without some idea of good and justice, there really isn't much to hold onto in this world."

"You always were the better man, Jarrod. You have a kind heart and do what's right." Ishmael dumped out the remainder of his tea. "I don't think the world is ready for someone like you." He stood up, dropping the cup into a bucket. "No camp fire tonight. Whatever you want cooked, do it now. We pack up camp at first light. Do you want first or last watch?"

"I'll take first."

"Then I am going to sleep." Ishmael stood up and dumped out the remains of his tea. "Wake me up at moonrise and try to keep the children quiet. Oh, one last thing."

Here it comes, Jarrod tried not to roll his eyes. *Another accusation, another dictate.*

"Forget what I said before about Bekka staying with me. You can keep her," Ishmael said, touching the wrap around his head. "Just watch her closer."

"What about Sarrah?" Jarrod asked. "Can she stay with Bekka?"

"No. She stays with Elly. I don't want them running off and causing us more trouble." He turned away and went to his tent.

Keeping them apart might be more trouble than he realizes. He kept his mouth closed, done with arguing for now.

The children were fed and put to bed. They had a cold supper of wild yams sliced up with roasted nuts, all preserved from past roasting, and the remaining berries. Bekka slept through supper. Jarrod set a plate aside in case she woke up hungry. He reheated water before it got dark, giving each of the children, Hannah included, a cup of willow blossom tea. Hannah left hers to cool without taking so much as a sip.

The cup still sat on the rock where she left it.

Jarrod turned his attention to the sky. A tapestry of bright orange and red stretched across the western sky as the sun gave one last burst of color before surrendering to sleep. Dark grey closed in from the east like a blanket being pulled over them. The first star of the evening appeared distant and shimmery. He used to wish on the first star he saw each night. Wished for a dance with neighbor's daughter, Samantha, at the Solstice Fare. Wished the rumors of war would blow past Heartwood. Wished his mother would leave the farm and go south to the iron mines and stay with her sister.

Samantha chose another boy, war took away everything, including his parents.

Wishes are like prayers. Jarrod watched the lone star shimmering so far away. *They draw unwanted attention from ill-tempered gods.*

"This is our last night here, together," Hannah said, breaking his reverie. She sat close, but not touching him like she had on previous nights before the arrival of their guests.

Jarrod nodded.

"I'm going to miss the quiet nights." She looked at Jarrod, her brow tightened. She twisted a blade of grass around her finger. "When we get back to Heartwood, where will we stay?"

"I hadn't thought much about it," Jarrod said. The girl's home was gone, burnt down. After recovering from the knife wound, he returned to the place without Hannah's knowledge and buried her parents—

what was left of them. Her father died in the burning home, so his remains were charred, while other creatures feasted on her mother. His childhood home was destroyed in the war. When Prince Thomas was defeated and Heartwood returned to peace, Jarrod started to rebuild the farm house, getting as far as clearing the land and setting up four walls and a thatched roof before Thramel's men recruited him. He even had a nice garden growing, which he was certain had gone to weed. "I guess it depends on what we find when we get back to the Pines."

If there is anything to return to. Heartwood Pines may not even exist anymore. For all I knew, Joanne could have razed it to the ground.

"What will happen to Bekka and Sarrah?"

"I don't know," Jarrod said. "We'll sort that out when we get there."

"I don't want to live with Bekka," Hannah said, her face scrunching up. "Please don't force us to stay with her while you rush into battle."

"What do you mean rush into battle?"

Hannah laughed.

"You know what I mean. You always run into the thick of things when someone needs your help." Her voice grew lower. "You don't even think about the consequences."

Jarrod tried thinking of a response, but he had no retort. As far as Hannah understood, he was always running off into some trouble.

"Were you there to kill my parents on that night?" Hannah asked, the grass tearing between her fingers.

Jarrod studied her eyes. No longer innocent, but filled with pain and worry.

"No," he said. "Like with many things, I didn't know what I was doing. It was my first night out with Fraster. They told me we were going to put a scare into some war criminals. Nothing about burning and killing. I guess it was my initiation into the group." He looked up at the sky. Darkness crept in closer. "I failed it."

He heard Hannah get up and when he turned his head, she stood over him, her hair crowned by the burning sunset. Without warning, she bent over and kissed his mouth. Her lips were soft, pressing lightly into his, and his heart quickened. She pulled back, searching his face. Dumbstruck, Jarrod sat there unable to form words or thought.

Hannah's cheeks burned crimson.

"I just... I just." She took a step back, then another, before turning and running off behind the outcrop. *Wait!* The word never formed from his lips that tingled still from her kiss. He clambered to his feet and nearly fell over. He didn't trust his legs to move. Everything seemed to spin in slow motion.

"I was right."

The shock of the words snapped him back into reality. He turned and saw Bekka walking towards him. A ghost of a smile played at the corner of her mouth.

"What do I do?" the question came out whiny and he cleared his throat. "I mean, she kissed me and she is....is..." A storm of conflicting thoughts and emotions rolled around his head. He sat down, running his fingers through his hair.

"I guess you're going to have to figure this out on your own." Bekka sat down next to him. He felt her warmth and wanted to lean into her. She put an arm around his shoulder, a friend drawing him in for comfort. "I wouldn't wait too long to talk with her about it. Girls are complicated creatures and we don't appreciate being kept waiting, especially when taking a huge risk, like she just did."

Risk! Jarrod frowned and scratched his head. *First the Blades Man, then the Shadow, and now Qetesh is conspiring against me.*

"I don't understand," Jarrod said more to himself.

"When I told Shane that I was pregnant," Bekka replied, "he didn't say a word to me. I was so distraught I didn't think he loved me anymore. I nearly packed up what little belongings I had and went back to my brother."

"But you were pregnant," Jarrod said. "This is... this is... different."

"The fear of rejection is still the same." Bekka looked him in the eye. "I would find her, talk about what happened. Otherwise, it will fester like a boil and you will never have the same relationship with her again."

"After this, nothing can be the same," Jarrod said. "Besides, she is like a little sister."

"She's not, so you need to stop comparing her to blood kin. Look at it from her perspective," Bekka said. "You told me you saved her life, you protect her here and provide food and shelter. All good reasons for her to be enamored with you."

And jealous of you. Jarrod remembered how Hannah stormed off after asking if he liked Bekka and just a moment ago, begging not to stay with her.

"I guess I'm not ready for any of this." His shoulders slumped.

"Then you need to explain that to her. She will respect your feelings more than if you ignored her."

"Alright, I'll go find her."

Hannah sat beneath the weeping willow, arms folded, and head resting against the trunk. Jarrod leaned on the outcropping, supporting his weak legs as his heart climbed up his throat. *I'm going to throw up!* He pressed a hand to his stomach, his gut tossing and turning. He drew in a deep breath, held it, and then slowly released. *I can do this.* His arms trembled and he pushed away from the rock. He shook the nervousness from his hands, stuffing them into his breeches' pockets.

As he approached, Hannah lifted her head and ran the back of her hand under her eyes. Wet tracks traced down her chin. She frowned, eyes shimmering as she waited for him to berate her, maybe even break her heart. Jarrod plucked at the blossoms, pink petals closed for the evening, and held a petal between his fingers. It tore in half and he let it fall, watching them flutter to his boots.

"I'm such a twit," Hannah said, ending the uncomfortable silence. "I should never have done that."

"Why did you?" He asked, trying to keep any accusation from his tone.

Hannah shrugged.

Jarrod waited silently for her to find the right words.

"It won't happen again," she said.

"I don't want this to be a wall between us," Jarrod said. "I was surprised by it and didn't know what to think or do... gods I still don't know. You're sweet and kind... with all these dangers and threat of war, I can't focus on anything else."

"Except for Bekka."

Jarrod's face warmed and he reeled back as though he had been slapped.

"I'm sorry," Hannah replied, hugging herself. "I see the way you look at her. The way you treat her like she is *there* and I... I want that."

Words were vapors he clutched at, slipping away like mist when his mind reached for them. His heart felt like a stone split open by the awl of uncertainty. *Hug her! Tell her that she is noticed.* He remained frozen. She was young and impetuous, and would end up regretting her youthful choices as the flowery dress of naiveté shed in place of the grey caul of adulthood—not that he was much older than her, just wiser in some ways. "Never wise in the ways of women," his father often quoted. At this moment those words were truer than anything.

"I don't know what to say," he said.

Hannah's lip trembled and she covered her face. Like a dumbstruck cow, Jarrod watched her cry. His mouth was full of cotton and his head stuffed with wool. Finally, he looked away. Down in the Yellow Valley, night smothered the land. At the edge of the stream, a tiny prick of light shown. Jarrod's eyes widened and his breath caught in his chest.

Sensing this change, Hannah asked: "What is it?"

He shushed her, clutching the weeper's trunk and peering over the hill. A camp fire flared up by the stream's bank. Four shadows moved among the newly birthed flames. He was in direct view certain they could see him should he move from the tree's cloaking canopy. The murmuring stream drowned their voices. He wasn't sure about the noise from above and thought it best to be quiet. Two men moved away from the fire, disappearing into the trees.

Setting a perimeter watch. Jarrod was certain now they were soldiers. *Bernal? No, he hasn't been gone long enough. Maybe Manor soldiers seeking out their companion. If they find him, it won't be long until they come for us.*

Footsteps sounded next to him. Hannah started to walk towards the hill's edge. Jarrod grabbed her hand, guiding her around the trunk. Pressing his mouth to her ear, he whispered: "Soldiers."

Hannah's eyes widened.

"Kellen! Lily!" She made a move towards the tents. Jarrod caught her arm, yanking her back. She made a squeak, prying at his fingers. He wrapped his arm around her waist, pinning her to him. She smacked his chest and said, "Let me go."

"Stop," Jarrod hissed.

Hannah wouldn't. She wriggled against him, digging her nails into his skin as she locked her arms trying to separate from him. Jarrod spun her away from the ledge so they wouldn't tumble down into the laps of the soldiers. His arms began to hurt as she struggled to escape. *Too much noise.* He imaged the soldiers below staring up at the commotion, swords drawn. The more Hannah fought, the closer she was to breaking free and rousing up the camp. He did the only thing that he could think of to calm her down.

His lips found hers and he kissed her.

Hannah no longer fought, but seemed to melt into him, arms once shoving against his chest, snaking over his shoulder. Her eyes closed and he could feel the warmth of her breath on his upper lip. For the first time he realized her body was soft, small, his hands fit around her waist, fingertips nearly touching. He felt a stirring and pulled back. Hannah stood mouth parted, eyes staring into his. Her heart beat against his chest. Small hands slid from his neck, down his shoulders and grasped his arms. Jarrod gave her an awkward half-smile and pointed at the tree. He mouthed the word "stay."

Hannah nodded, sliding down once more against the trunk.

Jarrod dropped into a crouch. He stepped deliberately, gliding his feet through the grass and around the edge of his garden. He peered over the rock side. Four men sat around the campfire. *Did I miscount? Were there more?* He waited, watching to see if anyone appeared. His knees and lower back ached from leaning down for so long. *What do we do? We can't stay here this night!* The answer was simple. Ishmael needed to know.

Jarrod crept to the weeper.

Hannah watched him, her head tilted in confusion.

"What was that?" she demanded, arms folded.

"I was counting soldiers," Jarrod said.

"No, what you did with me."

"You were making too much noise," Jarrod said. "I had to stop you from running off and drawing attention to us."

As soon as he said it, he wished he could take the words back.

"Is that all?" Hannah folded her arms.

Jarrod felt his face flush. *What more do you want?*

Hannah rolled her eyes when he didn't respond and threw her hands up. Then she stalked away.

Qetesh! What am I supposed to do?

"How many did you see?" Ishmael asked, annoyance at being awakened early turning his whisper into a hiss.

A stone jabbed Jarrod in the rib and he squirmed away from it, getting closer to Ishmael as they lay on the ground and watched the campfire beneath them. It had burned lower and two men were visible sitting on fallen limbs. A third was wrapped in a cloak on the ground a bit of a ways away.

"Four or six," Jarrod replied, rubbing his cold arms. He wanted to fall into a warm blanket and sleep for the next three nights. Sleep, he figured, would be as hard to come by a gods-forged steel for a plow.

"Which is it?" Ishmael demanded.

"I don't know." Jarrod's face flushed, grateful for the dark to cover it up. "I got distracted as I tried to count."

"If there are only four…." Ishmael went quiet for several heart beats. He looked from the fire, to the weepers and back to the fire. Finally, he shook his head and let out a sigh. "Gods, I wish I knew. Four we can handle. Six… is too much. We have to move, tonight."

"How?" Jarrod asked. "Won't we catch unwanted attention?"

"From where they're camped, they can't see us on the other side of the outcropping," Ishmael explained. "Otherwise, they would have come up here by now. Shadow's luck they didn't continue through the weepers and camp on the other side. They would have heard the horses or possibly seen our tents depending on how far back from the stream they camped. We still need to make sure everyone keeps as quiet as mice stealing cheese from the larder. You and I will have to scout the north and south paths to be certain were won't run into anybody."

Jarrod didn't like the idea of leaving the camp unprotected while they searched the trails, but Ishmael was right, better safe now than sorry later.

"I will check the south," Jarrod said.

"Hannah will stay with the children, keep them calm and quiet," Ishmael said. "I'll make sure she knows not to leave the tent unless they have to run. I don't think there will be a need to if we cover the visible routes in and out."

Jarrod crawled back and Ishmael grabbed his arm.

"If you find more of them then you can handle, hurry back and get the children, *our* children, on horses. Got it?"

Jarrod nodded.

"I mean it. Get my brother and sister to safety. Don't wait for me or anyone else."

"Fine," Jarrod replied. "You do the same."

"Mother's troth I will," Ishmael said. "You have until the Lover's feet hang over us, then I am taking everyone and going. Hurry along, but for Mother's sake, keep quiet."

No matter how soft he tried to make each step, to his own ears he sounded like a drove of pigs rutting in mud. Stones crunched the hard ground, tumbling down the path. Jarrod stopped and cursed silently, waiting for an alarmed shout or an armored soldier to leap from the next thicket to skewer him. He continued on, walking at a snail's pace, head swiveling to take in as much of the surroundings as the moon lit path allowed. He'd almost reached the bottom of the hill, when he heard swooshing of grass. Crouching beside a squat boulder, he watched the Eastern side. Though the stone was cold, his palms sweat. *The wind... please be the wind.*

Two soldiers approached and Jarrod swallowed hard, trying to mold into the rock. One pointed at the switchback and they stopped, craning their necks to follow it up to the top of the hill. Scrub brush and fallen rocks blocked any clear view.

One soldier took a step towards it. Jarrod dropped a hand to his sword pommel, ready to draw. Sweat slick hands slid from the pommel and he almost rattled the scabbard against the rock.

"I wouldn't go up there now," the second soldier said. "No telling what creatures we'll run into."

"That's what we're here for," the first said.

"Remember what happened to Gil when he poked around that cave." The second soldier's hands turned into claws and struck out like a cat pouncing on a mouse. "I'm not about to have my face chewed off. We can check it out when the sun rises."

"You've got the guts of a worm."

"Better to have worm guts, than to give my guts to the worms."

"Fine," The first soldier grinned and shook his head. "But when the Captain asks, you can explain how you nearly pissed yourself."

"He can explore up there all he wants," the first soldier said, walking past where Jarrod hid a few steps away. "Instead, he's sleeping by the fire, all wrapped up and cozy like a baby girl sucking his thumb and squeezing his dolly." He grabbed his groin and laughed. "We'll mark this spot and come back at sunrise. Not like anything will run off during the night." He pulled down his trousers and urinated on the stone.

Jarrod wrinkled his nose, holding back his gorge wanting to wretch up supper.

"Let's get back," the second soldier said. "I want to get a few winks before we have to march again."

"The problem with all these empty hills," the first soldier said, heading back the same direction they arrived, "is there's no women. Moko stomp them flat! I can only take so much of your ugly face, though you do have a pretty mouth."

"I got pretty teeth, too," the second said, chomping down. "So don't go getting your wax hard. Besides, I think we're chasing shadows and there's no one out in these hills but us and maybe a few Manor deserters."

"Does it matter?"

They were out of sight and Jarrod could no longer hear their conversation. He counted to twenty, before turning and running back up the hill. When he got there, the place was silent and had an empty feeling, like they all decided to leave him behind. The Lover's Feet hung directly overhead, the stars brighter than any others in the night sky. *Am I too late? Did he take everyone down the north side?*

He went to the children's tent and threw open the flap. A knife point nearly jabbed him in the leg.

"Watch it," he said, dancing back a few steps.

"You scared me," Hannah replied, stepping out after him. She refused to look him in the eye. "What'd you find?"

"We have to go." He took the knife from Hannah and she scowled. "Tonight. They'll be up here searching around at first light."

"Fine." She brushed past him. "Elly will you please help me get the horses."

Jarrod stayed and helped the other children gathered what food and water they could pack into saddle bags. Bekka cleared the tents so Jarrod could break them down. When Elly and Hannah brought the horses around, they loaded them up.

"Where's Ishmael?" Elly asked once they had everything stowed and ready to leave.

"He'll catch up to us," Jarrod said, he looked overhead and saw the waists of the intertwined Lovers were directly overhead. *We can't wait around. He told me not to wait.* "Everyone up on your horse. Those soldiers might come back around."

"We can't leave my brother," Elly said. "I won't leave him."

"Me, either," Azriel chimed in.

"We're not," Jarrod said. "He's scouting the path. He wanted us to get some distance and then he'll find us further east."

"Are you sure he said that." Elly folded her arms. "That's how we lost Michael and—"

"And I'm not Michael." Ishmael reached the ridge, stopped and looked around at them. "What are you waiting for? Jarrod spoke truly. Get on the horse, or walk, it doesn't matter to me. We're heading out. South switchback?"

Jarrod nodded. The soldiers would be back at their camp.

"Let's go!"

The children mounted the horses, while Bekka, Jarrod, and Ishmael walked. As they passed the weeper to follow the trail south, Jarrod looked at his little garden, wondering if what he planted would take root and sprout life.

Another garden abandoned. He sighed. *One day I may get to reap what I sowed.*

CHAPTER TWELVE

Omnipotent they called us. All power, but not all powerful. Flawed though we were, we created a perfect schema to increase our power; they worshipped us in guise of having their every desire fulfilled, or punished for reasons beyond their limited understanding. Nurtured by prayers, our essence strengthened until we nearly believed our own lies. Heads filled with hubris, we carried on the pretense of gods, never realizing that as we intervened in their lives, they shaped who we were for better, and for worse.
— *From "Prophetic Musings"*
Menrva

Where's Menrva? *Where is that prophet when I need her?*

Mother sat in her Rose Chair at the top of a raised platform in the Throne Room carved from ironwood, petrified wood as ridged as sitting on a blacksmith's anvil. Plush velvet cushions lined the hard seat and back to add an illusion of comfort. Fingers drummed on the wooden rest, intricately carved like twining rose vines, thorns jutting out at various angles. Should someone unintended sit in the chair, the vines would twist around the interloper, sharp points digging into ethereal flesh and shred them over and over until madness stole through their undying minds. The thorns drank blood from those they pierced and reshaped their flesh, Father had warned, though no one had dared test the warning. Father designed the Rose Chair for her specifically, as an anniversary present to celebrate their seeming immortality. The thought of him brought on an old ache.

"My love," he had said, pulling a sheet off the beautiful chair. *"We have truly ascended."*

She had giggled like a young girl and kissed his mouth. It was a glorious moment, but brief. So very brief. He carved another throne similar in design of the Rose, though darker in wood and lacking its sharp objects. The Shadow Throne, he had named it. Anyone besides Father who sat on its dark wood would slip away into some unknown prison only he could access.

The Shadow Throne sat empty beside her.

Mother didn't feel safe anywhere else in the Palace of Gods. The last encounter with the Mistress of Shadow had left her feeling naked, exposed. She touched her bare neck where the star of creation used to rest. The Shadow possessed both the star of creation and disc of darkness. *She doesn't know how to use them. She doesn't know the words.*

No matter how Mother tried to put worry out of her head, she kept envisioning the worse. Her children thrust out of heaven, crashing down like fallen stars to consume the Created below.

"Damn it all to Donn, why is it taking so long to find Menrva?"

Mother had sent one of her trusted children to summon the prophet from her cell up in Overlook Hill where the prophetess enjoyed gazing at the stars and weaving patterns for dreamers. A trip there and back would take half-a-day, but it seemed so much longer than when she sent her servant. Every moment counted when at war, even a silent war.

Wish I'd brought wine. She curled her legs beneath her on the velvet cushion and chewed on her nails—a habit from centuries ago. These moments, Father's absence hit her the hardest. She wanted to cry. Crying wouldn't help the situation. She needed a clear head to think. Needed a plan. The demise of her children and created would be on her hands, even if she didn't do it herself.

Menrva would bring her good counsel.

The door opened to the Throne room. Mother leaned forward, gripping the vines. A thorn pricked her finger. Blood trickled down the vine and dripped onto the floor. The lone, hooded figure slipped into the room and closed the door.

"Mother," Agni said, lowering his hood and bowing his head.

"Where is Menrva?" Mother stood up and clenched her fists. "Why didn't she come?"

"Forgive me, Mother, but I failed to find her." Agni kept his eyes lowered.

"Did you check her room here in the palace as well as at Overlook?"

"Yes."

"Where could she have gone?" The look of Agni's face showed fear as well as disappointment. "What's wrong, Agni?"

"There appears to have been some sort of struggle. Her residence on Overlook had paper strewn all about the floor and furnishings toppled over." He paused and looked briefly at Mother. "I believe there were specks of blood. I examined one of the papers, written in her hand, I recognized, dappled in tiny droplets of red, like the one on your finger... Mother are you hurt?"

Mother noticed the puncture wound in her finger. The red trickle plinked onto the Rose Chair. The wood sucked it up like tiny drops of rain on parched soil.

"A scratch," Mother said and tapped the wooden rest in impatience. "I'm fine. Please continue."

Agni nodded. "I called her name several times and no one responded. I returned to the palace as quickly as I could to investigate her room here in the Observatory. They appear to be untouched."

The conversation had an odd, twisting feeling. Too similar to the one they had when Father disappeared.

"Take me to her rooms."

"Yes, Mother." Agni bowed and opened the Throne room doors.

Mother moved briskly through the lengthy hallway, forcing Agni to nearly run to keep pace. Heraldries from long forgotten kingdoms and tapestries depicting scenes about their transformation into immortality hung along the walls. Mother stopped at one portraying the flight of souls after judgement. Elongated blue spectral forms stretched upward to the peaceful rest awaiting them in Nahrangi while black, distorted figures sank into the pit. Mother drew the tapestry aside to reveal a staircase. It was seldom used, known only to Mother, Father, Menrva, and Agni.

Blue light ignited in the narrow, spiraling staircase as they drew close and extinguished as they passed. Doors marked the passage of floors. Mother counted them, choosing the seventh. A cold draft escaped its edge and the golden handle chilled her hand so she pulled back.

"Allow me, Mother," Agni said, sliding his hand into a glove and then twisting the knob.

A tiny click sounded and the door opened. On the inside of the Observatory a bookcase moved inward to reveal a room complete with bed, three more bookcases, a writing desk and single hardwood chair. Menrva's room was neat and tidy. Several rolls of parchment lined her desk with quill and ink. The windows were all sealed, giving the room a stagnant feel. Stagnant, but frigid.

"I don't know how she can stand the cold." Frosted air puffed from her lips.

"She lived in the cold before her ascension," Agni replied.

"Very true."

Mother opened a sliding glass door and stepped out onto the balcony. An observation glass pointed towards the Entwined Twins constellation. *A sign? Or just star gazing?* Anything in the room could signify a bigger picture only Menrva could see. Mother returned inside and slid the door closed.

"Doesn't seem like she has been here in a while." Agni stood next to a shelf, holding a finger up with dust covering the tip.

Strange, she is usually so tidy and doesn't allow dirt in her room, unless—

Mother went to the writing desk. Several unused scroll papers were rolled up in the corner beside the ink well. Mother opened the drawers, finding more blank parchment, extra quills, and empty inkwells. She ran her hands along the edge of the desk and felt a metal latch. Pressing it, a spring popped. A click sounded as a small compartment opened on the side of the desk. The compartment contained tightly bound scrolls sealed in wax. Stars and moon, Menrva's signet ring. Mother broke the seal and read the strange glyphs.

"Mother, you look pale," Agni said, coming to her side and helping her keep her feet. "Are you ill?"

"No," Mother whispered and re-rolled the scroll, tucking it into her cleavage. She closed the compartment and took Agni's hand. "Help me back down stairs."

"Where do you suppose Menrva went?" Agni asked as they slowly walked down the stairs. Mother's legs trembled, threatening to send her tumbling down to the bottom if not for Agni's steady hand.

"Away," She breathed in and out, trying to stop the shaking "Somewhere we may never find her."

Oh my children, it is all my fault!

Agni gave a questioning look.

"We can't speak of it here. Get me to the Throne room and bar the door," she said, her heart heavy from the parchment's content. *It could be nothing, but then why would she hide it?*

They reached the bottom of the stairwell and pushed back the tapestry. The hallway was empty. She released his hand and began walking under her own power. As they approached the Throne room, Mother halted. She placed a hand on Agni's chest. Eyebrows raised, he glanced up the hallway where murmurs grew into disgruntled voices.

"Take this," she said, removing the scroll from her cleavage and pressed it into Agni's hand. "Go to my chambers and search in my bookcase. Find the book entitled *Life of the Created*. Tucked into its spine is a soul pendant. Use it to find Huron."

"Mother—"

"There isn't time for argument." The sound of voices grew louder. "Use the Pool of Reflection and give the scroll to him. Tell him it's about the farm boy. Huron must read it. Be careful, Agni. Avoid the Mistress of Shadow at all costs."

Agni furrowed his brow.

"Go!" She shoved him. "Leave me. I will be fine."

Agni bowed his head, a sad dutiful expression on his face. He took the scroll and turned away without a moment's hesitation. *Bless you child and may you find your brother before it becomes too late.* Mother took a deep breath, releasing it gradually. Her rapidly beating heart settled into a steady beat. *Let's find out what the trouble is all about.* She put on a smile and walked casually towards the disgruntled sound. Six of her children filled the hallway, an angry energy flowing off them like heat from a bon-fire. Hacawit, eyes blazing and hand on his lustrous red sword's hilt, led the way followed by silver-haired Sin, green-eyed Sierna, thick-bodied Moko, pale-skinned Donn, and Qetesh trailing, sheepishly behind.

"Why are my children gathered before me at such a late hour?"

"Seeking your wisdom, Mother," Hacawit said, smiling ironically. "We sought you out in your chambers, the Grand Hall and the Throne Room, yet here we find you walking the hallways."

"Such disturbing news have reached our ears," Sin said in her nasally tone.

She thinks she has something over me. Mother bit back a snarky reply.

"Come, let's speak of your troubles in a more private setting." Moko blocked her way as Mother tried to pass around him. She gave him a flat stare that would cause even the sternest of her children to flinch, but Moko folded his arms and shook his head. "Why are you acting like peevish children?"

"Because, Mother, you have been keeping secrets from us," Qetesh said. "I sensed it several nights back at the Pool. I didn't believe, or want to believe it. You cast a veil over one of the created to hide them. But love is not always blind, Mother. Love is strong enough to pierce even the darkest of veils cast over it."

"Whatever do you—"

"We know, Mother," Donn said, "so save your silver-tongued lies for those naïve enough to believe. Ever since Father went away, you have been powerless to stop it. We grow tired and want it all to end."

"You don't know what you are saying."

"We do, Mother," Sierna said. "We have outgrown you and like all children, must depose of our parents so we may grow and ascend beyond."

"She spoke to you," Mother said, the understanding of which she plain on their faces. "She filled your head with these lies."

"Not lies, but truth." Hacawit grabbed her wrist, yanking her close. "Where is the star of creation? Where is your power for upholding life?" He tore open the top of her dress exposing her throat and the top of her bosom. "Gone, I see." He turned her around for the others to notice as well, twisting her arm behind her. "You are no longer able to protect us, to sustain us." He passed her to Moko, who wrapped his large arms around her and lifted her off the floor.

Mother kicked at the air, the breath crushed from her lungs. *Oh, my children! My children I am sorry.* Tears sprung from the corners of her eyes. "You have done enough harm, Mother." Moko carried her to the Throne Room. When she saw where he intended to place her, she struggled harder in his grip, but was unable to break free. Moko stood before the Shadow Throne, waiting for some signal to set her into it, into an oblivion Father had created and only he could access.

"It's time for us to ascend beyond, Mother. Thank you for all you have given us," Hacawit said then nodded to Moko. Moko lowered Mother to the Shadow Throne and dropped her onto the black wood.

She tried to leap away as though tossed into a fire. Moko pushed her back, careful not to touch any part of the black wood. Mother's breath caught and an icy chill stole over her body. She became weightless, as though she would float away from the chair. A bright blue light surrounded her, and then dimmed. One last breath. She exhaled her proclamation.

"You have ruined us a—"

Darkness absorbed her.

Three mounted soldiers passed the dense thicket, close enough for Huron to hobble the lead horse. A quick swipe at the forelegs and the rider would be thrown or crushed beneath the weight of his mount. He had seen it happen hundreds of times in war, was even the victim of a well-placed spear. That would leave two more men. One would ride off to warn the vanguard while the other attempted to detain or kill him.

His hand rested on the pommel, fingers tightening for the draw. Killing one would bring twenty or more down on him. In this frail body, tired and sore from the slow march, he wouldn't get close enough to even see the wagons let alone rescue the captive children. The soldiers rode past, ignorant of how close they came to death. Huron closed his eyes and focused his breathing, slowing his heart so that it made no sound. He imagined the tight pain in his muscles as balls of light. One by one he extinguished them. The pain vanished along with the light, body becoming numb. It was a temporary trick he learned long ago, but one essential for surviving long marches.

They're going to have to stop sometime. The horses will need to rest and so will the soldiers.

Huron continued walking the tree-line. He knew how to trick the mind into ignoring the aches, but soon his body would need to rest as well. They would outdistance him on foot, leaving him lost in the leagues of wilderness. He needed to strike soon.

I need a horse!

The sky bled a bright red in the west when Huron caught up to the rear guard. He watched them picket the main road, posting two men to guard the way they had come. More were sent out to scout the woods in three groups of four. He was forced to backtrack a quarter of a league to avoid being detected. Every moment he retraced his steps, the weight of being absent from Jarrod dragged on him, like a slow erosion that comes when the battle lines thin and there are more enemies than friends standing. His greatest enemy sought the boy— she had revealed her hand too soon at the Forge. Huron had to make her pay for her hubris. Each passing day was one less he had to prepare the boy for the coming battle.

Huron ducked behind a rotting trunk as two soldiers approached from the west. His listened to their shuffling boots slip further off east. The compulsorily search made them lax. This would create a chain reaction, disarming the guards and lulling them into a false sense of security. Then Huron would fall on them like a waking nightmare, like a shadow... *No, I have to tread lightly*. His very presence among the Created intruded on the strife beyond the rights of gods. Should the brothers and sisters discover his actions, the results could be devastating.

I won't abandon the children to these men. He crept forward, keeping ahead of the scouts and using the spreading darkness to cover his movements. The scent of meat roasting over campfires told him he was close to the main camp. His stomach rumbled. Blood berries, a meager meal he had carried in his pack, were gone along with over half his water. This body required more sustenance than he had provided. Touching the soul pendant hanging protected in his tunic, he knew an easy solution. Easy solutions made for difficult choices.

Huron closed his eyes, focusing on numbing the needs of the body. Unnecessary distractions would be his doom. He opened them, hunger pains dulled, and he seemed to float beyond the flesh, a spirit tethered to the body by a thin line. He moved silently along the tree line until he came across the supply wagons. A single soldier guarded it. The man slouched, looking bored and inattentive. They put too much trust in the security of their parameter guards. Most likely the one guard protected against thievery from his fellow soldiers.

Not very disciplined, Huron thought, checking for any other soldiers lurking around. By his count, there were twenty-five soldiers. Nine were sent on patrol, four kept guard on the children bound wrists and ankles twenty yards further up, another two worked the cook fires and nine more set up camp.

A pair of torches were set in the ground at the edges of the wagon's perimeter about a full man's length apart. The light dissipated at the tree line, not enough for the lone guard to see Huron watching him from the shadows. The man was more interested in chewing his finger nails than what may be lurking beyond the light. Huron kept to the shadows, looking away from the fire so he wouldn't be blinded. Two carts filled with crates and barrels blocked his approach. He waited for his eyes to adjust to the light before flanking the guard's left side.

Quick and silent. Huron drew his sword from the scabbard.

Either soldier's instinct or the hiss of metal on leather caught the man's attention. The soldier immediately straightened, drawing in a breath to shout a warning while his hand dropped to sword grip. Huron's sword struck the guard through his mouth, severing tongue and piercing the base of his skull. Blood bubbled up around the swords edge as the guard's surprised eyes stared at him in dumb wonderment. His knees buckled and he began to fall. Huron caught him in a lover's embrace, easing his lifeless body to the ground. He waited, listening for any alarm to the brief struggle. No one came running, no shouts or weapons drawn. He wiped the blood off his blade using the man's trousers and sheathed it.

Lifting the top off a crate, he smelled salted beef and his stomach rumbled. The salt would worsen his condition and so he searched the barrels. One sloshed, smelling of brine and another had not scent at all. He cupped his hands and drank from the cool liquid. Water tasted better than any wine he remembered in his day as one of the created. He searched the wagons for skin or bladder. Tucked in the corner by the barrels were several extras. He quickly dunked them in the water and drank his fill. Next, he chewed on some salted beef, finding strength renewed.

Looking at the dead body, blood soaking into the dirt, the advantage of stealth was no longer an option. *Mother, this is going to be a long night.* Huron drew both his swords and entered the darkness again.

"Shut your traps," Dufree said, rapping his sword pommel against the wooden side of the wagon. The child gasped, scooted away, and whimpered in the corner. *Gods I can't stand children!* Constant demand for attention, their whining and crying and screaming made his head ache. They always smelled like dirty boots. These ones were extra smelly with their fear, shit, and piss. He didn't want to be the one to clean out the wagon after they returned to Nemus. Worse yet was the wolf's bane they had entwined in the ropes binding their wrists and ankles, the stuff was like wet dog cut open to feed the carrion birds. Not that he was complaining—the wolf's bane prevented the buggers from changing and slipping free, and kept them from gnawing on his throat. *Vicious vermin.* Marching downwind of the wagon was unbearable and the humidity made their smell worse. Dufree could almost slice the air with his blade and suck on it.

One little girl cried for her mother for the hundredth time.

"Your mothers are all dead." He tapped the wagon again. "Be grateful, little ones. Say your prayers to the gods *you* still draw breath."

He couldn't even hurt the little buggers. Smack them around to shut their mouths the way his father used to do to him and his siblings when they cried. Joanne wanted them brought back to Nemus alive and unspoiled. The thought of touching the creatures disgusted him. He made the other guards feed them bread and hold up water skins for their greedy, dry lips tongues lapping up the water that spilled down their dirty faces.

I like my fingers where there are, thanks very much.

The real reason he didn't haul off and split a lip was because of *her*, not Joanne, but the other woman's voice in his head. Gentle, firm whispers, *"protect the children,"* followed by images of what would happen if he failed in this duty. He wasn't alone in these waking nightmares. Every soldier he spoke with mentioned hearing the same woman's voice commanding them to watch over the children. Each had a special reward envisioned—and a terrifying punishment for failure.

Need to get these beasties north, then it's back to tavern wenches whose only complaint is where I put the coin.

Those women may or may not be clean, but he knew if the coin was good, then he could smack them as hard as he wanted, as long as no marks were visible above the clothing line. Good food, good wine, and good women. All the finer things in life were as distant as the camp cook fires, he knew were back by the rear guard, but couldn't see. He'd settle for potato stew and pickled eggs at this point. Anything to fill the hole in his gut.

The emptiness of this place worried him. They destroyed the only civilization for at least three hundred leagues around, leaving woodlands to truck through. Soon those would dwindle into desert sands before he saw so much as a village farm. He was used to the large cities in Seaptum, buildings taller than trees packed together like planks in a wine barrel with people as the glue. He didn't understand what Joanne wanted with the backwoods Nemus or these shifter children. Although part of him guessed they were not for her, but for the other woman. The one who insisted the children be protected.

Movement from the supply carts caught his attention. A lone figure walked towards them in the dark.

"Here comes our relief," Dufree said, nudging Graudy who leaned against the wagon, half-asleep. "Looks like one of us is going to eat and then sleep."

"Why would they only send one?" Graudy straightened up and stretched.

Dufree squinted, the man's cloak hung off the left shoulder, not the right. His armor wasn't regimental either. He walked with his arms behind his back, like he was hiding something.

"Blood and ashes, he isn't one of ours!"

The cloak fluttered from the stranger's back as he brought around a pair of long swords. He struck quicker than a cat pouncing on an unsuspecting mouse. Two of Dufree's companions crumpled as they engaged the stranger, long blades swiping, disarming and decapitating the first and skewering the second. Graudy ran past, sword drawn, and screaming a string of curses. The stranger fell into *Scythe* pose, sweeping aside Graudy's *Threading the Needle* and countered with *Thrash the Wheat*. Graudy screamed as his severed hand dropped at his feet, sword still gripped in it. *Reapers Cut* silenced him, sending his head tumbling from his shoulders.

The stranger didn't break stride, but came directly for Dufree.

Just need to delay him enough. Dufree lifted his sword and took the familiar *Ox Guard* stance. Fighting at night was as good as fighting blind. He had his fair share of brawls and knife fights in dark alleys, but sword play he kept for the daylight when he could see the blade. He parried the *Topping the Poppy* and took a wound in the side. Fire burned where metal rings bit into his skin. Dufree grunted, backing against the cart.

Children cried out and he smiled.

Keeping making noise, little ones, draw the attention of the guard.

The stranger struck high, and Dufree moved to *High Guard* before he realized his mistake. The blade changed course effortlessly into *Mist in the Moonlight*, the points of swords skewering Dufree's sternum and chest. It scraped the bone, alighting an internal fire that turned into a chilling, numbness, spreading through his body. His fingers convulsed and his sword clattered on the hard ground. Dufree chuckled, watery bile spurting from his lips.

"What is so funny?" the stranger asked.

"You may have ended me, but can you kill a dozen men?"

"I won't have to."

"You…noise. So much noise."

"All will be silent soon." The stranger twisted the blades and yanked them from his body. "Everyone else is dead."

He'd moved through the camp silently killing soldiers. No one had a chance to raise an alarm and few noticed his presence before he cut their windpipes, washing bedrolls in blood. He moved like a wolf among sheep, dispatching men as neatly as sheering wool. *Donn's platter is filling up.* Huron wiped his blood slick blade on the cloak of a permanently sleeping soldier. He killed the men at the cook fires next, taking both from behind with an upward thrust of his blades through the back of their necks. Red ichor bubbled in the soup pots mixing with the vegetables and grains. Then he hunted the patrols in the woods, stalking them and killing.

Two patrols remained missing. He guessed they moved ahead to secure the road from any surprise visitors from the northeast. He'd hoped to draw them out of hiding with the last slaughter of soldiers guarding the children. None came. Nineteen soldiers fell to his blades, like sheep carved up by a wolf. These sheep would no longer be following orders, orders from Dandulain, the Mistress of Shadows, no matter who the human was that dictated them. It explained how she found him in the city of light.

I was careless leaving a trail in Elysium. Huron studied the children cowering in the cart. Four girls and two boys huddled together in the far corners. The eldest girl stared at him with frightened, defiant eyes. This was planned out regardless of his presence in the village. Dandulain wanted these children for a reason.

"I'm not here to hurt you," Huron said, sheathing his swords. He tossed the guard's lifeless body off the cart and held out his hand. "Let me help you."

The older girl shuffled forward despite the protests from the other children.

"It'll be fine," she said. "If he wanted us dead, he would have done so."

When she got to the edge of the cart, Huron unsheathed a knife. The girl flinched as he brought it close. He cut her bonds and she thanked him after he handed her the knife.

She looked at it.

"Go cut loose the other children." He started to walk away.

"Where are you going?"

"Where I am needed."

"What are we supposed to do? Our home is destroyed, our parents are dead." Her lip trembled as she stared at him with yellow eyes full of fear and defiance. "Who will take care of us?"

He had heard that same question asked a thousand compounded in a thousand-fold prayers of grief and desperation. Each time he had no answer, not a single response. All he could do was listen as they cursed his name and died, or blessed him as they found miraculous resolve—neither of which had he earned.

If she *wants them as much as she desires my destruction...*

"You can come with me," Huron said. "I will find a safe place for you."

Mother help us all.

CHAPTER THIRTEEN

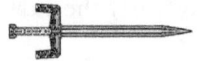

Moko shook in fury, discovering Qetesh lying naked in Virido's arms among a field of yellow forget-me-nots. Truly, she forgot her lover's vow. The ground trembled and heaved, tearing up the green glade and yellow blossoms as twin peaks rose to forever trap Qetesh in the broken field as punishment. Her lamenting tears shattered his heart and he relented, loving love too much. He released her, swearing never to fall for another's wiles again.

— *From "Origins of The Mountains of Destiny and Dawn."*

"We're lost."

Thramel felt it in his gut like a blade twisting his innards. They rode south for a day and a half without so much as a single sign. An endless measure of dust, scrub weeds, and flowers—bright yellow flowers as though the stems swallowed the sun whole and spat it up again on their stalks. His eyes ached and his head throbbed. He rubbed his temples wanting to rant and rave at Snout. The trail was cold! Dead as the rotting corpses back in Blackwood and their quarry too long on the run. Thramel wiped sweat off his brow onto a stained sleeve. His options were running out. Land and mines would be forfeit. The more he thought about why she sent two personal guard, the more he realized that their duty was not one of protection, but as executioners should the time expire as the new moon rose.

Snout stopped. Nose tilted up and eyes closed, he sniffed the air. He clambered off his horse to crouch, touched the ground and brought his fingers to his mouth. Thramel cringed watching Snout lick the tips, smacking his dry lips. Then the tracker dropped on hands and knees, smelling the dirt, snarfling like an old hound dog with nose pressed to the ground. He sneezed and sat up, a look of disappointment on his slack-jawed face. Muttering a curse to the goddess of animals, he climbed back on his horse and led them further south.

"We're lost," Thramel repeated, louder and spitting on the "t".

The rat-catcher made no reply, returning to his horse, and continued the journey. Silent *Mors Faunis* waited beside him, metal snarls aimed like pack members waiting for a signal to pounce. Thramel kneed his horse in motion and they rode parallel, an honor guard more awaiting the prisoner for execution. Except he wouldn't go down so easily. He had faced a wyrm and lived. Two wolves might prove a bit of a challenge, but Thramel had an idea on how to tame these beasts. *Not that there's much of a place to hide out.*

The Yellow Valley all looked the same. The only reason he knew they weren't riding in circles was because of the large mountain to the west of them served as a guiding landmark. Grass rolled along the hillside like one long yellow sea, as though the gods decided to piss down the hillsides and watch it run. He hated it. Hated the dry smell, the white moths that flitted past, the yellow hogs-bell flowers with the black-stripped golden bees pollinating them. It gave him gout just to see it all. A great big jaundice patch of earth. The grass itself felt dry enough to burn. Thramel wondered if he lit a fire, just how much of the valley would go up in flames before the fire died. *Would it burn to the ocean? Suck up the water and leave behind only salt?*

"So, are we just going to ride until we reach desert?" Thramel asked. Snout ignored him.

"Maybe they got eaten," Thramel said. The first night he slept under the stars in the Yellow Valley, a wild cat's shriek nearly caused him to piss himself. He'd crossed the path of one six years back. It had snuck into the open window of one of his workers and stole away with her baby. Thramel had followed the beast's trail, blood from the doomed infant, to a mine. Yellow eyes gleamed in the torchlit as it glared at the freighted, angry group of men. Red dots speckled its golden-brown snout. The gory remains of the baby caught between its massive paws. When the cat stood up, it reached about nine hands. Given a saddle, Thramel could have ridden it like the storied beast-wranglers and their travelling show of mystic and wonder. It took every man there to kill the wild cat and most didn't escape injury.

"Pray to the gods they didn't," Snout finally replied. "For your sake."

"If they're skin changers as you say, what makes you think they didn't just turn into beasts and run off with a new pack?"

"For one," Snout held up a pudgy finger, "the woman was pregnant."

"So they can't change while whelping? Beasts get pregnant just the same."

"As far as I'm informed, it's hard on the baby and the mother. They eat some sort of berry to ease the transition and that berry's poisonous to unborn children."

"What berry?"

Snout shrugged.

"Nothing but old wives' tales," Thramel said. "So far nothing you told me makes any sense. Rebellious soldiers run rampant over the manor and here we are chasing phantasms. Is this an elaborate punishment from Joanne? It seems like a gods-awful waste of time."

"Only times wasting in those on holding your mines," Snout said.

And my head, Thramel thought. "I guess you better find—"

Snout raised a hand to silence Thramel. They approached a grove of weepers and he leapt from the saddle, sprinting to the closest tree. Snout stroked its trunk, examining a branch carefully. He sniffed the tree and licked the wood. A big, dopey smile crossed his lips.

"Here!" Snout shouted and circled the tree in a strange dance. "Here, here, here."

"What are you bleating about?" Thramel leaned over the saddle and tried to see what got Snout all excited.

"They came this way." Snout held up the broken twig. He traced an upside-down "Z" carved into the trunk. "Shadow Manor. See, this is the mark for Shadow Manor. The broken twig tells the direction they went. East, inside the weeper grove."

"How long ago?"

Snout shrugged.

Gods! Why do you taunt me? He looked up, certain his lament fell on deaf ears. If not deaf, then most certainly indifferent.

"Quit pissing on the tree and let's go!" He grumbled at the pair that could hear him.

Snout sniffed and walked past in a huff.

Tracking went very slow. Snout examined several trees before finding one with similar marks. He'd sniff the ground, pausing to stare at what Thramel believed to be nothing except twigs and grass. He circled several trees before shaking his head and meandering off in an entirely different direction. They managed less than a league when sun reached midday. It almost felt like Snout deliberately led them in circles. Thramel ground his teeth and tightened his fists on the reins, sure that he would fray and snap in half.

Birds squawked overhead as they passed. *So much for any element of surprise.* Small, yellow feathered blurs darted from branch to branch, following them and chirping complaints until they were out of their territory. *Gods-damned birds, wouldn't be a mouth full to cook up.*

By nightfall they had made little progress and Thramel called a halt.

"No use getting lost trying to find where we're going," he said when Snout tried to protest.

Sleeping under the cover of the sagging branches was more difficult than in the vast open land of Yellow Valley. Moonlight created shadow puppets as a breeze blew through, swaying the branches so everything seemed more alive at night. He'd closed his eyes and began drifting into sleep, then some noise would startle him awake. Snout slept soundly, his snores competing with the rustling branches. As usual, the wolves were nowhere to be seen.

Thramel got up from his bedroll and staggered off behind a weeper. He unbuckled his belt, dropped his trousers, and urinated. The problem, his groggy mind worked over, was that once they found these runaways, how could he use them as leverage against Joanne? The *Mors Faunis* wouldn't sit on their haunches while he walked away with the captives. He didn't trust the Death Howlers not to kill him even after he helped find the woman and girl. Thramel lifted his trousers and froze. A twig snapped somewhere to his right. He buckled his belt and loosened his sword in the scabbard. Hugging the weeper, he scanned the trees and shrubs.

Wolves returned after their hunt? Or is it something else hunting us?

Another sound, the rattling of leaves only closer, approached their camp. Thramel gripped his sword hilt and drew it as quietly as he could manage, keeping vigilance. Something moved in the moonlight close to the camp. He saw a shape walking on two legs. *I should let it slit the rat-catcher's throat, but then I'll never find the girls.* Thramel moved to intercept, walking on the balls of his feet and stepping softly over the leaf ground. Not softly enough. A stick cracked under his boot and the figure stopped, staring directly at him. Then it turned and ran off, disappearing into the shadows before Thramel could catch it.

He shook Snout awake.

"Someone's out there," he said. "He came into our camp and I don't know where our little pets are to help keep watch."

"Do you think it's them?" Snout rubbed his eyes and sat up. He explained more. "The woman. Maybe she's looking for food. They've been out here a while all by themselves. No food or shelter."

What about the men following them? Thramel recalled what the Manor Lord had said.

"She's supposed to be pregnant," Thramel said. Snout nodded. "This one didn't move like a pregnant woman."

"How does a pregnant woman move?" Snout asked

Thramel mimed a big belly and waddled. "This one moved from shadow to shadow, like the Dark Mistress herself."

Snout made a circle with his fingers and spat through them.

"Don't invoke her name. Not here, not at night."

"Afraid she'll come get you?"

"Yes."

"Then you can keep the first watch while I sleep." Thramel unbuckled his belt, setting his sword aside, and lay on the bedroll, listening to Snout grumble.

"What about the thing out there?" Snout whined.

"What about it?" Thramel loosened the sword in its scabbard and kept it close at hand.

"Won't it come back? Shouldn't we at least try to find out what it is?"

"Not when you get us lost in sunlight," Thramel said, rolling away from Snout. "Shadow take me for a fool if I got lost with you by moonlight."

Once more he imagined the farm boy standing before him, sword pressed at the girl's chest. Only this time, Thramel gave the boy a nudge, shoving the blade forward.

Bernal leaned against the weeper, rubbing the side of his head. The throbbing subsided a little. It got so he could hardly think, like a thick fog settled over his thoughts. For three nights he wandered around this godsforsaken place, no food except for some nuts and berries he'd scavenged along the stream bed. He was tempted to return to the camp and steal some items, a horse even, but they were gone. He'd missed a crucial opportunity.

Cruel fickleness of gods. He crouched and listened for the sound of pursuit. The steady hum of crickets kept him company. He could thank Janus for this as well.

The same blessed luck which allowed him to track Bekka and the child after Fraylin led them into the beasts' den, flipped like an ill-fortuned coin when those boys got the jump on him, knocking him unconscious and trussed him up like a pig to slaughter. He thought it'd turned for the good when Bekka thumped the one, Ishmael, on the head, allowing Bernal to find freedom.

Then two-faced Janus spit in his eye.

On the night of his escape, Bernal waited patiently for everyone to fall asleep, leaving only one boy on watch. It usually occurred after sunset. He'd wait for the fire to die down, except there wasn't any fire. When he was about to circle around the hill and check on the camp, the soldiers had arrived. Bernal didn't know these men, but he noticed they were dispatched from Joanne's personal forces. The lightning bolt through the golden sun gave them away. They were in the valley for only one reason: to capture the Blackwood fugitives and return them back to her. Once in the Keep, he would never see his betrothed again.

One clear plan of action remained. Bernal had created a diversion, drawing the attention of the two soldiers on watch by slipping through the trees, making enough noise so they followed him and he led them on a wild chase north of the weepers. He'd dug a hole earlier, and filled it with shrub he cut with the dagger he took from Bekka. He slipped in his hole like a rabbit evading the fox. Dagger ready to jab in the eye of the first man to stumble on his position, he hunkered down and waited. Footfalls stumbled through the underbrush, almost close enough to fall into his hole, but they moved on. Night birds began to chirp and Bernal waited a little longer.

Once again Janus got the better of him and he fell asleep, waking with the sun overhead. Then he clamored out of his hole and ran back to where he spotted the soldiers. Charred remains of a camp fire marred where they stayed the night.

He climbed the hill to the campsite, keeping to the cover of large rocks, arriving to find another abandoned campsite. The children were gone, stolen away while he was playing hide-and-go-seek. He sulked in the weepers, ready to give himself up for dead. The dagger's sharp edge against his wrists, a quick swipe to end it all—he would curse Janus in person. As he was making up his mind, more familiar faces showed up in his woods.

Sweet Janus swiveled her head and puckered her lips, begging for a kiss. Joanne's tracker, Snout, slept under the same trees as Bernal. Like the goddess herself strolled the paths, his luck changed, but was it for good or ill? He tried to get a closer look, to verify that his assumption was more than idle hopes from a muddled mind, though the snores were enough to identify the old hound. Snout's companion spotted Bernal and Bernal ran away, rather than pick a fight.

Although there weren't any other soldiers with them, there must be a connection to the ones from the previous night and Snout's arrival.

They all want to take my precious Bekka away. They can't have her. She is mine by god-rights, even if she carries that bastard creature in her belly. Some rue root will clear up that disease sure as water washes away shit.

First, he had to find her before anyone else did. The problem in this plan was he had no idea which direction they went or where they were headed. He didn't learn much of where his captors came from, though he was almost certain they were Nemorians. *Narrowed down the needle and the hay field.* Once more, it would take Janus' own luck to find her.

Sure enough, the two-faced bitch stared him in the eye and kicked him in the groin.

Bernal heard a twig snap to his right. He turned and saw a wolf standing twenty yards away, except wolves didn't walk on two legs. *Mors Faunis? What's it doing out—*

A sword tip jabbed against his back. Bernal straightened up, keeping as still as possible with a blade close enough to cut out a kidney. Strange huffing noises sounded from over his shoulder and the distant *Mors*

Faunis replied in kind. Bernal felt his legs weaken. An encounter with Death Howlers didn't end pleasantly.

"My name is Bernal Werden," he said, hoping they understood his language. "Shadow Manor Guardian—"

The point poked his ribs and a warm trickle of blood ran down his back. Bernal winced, but kept his mouth shut. As the first *Mors Faunis* drew closer, a hand fell on his shoulder, shoving him further into the grove. The metal wolves head leaned in enough for Bernal to see the dark holes where eyes should peer out at him, eyes he couldn't see. The *Mors Faunis* retreated and flashed a hand signal. The sword point moved away, but the strong grip remained on his shoulder, guiding him in a direction back towards Snout's camp.

Bernal swallowed back laughter. The irony of the gods. *Oh my love, we are destined to be together, if they don't kill me.*

"Look at what the wolves dragged in," Thramel said. "Didn't I tell you not to play with your food?"

Snout snorted. He had informed Thramel of the former Manor Guard's position and his role in chasing down the escaped rebels.

Bernal grinned. He was grimy, smelled like a wild cat pissed on him and then tried to bury him. The left pant leg was torn up to his knee and his tunic had several rips along the seams, the right side nearly falling off. Dark circles formed under his eyes and his hair stuck up in duck tails around his ears.

"I must be in the company of some grand, illustrious figure," Bernal said. "Sleeping under the stars, nothing but bedrolls and accompanied by a hunting party of mutes and a hound. What is your name, oh mighty lord of the—"

Thramel backhanded him. The meaty smack sent Bernal's head rocking back. He would have toppled over if not for the Death Howler catching him. Bernal sucked in his lip, a child about to cry. The grin faltered momentarily before returning. His eyes burned with hatred. He touched his lip, dabbing at the blood that trickled at the corner.

"Choose your words carefully, soldier." Thramel rested his hand on his sword pommel. "As far as anyone else knows, you died out here looking for the woman and child. We came across your remains, didn't we Snout."

"Wild cat got him. Or maybe the girl shifted and ripped his guts out. Very messy."

"Kill me and you won't find her," Bernal said, locking eyes with Thramel. "Not even this old hound could sniff them out."

"Sounds like someone is trying to make himself valuable." Thramel gave Snout a wink. "By the look of him, he's alone, lost and confused. He failed his mission. Poor bastard doesn't even have his sword!" Thramel laughed and Snout chuckled. "I've seen a pot of piss worth more than this man's life. I wonder if we start cutting off fingers and toes, what precious information he might have for us."

Bernal spat.

"You can yank my cock all you like, but that ain't the way to get me to spill for you."

"I'll do more than yank it." Thramel drew his sword and placed the tip on Bernal's groin. "I'll shave the bugger so you can piss through a hole. Tell me where she is, or where you think she is, and don't lie. Snout here will smell it and then I get to slicing."

"Gone."

"You're going to have to be more specific." Thramel slid the blade down over the front of the guard's trousers. Bernal tried to back away, but the *Mors Faunis* held him. "Dead gone? Run off gone? Swallowed by Moko?"

Bernal shook his head.

"Quit trying to get me off and I will tell you."

Thramel stepped back.

"Two boys took her and the girl," he said. "Several nights back they ambushed us in the dark, killing Dayrll and knocking me out."

"He's telling the truth," Snout said.

"Why didn't they kill you?"

Bernal shrugged.

"They plied me for information. I told them about the girl, that they were skin-changers, but they didn't believe me. I hope the girl turns on them and tears their throats out." Bernal turned his head and spat. "So they kept me tied up in a tent, but I could hear them arguing. They had other children in their camp, too. It's like they were war refugees trying to make a living in the hills."

Thramel heard stories about older siblings taking brothers and sisters out into the wild lands so they didn't get sold off as slaves. These little bands didn't always last long, succumbing to starvation or whatever other tragedy the gods planned for them.

"What were they arguing about?"

"Mostly what to do with me. I think the older one wanted to take me to the weepers and cut my throat. He didn't trust the woman, either. The other one lacked the smarts. I didn't get a good look at him."

"How did you get away? Don't tell me they just let you walk out of their camp."

"I escaped when the woman tried to kill me."

Thramel laughed.

"Did she use her tooth and claws?"

"No, a knife."

"Where were they camped?"

"Up on the hillside. I can take you there, but you won't find anything."

Thramel looked at Snout.

"I might be able to pick up their trail," the rat-catcher said. "Depends on how long ago they left."

"Two nights back."

"Any idea their direction?"

"They didn't pass this way… I would have seen them."

Thramel sheathed his sword.

"Get some food and drink in him. We leave at sunrise." The *Mors Faunis* released Bernal and Snout led him to the sacks of food. Thramel approached the Death Howler and whispered. "If he tries to run away, gut him."

The *Mors Faunis* made no reply.

Makes me wonder if there's anyone home or I'm talking to a tin can.

The hillside was empty as Bernal had claimed. Pickets and a makeshift stable for horses, a partially completed hovel built into the hillside, and a garden, marked the signs of occupation. While Snout sniffed around the camp, searching for which direction their quarry escaped, Thramel examined the garden. Mounds of freshly built dirt followed the neat little rows.

Jarrod, he pondered, kneeling beside the tilled ground. *Stupid farm boy knew his way around dirt and shit, but he never could hold a sword right. How he killed eight of my men in the tower was an amazing feat... No! The boy had to be God touched. A god obsessed with war and death.*

"When I find you. I'm going to kill him myself." Thramel stood up and kicked over the mounds of dirt, trampling the rows until nothing remained except his boot prints.

"I think I smelled where they're going!" Snout shouted from down the south side of the hill. Thramel stood at the edge, watching Snout crawl along the ground, following the switch back and stand at an attention, looking east.

East. Thramel scratched his chin. *Heartwood Pines.*

"Could it be him?" Thramel squinted his eyes against as the bright sun broke through the clouds.

"Who?" Bernal asked, standing next to Thramel and chewing dried fruit.

Thramel ignored him. *The gods wouldn't be so kind, or cruel.*

"The children should slow them down," Bernal said. "We could catch up to them in a day or two."

"How many were there?"

"Five," Bernal said. "Six counting the changeling whelp."

"Bring the horses," Thramel said.

Bernal shoved the rest of the dried fruit into his mouth and bowed, flailing out his arm dramatically. He slunk away under Thramel's hot glare. Thramel turned back to the torn-up garden. *Five.* The number rang true. Again, it seemed too good. Of all the places to find them. Thramel shook his head. *No time for fancies. Get the girl and the child, Shadow grant me that boon.*

"Snout!" The tracker looked up, dopey eyes wide, a wildness dancing in them. "That nose of yours better not fail or I'll cut it off and feed it to the wyrm."

Snout brayed laughter.

"Let's hunt some children." Thramel grinned. They were close enough he could almost smell them.

CHAPTER FOURTEEN

Prophesy. To speak vision into words. To explain the unexplainable. When regarded as truth, words strangle what should be as quickly as the creeper vine suffocates the mighty Redwood. When proven false, regaled as petty words mistrusted until swayed by more foretelling. Thus creeps fear and mistrust and zealot-like adherence to the implied meaning, distorting the possible with the not possible. Devastation in the wake of creation.
— *From* "Treatise on Prophesy."
Menrva

"Milady, the regiments are gathered and awaiting your inspection." Captain Davis stood in the door way to Joanne's chamber. A young battle veteran, short cropped black hair, fair-skinned and a strong jaw. A small scar under the corner of his left eye marred his perfection. Despite the scar, Joanne found his appearance attractive, in a naïve way. Were she a young tavern maid, she would've fallen into his arms. She could easily use her power to coerce him into her bed. Since Fraum's death, Joanne has had her share of lovers. No man, though, sated her burning desire, her thirst to possess that which was denied. Only the divine truly satisfied her. The seductive draw of the shadow. Still, Captain Davis had his own intriguing traits.

"Thank you, Captain." Joanne strapped a belt around her waist and sheathed daggers at her hips. She knew he waited for her command to dismiss him. He would stand there all day and night, wavering from exhaustion until she gave the word. "Do you find me attractive?"

"Milady, I-I—"

"A simple question." She looked at his brown eyes, a lovely color that would impress the simplest girl. "Yes or no."

"Yes," he said. "You are a beautiful woman, your Highness."

"Since you find me to your liking." She walked over to him, placing a hand on his firm chest. His heart beat quickly like a bird flapping its wings to escape the cat's claws. His eyes remained forward, staring at some distant point as though Joanne's actions were not distracting. She leaned in, smelling the astringent soap he used to shave the stubble from his chin. "Would you tell me all your secrets?"

"Secrets, milady?" He swallowed, eyes widening. He trembled slightly. She could tell he wanted to slink away. Duty held him firmly in place. Joanne smiled at his confusion, and his fear. Fear was important. Fear inspired awe and awe led to loyalty. A loyal army was a disciplined army. Discipline won wars. "I'm not sure I understand."

"Sure you do. Let me give you an example." She leaned in closer, her inner thigh brushing his inner thigh as she dragged her fingertips down to his stomach. His breathing changed, becoming panicked, heavy breaths, almost groans. "Where do you like to be touched? To bite? Feel my nails tearing into your back as I cry your name?" She stood on the tips of her toes, whispering into his ear as her leaned his head away. "What terrible things have you done to a woman? What promises have you broken? How did you crush her fragile heart? Oh, and most importantly, Captain, where are you marching to in a fortnight?"

"I've done nothing wrong." He was sweating and licking his lips. "I swear by the Mother."

"Lies," Joanne hissed, ripping his sword out of the sheath. It clattered to the floor next to the hearth. "Lieutenant, bring in the girl."

Lieutenant Ferns half-carried, half-dragged in a distraught girl, weeping and moaning around a gag in her mouth. Dark purple bruises marred her cheek and her split lip bleed around the cloth. She shot startled glances back and forth between Joanne and Captain Davis. Captain Davis went pale.

"So now you understand, Captain," Joanne said, circling the air with her index finger. Two Death Howlers stepped out from their silent corners and gripped his arms. Captain Davis stood, dumbfounded by the events happening so quickly. "You should know better than to use pillow talk to discuss important plans. This maid may have been sending warning signs to those who usurped what rightfully belongs to me. You know what that is called, don't you Captain?"

He nodded, legs giving out and was held upright by his captors.

"Fortunately for you, she was only writing love notes and placing them under a rock where presumably you would discover them later," Joanne said. "I cannot have word that one of my Captains flaps his tongue so willingly." She drew a dagger and held the blade between her fingertips. "So I'm going to cut it out."

One *Mors Faunis* twisted Davis' arms behind his back and forced him to his knees while the other pried open his jaw. Joanne caught his tongue between her fingers, dry and wiggly like a worm drying up on a stone. She yanked it clear of his teeth and snipped it quickly at the root. Blood poured out of Davis' mouth, puddling on the floor. Groaning, choking sounds came from his throat. She tossed his tongue at the maid's feet. The girl screeched and tried to scurry away, but Lieutenant Ferns held onto her. Her eyes rolled up to the whites and she went limp in his arms.

Joanne grabbed a hot poker from the fire place.

"Keep your mouth open before you drown in your own blood." She stuck the red tip on the sliced stub. It sizzled, filling the room with burnt flesh. Davis screamed and bit down on the metal. Teeth cracked. She pulled the poker back, striping off flesh from his lips melted on the heated sides. Joanne set the poker back in its stand and went to the trunk by her bed. She opened it, lifting up a silver wolf's mask. Davis stared at it in tears wetting his cheeks. "Put this on him. I will be there to complete the ceremony in a few moments."

They dragged him out of the room.

"No use in wasting a good warrior," Joanne said.

"What shall I do with her?"

"Give her to the men to temper their desires." Joanne wiped blood off her dagger with a cloth on the hearth. "When you are finished, Captain Ferns, prepare my soldiers for travel. Also, find yourself a suitable lieutenant."

"Yes, your Highness." Ferns bowed and lifted the unconscious girl over his shoulder, carrying her out of the room.

"Discipline and loyalty," she said to her father's painting and sheathed her dagger.

Dark clouds rolled in from the east. A cold wind carried the smell of rain. Static energy gathered in the air and she noted the streaks of lightening in the distant clouds as she stepped out onto the balcony. Black banners bearing the golden sun insignia dotted the parade ground below, flapping in the breeze. Joanne gripped the metal arrow catcher and surveyed her soldiers. Four thousand shield bearers and twenty-five hundred spears formed up into ten units spread across the dead pastures in a vast sea of dark blue and silver. Another thirty-five hundred archers, each carrying two quiver full of arrows, flanked the shields in two groups. She had recalled the majority of her Nemus invasion force from the surrounding manors, leaving behind a small occupying battalion to battle the rebels. Twice the numbers remained in Septum, as assurance against invasion from the outer regions.

With Nemus nearly in her grip, her next step was to conquer the north and south. To accomplish the task, she needed as much of her army intact here in Nemus before marching south. A messenger returned late in the morning bearing news of success in Elysium.

Everything was flowing according to her Mistress' plans.

Only Heartwood Pines remained to be pacified.

Once they view the magnitude of my power, they will bend or I will break them.

"General Hale, what are the scouting reports?" Joanne asked.

"I apologize, your Highness, but we have no accurate account," General Hale replied. "None of my scouts have returned. The reports from your brother during the last incursion suggested that they could muster a force no larger than two thousand."

"Those reports are over four years old," Joanne said. "Dispatch a dozen scouts if you must. I require a full report on the enemy's number, strengths and weakness before we arrive. The rain will delay our progress and provide your scouts with ample time to gather information."

"They will be sent at once, your Highness." General Hale signaled a messenger who gave him a roll of paper. He wrote a quick note and sent the messenger away.

"Have them prepare my horse." Joanne surveyed the parade ground, nodding, satisfied with what she saw. "We march at midday."

Covered wagons rolled over the hard crusted sand. Wheels rattled and jounced at a steady speed, kicking up a dust tail visible for at least a league. It was an unavoidable risk Huron wished he could have avoided. Children of Elysium huddled against the wooden planks beneath canvas covering and protecting them from the sun's glare. Stripped of his armor, Huron rode beside the cart, a white towel wrapped around his head. Three days under the angry sun cut into their supply of water, leaving a few skins to be rationed between the seven of them and a barrel for the horses. He wished he could ration more, but the horses need to drink to survive. Without horses, they would be hard dried corpses wasting away in the desert heat.

Donn would have a new flavor on his platter. I wonder what a god's heart would taste like.

A young, black-haired girl peeked out of the canvas. Yellow-tinged eyes looked at him like a hungry cat. She gripped the edge of the cart, finger nails long and jagged clicking against the wood.

"When are we stopping?"

"Not now." Huron tried to keep the irritation from his voice.

"When?" She whined. "All this bouncing around and I have to pee."

Short, prickle plants, brown spider grass, and twisted thorn trees grew in clusters marking the edge of desert and plains. Ground squirrels poked tiny round heads out of burrows to watch the wagons slowly move past. He could see for leagues ahead unobstructed. Foothills waited in the distance like rotted teeth in a brittle jaw. Beyond them was Nemus.

"Please." Her small voice pleaded.

Huron frowned, contemplating the innocent face and rode up to the lead horse, gripping the reins, he slowed the wagon. The young girl shoved back the canvas and the children poured out, jumping down into the sands. Huron dismounted and took a water skin from the wagon, unstopped the lid and drank three swallows.

"Cut back on their water rations," he told the girl. "We cannot stop again until nightfall."

"We hardly drink enough—"

"This was our fourth stop since we started well after sunrise. We're moving too slow," Huron said. *They are children.* He shut his mouth, stopping his diatribe of harsh criticism. The girl's shoulders slumped and she stared at her bare feet. None of them wore shoes or stockings, the result of being stolen from their sleeping beds. "Go water the horses."

"They don't like me." She whined, digging her toe into the sand. "We were never allowed close to the stables because the horses acted strange, stomping and shaking their heads."

"You have to earn their trust."

"How?"

"Give them something they want." He handed her a pail.

A strong gust of wind swirled the sand. Several children cried out and hid in the wagon, drawing the canvas over them so the tiny grains pattered against it. Horses whickered and danced, knocking the water bucket from the girl's hand.

There's something not right about this wind. Huron pulled the corner of the rag over his eyes and nose. Gritty sand scrapped against his red, chaffed skin. As quickly as it started, the storm ended. The unease remained. His skin prickled, the hair on his arms rising. A tinny, scorched metal smell filled his nose and his teeth ached. He faced south, drawn to the unseen force… and then he saw why.

A hooded man stood in the prickly thorn bushes, face hidden by the brown cowl wrapped around his nose and mouth. The stranger crouched, hand on sword at his hips. Brown eyes darted around. Huron drew his twin swords, preparing to *Reap and Sow*. The new arrival's eyes widened. He stood up, shorter than Huron by over a head, and pulled the cowl down, revealing a look of desperation.

"Brother Agni?" Huron lowered his guard for an instance before returning to his stance. "Or are you some trick of the Shadow?"

"I assure I'm no trick." He took out an identical soul pendant attached to a silver chain around his neck. Blue light swirled within the crystal. He tucked the crystal back under his tunic. "I don't remember the last time my feet touched this strange world." He stepped over the cactus, catching his balance as a chunk of dirt broke off unexpectedly.

"The ground seems to shift beneath me. Almost as if I have been at sea for a very long time."

"That we have, Brother. The world is not as we once knew it to be," Huron said, clutching Agni's extended arm and pulled him into an embrace. "What brings you here? Is everything well?"

"Mother." Agni frowned, shaking his head. "The last I spoke with her, she had insisted I come to you at once. As is my duty, I obeyed her, to bring you this." He took out a scroll from inside his tunic and handed it to the Blades Man. The wax seal was already broken. He unrolled it and began reading.

"Where did she get this from?"

"Menrva's rooms."

"Menrva gave this to Mother?"

"No," Agni said. "Do you have something to drink? This heat is oppressive."

Huron tossed him a water skin. Agni took a long swallow.

"I sought the Prophetess at her home," he continued, handing the skin back to Huron. It was woefully low. "I didn't find her there. Mother had us look in her rooms and that is where she found the scroll."

"Where is Mother now?"

"I left her at the Palace." Agni hung his head, knuckling his brow. "Angry Brothers and Sisters called for her at the throne room. I left her with them."

"Who?"

Agni shook his head.

"I couldn't see. She made me leave—I shouldn't have left her."

"You did well, brother, don't fret for Mother. She is strong and *every* child knows her power."

"I should return and attend to her."

"No. Stay." Huron placed a hand on his shoulder. "We shall go back together when my task is finished."

"Yet, Mother—"

"You can do nothing more for her. Besides, you found me through the Pool of Reflection. If you return through it, then the others will know you were helping me. This would draw the attention of she-who-dwells-in-shadows and put my entire mission at risk."

"You mean interference with the Struggle." There was no judgement in his voice. Part of him must've known, especially since he was the personal messenger to Mother. One would have to be addle brained as well as blind not to connect the requests made by her.

"Our very existence interferes with the natural order of events. Should what is written here be accurate, then Menrva is gone, most likely taken by the one I fight against." Huron held up the scroll with the seal broken. Mother's hands must had done so. "You didn't read its content, did you?"

"No." Agni stiffened, obviously annoyed by the question. "I brought it directly to you."

"Peace, brother, I meant no offense," Huron said. "I only ask to discover your knowledge of the matter. It is imperative that I guide the one who will save us all."

"You have chosen a new Champion," Agni said, brows furrowing. Huron nodded.

"This one is very different from the last. She only destroys while this one protects. Through him, all life will be persevered."

The girl gave a shout. Huron hurried over, hoping the horse wasn't trampling her. He found it licking her hands as she giggled. She stroked the horse behind the ears. "You were right," she said. "Now he acts like I'm his salt lick."

"I could really use your assistance," Huron said to Agni, patting him on the shoulder, "getting these children to safety."

"These are no ordinary children," Agni said, taking in the curious faces peering at him. Iridescent yellow and green eyes measuring him, chins raised as the scented the air.

"Yes, I know that very well. Which is why I am keeping them away from *her*."

"Very well, I will gladly assist you, Brother."

"We rest here a moment. Eat." Huron opened up a crate with salted meats and took a smaller water skin, handing it to the youngest child. She went to take it from him, but he pulled it back. "Don't drink too much. After he eats, we ride non-stop until night fall."

The girl nodded and he let her have the skin. She smiled, drinking a small mouth-full before passing it to the next child.

A crescent moon hung overhead adorned by stars. The bright twinkles reminded him of Mother residing above in the Palace somewhere in that space of darkness between the light. Nights seemed longer than what Huron remembered. He wrapped a cloak around his shoulders, leaning close to the fire and caressed the soul pendant around his neck. From what Agni told him, Mother's plans were compromised, which meant that the other Children knew he was here, or would soon enough.

What's going on up there? What I'd give to know you were safe, Mother. He opened the scroll again and read it. Mother taught him how to decipher the old language. Reading the First's script for those not of the First, those chosen by Father and Mother to Ascend, was very rare. Menrva was the only other Ascended he knew who could read the language of the First. Mother always favored him, viewing him more than the brute warrior set on killing and winning battles. Battles were the result of poor political strategies devised by the weak minded, a failure to accomplish the goal through outsmarting the opponent and obtaining the higher power before they knew they had lost it. Order was a sign of intelligent creatures. War was for the enslaved, the oppressed, to rise above their circumstances. Mother believed this sentiment, which was why she taught him how to read the First's script; how to think instead of mindlessly taking orders.

As a man, he fought battles for a ruler and a land, neither of which no longer existed. As a god, once more he embarked on a war, but one that held much meaning. A war for survival of both the Created and the Gods, if what was in the scroll was accurate.

The children slept in the covered wagons. One softly wept while her companions whispered comforting words. *Children shall weep and gnash teeth at the failings of their Mother.* Weren't these children of the Created also children of Mother and Father? The Ruin Prophesy, as he understood it, didn't encompass the Gods alone. Everything would be destroyed.

"I have not drunk fermented liquids in many centuries, I almost forgot the taste." Agni sat across from him, holding a wine skin and drinking heartily from it. "And the effects on the head."

"Partake too much and the morning light will be like a spear jabbed between your eyes."

Agni nodded and grinned.

"That advice comes much too late, I fear." He offered the skin to Huron, who turned it down. "I don't mean to pry, but what is it you read? I know Mother seemed very distraught after finding the scroll. I hope I hadn't risked my well-being coming here for a silly love note."

"I swear to you it is no mere trinket, Brother." Huron tapped the page of the scroll. "Here is a message from Menrva regarding prophesy."

"Which one? Sister Menrva was very fond of dreaming up stories regarding our demise. I don't know if she half-believed her own words, but she stirred up Father and Mother enough for them to record her words into the Book."

The Book, as the children referred to it was the Tome of Essence. A large history of the First men. Huron had read most of it while learning the script.

"Sometimes I wish they were stories," he said. "Especially this one."

"Enlighten me."

Huron hesitated.

"I believe it would be safer for you the little you know about it."

"That bad?" Agni shrugged and swallowed three more gulps from the skin, wiping his chin where it dribbled. "I am going to turn in for the night. May Mother watch over us." He lay out a bedroll beside the cart and began snoring.

Huron continued reading the scroll, committing every word to memory. Then he tossed the paper into the fire where it curled up, smoldered, and feed the flames. He looked up at the stars and hoped Mother was looking down on him. A shiver ran down his back. Part of him sensed nothing was as it should be among heavens and creation.

Just a little longer, then I may return home.

Menrva placed a hand on the cold stone. She couldn't see anything, but could feel the water beneath her bare feet, hear it drip from the ceiling. A five-count passed between each echoing plink. The water smelled brackish, like she was being pickled in her prison. A shiver ran through her and goose flesh poked out on her skin. The only time keeper she had was the consistent drip every five count.

One thousand and fifty-nine. That's how long she had been awake. She couldn't tell day from night. It was always dark. Sometimes she'd stub her toe moving around the cell. She tried counting the number of steps between walls, but kept losing track as the next drip added onto her time count. Keeping both sets distinct was difficult for her deprived mind. The room had one dry spot where the floor slopped upward. Curling her knees to her chest and leaning against the hard, cold, stone wall, she slept, sometimes waking when her face plunged in the cold, brackish water.

One thousand and sixty. She counted partly to keep her sanity. The numbers in her head were like an anchor to reality that swum in and out; they were the moon drawing the tide and washing away everything she knew, leaving bits of grainy sand of what was once her existence. The darkness tried to swallow her. Even with her eyes open in the dark, white flashes flickered across her vision, a marking of a new prophetic sight to fill in the blindness. She fought the visions until her head hurt and wetness dripped from her nose, leaving a coppery taste in the back of her mouth. She fought them because she had no way to record what she viewed. Without her fingers trailing a quill across blank parchment, her mouth would force the phrases out, like bubbling gas that would explode her insides unless released. Speaking prophecy was more dangerous than recording it on parchment. Parchment she could burn. Spoken words may reach the wrong ears triggering an alternate branch in the Prophesy, creating a dual paradox where one vision's truth and another vision's contradicting truth, rather than cancel each other out, birthed a new path.

This catastrophic event was already happening. Ruin and Ascension grew on parallel courses, both existing to contradict one another. Ascension dealt with the rise of created humanity, while Ruin spoke of the fall of the gods. How could one ascend into what no longer existed? The resulting prophesy was Transcendence, as Menrva called it. The very idea was like cold hands clenching her heart. The end consequence was unclear to her. It could be the undoing of everything Mother and Father built.

One thousand and sixty-one. She huddled in her dry corner, legs drawn up and rocked back and forth. Her head felt like a ripe melon with someone thumping on the rind to test how hollow she was inside.

One thousand— grinding of stone against stone. She placed her hands over her ears, blocking out the grating sound and clenching her teeth. She watched a stone slab slid open. Grey light slipped inside, too bright for her sensitive eyes. So long in the dark, the light felt unnatural, burning her. Menrva pressed her face against her knee.

Splashing approached her, not the simple drip that echoed in her chamber, but something larger sloshed towards her. She slunk against the wall, pressing into it until her spine hurt. Gloved hands gripped her wrists and she screeched, a strong force hauling her to her feet. She turned away from the light.

She set her heels against the stone in a futile effort to resist. The hands dragged her forward, catching her into a pair of strong arms.

"Open your eyes, Menrva," demanded a strangely familiar voice— one she had heard countless times in her nightmares. "Look at me. Come on, open them."

"No," Menrva said, shaking her head.

The arms lifted her up, half-carrying, half-dragging her across the stones, her toes dragging in the water. Powerless, like a rag doll toted by a child, she was removed from the chamber. Stone ground against stone. Her soles touched dry ground. Quivering legs refused to hold her up and she collapsed, her rear striking hard wood, jarring teeth together. Bright light shone through her eye-lids. A white flash struck through her head. She gasped and forced her eyes to open before the vision could begin.

Standing before her, dressed in a black cloak and leather armor, Dandulain, the Mistress of Shadows, smiled at her. "That's a good girl."

"You shouldn't have taken me away," Menrva said, teeth chattering. The air around the goddess felt colder than the dank chamber. "Mother will be upset."

"Mother has other problems of her own to worry about." The Mistress of Shadows yanked Menrva to her feet and plunked her down on a cushioned wooden chair, angled to the corner of a small table. The room was otherwise bare except for cupboards lining the walls and a single door. The Mistress of Shadows opened one cupboard and took out what appeared to be a book. She set it on the table. "Besides, you are going to help me."

Menrva gasped. "Where did you get this?"

"I borrowed it." She smiled, one lacking mirth. "Mother was so very generous to lend it to me."

"I don't believe you." *Mother rarely let the Tome of Essence out of her sight. Only a few could actually understand the language.*

"I didn't bring you here to *believe* anything." The Mistress of Shadows sat on the edge of the table, taking out a dagger. She twirled the point on the tip of her finger. "You have one purpose. To read."

"Why would I do that?"

"Oh, you poor fool." The Mistress of Shadows slammed the dagger point into the table. Then she grabbed Menrva's face, turning her chin up so she stared into dark eyes glistening with menace. "I see the pain, the way you force your thoughts away. You fight to hide what you cannot control." She rubbed the blood crusted under Menrva's nose with a gloved thumb. "Do you think you resisted the visions this entire time? Oh no, dear Sister, you fought valiantly, but as you slept, you mumbled. The words were faint, but clear. So very clear. Here, let me recite a snippet I heard fall your very own lips. *The dreamer speaks of Shadow and Light. Soul binds to flesh to walk among the Created, bearing ruin.*"

Menrva's heart grew heavy and she wanted to crawl into a ball. That was a section of the Transcendence Prophecy. The Mistress of Shadows must have heard it from her. Only Mother knew of the prophecy, though not what it meant. She wrote it all on a scroll secreted away in her rooms.

"I know that we, dear Sister, are more than capable of becoming as we once were. My own mentor proved it by creating me." The Mistress of Shadows clapped her hands together in mock adoration, fluttering her eyelids and puckering her lips. After the brief display, the predatory glare returned. "Either you read to me what is written in this book about becoming flesh again, or I will dump you into the deepest hole and listen to your mad ravings and record them myself."

"Please," Menrva said, eyes brimming with tears. *Don't make me the harbinger of the end!* Her lips trembled as she spoke slowly, staring at the single door. "Don't do this."

"Or, I have another solution." She lifted two charms, dangling from chains cinched around her neck and held them out. Menrva recognized the black, flat disk and blue crystal swaying in front of her nose. She had seen them too often in her visions, suspended in darkness like they were now, gripped in black gloves: the disc of darkness and star of creation. The Mistress of Shadows placed the two pendants next to the Tome of Essence. Taking the dagger from the table, she waved it loosely around. "I could end all creation by destroying these little icons. Father told me how the universe is held together by a thread and would unravel at the cutting of these simple strings. Those were his last words before I stuck my daggers into his eyes and pried his brain out of his skull. I guess these must be the strings he spoke of, since it was by this power here that all of that out there was created."

She held the dagger point over the disc and star.

"Shall we find out if he told the truth?"

Menrva closed her eyes, squeezing out tears.

"Have it your way." The Mistress of Shadows raised the dagger higher until her arms were fully stretched, poised to bring the point down.

"No!" Menrva gripped the Mistress of Shadow's arm, too weak to prevent the downward thrust, but diverting it enough so the blade struck wood giving a loud *thunk!*

The Mistress of Shadow's eyebrows raised, lips curled, and a mad light in her eye.

What am I doing? Menrva's chin rested on her chest, tears dripping off her cheeks. *Better for her to destroy us all!*

"I—I will read for you."

The Mistress of Shadow snatched up the disc of darkness and star of creation from the table. She smiled. "I knew you would see it my way."

White desert sands changed into yellowed grass. Short prickle bushes gave way to multiple spikey flowers, white and yellow mixed with orange. Butter flies flitted among the blooms chased. Bees hummed madly as the cart rumbled past. Several small birds fluttered rapid wings and lapped at the sweet nectar. In the distant, foothills rose in the forefront of an even larger formation stretching up to lose its head in the clouds. The Mountains of Dawn, known to Huron and Agni as the Dragon's Teeth, marked the entrance to the fire of the Desert of Sorrow, which had lengthened by several leagues since they last strode the mortal coil.

Long-legged antelopes grazed in a herd of twenty, circled around another four fawns. The children leaned against the wagon side, eager to run among them. They would have chased one down and devoured it if he allowed them the chance.

"That stag has antlers bigger than some of you," Huron said. The stag lifted his head, a mouth full of grass as he warily watched them. "He'll spear you before you got close enough to spook his herd."

"My parents used to take me out hunting," the girl said. "We took down creatures twice his size."

"That experience will benefit you on another day."

"We are just so bored." The girl huffed, laying her head on her arms. "All we do is ride in this wagon from sun up to sundown."

"Would you rather run alongside it?"

"No."

"Thank the Mother for your respite and be quiet."

The girl gave a frustrated grumble and ducked back inside the wagon canvas.

"Did you have any children when you walked among the created?" Agni asked. "Before your Ascension, of course."

"No," Huron said. "I ascended without siring an heir to my destructive path. Which is why I regret creating any after I ascended."

Agni nodded and they rode along in silence.

By midday the clear sky turned black as a large shadow of birds circled above. Black birds cawed, gathering more from the wispy grass. They made a dark funnel rising up and then flew east. Smoke gathered beyond, puffing up into grey billowed clouds.

"What do you think it is?" Agni asked.

"A sign of battle." Pleas made in the Blades Man's name tugged at him. Cries of blessing for a brave death. Prayers for strength to bring victory. Voices rang in his head like wine fumes intoxicating, provocative. The draw of blood and steel. "Those birds go to feast on the fallen."

"We should continue on." A nervous timber shook Agni's voice.

"Remain here with the children." He heeled the mare into a canter. "I must find out who is fighting. This could benefit our cause."

"We interfere too much in the Struggle!" Agni shouted in vain. Huron galloped beyond earshot, focused on the sky. Black birds continued to caw overhead, forming a large cloud and he its shadow below. Dandulain once used the eyes of such creatures to spy on him and destroy his work. He watched the patterns for any that may stray from the murder gathering. None were discernable. *It is too late to concern myself now. She may be watching me or not. If she is, let her see me and not the children in the wagon.*

He continued on, closing in on the source of the clouds.

Smoke thickened, rising from a two-story house. Huron stopped a good distance away and observed the events. Thirty soldiers wearing dark blue uniforms and chainmail rampaged through the fields, launching pitch coated arrows. Several struck the house's side and caught the wood shingles ablaze. Fire broke out on the roof and bloomed on the walls where more arrows marked it. A man screamed, flaming shaft jutting from his chest, fire crawling up his neck, as he fell from a shattered window. Other defenders, greatly outnumbered, charged a small group of archers, cutting them down, and retreating to the cover of the house.

Huron heeled his mare into a trot, then a sprint, closing the distance. The orange sun on the soldiers' cloaks marked them as the same factions that burnt Elysium. Rage boiled up inside of him. He drew his blade, loping off the head of the first man. Blood spurted from the decapitated neck. Two more fell to his blade, struck down from behind, before the attackers turned to face the new threat. Huron charged a cluster of archers. Bows twanged and hastily aimed arrows flew past. His mare knocked one man over as he batted aside a sword aimed for his thigh.

A great cry rose up as men charged from the burning house, taking advantage of the confusion to launch a counter-attack. The soldiers bearing the orange sun tried to re-form into a defensive line. Huron cut a swath through them, scattering them like flies from a corpse. An arrow grazed his left bicep. He continued to hack away while blood flowed down his arm. The battle ended as the last soldier fell. The battle rush filled him and he circled his mare around, seeking another foe to kill. His chest heaved and his arm burned. All around lay bodies in dark uniforms. Blood soaked the ground, the groans of the dying filled the air, along with sweat and urine.

The defenders, twelve in all, many dressed in thread bare gray uniforms, mismatched armor, and pitted weapons stared at him. A young man, face streaked with blood and dirt stepped forward, sheathing his sword.

"Gods bless you," he said, taking a knee. "We owe you our lives. If you hadn't arrived when you did, we would all have died inside my father's house."

"Why were these men attacking you?" Huron asked.

"They belong to Joanne, new master of the land, or so she claims. My name is Keith and I'm a warden of the south post, overseeing the reconstruction of the South Manor. These are my men, or what remains of them. We were told to surrender our posts and join their ranks, or forfeit our lives." He folded his arms and grimaced. "Some of the men did. Those who resisted were hunted down, their families threatened or killed."

Huron inspected the rag-tag group. All were young men, faces bearded or covered in stubble. Clothes hung off lean bodies, gaunt faces beaming with the joy of victory.

"When was your last good meal?"

"How long ago did we raid that supply off that caravan?" Keith asked a youth closer to swaddling clothes than shaving.

"A moon ago," the youth replied.

"Mother smiles on you," Huron said. "You are about to dine well."

Keith, the first warden of South Manor helped his men tend the wounded and buried their fallen brothers while Huron brought the children and Agni up with the remains of their supplies. They cooked barley soup and drank the remains of the wine. The girl cleaned and bandaged his arm.

"You should be more careful," she said. "Or at least wear your armor next time."

As the children loaded back into the cart and Huron prepared to leave, Keith approached.

"It's no longer safe for us to stay here," he said. "Can we travel with you?"

"We are going far east. I'm not sure we have enough food for everyone."

"Food is not a problem," Keith said. "We know of some outposts where food and weapons are stored. We tried raiding one, but our numbers were too few. That is how they found us at my father's home."

"I am only one man," Huron said. "How do you expect to attack these places with fourteen?"

"Don't worry about numbers," Keith said. "I know we can get more men to join us. We broke up into smaller groups so it would be harder to catch us all in one spot. I tried to rally them for a strike, but none would join out of fear of exposing their hiding places."

"Why would they now?"

"Hope," Keith said, clapping Huron on the shoulder. "Hope is their reason."

CHAPTER FIFTEEN

Parched soil drank up the rain as quickly as it fell. Large drops plinked against hundreds of metal helms and shields. Grim faces stood in silent ranks, glaring across the vast, empty field, soon to run red. They awaited orders to march, orders to draw bow strings and darken the air with more than clouds and rain cold death in place of water on the opposing side, orders to form rank, horses churning up mud and fill the silence with screams of the dying. War is an awful thing of beauty.

— *From "Chronicle of Battles: Blood Line Wars."*
Master Hemmelstein, Scribe to Lord Alfred

𝒥arrod sensed Hannah's eyes on him. He walked beside the lead horse, alone and transfixed by the slow clop of hooves and boots whisking the thin grass. He was tempted to look back the way a retreating soldier looks over his shoulder for the pursuing troop, right before a spear jabs him between the ribs.

Eyes forward, focus on walking. He flashed back to the kiss. The softness of her lips, her warm breath, and how he desired more. More of something he couldn't have. *Not as long as I am hunted. Maybe after—*

After what? He couldn't focus on the future with war and gods nipped his heels. As far he knew, he didn't have a future. Hannah hadn't spoken more than a few words to him since the night they had to abandon their camp at Garden View—named in memory of his last garden. Jarrod didn't know what to say, how to take back the callous words spoken in haste. Was it love he felt for her? Or was he in love with the idea of having family?

He didn't know anything except he felt more alone in the company of people than he did on the quiet nights rebuilding his farm.

The nights in the wild he slept alone in his bedroll, up half the night watching for danger. Garden View had felt more like a home than any place he lived since the War of Ascension began. Bekka, Hannah and all the children, even soured faced Ishmael, were his family. He missed it: the sleepless nights and anxious days, patiently awaiting a message that never arrived. Oh, but the gods sent him one, a very strong message. Dark clouds rolled in from the east marking a terrible storm to catch them before they ever reached Heartwood Pines.

Tomorrow, maybe later tonight, rain will fall and force us to stop until the storm passes. That would put Ishmael in a mood. As it was, they weren't moving as quickly as he desired.

They gained eight leagues per day, which wasn't bad due to the frequent stops required by Bekka and the children. Bekka couldn't ride because of the danger it posed to the baby, and as far as Jarrod knew, she didn't have another false labor. A blessing from the gods. Azriel and Lily rode much of the time, but they grew impatient and irritable at a constant pace. During these breaks Ishmael would scout ahead and Hannah busied herself tending to the children's needs, avoiding Jarrod and his attempts to speak to her.

Neither of us is ready.

Something touched his arm and he jumped, reaching for the hoe tucked in the horse's saddle. Bekka pulled he hand away, a worried expression creasing her brow. She wore his trousers and shirt, tight around her belly and chest, revealing the swell of her breasts. Her braid swung back and forth as she waddled to keep pace.

"How are you holding up?" she asked.

"What do you mean?" Jarrod slowed down so she didn't have to walk so fast.

"I see the way you two keep avoiding each other," Bekka said, motioning back to Hannah. "Couldn't split that stone wall with a pick ax."

"Maybe it's better this way," Jarrod replied.

"For now," Bekka said.

"For now," Jarrod repeated.

They continued along in silence.

"I wanted to let you know that Sarrah and I will be leaving soon."

Jarrod feared this conversation.

"It's not safe."

Bekka placed a finger on his lips. "Keep it quiet. I'm telling you because I owe you for all that you've done." Bekka shook her head. "Besides, we're only slowing you down."

"You don't have to go."

"I do. For Sarrah and this little one." Bekka touched her belly. "They'll never be accepted by outsiders. People will hunt them, persecute them for being different. We need to be with our kind. It's the only way I can guarantee their safety."

"How will you get across the desert?"

"We'll find a way," Bekka said. "Don't tell Ishmael."

Jarrod didn't think Ishmael cared one way or another now they were doing what he wanted by returning to Heartwood Pines. Bekka could steal away in the night with half their supplies, and he doubted Ishmael would notice.

"When are you going?"

Bekka shrugged. "Best if you don't know. I'm only telling you because you saved us. You are a good man, Jarrod. I feel blessed knowing that there are people like you out in this world. Also, don't take too long in talking with Hannah." Bekka twirled a copper ring on her finger. "You never know what the next day will bring."

"Don't I know it," Jarrod said. "Perhaps when all this is over, I might come visit your village. What's it called?"

"Elysium," Bekka said. "The main road past the desert takes you directly through it."

"Mommy!" Sarrah called from the rear. Jarrod noticed how the girl had started taking to calling Bekka by the new title after they left Garden View. It fit her well. She cared for the child like a mother.

"Coming, Sarrah." Bekka leaned in, warm breath tickling his ear. "Keep this conversation between us." She squeezed his hand and smiled. The wrinkled corners depicting a strained suppression of happiness and sorrow. Bekka took a few steps back, hands resting on her belly and watched as Jarrod's motion carried him further away. Then she turned her back, and went to attend Sarrah.

Jarrod caught Hannah staring at him. She stepped behind the horse carrying her sister, but not before he noticed her disappointment. The idea that she was disappointed agitated him and he felt the need to explain that he was just talking with Bekka. That only made him angry at the need to explain his actions. Jarrod watched the dark clouds draw closer, and yanked his cloak edges tighter around his slouched shoulders. A damp chill filled the air. Anger warmed him and he walked faster, putting a little more distance between himself and those who followed.

The first drops of rain hit before nightfall. A cold wind blew grey clouds over them, darkening the sky. In the last of the light, they followed a shallow stream to a hillside where a once large river carved a hole in the stone wide and tall enough for them to walk the horses through. Jarrod lit a torch and went in first, searching the ceiling for bats. He ducked, half-expecting to hear high pitch screeches as webbed wings beat against his head.

Stalactites hung of the smooth stone above, ill-formed and crumbling. A strong mineral smell wafted in the cool breeze. Ishmael followed behind, footfalls echoing off the walls. He had an arrow notched in case it the cave wasn't as empty as it appeared. Jarrod stepped in water and he lowered the torch to examine the ground. Salt deposits sparkled in the torch light, but the water was a small puddle not so big as to cover both boot tops. He followed a warn, thin groove in the stone where water flowed to the form the puddle. He reached the solid stone back and saw water trickling from several fist-sized holes. No light shown from the holes which meant the water came from somewhere higher, carving its way through rock and depositing in the center.

"We'll stay here the night," Ishmael said, his voice bouncing off the walls. "You can spread the canvas from two of the tents there near the opening to dampen the noise we make and serve as an early warning in case something does call this place home."

"What about the rain?" Jarrod poked at the holes. Calcified stone rubbed beneath his fingertip.

"I don't think this place will flood, if you're worried about it," Ishmael said. "We'll be long gone before enough water comes through here to flush us out."

They hobbled the horse against the back wall and fed them. Kellen showed Lily and Azriel how to remove the saddles and brush the horses properly. Ishmael went out to scout the area, again, alone. Jarrod offered to go along, but Ishmael ignored him and went off.

You'll only be in the way, he imagined Ishmael responding to his request.

Jarrod gathered kindle to start a fire, using some of the wood they brought along from Garden View. He fanned the sparks into a small flame. Hannah rummaged through the food sack, bring him wild mushrooms, nuts, and some barely. Again, she said nothing, but laid the items at his feet and moved away. He cracked the nuts and heated them with the mushrooms. So many words of what he should say ran through his mind.

Ishmael returned as they finished cooking.

"The perimeter's clear." He sat by the fire, warming his hands. "Those clouds are coming in fast. Looks like a Planter's storm."

Planter's storms were a farmer's dream. They came in before seeds were sown, drenched the land for three or four days, conditioning the land for planting. The most bountiful harvests followed a Planter's storm. Occasionally, Planter's storms came late, ruining crops and drowning newly planted seedlings. Jarrod's father held off planting as long as he could in anticipation of a Planter's storm, but not so late in the season where the fledglings would wither beneath the hot sun.

My little garden will be obliterated. Jarrod watched the dark clouds, sad at the idea of the seeds being washed down into the stream.

"So, we wait it out." Jarrod handed Ishmael a steaming bowl.

"No. We don't have that long," Ishmael scooped food into his mouth. "Remember what I said about the cave filling up with water? A storm like this will bring the flood a lot sooner than I thought. I don't know about you, but drowning in my bed is not my ideal way of dying. Before we leave, we cut up the one tent to cover us against the worst of it. At night spread the others overhead so we have a dry place to sleep."

"Better cook up more gruel," Bekka said. A strong breeze howled past the entrance, kicking up ash. The horses whinnied uneasily and the rain began to fall in a steady patter against the stone. The fire sizzled as rain drops struck the burning wood. "Doesn't look like we'll have any extra dry wood than what you've already gathered."

Jarrod used the wooden poles and spread the canvas out so it was flat rather than propped up. He set both against the entrance, hammering two spikes on either side of the stone to use as a tie down so the contraptions didn't blow in on them. Next, he strung a leather thong, tying them together, and left an opening for the camp fire smoke to escape. They ate, listening to the rain strike the canvas, and then set out bedrolls. Hannah told the children stories about three young girls and a boy finding a faery stone and setting off on a journey to return it to the King of Fey. As they travel through the enchanted forest, they meet trolls and must answer three riddles.

"I am tears that come from no eyes, fall down and never flies, brings life but too much and you die," Hannah said in an affected, deep voice, the way a troll might sound.

"I know! I know!" Lily said, sitting up excitedly. "It's rain."

"Very good," Hannah said, kissing Lily on the forehead. Lily giggled. "That is where we end the story for tonight."

The children groaned, pleading for more. Hannah resisted.

"You need your rest," she said, tucking them in. "More walking ahead of us in the morning."

"Oooo, but it's raining," Lily complained.

"Then you better enjoy the warmth now," Hannah said. "I don't think we'll find much after we leave here.

"Are we almost home?" Azriel asked, yawning. "I miss father."

"Soon," Hannah said, looking over to Ishmael.

"Before the next full moon, we should be there," Ishmael replied.

"When is that?"

"You can't see it, but it's at Fetch's bow," Ishmael said, unstringing his bow and sliding it into a canvas case. "That means about ten more night, depending on how much the rain slows us down."

"Tears from no eyes," Azriel said and closed his own.

Ishmael yawned and began to move towards the front of the cave. Jarrod put a hand up.

"Get some rest. I'll take first watch."

"Something always seems to happen when you take first watch," Ishmael said. "I'm in no mood for more surprises. You sleep and let me watch."

"Blame me for that as well!" He understood Ishmael didn't mean it in any critical manner, but Jarrod hadn't had enough sleep for banter. "You'll be less than six hands away, if something happens, you'll know about it immediately."

"Fine." Ishmael patted him on the shoulder. "Try not to fall asleep and get us all killed."

"We haven't died yet."

"That's reassuring," Ishmael said, covering up in a blanket. In a brief moment he was sound asleep.

The fire died. Jarrod kicked the ashes to let the remaining warmth escape. He wrapped his cloak around his hunched body, listening to the wind rattle the canvas and rain pelt against it. He nodded off, strange images of flapping wings and weeping children. A noise startled him awake. He looked over at the children, believing one had cried out in her sleep. Soft breathing told him they remained asleep. The noise sounded again. A loud whiney followed by angry voices. The wind and rain carried the voices, muting them so he could make out the variance against the drops pelting the canvas.

Jarrod reached for his hoe. For all he knew, they could be waiting on the opposite side of the canvas, wondering at the strange covering. He couldn't see anything more than the billowing of the tent, breathing in and out with the air like a giant lung. The wooden frame held it in place and the tethers strained, but didn't break.

"Get that damnable creature up!" growled a voice. "If it won't get up, put it down for good."

The whining reached a high pitch shriek and then ceased. Jarrod waited, heart racing that their own horses would respond. He heard their heavy breaths, but they remained quiet. They must've sensed his fear.

A hand touched his arm and he jumped.

"How many are out there?" Bekka's warm breath against his ear.

Jarrod shook his head.

Azriel began to stir and he heard Elly whispering softly.

"Leave the damn thing." The voice sounded closer. Jarrod stared at the tent snap back in the cave like water slapping against rocks. It sounded so loud. How could they not hear it outside? How could they not notice the movement? "I'm getting soaked to the bone."

Now they will try to enter, discovering the way blocked. Jarrod tensed, his hands sweating on the wooden handle. Bekka leaned against him; her soft body ridged as a board. He needed to wake Ishmael, but couldn't move. He couldn't tell how close they were to cave. Any noise he made could alert them, ruin any element of surprise.

Where are they?

"Mommy," Sarrah whispered close by. "What's happening?"

Bekka retreated back to her.

Jarrod crawled close to the canvas. It billowed in at him and he peered around the edge. Rain wet his face, a cold kiss. He blinked, water streaming from the dark sky at an angle. It was too dark to see anything. He caught a glimpse of light an indistinguishable distance away from the cave's entrance. Four figures stood around a shuttered light, bent over and working straps off a lump on the ground.

"Move it, now," bellowed an angry voice off to Jarrod's left. He couldn't see anyone, but the men stood up and hurried away, hunched over and carrying a bundle. Jarrod watched the light shrink and disappear into the rain slick night. He moved back behind the canvas.

"They're gone," Jarrod said, speaking quietly.

"How many?" Bekka asked.

"Five, I think," he said.

"What're they doing?"

"I don't know." Jarrod sat and continued to watch the canvas billow in the storm. "Whatever it is, they're not doing it here."

Jarrod woke up shivering. Somehow, he was wrapped in his bedroll and it was wet. The dampness creeped into his side, causing goose flesh to rise on his bare skin. He unraveled from the wet roll, sat up and found himself alone in the middle of the cave. Everyone else was asleep further at the side, dry, except for Ishmael. He leaned against the hard stone near the silent canvas, no longer puffing up its cheeks blustering to the storm. Snores and the trickle of water filled the cave. Jarrod's eyes followed the water to the source. Sure enough, just as Ishmael had predicted, it flowed from the holes in the back of the cave, quickened by the continuous fall of rain. It wouldn't be long before the small stream would swell and wash everything from the cave.

He pulled on dry cloths and boots. Then he walked past Ishmael, whose chin rested on his chest as he slept. Jarrod quietly untied the thong holding the canvas structure together and pushed them aside.

Rain no longer fell in large drops, but had eased, turning into a cool mist. Grey light shown through the haze. He didn't have to go far to see what troubled the men last night. The corpse of a horse laid fifteen yards beyond the cave's entrance. Glazed eyes rolled up in its head and Jarrod noticed its front leg bent at an unnatural angle. They had stripped it of tack. The straps of the saddle had been cut and it appeared as though they tried to move the horse to get at the contents on the other side. Jarrod tugged at the saddle, but it was stuck firmly in the mud beneath the horse. Closing the horse's eye, he left it and returned to the cave.

"What were you doing out there?" Ishmael asked as he came in.

"Checking on something," he said and piled up the last of the dry kindle.

"And?"

"Nothing." Jarrod struck flint together, sparks leaping onto the wood. A small flame flashed and he cupped his hands around his mouth, blowing the red embers until more wood caught fire. He looked over his shoulder and Hannah was up, helping her sisters

"I fell asleep on my watch." Ishmael yawned and stretched. "Why didn't you wake me?"

"I didn't think it was important." He broke up more wood and stuck it into the fire. "So I thought might as well let you sleep."

"Something happen last night?"

Jarrod glanced at Bekka. He shook his head.

"Fine. Don't tell me." Ishmael examined the canvas, poking his head outside. When he brought it back in, his hair was damp. "At least we didn't die."

"No, we didn't," Jarrod said.

"Here, let me prepare breakfast," Ishmael said, taking a pot and setting it outside to catch rain. "You should try to get more sleep. When I got up, you were half-asleep. I had to drag you to your bed."

"In the middle of the puddle?" Jarrod asked, sharper than he intended.

"That was your doing, not mine." Ishmael pointed at the wall furthest from the gathering water. "I set your bed up dry, like you wanted, away from the others so you wouldn't wake them. Exactly as you told me."

Jarrod didn't remember speaking or even moving last night. He closed his eyes and saw the lamp light. Heard the voices in the rain.

The scream of the horse and its silent dead gaze, telling how it could've been them, lying in a pool of blood. White corpses hidden away for wild animals to feed on.

"I don't remember," he said and got up from the fire. He placed the dripping bed roll on the floor beside the fire. Ishmael rummaged through their saddle bags and took out several bags of wheat.

"Well, you did," Ishmael said. "You also muttered something about lights I the rain and screaming, not to let it get inside."

Jarrod sighed. He glanced at Bekka and the children picking up their sleeping area. "There were men outside."

"Yeah, I figured." He brought the pot back in and began filling it the rest of the way with ta water skin. "Did you get a good count this time?"

"Five," Jarrod said. "They headed west. We wouldn't have known anything about them if their horse hadn't broken a leg."

"Were they Manor Guard?"

"I don't know. I couldn't see their faces or uniforms."

Bekka sat across from them.

"Any idea who they might be?" Ishmael asked her.

"No," she said. "If they weren't Manor Guard, then I don't know."

"We aren't close to any out posts or other Manor," Ishmael said, scrubbing the stubble on his chin. "My guess is they were looking for someone. Even if they weren't, we have to think like they were and keep moving, get beyond the Yellow Valley. We can slip past their patrols in Widow Forest."

"Be there by night if we leave soon enough" Jarrod said. "Otherwise, we might get caught out in the rain."

"As long we trust each other," Ishmael said. "We'll be fine."

Jarrod flushed at the stinging comment. *I earned that blow.*

After they ate, Elly saddled the horses and helped Bekka wrap the children in cloaks. Ishmael dismantled the barrier, while Hannah and Jarrod folded up the wet material. Their hands touched. Hannah looked up at him in earnest. A sad, longing in her eyes. Unable to speak his true feelings, he entwined his fingers in hers, squeezing. Hannah squeezed back and smiled.

"Thank you," he said, taking the folded tent from her.

"When you are ready, I am willing to talk," she said.

"Let's get past this storm, first."

Hannah nodded and went to finish packing.

Rain fell harder as the left the cave. The children rode, hunched over the horses. Jarrod shivered, exhausted from so little sleep. The rain and cold didn't make it any easier. He slogged along, taking up the rear while Ishmael walked beside the lead horse. Bekka and Hannah were in the middle. The ground became soggy and slick with rainwater, slowing their pace to a crawl.

Almost seems better taking out chances in the cave. Jarrod kept his head down and watched the mud squish beneath his boots. Their nice dry cave would be flooded either that night or the next. *Drown in the open, or drown in the cave, either way Donn would dine on rain brined hearts.*

They moved down a sloping trail, away from the hills. The land opened into sloping plains that separated the Yellow Valley and Widow Forest. Jarrod could make out the shape of trees in the distance. Copses sprouted along the plains with a dozen ash trees or so, but nothing as grand as the hard oak comprising the Widow Forest. Wild boars lived within the Forest, tusks as sharp as knives; many men hunted the boar in the Spring Hunt and ended up skewered at the end of its tusk, leaving behind grieving widows and children.

Chac, enjoy drowning us all in your tears. Jarrod blinked as a drop struck his eye and rolled down his cheek. The rain god never had very good timing. One positive about running for his life, Jarrod realized, was that he hadn't thought about the other gods trying to ruin it. *Man or god, it makes no difference. They're all trying to kill me in the end. Except I'm still standing. Even if it's in a rain storm.*

They approached the first thicket. Jarrod expected Ishmael to circle south around the trees. Roots and dense brush would slow their progress. Instead, Ishmael led them inside. Rain rattled the leaves, the foliage drooping under the deluge. Red blood berries, weighed down low branches, wet wood ready to snap off under their weight. Jarrod plucked one and sucked in its sweet juice as he listened to the rain slacken. It was a little drier, the ground slick with wet leaves and evergreen needles. Ishmael stopped the train and came back to Jarrod.

"We should break here." Ishmael pointed where the trees thickened. "Spread out a tent and have a quick meal before moving on."

"We could stay the night," Jarrod said. "It's close to Widow's Forest."

"No," Ishmael said. "The children need a break from the rain, that's all. Don't want to get too comfortable. Who knows what we'll find out there before it grows dark."

"It'll be nice to be dry again," Jarrod said, thinking, *if only for a little while.* "We shouldn't wait here on the edges where we can be seen."

"Stay on this path while I have a look around," Ishmael said. "Set up one tent and I'll join you shortly."

Further along the trees thinned. They found a clearing and spread out a tent on the ground and erected another. Cold gruel and water served as their meal. Jarrod wished they could have a fire, to dry off before plunging back into the rain. He removed his cloak and set it to the side.

"Did you see Ishmael come back?" Elly asked.

"No," Jarrod said, taking a bowl from Hannah. He spooned in a mouthful of cold, clumped wheat, began to chew the tasteless bit and swallowed. Elly stared at the tent flap, leaving her bowl untouched. Jarrod patted Elly's hand. "I wouldn't worry, he always comes back."

"I wonder if this is how Mother used to feel every time Da and the boys were out fighting battles," Elly said, a grown-up sadness reflected in her tone. "I don't think I'll ever marry."

"Don't say such things," Hannah said. "It all seems difficult now, but it'll get better."

"I mean it," Elly said, her voice hardening. "I have enough to worry about without marrying a man who'll go off playing war like these boys in my life."

"That worry will never go away," Bekka said, touching her belly. "Marry, or not. There will always be someone you love. Someone to keep you awake, worrying. It's about finding the moments of joy in life. That's what they're fighting for."

Footsteps approached.

"I think that's him now," Jarrod said. He gave the bowl over to Hannah and began opening the flap. His hand froze.

"Oh, how the mighty gods laugh," a familiar voice called from outside the tent. "We're one big, cosmic joke. And I'm here to deliver the punch-line. Come on out, little farmer boy, and surrender your goods."

That's not Ishmael! Jarrod grabbed his hoe. Bekka caught his arm before he could charge out. She pointed at the shadows on either side of the flap. They'd anticipated a blind attack. *Probably have swords ready to skewer me. I wouldn't make it more than two steps.*

Lily began to whimper and Hannah hushed her. Kellen pulled her younger sister into her lap so Lily could hide her face. Kellen looked to Jarrod. All the children, including Hannah, trembled like terrified rabbits trapped in the hollow of a fallen tree, the hounds sniffing about.

Blades Man, if there's any time I need you more, this is it and only.

"Listen up, thieving murders," another familiar voice shouted. Bekka cringed, her nails digging into Jarrod's arm. "You had your chance to give over the rightful property of her Highness. Pray to your gods and release them to us."

The tent shook as the ropes were chopped. Poles shuddered with each blow, material slackening, sinking in and ready to enfold them like a net.

"Out the back," Jarrod whispered to Hannah, using the hoe to prop open the rear. "Get to the horses."

Azriel and Lily crawled through the mud first, then Kellen and Sarrah slipped out next. Elly dove, helped to her feet by Kellen. Surprised curses followed them, feet pattering in the mud away from the tent. Hannah paused briefly to look at Jarrod.

"Go," he said. "I'm right behind you."

"You better be." She ducked under the flap, crawling part way in the mud and then screamed. Pudgy hands grabbed her arms and began dragging her. Jarrod lunged for her legs, but she slipped away before he could wrap his arms around them. Her boot heel caught him under the chin, teeth clicking and flash of white light behind his eyes.

Hannah screeched, calling his name. Jarrod shook his head, clearing away the white flashes. He rolled out one side of the collapsing tent, leaving Bekka behind. As he rose to his knees, he stared about at the chaotic scene.

Hannah struggled against a man, little taller than her, mouth open, either laughing or growling, as he tried to contain the squirming girl. She bit his hand and he cuffed her upside the face, dropping her to hands and knees in the mud.

"Leave her alone," Jarrod said, swinging the hoe. The man ducked, dropped on all fours and scrambled away.

Jarrod tried to take Hannah's hand. From the corner of his eye, he spotted a blade crashing down on him. He turned, spinning the hoe's handle to deflect the blow. Splinters flew from the wooden handle, the jolt shivering up his hands to his elbows. He side-stepped, getting a good look at his attacker.

Mother! How? Feet tangled and Jarrod slipped on rain-slick leaves. He slammed the hoe's head down to catch his balance.

Thramel grinned at him, a wild light in his eyes as he thrust the blade at Jarrod. Jarrod twisted so the sharp edge sliced his tunic and scratched his ribs instead of splitting them. Thramel advanced, two-handed thrust aimed for his leg. Jarrod tried batting it aside, but the blade struck the hoe. The wooden handle shattered.

More screams came from the west. Two men wearing metal wolf helms appeared, carrying Sarrah and Lily, both girls crying. Bekka emerged from under the tent and stood still as one of the wolves put his blade to her throat. In a matter of moment, the fighting was over. Jarrod dropped the broken pieces of his father's hoe. *The Blades Man abandoned us. He must've figured out I'm no warrior.*

"Should never had betrayed me, farm boy." Thramel punched him in the gut. All breath rushed from him. An intense fire spread across his midsection, and he vomited sticky gruel. Jarrod dropped to his knee, wetness soaking through his trousers. A mud coated boot sped towards him, colliding against the side of his head. Pain exploded in a bright flash of light and winked out.

No warrior.

Jarrod tumbled into the depths of darkness.

CHAPTER SIXTEEN

Death is an extension of life.
—From "Life and Death"

"That's what I need?" Dandulain asked, leaning back in the chair. She shifted her weight forward, the chair dropping to all four legs. The loud thump made Menrva jump. Pages in the Tome of Essence fluttered as her ink-stained fingers flew up to stifle a yell. "You're not leaving out any important detail?"

"No, Mistress... I mean yes... there's more," Menrva said, shaking as she tried to find her place. She flattened out one page, her finger tracing the symbols right to left. "It says the soul must match the wearer. One of exact intentions so the sacrifice may not twist the wearer against his or her will. Also, should the pendant be destroyed and the soul released, the consequences are unknown." Menrva glanced up from the page. "Though I think it would have a dire effect on any created close by. A soul seeks a body the way someone who's lost in the cold seeks a dry house and warm hearth."

"I don't intend on breaking the thing," Dandulain said, looking down at the strange symbols scratched out on the page.

"Then you plan on staying with the Created forever?"

"Don't be silly." Dandulain flipped the book cover closed. Menrva pressed her hands together under her breasts, watching Dandulain place the Tome in the cupboard. "I will need to return to the Palace as soon as events below are resolved."

"Then you will need to break the pendant," Menrva said, an insolent tone in her voice.

A risk I will have to take. Dandulain turned a key in the cupboards lock until in made a soft click and then put the key in a pouch. She turned on Menrva. The prophetess was getting a bit impertinent for her own good. *Some fear will fix her up. Let her know who her true master is now Mother is gone.*

"If I remained as one of the created," Dandulain said and walked behind Menrva's chair. The prophetess tensed, tracking her with her eyes while sitting pert. *You better worry. The future may be in your sights, but you are blind to here and now.* "Then who would release you from your hole?"

"What do you mean?" Menrva's stiffened, fingers pressed tight to her chest. A moment later, her eyes widened as she figured out the intention. "No, please. I did as you asked. Don't put me back down there."

"It's the only way I can assure your safety." Dandulain laughed. "Oh, you don't know about the squabble. With Mother's betrayal known throughout the palace, and she nowhere to be found, our brothers and sisters fight each other over control. They don't realize I have all the power, yet."

Dandulain held out the star of creation and disc of darkness and chains latched them around her neck. She let them dangle for a moment, so the prophetess could take in her dire importance, before dropping her raven hair over them.

"You, my dear child, are my key to unlocking their secrets. I must keep you safe."

Menrva tried to stand up, but Dandulain grabbed the prophetess by the back of her neck, tipping the chair over as she dragged the frail goddess to the stone wall. Menrva grabbed Dandulain's wrist and tried to pry her grip off, kicking and whimpering.

Everyone struggles, even the fly trapped in the web, wrapping itself up tighter. Dandulain tapped a stone and it depressed into the wall. A section grated open.

"Think about all the good you are bringing into the world while I fight to restore balance... how it used to be before Mother and Father destroyed it." She pulled Menrva to her feet, holding her to the bleak darkness. Terrified eyes looked blankly at the Mistress of Shadows as weak fingers scrapped along her black armor. Dandulain kissed Menrva's forehead. "They have you to thank for helping me."

She shoved the prophetess inside the dark hole, then tapped the same stone to seal the wall. Menrva shrieked as she plunged into cold water. Her cries cut off as the wall *thunked* in place.

"Curses will drip from their furious lips more than words of gratitude," Dandulain said, stroking the cold stone. "They will all fall on their knees, crying out in despair, and worship the darkness as Shadow rises."

She smiled at the last phrase. So much delight, her heart ached with it. *So close to Ruin.* One small task remained.

Dandulain went to Mother's study and rummaged through cabinets to find the crystal shard Menrva described from the Tome of Essence. She hurried through the hallways, pausing at the echo of an argument came from the Throne room. As much as she reveled in the thought of listening in, she had other matters to attend.

Don't worry, children, Auntie will return and see your little game plays out.

She entered the large room near the basement of the Palace, Boot heels clicking off the marble floor. She circled the room, testing each section by listening to the change in her steps. Near the center, a hollow sound came to her and she saw a single white square next to the various shades of grey. She triggered the release switch. A square patch of marble parted, revealing stairs going down into darkness. Dandulain descended to the bottom. Strangely enough while all the other children fought and argued for control above, the one who was a part of the unseating of Mother, and who could have greater gain, hid away in his cell.

Donn sat up from his table, surprised by her entrance.

"What do you want?' He asked curtly. "Haven't you caused enough trouble?"

"I haven't even started." Dandulain smiled.

"I have nothing more to offer you. Except maybe a piece of my heart." Donn held up the silver platter containing a small heart. "It belonged to a child. She drowned in a flood trapped beneath a tree uprooted by the rain storm. This kind always taste the most bitter-sweet."

"Tempting as it sounds, I will pass." She wrinkled her nose. The room smelled of death and decay. He covered the heart, taking some of smell with it. "I need your assistance. A soul of a different sort than the one you have to offer."

Donn narrowed his brow.

"I don't like where this conversation is headed."

"Give me what I need," Dandulain said, stepping from the gloom into the ill-lit room, "and you may go back to your judging of souls."

"Until the next time you require something of me." He sat back down, crossed his right leg over his left, foot jangling nervously. "The one constant I learned down here is that there is always a demand for more. Creatures such as yourself are never satisfied with anything they gain. It is all fleeting like grasping at grains of sands before the sea waves carry them away. You hold one grain in your hand, but it is not enough to build your castle. It'll never be enough."

"You presume too much," Dandulain said. "Just because you eat the hearts of the dead, doesn't mean you are wise."

Donn laughed.

"I never professed wisdom."

"That I know, otherwise you would have given me what I demanded." She hooked her thumbs through the belt. His eyes glanced at the daggers and he smirked. As long as she needed what he possessed, threatening him with physical harm was pointless.

She approached the simple wood table dressed with silver fork and knife. "I grow impatient with your boring prattle. Do as I ask, without any more delay."

"Time is a resource I have in abundance."

Dandulain lifted the cover on the silver platter.

"What you have in abundance, I may take from this one." She took up the fork and stuck its long tines into the heart. It was so small, so perfect. "Let's see if she gets a true judgment."

"You have no say in where her soul rests," Donn said.

"I have no say, and you won't have a true judgement. Was she truly innocent because she was a child, or did she drown little puppies just to feel them squirm? Any choice you make you'll have this question in the back of your mind. 'Was I right?'" She lifted the heart to her lips. "Give me what I desire and you shall win back her heart."

Donn's chin clenched and he stood, weighing his options. She opened her mouth and set her teeth on the soft flesh.

"Fine." Donn reached out and took her hand, pulling the heart from her lips. "What do you want?"

"A soul from the depths of Arula."

Donn raised his brow in question.

"That is all?"

"Yes," Dandulain replied.

"Oh, why didn't you say so from the beginning?" Donn asked, grinning to reveal red stained teeth. He set the heart on the platter, picked up quill and ink, scribbling on a note card. "Those are in abundance. In fact, you may choose a savory one for your palate. One thick in memory and coated in justice."

"Why are you not contending for the throne above?"

"Down here," Donn said, holding his arms wide and turned slowly around, "I rule a world of darkness and despair."

Soon that will be all the worlds.

"When I become Queen of the gods, I would choose you for my king," Dandulain said, taking the note from his cold fingers. "Except I know you would eat my heart out."

Donn laughed as he released the parchment. He sat down, taking up knife and fork, slicing off a piece of the right ventricle and shook his head as he chewed.

Dandulain took the note to the double door. She opened it and followed the bright white light to a clearing in a green field. A golden-haired woman, dressed in white robe and silver breasted armor stood vigil, spear in right hand and shield over left forearm. Seraphim blocked Dandulain's path, bright blue eyes watching her approach.

"Why are you here, Shadow?"

Dandulain said nothing. She held the note out between her fingers. Seraphim snatched it and read, frowning in disapproval.

"This way."

Seraphim led her down a stone path. The air was cool and green grass filled the flat land that seemed to continue on infinitely. Donn would refer to it as the Pasture in his sardonic tone because this was where the souls waited for the judgement. "They are like sheep in the green fields to graze while the master sharpens his sheers," he'd say in a drool manner, pale lips cracking a smile.

Gehenna the Created called it, or "the place of waiting." Several ethereal forms wandered the grass, looking lost or ashamed. One passed close; her skin prickled as it brushed her arm. Dandulain's hand dropped to her belt as she leaned away from the specter. It continued on, no more noticing her than a speck of dust. The stone path stopped abruptly, dropping off into nothingness.

Arula spread out before her in an endless void.

"Reach your hands into the pit and call the name," Seraphim said, standing to the side. "Say only the one you desire and no other, unless you wish to join them for an eternity of darkness."

"That doesn't sound like my idea of a good time."

Seraphim made no response, staring blankly at her.

You. I will make my cup holder. Dandulain crouched at the edge of the pit. *It couldn't be any worse than this appointment.*

Arula's air was thicker, frigid as a crypt. A grey mist swirled around the rim and she smelled despair like spoiled eggs. Voices cried out in anguish, babbling senseless words. She placed the empty crystal into the darkness and whispered the name Donn gave her. A force tugged on the crystal, nearly yanking it from her fingers. She held it firmly. It grew warm and took on a dark blue glow. She pulled back from the pit, holding the soul pendant in front of her.

"You once caused me great anguish," she said. "Now you will serve my cause."

"Leave here at once," Seraphim said, the spear lighting up in a flame. "Your stay is revoked."

"I have all I ever wanted." The crystal grew warm in her palm, like she'd reached up and stole the sun from the horizon. That's how it will be once she completes her task. Thrusting the sun from its pedestal, snuffing it out like a great candle, casting both gods and the Created into a pit of despair.

"Oh, my love we will meet on equal ground." She tied a silver thread through the end of the pendant. A dark, purple glow lit the crystal from within. "When I do find you, oh the fun we'll have."

The world blurred, thick and filmy like phlegm caught in the throat, clogging his vision. *I fell,* was Jarrod's first thought. *I tripped and fell into the stream, cracking my head on a stone.* The pulsing ache lent some credence to his reasoning. Water dripped from his hair, sliding down the bridge of his nose and over his lips like a wet kiss. *Mother will tan my hide if I ripped my breeches again. Bad enough I have to slink inside with my*

clothes all wet.

Somewhere, someone moaned.

Jarrod peeked one eye open. Grey light drove a spike through his head and his throat rattled. The moaning was his own response to the stupidity that landed him in the stream. Mother's blessing, he didn't drown. Fluttering his lashes, he let the world come into focus. His head lolled forward so he stared down at his bound hands resting in his lap. The rope chaffed his wrists as he tried to separate them.

How did these get like this? He let them lay still.

Shivering, sitting in all the wetness, he tried to stand up. His legs refused to obey. He swallowed and something swollen filled his mouth. Teasing it with his tongue, the rough barrier refused to move. It peeled his mouth back in an unnatural smile.

A whimper came from his right. Heavy headed, as though an anvil rested on his neck instead of his skull, he lifted his chin and turned towards the sound. Hannah leaned forward, straining against the tree. Her hands and feet were tied and a gag filled her mouth. Wet, sunken eyes stared at him, delivering a desperate message for hope. Hope that Jarrod could save them both from drowning in all this wetness. He tried to tell her everything would alright—the lie natural on his lips. Words wouldn't form. They were stuck behind the barrier, leaving his mouth unnaturally dry with all this water to wet it.

He let his head nod back against the rough bark. Leaves sagged overhead as water continued to pour from the sky. They patted Jarrod's face, cold tears running down his chin.

Not a stream but woods. He closed his eyes as some memory returned. *The only thing we may drown in is blood.*

Sarrah and Lily were tied on trees opposite trees from Hannah, and as his head swirled, he saw Bekka across from him, her mouth gagged, feet and hands bound like the rest. To his left sat Ishmael. Ishmael's face was also pale, a dark red patch on his side of his head. He saw no one else. Azriel, Kellen, and Elly could've escaped.

What hope have children against these adults wanting us dead? Elly, keep running and don't come back. We will be nothing more than corpses moldering alongside the mushrooms on these trees.

Footsteps crushed the wet leaves next to him, and Bernal's face filled his vision.

"Doesn't taste very good, now does it?" Bernal grinned, tugging the gag in Jarrod's mouth. "I made sure to wipe my arse on it before shoving it in your mouth." He laughed, patting Jarrod's cheek. "I'm just yanking your pecker. It's from an old tunic your good friend Thramel sacrificed to make you more comfortable. Although I cannot give my word it never touched his arse."

Jarrod looked away from Bernal to Hannah. Her face was streaked with dirt and her braid unraveled with thick strands of hair sticking out to the sides. The left hem of her dress was torn up to her hip, exposing her thigh and small clothes. Hannah trembled, wriggling her hands back and forth in the bindings. *Don't waste your efforts.* Hannah seemed to read the thought, letting her hands flop on her dirty dress and laid her head back against the tree.

"Don't worry about your little girlfriend," Bernal said. "A pretty creature, soft and supple curves, though they be too small for my liking. She's not yet ripe for the plucking. I speak for myself, since she isn't my prisoner. That one," he nodded towards Bekka and grinned solicitously, as though she were a slab of cooked meat roasting over a fire. "She's my prize. Betrothed by her brother's good graces. Once I give the thing growing in her belly over to Joanne, she is mine to do with as I wish."

Jarrod glared at Bernal. He couldn't speak, but even if he could, he wouldn't give Bernal the satisfaction of giving in to his goading. *Blades Man give me the strength to kill this man.* As with much of his prayer of late, they fell on deaf ears. He didn't feel the strength like he had in the Tower, his mind disconnecting as another took possession of his flesh, slaying eight archers. He remained the numb farm boy, useless with his broken hoe. The only ground he was fit to fallow would be his flesh melting off and bones crumbling to feed these trees.

No longer a tool, for now I am broken.

"I guess your friend should've taken my offer, or at least killed me when he had the chance," Bernal said, his sour breath wafting over Jarrod's nose making him wish they had covered it as well. "By the way, he's not looking so swell. I think the wolf's bite done him in."

Wolf's bite? So that is how they brought Ishmael down.

"Get away from him," Thramel shouted. "Go help Snout saddle the horses. We need to leave here before it gets dark."

A distant, hazy memory teased his brain. He remembered hearing the voice not long ago, somehow close, but not visible. Jarrod ground his teeth on the rag. This was the very same voice that shouted outside their cave last night. Thramel had tracked Jarrod and guessed they were returning to Heartwood.

"Thanks for watching over her, kid." Bernal patted his cheek again and stood up. "May the gods judge you worthy." He untied Bekka's legs and forced her to her feet. She struggled, but he pulled her by the rope, nearly dragging Bekka. Her heels leaving a trail in the soggy leaves.

Gods judge me worthy! Jarrod wanted to laugh and succeeded in groaning. The gods had abandoned him. He was at the mercy of a madman. Jarrod looked over at Ishmael again. His eyes were closed, but his chest slowly rose and fell. He lived. *For how long?* Unless he tended the *wolf's bite*, Jarrod was certain Ishmael wouldn't last the night. *I don't even know if I'll last the night.*

Thramel loomed over him, a gloating smile and bemused eyes, like a cat that caught the elusive mockingbird.

"I don't know why he bothered to gag you. Isn't anyone out here to hear you scream, except for Joanne's soldiers." Thramel bent down and pulled the rag from Jarrod's mouth. "Those work for our side."

Jarrod glared at Thramel.

"This is where you're supposed to beg for your life, or at least the lives of your friends." *Don't say a word, don't let him hear the terror in your voice.* Thramel rapped his knuckles on the top of Jarrod's head, sending white flashes of pain streaking past his eyes. "Did I hit you too hard? Knock something loose?"

"Why bother?" Jarrod's voice was raspy. "You'll do what you want anyway."

"So you are not dumb after all."

"Fool enough to believe in your lies back in Heartwood Pines."

"Big difference between someone who's dumb and someone who's a fool. A dumb man has lost power of speech, whereas a fool doesn't know when not to speak. I think there was one time you played me for a fool," Thramel said and gave a heavy, theatrically sigh. "Look, the gods have decided we need to correct that error on my part. They led you and the traitor's daughters back into my grasp."

"You're the traitor," Jarrod said, knowing it wasn't wise to provoke the man who tried killing children. "Joanne's sheepdog, stirring up the livestock in Heartwood while all the time allowing the wolves into the yard."

Thramel laughed.

"Yes, you are all sheep. Sheep dully grazing in the field, munching along as though the grass would always grow green, never understanding the yard is nothing more than a field of shit, stinking and overrun with weeds. The wolves merely had to show up to take it. You see, Heartwood is the last village to fall. It's like a tree that's been hacked in half and waits for a wind to blow it down." Thramel slammed his fist into his open palm. "Joanne is that wind. She already occupies the Keep, the manors, everything but that one lonely pile of tinder. She's smarter than Alfred and crueler than Thomas. Do you think you can stop her? Two boys and a bunch of children? Gods no! You fooled me and that's my fault for trusting your stupid farm boy act.

"Here we are for a second round, a do over. Only this time I'm going to help you." He whistled and the two creatures wearing metal wolf helms approached on either side. Water *tink-tink-tink*ed against the vicious snarl and sharp metal teeth. Thramel drew his sword and handed it to the one. "Make sure he holds this tight. Wouldn't want it to slip and cut him."

The wolf-man took the sword, knelt beside Jarrod and placed the weapon into his bound hands. A musky smell emanated from the creature and Jarrod tried to look into the eye holes. Crinkled folds forming from the snarling snout led to dark, empty sockets. The wolf-man's fingers wrapped around Jarrod's hands, angling the sword away from his chin.

What game is he playing?

Thramel slowly cut Hannah's bindings. Understanding struck like a punch to Jarrod's gut and he wanted to wretch. He wriggled to the side, twisting his hand the sword tilted and nearly fell, but for the wolf-man's firm grip. He swung his right shoulder into the wolf-man, knocking him off balance for a moment. The creature recovered quicker than Jarrod anticipated. Before he could swing the blade around, it grabbed his shoulder slammed him against the tree, sending a flare of pain up his spine.

"Don't do this," Jarrod said, growling as he fought against the strong arms holding him in place. "You want me to beg? Fine, I'll beg! Let her go. I'll do whatever you want. Just let her go."

Thramel pulled Hannah to her feet. She squealed as he bent her arms behind her back, shoving her along until she stood in front of Jarrod. Freckled face pinched, she looked so young. Frightened tears welled in her eyes as she stared at the sword point. She squirmed, kicking back at Thramel, her legs too short to reach.

It was the event in the Tower reenacted when Thramel had handed him a sword and told him to kill the girl to prove his salt.

"Fool me twice, shame on me." Thramel pressed his knee behind Hannah's and slowly bent her over. She thrashed, swaying away from the sharp point. Her legs buckled and she dropped to her knees, water spraying and soaking her ruined dress. Thramel yanked her to her feet. "It is only fair that you complete the promise of faith you made to me."

"Please," Jarrod said. "You don't have to—"

"Yes. I. Do." Thramel shoved Hannah back over the sword, the tip hovering close to her heart. She screamed and he pulled her short of being skewered by the blade. "You had your chance, farm boy. All you told me is you need a little assistance, a shove so to speak."

Hannah cried, lips trembling. She shook her head, mumbling "no" through wet, thickened voice sounding like a little girl. Sarrah and Lily both whimpered, but Jarrod caught Hannah's eyes. *Gods, I got to figure something out! Please don't make me kill her!* Last time it was the cry of an attack that bought them precious time. Who else knew where they were except for children? Only children.

"Thramel, please!" Jarrod shouted, straining his arms to swing the blade's point away from Hannah's heart. The wolf-man gripped his fingers, nearly crushing them with its metal gauntlets. "She's done nothing wrong. Let her go, please."

Thramel grinned.

"As you wish."

He released Hannah.

"No!" Jarrod jerked his body, tendons popping in his hand.

He was too late.

The sword grew heavier as Hannah's weigh drove her down onto the blade. It pierced her left breast, missing her heart and scrapped past ribs, the bloody edge exiting below the shoulder blade. Hannah's eyes widened and she moaned, a scream caught in her throat. Warm, wetness slid over the hilt and coated Jarrod's hands in sticky ichor.

Gods! What have you done! A strained whimper escaped his throat.

The sword dropped as the wolf-man backed away. Hannah tilted, pinned on the blade like a butterfly, then she fell sideways into the mud. She began to quiver, sword jutting from her chest. Blood poured out of the wound, mixing with the brown and green, turning it dark red.

Jarrod scrambled to his knees.

"Hannah, look at me!" Jarrod screamed. "Look at me!"

Hannah's eyes rolled up into her head as she quivered in the mud. Jarrod searched around for something to stem the blood flow. He tugged at his own stained tunic, wet and slipping through his bound hands. Thramel stepped in and gripped the hilt. In one, quick motion he ripped the blade free.

Blood splattered Jarrod's face, spread across her small chest in a rose bloom.

"It's your fault she's suffering now," Thramel said, shaking blood drops from his steel. "Could have been a nice, clean kill. Straight through the heart."

Jarrod growled and lunged at Thramel. Thramel kicked him in the side, sending a rush of air through his clenched teeth. Jarrod doubled over, coughed, a fire burning in his gut. He forced himself to his knees, preparing another strike. *Strike me down, too. Kill me!*

Hannah made a squeaking noise, and called his name.

Slipping along on his knees, Jarrod made his way to her. Her eyes were open and full of pain and fear. The front of her blue riding dress turned red, a rose spreading across her chest.

"You'll be alright," he said, taking her hand in his own. It was cold.

Hannah shook her head.

"I'll help you like before." Hot tears stung his eyes and he blinked them away.

"Jarrod," she said, squeezing his hand. "I... I'm dying."

"Gods, no."

"Thank you," she whispered, shivering in the mud, rain water mixing with her tears. "I love you."

"I love you, too," he said, kissing her hand. "I'm sorry. It's all my fault."

Hannah shook her head, again.

"Save my sisters," she said. "Protect... protect.... Pro—"

She closed her eyes and her breathing ceased.

Jarrod collapsed onto her. Blood soaked his hair and he tried to gather her up from the mud. His bound hands were clumsy, slipping in the mud and the blood. Thramel's rough hand grabbed his shoulder and yanked him back.

"I let you have your last moment," Thramel said. "Now it's time for you and me to have a serious conversation."

A loud, angry shout echoed through the trees. Thramel turned, sword drawn. Snout wandered out, holding his nose as a red flow stained his fingers and dripped from his chin.

"He's gone! The bloody bastard's gone!"

"Who?"

"Bernal," Snout said, "and he took the girl."

CHAPTER SEVENTEEN

Grief is as sharp as the carpenter's knife, carving out a hallow seat where once Joy and Love resided.
          —Unknown

It's all over! Everything is in ruins! Qetesh crawled along the stone floor, among the chaotic screams and sounds of battle. She tried to call out for Moko, but her mouth, full of salty tears, made a weepy, wet squelch. Love blinded her to everything. Now she was unable to see anything.

Not so long ago, lost in the basking love radiating through her body like a warm blanket on a cold night, Qetesh sat cross-legged in the Throne room, listening to Hacawit drone on about Sin, Donn, Seraphim and countless other Brothers and Sisters. All the boring talk about who should be their allies and which were potential enemies. The warmth and monotonous speech made her drowsy. Sharp, irregular tones kept waking her up. Hacawit leaned back in a plain wooden chair in the throne room situated in front of the Thorns or Shadows. Moko slouched against the wall, scratching his head

"Agni," Moko said, "Agni will support anyone who tells him."

"You're reaching, Moko," Hacawit said. "He's one of Mother's and ran messages for Donn because she wanted the Heart-eater watched. Even the cockroaches in the basement need to be controlled before they overrun the house."

"Stomp them." Moko lifted his thick, tree trunk leg and dropped his stony foot down like crushing a bug.

The room shook.

Qetesh pressed her hand on the floor, nails grating against the stone. She looked at Moko, picking himself off the floor.

"It wasn't me," Moko said, dust powdering his bald head. "Was it?"

"No, you dumb block!" Hacawit rose so fast from the chair that it clattered against the stone. "This shouldn't be—"

Qetesh groaned. A knife pierced her heart, digging through her chest and carving a hollow throne for Pain to throb. The Throne room darkened to red. She gasped, sucking chilling air and shuddered as another wave of pain cut through her breast. *I am dying,* was her first thought. Hot tears squeezed out the corners of her eyes. She was a goddess. Goddesses don't die, at least not from heart pain.

"What's wrong?" Hacawit asked, voice emanating from a distant, resonating echo. Her vision narrowed on him rising. Hacawit stumbled, the room shuddering in rhythm to Qetesh's shallow breathe.

She pressed a palm against her breast, trying massage her perforated heart. The pain diminished some, leaving an afterglow still burning, embers waiting for the right amount of air to stoke life and placed a fiery crown on Pain's head. Hacawit knelt beside her, a large hand supporting her so she could sit up. He spoke more inaudible words. Tears flooded down her cheeks uncontrollably. She drew in short breaths, gasping from her rounded mouth, trying to birth the monstrosity inside her.

"What's wrong?" Hacawit repeated his question.

Qetesh shook her head, unable to speak.

The throne room shuddered again. A crack ran down the back wall and spilt the platform between the Shadow and Rose thrones.

"Sounds like the palace is coming down," Hacawit said and lifted Qetesh. She sobbed, tried to force the mewling noise to stop by holding her breath, but instead she gave pitiful squeaks. He carried her out Throne room.

Moko lumbered behind them to the hallway.

"What's making all this noise?" he asked.

"I don't know," Hacawit said, shifting Qetesh in his arms. "We have to leave, before it falls on our heads."

"Why is she crying? Is she hurt?" Moko replied asked, bouncing against the wall as another jolt shook the Palace.

"Nothing I can see," Hacawit said. The hallway shuddered, nearly knocking Hacawit over. "Take her while I figure out a place for us to go."

Strong, rough hands cradled her thighs as Qetesh felt the pain and tears near an end to their course. As they diminished, a strange feeling followed. It was like a candle flame that once burned robust, lighting a lover's writing desk as he composed poems about his mistress's eyes, now snuffed out, leaving nothing but cold, hard wax. In its place, a void. Empty. Hollow. Where there was once was warm love, nothingness resided. Something was missing. Something that was so full of vigor it nearly drowned her with yearning.

"I don't feel her love anymore," Qetesh said in a toneless whisper.

"She never really loved any of us, except for him," Hacawit said. "He was her favorite."

Qetesh looked at him dully.

"Not Mother. The girl," Qetesh explained. "The girl is dead."

Her own grief rose up inside at the loss of such a strong love. The grief was short lived, lost in the deep oblivious void leaving her empty. Even the light shining off the marble became a dull white wash.

The floor cracked, stone crumbling like dried bread. Moko pulled up short of tumbling down gripping her tight enough to leave bruises. Hacawit leapt over the gap, skidding to his knees on the opposite side.

The Palace's going to consume us all. The idea should be horrifying, but she felt nothing. One darkness or another would own her.

A great shadow rose up from the hole. Black robes fluttered as they reached their pinnacle.

"What are you doing, Mistress?" Hacawit demanded, hands creeping behind to his cutlass. "Do you know the cause of this?"

Dandulain smiled, such a dreadful grin causing Moko to retreat a step from her. Her presence both sucked in the light and radiated it from her in the same instance. The Palace gave another heave, walls shifting up and then crashing down. Large stones tumbled and smashed apart as they struck just a few yards away. Moko squeezed her to his chest so hard her face was buried in his fur jerkin smelling of old dirt and fire. She turned her head away and saw fear crack his ancient face.

"It's finally happening," Dandulain said, euphoria lifting her voice up.

"The end," Qetesh said.

"Yes, beautiful one," Dandulain said, stroking Qetesh's cheek. An electric jolt twitched her eye and Qetesh's vision winked out like a comet melting in the night sky. "The Ruin Prophesy is almost complete."

Qetesh blinked, but her vision remained dark. Metal scarping on leather, the sound of blades drawn. "What's happening?" she asked, and for a moment she was falling. Her bottom struck the floor, jarring her teeth together.

Her ears rang as metal clashed. Someone screamed. A loud thud landed next to her. Warm, wetness seeped beneath her heel as she scrambled away on hands and knees. Tears streamed from eyes unable to see. *Moko!* The name swelled on her tongue, but she swallowed it back in salty tears. She reached out, hoping to find some idea of direction, her hand touching nothing. She tried to set it down, but it kept going, hovering over empty space. She pulled it back, teetering on the brink of the hole.

A hand grabbed her by the neck, twisting her head and held in place as a kiss pressed her cheek.

"You're right all along," Dandulain's hot words brushed her ear. "You shouldn't have trusted me. Oh, but love is frivolous. Without you, I would never have found *him*. Like Mother, you played a greater part in my transformation. Thank you."

Cold lips pressed against Qetesh's mouth and she yanked her head away.

"Important steps remain to be completed, so I must bid you farewell."

The hand released Qetesh and she thrust her palms out to brace herself for the hard fall, but they found the empty space. Momentum carried her head over heels down into darkness.

"Listen to me and do exactly as I say," Bernal said, nearly dragging Bekka. "You can fuss and fight all you want, but if you want to save that little girl, you need to play along. Otherwise, you won't see her olive face again. Joanne will see to it."

What he told the boy about Joanne giving him Bekka after she whelped the bastard's beast he'd made up entirely. Joanne was more likely to cut off his sack and hand that back to him, than give up the woman. *My woman, betrothed to me by her brother.*

He drew a knife and Bekka balked.

"Don't worry, this isn't for you, though you would have stuck me good when I was all tied up." He went down the line where their horses were tethered to trees, cutting the leather thongs and giving each beast a whomp on the withers to spook them off. The last horse, one with full saddle bags, he left alone to use as their escape.

"Up you go, girl," he said, grabbing the back of Bekka's dress. He cupped her bottom, fingers squeezing as he lifted her to the saddle.

"Hey! What are you about?" Snout, the droopy-eyed tracker, staggered out.

"Don't move," Bernal said to Bekka. The old hound was alone. *No tin wolf around to guard his flanks. Janus rolls along on my side yet.*

"I am just preparing the horses to leave," Bernal said. "Whenever Thramel's done playing his children's games."

Snout stared at the horses running off. He snarled and drew his sword. Bernal waited for Snout, holding the knife out. Snout swung *Snipping the Willows*. Bernal caught the sword's edge on his knife, executed a *Reverse Windmill*. The sword tumbled from Snout's grip and Bernal struck him on the nose. Snot's head rocked back, blood spraying outward. He gave Bernal a goofy squint and then wobbled.

"What'd you do my no—" Snout dropped like hound exhausted from the mornings chase.

"That was easy." He turned, smile falling from his lips. He cursed Janus. *The ol'she-bitch is swirling my luck faster than a drunk pissing up a wall.* Bekka no longer waited on the horse. Bernal caught a flash of her running between the trees.

He gave chase.

Old times. He slipped on the wet ground, rounding the first tree. A slimy root caught his foot and he flew forward, sliding along on his hand until he regained his balance. Bekka wasn't having a better time of it either. He watched her slip, going down on one knee and try to push herself back up. Her bound hands made the task more challenging, nearly impossible. Bernal closed on her like a hawk catching a little mouse. He wrapped his arms around Bekka's waist and lifted her up. She twisted, elbows shooting out and heels kicking the sides of his legs.

"I told you to stay put." He brought the knife to her belly. "Try it again and I'll cut the creature from you as we stand."

Bekka stopped struggling. He got her back to the horse and heard Snout moaning. He tossed her up on the saddle and clamored behind her.

A loud scream came back from the camp. Followed by sounds of a struggle.

"Sarrah!" Bekka shouted.

Bernal clasped a hand over her mouth.

"None of our concerns," he said. "Most likely he killed the boy or the older girl. He needs Sarrah so she will remain safe. Same as you as long as you don't struggle. Do you understand?"

Bekka nodded and he released her mouth. Bernal heeled the horse into a quick trot, placing as much distance between them before his plot was discovered.

"He's gone!" Snout covered his nose, red streaming down his chin. "Bloody bastard broke my nose!"

"Tie him to the tree," Thramel said. Jarrod sat limp in the mud and two hands dragged him back against the tree. Rope entwined around his midsection and shoulders three times, tightening into a knot. He hung his head, listening. "Get the horses and run the bugger down."

"No horses," Snout said.

"Shadow take you," Thramel cursed. "What kind of watch dog are you? Should have you put in a sack and drowned in a well. Will someone get me a horse?"

The wolf men ran off. Thramel stood next to Jarrod, blade on his neck.

"I'm not feeling generous enough to cut your throat and have you die next to your girlfriend." He sheathed his weapon. "I think you need to wallow in your grief some and think about the misery you caused me by your betrayal. As you think, know this, everyone you loved and ever fought for back in Heartwood will all be dead in a few days. Not a single thing you can do to prevent it."

Jarrod made no reply. He kept staring at Hannah's lifeless body, blood seeping out and pooling in the mud.

"Jarrod!" Sarrah screamed. His heart ached as he watched helplessly as the child was tossed over Thramel's shoulder. Her tiny face twisted in horror and her wet, red-rimmed eyes pleaded for him to do something.

I can't... I couldn't even save Hannah.

"Jarrod!" Sarrah shouted again as Thramel carried her off. After they slipped out of view, he heard one last shriek. "Mommy!"

Snout glared at him, as though his pain was caused by Jarrod as well, and turned to follow Thramel, leaving Jarrod alone.

Rain fell harder, cutting through the leaves in cold pellets. They *thunked* him on the head, dripping down his neck like cold kisses. He shivered, flesh rising in goose bumps. Rain soaked through his tunic and trousers, sticking them to his skin. He wouldn't last long exposed to the cold and wet. A chill and a fever would overtake him, he had seen it happen to stronger men than himself during the war.

He looked at Hannah, heart heavy in his chest, like he was drowning inside out. His mouth trembled as he let out a gasp. "I'm sorry." Words were empty. Meaningless. *I couldn't do anything.* That part he understood as truth, but only partial truth. The reason she was in the woods were because of him. She could've died on the same night as her parents, but he rescued her and was responsible for her. He failed in many things regarding Hannah. He deserved to die, not her.

Should've killed her in the tower, a deep aching part of him dug up. *Then she wouldn't have had to suffer so much.*

Any suffering was caused by your idiocy. Ishmael's voice deprecated him. *Her linger touch, snuggling up next to you as you slept out on watch. Awkward kisses. You ignored her love. Had you recognized it and returned it, perhaps none of this would have occurred. Qetesh punishes the fool for unrequited love, taking away everything.*

The last thing he remembered saying to her was they would talk after the storm had passed. How he wished he could go back and tell her all the things he felt now. It amazed him how grief, the great clarifier, freed words from their bondage when the end was reached.

The storm raged on, heedless of their insignificant lives.

I will dash out my brains on this tree before long, Jarrod thought. *Spilt open my empty skull and let everything wash away.*

Jarrod looked over at Ishmael. He was slumped over, making it difficult to view his chest. For all he knew, Ishmael was dead. *I'll be joining you both.* Then they can be a great feast for the wild cats and bears.

"Save my sisters." Hannah urged in her last words. The one left unformed: Protect. Nothing remained to protect. Even Lily grew silent. *Why didn't he kill her as well?* Because he had Kellen and Hannah in the Tower. Thramel didn't know Lily was Hannah's sister, otherwise, he would've killed her too.

Elly's a smart, brave girl. She'll help the children find their way back to Heartwood. Gods grant one last kindness that they don't return here to find brother and sister slain. Like Thramel, the gods were all out of charity.

Tears ran their course and another great weight fell over him. Exhaustion, as grief and anger sapped his strength, caught up to him. Jarrod's eyes closed and he forced them open. *Once they close, they may never open.* He took in Hannah's body, ready to surrender the fight for good. Remove the yoke and lay down in the fields. The rain, he noticed, washed the dirt from her face and cleansed the ground where she lay. The dark red blotch across her dress marked where her life-force had bled out. Once again, it looked like a rose patch blooming over her breast. *She has gone to the flower gardens of the gods.*

His eyes closed and he succumbed to the sweet release of oblivion.

Her hands were warm, skin pale, knuckles pink as her fingers entwined his. Twirling beneath a clear blue sky, she giggled and drew Jarrod in, forearm to forearm until their elbows touched. Red freckles stood out on her pale face, green eyes gleaming in delight. Pink lips spread wide in a smile, though the corner had a red dash the could've been a stray freckle, except it gleamed wet in the sunlight. Jarrod leaned in to kiss those delightful lips, but she threw her arms out, dancing beyond reach as she spun around in his hands, white dress billowing like a cloud.

Jarrod laughed, grass whisking beneath his bare feet. Once more he drew her in tight so their elbows touched, only this time let go with his right hand and caught her around her waist, pressing pelvis to pelvis. He leaned in and she closed her eyes, head tilting in anticipation.

"Jarrod."

His name sounded like rumbling thunder, distant but approaching.

"I'm here," he whispered, mouth was close to hers, the cold breath on his upper lip. She smelled of cloying rose petals. He looked down and saw a red patch spread across her right breast.

A rose. She waited for the kiss, lips slightly parted, breathing softly though her chest did not swell or fall. No natural ebb and flow, just cold air puffed from her nose and lips.

"Jarrod."

More thunder and he looked around. The field of wildflowers and butterflies darkened, cracking at the edges. Petals wilted, browned, and dropped around shriveled stems. Butterfly wings crumpled, dropping like sorrowful drops of rain into the puddle of decay.

Without warning, her hands broke free of his and Hannah twirled away. Jarrod reached for her and missed. Green eyes looked at him filled with dew that leaked from drooping eyes and melted down her cheeks as the distance between them grew.

"Wait!" Jarrod shouted and ran after her. His feet were heavy blocks of stone. Legs strained to rise up from the earth, rooting him in the dark mud seeping over boots and up his calves.

Seek for me in the green beyond the stars. A thought, soft as a Sower's Breeze, tugged at his heart.

"Jarrod."

The voice boomed louder and darkness overlaid the blue sky. He felt dampness on his cheek and thought it was rain until he tasted the saltiness. The air shimmered, cold and smoky, yanking him away from roses and wildflowers, away from green grass and Hannah's soft touch— into a wet place. A place of fire and sadness.

"Jarrod!"

His head snapped up. Wood crackled and popped. Orange flame blurred and cleared. Thick smoke rising to a hole above, meshed to keep out the rain. Something heavy covered him. He shifted and a blanket chaffed his bare skin.

Opposite the fire from a man in black armor sat cross-legged, twin crossed swords on the breast plate marking his insignia.

"I died," Jarrod said, though this time felt much different. No stone white light, no stone chair to be judged upon. "I must've, how else can I see you?"

"There are other ways." A deep, calm voice— the very one that drew him from his dream back into the nightmare of life.

"Why didn't you let me die?" Anger swelled in him, renewing his exhausted limbs. He sat up, the blanket pooling down into his lap. The fire was warm on his bare chest. He could feel it burn through the numbness as anger coursed his veins. "You abandoned me when I need you most. Why save me now?"

"Because you are needed." Calm, placid. Arms folded and eyes half shut as though in deep meditation.

"So I am nothing more than a tool. Abandoned in the rain until you want me for something," Jarrod said, fury rising at the tranquil reaction, the peaceful, almost prayer-like trance the Blades Man embodied. He picked up a stick and hurled it at the god who once possessed him. The wood clacked off metal, falling into the fire and kicking up sparks.

The Blades Man peered at him from beneath half-shut eyes. Jarrod wanted to jam a knife through them, hear the satisfying pop as they deflated into gelatinous red gore. As a candle consumes it wick and melts the wax, his fury consumed any remaining strength. He collapsed on the floor and pulled the blanket over his head. "Find yourself another tool. I'm broken."

"I know you are hurting." Patient, annoying voice. "It was never intended for the girl to die."

Jarrod ignored him, allowing the grief to swell over him again like a damn broke open and a flood of emotions sweeping away the outside world. *Hannah died because of you. Because you weren't there when I prayed, when I begged.* Jarrod could never forgive him.

"Your other friend, Ishmael yet lives," the Blades Man said. "So do the girl's siblings."

"Hannah," Jarrod said from beneath the blanket. "Her name is Hannah, not 'the girl.'"

"Hannah," he repeated, solemnly.

"Why weren't you there to help me? To help us?" His chest felt heavy and he gave a sobbing sign. "I am too weak to fight. I'm no warrior, just a feeble farm boy. "

"I got side tracked." He sounded contrite. "Even the gods cannot be everywhere at once."

You make damn sure to find me when you want me. Fine, you want to use me, let me get something from it.

"Now you are here," Jarrod said, turning over to face the Blades Man. Dark brown eyes stared at him, "you can help me avenge her death. Teach me to be a warrior like you. Give me the strength to kill her murderer."

The Blades Man frowned and picked up a stick, poking the flames.

"Long ago," he said, focusing on the fire, "a young girl survived while her entire village was slaughtered by brutal men. They caught her, locked her away in one of the houses and planned on making her a child bride. The girl prayed for my aide. So, I gave her my blessing and she killed the men holding her captive. I proceeded to train her in the art of combat and weapon craft. She had a strong brave heart masked in sorrow."

The Blades Man sounded distant, as though reliving the events.

"She used these skills not for defense, but to kill the men who attacked her village. Her revenge didn't end there. She shed the blood of the innocent people, women and children who lived in the same village as the attackers. She made them sacrifice in my name. I refused the souls and she became mad with rage, taking out her anger intended for me on other, more accessible targets.

"She robbed and murdered men encountered along the road, and as she grew into a young woman, she joined mercenary forces and eventually honed her skills, learning the ways of killing from the shadows."

"What happened to her?" Jarrod asked.

"Eventually, a man of greater skill fought and slew her," the Blades Man responded, regret in his voice. "When she died, she ascended and became a wrathful goddess."

"Who was she?" Jarrod knew, but he wanted to hear it confirmed. He wanted to be certain it was she who sought him, the one who pierced his thoughts briefly, causing him to collapse down by the stream in what felt ages ago. Also, he knew it would cause the god pain to name his failure. Maybe then he would have an inkling of Jarrod's state.

"You know her. The very same woman who is coming to kill you, Jarrod, and all of creation," the Blades Man said. "Revenge is a step on the path to darkness and shadow. I will not allow that to happen again."

"What do you want me to do?"

"Forgiveness is the first stage of release."

Jarrod laughed and rolled over. Forgiveness. How could he forgive him when he let Hannah die?

Save my sisters. Her last words. If only he had the skills, the ability to fight well, he could protect them. Then Hannah wouldn't have died in the rain, by his own hands nonetheless. He wouldn't have had to rely on gods or man.

Jarrod furrowed his brow. "How did you find me?"

"I showed him the way." Elly entered the tent, holding two steaming bowls. "After we fled the woods, I didn't know where to go, so I took Azriel and Kellen back to the cave to hide and wait for you to escape. We crested a hill and discovered their camp. At first, I thought they were more of Joanne's soldiers, but then I stumbled across him and I recognized him from the story descriptions father used to tell Michael and Ishmael."

Jarrod looked at Elly's sad face as she handed him a hot bowl. It had vegetables and mushrooms in a thick stew. Jarrod took it, although he wasn't hungry.

"He came with me as soon as I told him the story, only we were too late." Elly sat down and hugged him. Tears wet his shoulder. "I'm sorry I didn't get there sooner. I was lost and scared…"

"Where are Lily and Kellen?" Jarrod asked. "I want to see them."

"They mourn their sister," the Blades Man said.

I should be with them. He stood and the blanket shifted, revealing his nakedness.

"Clothes," he demanded.

"Drying over there," the Blades Man said. "You were drenched and feverish. Still, you shouldn't exert too much."

"Let me get you another outfit," Elly said, cheeks red but not looking away. "You eat."

Jarrod ate without tasting the soup.

"There was another woman and a child with us. Bekka and Sarrah," Jarrod said. "The guard from the manor said the girl was a skin changer and the baby inside Bekka was also one. Joanne wanted them both."

"Elly spoke of them," the Blades Man finished his soup and set the bowl aside. "I have sent out scouts to search for their captors. So far none have come back."

Jarrod was certain that Bernal was heading north with Bekka, probably back to Shadow Manor or a village close by. Bekka was his betrothed and Jarrod doubted the soldier would give her up so easily. Finding out where would take a while. As for Sarrah, Thramel possibly took her back to the Keep. Once they had her was inside the Keep, he would never be able to get to her out. Not without several thousand men to assault the Keep's defenses.

Elly re-entered, clean tunic and trousers folded over her arms. She turned around as he dressed.

"I think I am starting to understand what Joanne wants with the woman and child," the Blades Man said. "She sent an army to burn and kill all the residents in a southern village called Elysium."

Jarrod slipped his head through the tunic.

"Bekka spoke about taking Sarrah to Elysium. She said it was a sort of sanctuary for her kind, created by Sin."

"It was a sanctuary," the Blades Man said. "Now, it's nothing but a charred tomb. The soldiers took the children as prisoners."

"What for?"

"Joanne is the Mistress of Shadow's champion."

Silence, except for the fire crackling, filled the tent.

"Are you sure?" Jarrod asked. *Another reason to fight against her, to want her dead. It would explain her quick ascent to power.*

The Blades Man nodded.

"So why can't you just kill her?" Elly asked. "Strick her down with a lightning bolt or something."

"That isn't possible, since I don't have the ability to command the weather," the Blades Man said. "Also, we have become linked to our Champion."

"Killing Joanne would destroy the Mistress of Shadows?" Elly asked

"No, she would ascend and become a goddess."

"Which means we would have two powerful deities working against us," Jarrod said.

"Essentially."

If I die, Jarrod reasoned. *I become a god. As a god I could come back and take my own vengeance.*

"We are most vulnerable in this state of being," the Blades Man explained, seeming to read Jarrod's mind. "Since I do not maintain my powers as an Ascended down here with the created—"

"Then I couldn't be ascended." His shoulders sagged with disappointment

"Which means both of you would die," Elly finished the idea. "You have to get back to wherever you live so Jarrod doesn't get killed and disappear on us."

"You taught the Mistress of Shadows, giving her the very skills she now uses against you." Jarrod glared at the warrior god. "This isn't the first time you walked down here."

The Blades Man kept silent.

"Gods! You are no more than children playing with dolls and tin soldiers. You create us, we suffer at your hands and die for reasons not even you understand." Jarrod tightened his belt and threw a cloak around his shoulders. "We would be better if every last one of you just went away."

He stormed out of the tent. Rain pelted through the tree leaves and he pulled the hood over his head. Waning light told him it was nearing dark. Among the trees he noticed tents erected. Dozens of them, each with smoke rising up from their peeks. A soldier dressed in a grey uniform and dark green cloak nodded at Jarrod as he walked past. Elly exited the tent behind him.

"What is all this?" Jarrod asked

"The soldiers we found," Elly said. "They have plenty of food, clean water, and dry wood. These are the ones he posted to protect you. Even more tents are up outside the trees. You'll see them when I take you to Lily and Kellen." She paused, voice lowering. "You want to see her, right?"

Jarrod nodded, a chill coursing through his bones.

Ishmael looked dead. In the fire light, his skin was pale and dark bruises formed under his closed eyes. A blanket covered him from the waist down. His torso was wrapped in a bandage, a dark red bloom on his rib cage.

"They're uncertain if he'll survive the night," Elly said, lightly touching her brother's foot under the blanket. Tears stood out in her eyes. "He has a fever and lost so much blood."

Words escaped Jarrod. He wanted to tell Elly how Ishmael was strong and he would live, but couldn't bring himself to do it. Instead, he put an arm around her shoulders. His mind wasn't on her grief. He came to the tent for one purpose and Ishmael wasn't the reason. Sobbing came from the far corner. Two small forms huddled together on their knees. Kellen spoke soft prayers to Donn and Lily's shoulders heaved with heavy sobs. Stretched out in the corner was a form shrouded in white.

Oh, Hannah! Jarrod held back a cry and broke away from Elly. His heart felt like glass ready to shatter. Tears blurred his vision and he walked on stilted legs that threatened to topple him. Lily looked up at him, tiny face red and streaked. She grabbed his leg and Jarrod fell onto his knees beside her. Lily wrapped around his arm and cried against him. Kellen stopped praying and glared at him.

"She loved you," Kellen said in an accusatory tone.

Tongue thick in his dry mouth, Jarrod nodded.

The shroud seemed too small, as though Hannah shrunk in death. He reached out to touch, but drew his hand back.

This isn't her.

Hannah was in the green fields waiting.

Kellen took his hand and lifted his arm around her shoulder. She leaned against him, softly crying. Jarrod sat there, holding the sisters as they mourned. He couldn't hold back his grief and together all three wept for their lost love.

The girls fell asleep and Jarrod left them. He went over to Ishmael and found his sword sheathed in the belt. He buckled it around his waist. Elly woke up from beside her brother and gave him a questioning look.

"When they wake, and ask where I've gone, tell them I went to seek retribution," he said to Elly. The next part felt like a lie, but it had to be made. "Tell them I will come back for them."

Elly nodded drowsily and Jarrod kissed the top of her head.

"Thank you for everything you have done."

He went out in the rain.

The horses were paddocked near the edge of the trees. A lean-to was constructed over them to keep the worse of the rain off. No one tried to stop him as he saddled a horse. He led it away from the lean-to and stopped. Standing in the rain, black armored and holding a saddle bag, the Blades Man walked past Jarrod. Jarrod watched him cinch the saddle straps on another horse and ride up next to him.

Neither spoke as they rode away from camp.

CHAPTER EIGHTEEN

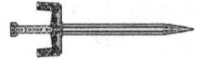

*Janus faces both what is to come and what has happened. She grins and
sneers, laughs and cries, blesses and curses. One moment presses soft kisses
against your hand and the Next, you must count your remaining fingers.*
　　— From "Treatise on the Gods"
　　　　Matheus, scribe to Samson the Wise
　　　　5th Season of the Council

Sower's rains. The strong deluge brought Joanne back to her
childhood, staring out the window as sheets of water feel from the sky.
An unattended book in her lap as she dreamed of it being dry enough
for her to run out in the gardens without being scolded for shoes
covered in mud. Years would pass and she'd succumb to melancholy,
tearing out the fine hairs on her doll's head in boredom.

"Chac is trying to steal the land from his brother Moko," her mother
would attempt to entertain her foul tempered child—a rare occasion
her mother spoke to her. "Chac used to own everything, all the land
was covered in water until Moko stood up to his older brother and
demanded a place of his own. When Chac refused, Moko jumped up
and down, shaking the water until it parted, allowing land to rise above
like a cork popping up from a wine bottle. Chac swore vengeance, that
he would flood the land until he reclaimed it all."

Joanne once believed her mother had wasted those precious words
on a child's tale. She was wrong. *Mother spoke a life truth.* Joanne sat in
her tent, reading over supply reports. The rains thumped like hundreds
of fingers peeling at skin. She ground her teeth at the idea of waiting.

Three and a half days had passed since her army marched from the Keep. They gained ten leagues when the rain fell, light at first, their trek unhindered. Grey clouds thickened, bloated by water until their pregnant bellies could no longer hold back. They released a torrent, forcing Joanne's army to halt at the side of the westerly road. The lowlands grew marshy, wagon wheels bogged down in the mud and men had to force them out of ruts using makeshift runners. The supply train took half a day to catch up to the main front.

My forces could've overrun Heartwood Pines even before the food and water arrived. She flipped through papers, skimming through numbers. Overconfidence brought about Thomas's early demise. She wouldn't make the same error. A little patience could mean a great victory.

Heartwood pines remained forty leagues east. Another two days in dry weather, three with the roads ground into mush, her forces would arrive and she would assess the situation. As long as the rains kept pouring down, she wouldn't risk the roads.

Chac, make your tantrum short and I promise to drown a hundred men in your name.

"Your Highness," General Hale entered the tent and knelt. "One of my scouts has just returned."

Good news, for once.

"Rise." She set aside the supply papers and dug out a rolled-up parchment. She spread it out on the table, revealing hand drawn landscape with trees and river marked. The map, one her brothers had created and she had found tucked inside a bookcase, contained detailed sketches of Heartwood Pines from the wooden walls that Thomas had burnt down, to the Twin Rivers, where they bisected the Pines in half forming North and South pines. Two strongholds had been built using stone scavenged from the East Manor. The South Tower was nearly impenetrable when defended by archers up top. *Yet the fool Thramel managed to lose it. To a farm boy of all people.*

Another fortress was marked in the north, though she questioned its accuracy. Her brother was defeated at the river's fork—very unlikely he ever saw the place.

"What did he discover?" she asked.

"Homes and farms are abandoned south of the fork," General Hale said, tracing the area beneath the words Twin Rivers. "The watch South

Tower appears unoccupied. He didn't witness any activity to or from the tower."

"Did he approach the tower?"

"No, because he didn't want to alert any possible guard of his presence."

Wise, Joanne thought, *however we cannot rule it out.*

"Send two more to investigate it," she said. "If they didn't know we were coming, they will soon enough." She tapped the north part of the map. "What about here? What news of this area?"

"Those scouts have yet returned, your Highness," General Hale said, sounding apologetic.

Which means they will not. The rag-tag band of farmers, miners and sheepherders most likely watched this part of the woods, setting up guard north of the fork. This simplified matters. One point of defense and one point to attack. The rains would swell the Twin Rivers, delaying her approach. She may have to build a bridge or two—

"Your Highness!" a messenger burst into the tent. Three *Mors Faunis* stepped from the corners, drawing weapons, and converging on him. The man dropped prostrate and tossed back his wet hood. "An urgent message, for you from one of your men, returning from Shadow Manor."

"Where is he?" Joanne bristled and the messenger trembled. "Was he alone?"

By the sweet Mistress, if Thramel came back without the girl and woman, I will slice off his tongue and serve it up to the dogs!

Before the messenger could respond, a loud commotion sounded outside the tent.

"Get your dirty paws off me!" She recognized Snout's voice, though it sounded thick, slurred like he was drunk. She didn't think her tracker gave in to drink, but travel changed a person. *If I had to spend a moon with Thramel, I'd probably give in to drinking as well.* "She's expecting us! Step aside else you get a tin helmet!"

A red faced, swollen nosed Snout entered, tugging a terrified child close behind. She had olive skin and raven black hair, her eyes green and bright, shaped like almonds. Joanne knew by the golden flecks she was the girl her Mistress wanted.

Two soldiers followed, looking flustered. They noticed Joanne and dropped to their knees, head bowed. "Apologizes, your Highness," one spoke to the canvas flooring, "he insisted on seeing you."

"Shush your mouth," Snout said, lifting the girl up by the sides and holding her out in front as though she were some disgusting thing he didn't want to handle for very long. She hung in his hands like an over-sized doll. "Look here at what I bring her."

"Leave us," Joanne commanded. The guards stood up and hastily left. She turned to Snout, noting how he didn't bow. *He's grown presumptuous.* She considered putting him back in his place, but more pressing matters were at hand. "Where is the fool I sent with you? Did he die on you? And the woman?"

"That's where it gets complicated." Snouts droopy eyes, bruised and streaked red, focused on the girl he set before Joanne. She shied back against Snout's leg. "This one here was traveling with some young men and their children. We waylaid them in a grove twenty some leagues south, but a man-of-the-watch from Shadow Manor mashed my nose, stole the woman and chased off the horses. Thramel is in pursuit, and on account of my nose being broken and not so good at sniffing at the present, I brought you this little one."

Undone by incompetence. Joanne touched her cheek where her Mistress reminded her about the price of failure.

"Take a detachment of thirty strikers and ride them down. Get the woman back." *She's the most important one. At least the thing growing within her is important.*

"Begging your pardon, but that won't work," Snout said. "I don't know exactly where they went, only that they went north, most like to Shadow Manor, if I guess the man's intentions. Thramel is tracking him and has one of your Death Howlers to assist him."

"That's not good enough!" Joanne shrieked. Snout took a step back and the girl began to cry. "I need them both, not one. Both! You will mount up and lead thirty strikers and find her."

"Please, your Highness—"

"Go! Now!"

"Aye, your Highness." Snout bowed, cringing at her fury. He backed out of the tent, his eyes fixed on his boots.

The girl stared at her, bright green eyes wide and watery. Her tiny wrists were bare, not bound by wolf's bane as she instructed her soldiers do to prevent undesired changes.

"Come here, child," Joanne said, hand on the hilt of her dagger and the other reaching out to the girl. The girl remained fixed to the floor. Joanne knelt to be eye level with the child. "I know what's it like be all alone in an unfamiliar world. How scary it seems around people you don't know."

"I want my mommy," she whispered, her lip trembling and more tears brimming.

Mommy? As far as Joanne knew, the child's parents were dead, slaughtered in Blackwood. *How sweet. How touching she calls the woman mommy. What sort of mommy abandons her daughter?*

What sort of father would sell his daughter's virginity for a small price for something as trivial as peace? A darker voice asked.

"So do I." Joanne smiled. "Do you understand why you are here?"

The girl shook her head.

"It's because you are special," Joanne said. "What is your name?"

"Sarrah," the girl spoke softly.

"Well, Sarrah, you are a very important little girl." Joanne moved forward and Sarrah took a startled step backwards. "You have a choice, Sarrah. You can be a brave girl and do as I tell you. Or you can be a disobedient child by trying to run away. There are consequences for either decision. What will it be?"

The girl lowered her head and sniffed back tears. She looked up, a dangerous gleam in her eye. Joanne grabbed twine from her belt, leaping forward to grab the child before Sarrah could fully change. Little teeth grew into fangs and finger nails into claws. Joanne wrapped the wolf bane twine around the girl's hand. She let out a pain filled howl that raised the hairs on the back of her neck. The girl slashed out and caught Joanne across the shoulder, claws ripping through cloth and flesh. Heat and pain were immediate. Joanne knocked the girl to the ground, twisting her arm around so she bound both hands. The wolf bane halted the girl's transformation, forcing her to return to her human form.

Sarrah struggled, but Joanne was bigger than her and pinned her arms down with one hand and sat on her legs. She brought out her dagger and held it close to the child's eye.

"That was very bad." The girl screamed as Joanne drew the blade down her cheek. "You will learn to be obedient." *Or I will make you ugly, like him,* her father spoke up. "What will it be, little one?"

"I will be good, make it stop!" Blood rolled down the side of her face. "Please, I promise to be good."

"I know you will," Joanne put the dagger in its sheath. "Just like I did."

Bekka felt numb. Rain plastered her hair to her face and soaked her dress to her body, but she couldn't feel the cold, the arm holding her up on the saddle, or the body pressed against her back. Her mind was caught in a loop. Running through the trees, wading in thigh deep water, the ring of steel, screams in the woods. More people died because of her. Hannah. Ishmael. Jarrod. *When will it end?*

Worse still, Sarrah was with those monsters.

"Where are you taking me?"

Bernal didn't reply.

The sky was clouded over and she couldn't tell if it were early morn or midday. It was gray. Only gray. The horse sloshed through murky grass making slow progress. Bekka looked around for landmarks to tell her the location. Ahead appeared a misty form of trees. A foul order wrinkled her nose.

"Not even rain can rinse the stink off you," she said.

"That's not coming from me, my dear," Bernal said, sounding amused. "That is the Black Marsh, a place where you'll call home until I find us a new place to hide."

"What about the black wrym?"

Bernal chuckled.

"Children's tail made up to scare travelers, nothing to worry your pretty little head over."

Bekka felt a kick and touched her belly. She was relieved that the child still lived after all the stress and abuse she took this past moon. *Hold on, sweet child, I will find us a way out of this. Then we will find Sarrah.*

The smell only grew worse the closer they got to the marsh. Bekka leaned over and wretched, dry heaving. Bernal relaxed his grip on her and she began to slide off the saddle. Before her weight toppled her over, he caught her around the waist.

"Careful now, the ground may be wet but it's still hard," Bernal said. "Wouldn't want you to bruise your belly."

"Why should you care? You want him dead anyway?" Bekka said.

"How sure are you it's a boy?"

Because I dreamt it. She refused to answer.

"Boy, girl, it matters none to me," Bernal said. "I'd no sooner kill it than lose my head. The child is my barter for our freedom. Once you birth the beast, I plan on leaving it on Joanne's doorstep so she won't hound our heels with her wolves."

"I won't allow it."

"You don't have a choice."

"Let me down, I have to urinate."

"Squatting in the open will not happen," Bernal said. "Wait until we reach the trees of Black Wyrm. Then you can water the abominations all you like."

The abominations, Bekka noticed were stunted black trunks, twisting away from marsh. She understood their desire to escape the smell: a mix of spoiled eggs and rotting wood. Her stomach felt ready to heave, but she choked it down.

"You'll get used to it after a day or two," Bernal said, nose wrinkled and grimacing. "Either this, or the gallows."

For you.

She didn't want to imagine what might be in store for her. Joanne wanted her more than just to hang her for killing the guards at Blackwood. Bekka sensed a stronger force, one beyond mortals. Like Jarrod, she had visions of a dark shadow hunting her. It wasn't the benevolent Sin from Shane's stories. This god wanted her baby and Sarrah.

Now she has one of us. Mother watch over her. Sin light my path to her.

The water inside the Black Wyrm Marsh sloshed over the path. A murky, brown almost the color of dried blood. Yellowed leaves softened the rain, but they continued to flood the sopping ground so the horse's fetlock sloshed through the water. Sound was amplified and echoed around them.

"Let me down," Bekka said. "I have to go right now."

"All this water will do that to you," he said, guiding the horse off the path and to a hillock rising above the water's surface. He helped Bekka dismount. She ran off into some sparse shrubs. "Don't wander too far," Bernal shouted. She could see the smug grin on his face as he waited for her atop the mount. She was grateful for the fact that he didn't follow her. "Wouldn't want you getting lost and falling into the marsh. No telling what snakes and slithering creatures lurk in there."

Safer than the slithering one out there. Bekka ducked down like she was squatting. Instead of removing her small clothes, she crouched and made her way through the shrubs, careful not to disturb them. She glanced back and could no longer see Bernal or the horse. The only sound she heard was rain striking the water and her boots splash into the water as she descended the hill. He would come for her soon. This was her only chance at escaping him. He wouldn't leave her alone for a moment after this, so she had to make good on it.

"Are you alright in there?" Bernal shouted, startling her. "Do you need me to assist with holding your skirts up?"

His patience wouldn't last much longer. She had to find a way out.

Stunted trees grew black and twisted in the water, their roots well below the waterline. A black vine dangling from a branch drop into the water. Bekka watched it drift across the murky surface towards her. The way it moved, coiling from side to side, it wasn't a branch but a thick black snake nearly as long as she was tall. It flicked a tongue the length of her hand, scenting the air.

Not going that way. She began moving north, crouching behind the shrubs. The snake turned along the hillside, following her. It swam quickly in the water. *Maybe this wasn't such a good idea.*

She searched around for a stick, or something to fend it off. Nothing was in reach. She stood up and began to run through, her boots sinking in the water. Soft mud sucked them in and tried to strip the boot off her feet.

Rather than finding dry ground, the water grew deeper, rising to her boot tops, brown, stinking water spilling over the lip and soaking her feet. Bekka glanced back at the hill. It was too far away. The snake gained on her, cutting her off from the higher ground. She sloshed towards the path, the water growing shallow again. She imagined the snake catching her, wrapping her up and drowning her under its weight. Or sharp fangs sinking into her thighs, venom paralyzing her.

I don't want to die, not in this stinking marsh! She put her head down and pushed headlong, sweating as she kicked up her knees. No matter how hard she waded through the water, she seemed to move too slow.

Sloshing sounded louder, closer. She turned to face it head on. Raising her hands into fists, she froze, stunned as the snake swam past her. Something else moved in the water behind it. A submerged log drifted behind the snake, too fast. It slithered along the surface, leaving ripples in its wake.

Bekka stepped back. A hand gripped her arm and she screamed. Bernal spun her around, grinning and revealing his yellowed teeth.

"Thinking of running off?" He twisted her arm and turning her so her back bottom pressed against his mid-section. "That's not a good idea. There are worse things than tales of black wyrms that stalk these marshes."

"I saw a snake," Bekka said, biting back another scream. In her peripheral, the log closed in and started to rise above the water's surface.

Bernal laughed.

"A snake? You ran away from a snake?"

Bekka's eyes widened as a large, black head rose up, water dripping from its scales. The patter of rain covered some of the sound. Yellow, reptilian eyes narrowed on them. Needle point teeth lined its open maw. Bernal jerked at the sound and turned to see the creature. He shoved Bekka back, stumbled, reaching for his sword.

"Janus! Godsda—"

The black wyrm lurched forward and snapped it jaws over Bernal's torso. Blood splashed Bekka's face, dispelling her stupor. It lifted Bernal from his feet, legs convulsing so one boot tumbled down and splashed in front of Bekka. She turned and ran.

She reached the main path and for moment panicked. How was she going to out run the creature? Where could she go? She saw the horse tethered to a stunted black tree and ran to it. She tore the leather reign from the branch and glanced over her shoulder. The black wyrm stomped through the brush and entered the road, moving slower on land than it had in water.

Bekka clamored into the saddle as the horse tried to bolt. She clutched the saddle horn, bouncing as the horse sprinted down the path. Slick from the rain, she lost her grip. Throwing her arms around the horse's neck, she held on. *Mother watch over me! Sin give me strength!* She closed her eyes, waiting for the warm, meaty breath just before teeth clamped down on her. Rain pelted her and she opened her eyes. No more trees lined her path, empty grasslands slick with mud and water.

The horse carried her clear of the Black Wyrm Marsh and eventually slowed down. She caught a loose reign, pulling back on the leather thong to force it to stop. Hands shaking, she climbed out of the saddle and sat down on the wet ground, legs unable to hold her up anymore. They stopped atop a steep slope and she looked back, expecting to see the black wyrm charging after her. The marsh was a distant point below. Nothing came out of it.

Please, let my baby be alright. She touched her belly. The hard ride jostled her good and she heard how pregnant women sometimes lost the baby from the hard motion, tearing it from the womb in an untimely manner. As if in response, she felt a kick. Bekka laughed in relief.

"Strong, little one," she said, rubbing her belly. "Strong like his father."

She placed her hand to her cheek, her fingers touching a drying fleck. She peeled it with her nail and looked down at the dark red spot. *All that remains of Bernal.* She laughed and cried in the same instance. She scrubbed her face with her the damp cloak, staining it maroon.

What am I going to do now? The rain had ceased, but it was growing dark and a chilly breeze picked up. She had to find shelter and wood to make a fire. She had no idea where the nearest village was to get help. South of Black Wyrm Marsh was the Keep and east was Heartwood Pines. That's where Jarrod was planning on taking her and Sarrah.

"Jarrod is dead and I don't know where to find Sarrah," she said. The Keep seemed more likely. In the clutches of Joanne. *I won't be much help if I die. First things first. Shelter and warmth.*

The idea of survival slipped away at the sound of riders approaching from the south. As they breasted the slope, the lead horse stopped and its rider looked shocked, then he grinned.

"Look as what we have here," Thramel said. "The gods sure are smiling on me."

CHAPTER NINETEEN

Like stars falling from the heavens we will burn.
—Ruin Prophesy
Menrva

*"**You!**"* Sin pointed a trembling finger at Dandulain. Red-streaked eyes and frown lines marred her pale skin. She was sitting but as soon as Dandulain entered the pool room, Sin launched to her feet. "What did you do to my children?"

The pool cleared on a familiar sight. Charred remains of Elysium under a fine grey powder of ash. A diminished nude form lay curled up on the cobblestone. Wolves and other carrion eaters have yet to descend on the village. Dandulain doubted they ever would due to the nature of the dead. *Leaving them to the flies and maggots.*

"You are accusing me of such a grievous attack." Dandulain scoffed. "I stand before you while the Blades Man walks among the created, killing as he pleases."

"Don't spin your lies!"

"You saw him when I opened the pool. Moko, Qetesh, Donn, Sirena, Hacawit all witnessed him walking in the woods." Dandulain rolled a crystal between her fingers.

"What about Blackwood?" Sin dipped her fingers into the pool and the water frothed, closing over Elysium and ripped apart to reveal an abandoned wood, rain dripping down on empty cottages and cabins. The residents had a deserted sense. No smoke rose from chimneys although it was closing in on nightfall. "The bodies of my children decay, nude flesh melting off their bones."

The image shifted to indistinguishable corpses. A few, Dandulain noted, wore uniforms. None of this surprised her, just ignited her fury over the lost young. One in particular, still in the womb.

"It appears the created rose up against your children and slew them."

The palace shuddered and bits of stone and gravel showered down. Dandulain laughed and clapped her hands. All of creation was about to collapse under the weight of the Ruin Prophesy and this moon speck worried about her children.

"What's so funny?" Sin asked. "Are you laughing at my pain, my loss?"

"You have no idea about pain and loss." She approached Sin and the pale goddess placed her hands on hips, invoking further defiance. Mirth rained from Dandulain and she grabbed Sin by the back of her neck. She tried to break the grip, but Dandulain bent her over the Pool of Reflection. The pale goddess cried out as her knees struck the stone and her face plunged into the water, gurgling her noise into wet bubbles. The image disappeared under a froth of bubbles. Sin flailed, trying to grip the pool's edge.

"Do you understand pain now? Your lungs burning for air, resisting the pull of water ready to fill them up?" Dandulain shoved her elbow in the middle of Sin's back, forcing her head deeper the water rising to the base of her neck. Her nails racked against the leather gloves. "The more you struggle, the harder it becomes to resist."

She lifted Sin up, water streaming from her hair hanging in wet clumps, and tossed her to the side. Sin hit the stone wall and bounced back, a loud crack in her shoulder as it hung, limp at her side.

"Do you understand pain, Sin?" Dandulain asked.

Sin sniffed and nodded.

"I don't think you really do, but I don't have time to teach you anymore." Dandulain clasped the soul pendant around her neck. "I'm needed elsewhere."

"You lied to us, fooled us into believing Mother was taking sides," Sin said.

"I did nothing. You all came to the conclusion that you wanted to believe." Dandulain dipped her hand in the pool. The water parted onto an open field. "Besides, Mother did choose a side. The truth is, so did you. She's gone and everything she built is also about to slip away into oblivion, because you wanted what she had. Now you shall have exactly what Mother has."

"Why?" Sin asked.

"Because," Dandulain said, climbing up onto stone edge. "I want everything."

She plunged into the cold water, waves rushing over her head, and she fell.

"Shadow descends on created, shadow descends on created, shadow descends on created." Menrva whispered in the dank, cold cell, her arms wrapped around her midsection as she rocked back and forth. Her eyes were open, but all she saw was darkness. "Shadow descends on created."

Ruin has begun! She shivered, shaking her head. Her voice was hoarse and cracked as she repeated. "Shadow descend on created." *Ruin is a lie, a ruse, since nothing may completely be destroyed, only changed, transformed.* Books written by wise men professed as much knowledge. Fire consumed, but created heat and ash.

"Shadow descends on c—" She gasped. A new vision superseded the darkness. He eyes rolled up to the whites as her head tossed back in exhilaration. *The darkest night ends in dawn and shadows run from light. There is no dawn, there is no light there is...*

"There is awe, there is nothing, there is everything, life, death, creation, uncreated." She babbled on, voice rising with each new concept, a new vision accompanying every word, until it crescendoed into: "Transcendence!"

The word echoed off the stone walls and as it faded away, her chin dropped to her chest and she slid sideways, tongue pointing out between her teeth and a trickle of blood running down the corner of her mouth. Eyes stared blankly at the dark stone beneath her sprawled legs, hands resting in her lap.

Water trembled as the palace gave a mighty shake. Tiny drops ceased, and then began to fall.

Riding blind. Jarrod kept his eyes forward, keeping doubt at bay. One direction, one destination focused in his mind. The Keep. He was certain that's where they would take Sarrah. *Sarrah, for certain, but not Bekka. The guard stole off with her. Gods knew where they went.* Only the gods didn't know. They didn't seem to understand much of the creatures they set loose on the world. *Just as selfish and near-sighted as those made in their image.*

The Blades Man kept several yards behind him. A silent shadow in black armor. Questions about Ascension plagued Jarrod. What could he do as a god? His role in the pantheon? The farmer? What powers would he have? How could he help people? Would he ever know true death? Jarrod shoved them aside, too angry and sad to speak.

They crested another hill about five leagues from the Keep, or so he hoped. He'd never been there and the maps he did see were crudely drawn on sheep skin. Guard outposts would be the true indicator of distance. At least one at every half league interval, according to the sheep skin map. He still lacked proper reports, for example the number of garrisoned troops.

"You don't know what you're doing," Ishmael's voice criticized.

Doesn't matter. I will fight my way through, or die trying.

"What good will you be to the girl?"

What good am I now? Better to try something instead of running and hiding. The foxes still dug us out of our holes and ravaged us. I'm not going alone. I have the god of war with me. That should count for something?

So far it only added up to heartache and disappointment.

The towers were the least of his problems. Joanne would have thousands of soldiers at the Keep and not even the god of war could handle those numbers. Also, he doubted they could walk up to Keep, knock and ask for Sarrah to be returned to them. He wouldn't be dealing with ignorant lay-bouts that he could convince to take him in.

I probably need an army, bigger than the one we left behind. The only one of significant size left to defend Nemus from Joanne was in Heartwood pines, if they haven't been slaughtered yet.

The rain seemed to let up some. Jarrod glanced at the puffy white clouds mingled among the gray. It was too earlier to proclaim the Sower's rains at an end. Usually, a small break came before the final deluge. A golden streak trailed between the white and gray clouds, almost like a single ray of sun light prying apart the thick layer blocking the sun. Jarrod shielded his eyes for a better view. *Not a ray of sunshine, maybe a hawk diving down on an unsuspecting prey?* At the angle of approach, it would strike ahead of them.

"We need to go back," Huron said, the sound of his deep voice filled with angst startled Jarrod. It was the first time the Blades Man spoke in over a day. His next words were not as inspiring: "That way is not safe."

"It's just a bird," Jarrod said.

"Something is wrong." Huron rode past him, speaking more to himself. "She shouldn't be down here."

"Who?"

"Dandulain, the Mistress of Shadows."

The name was ice on Jarrod's neck, sending a shiver through his body. *I'm coming for you. When I find you, I will break your blade and shred your flesh from bone.* Menacing indigo eyes glaring from some dark nightmare. Here she came to put paid to her words.

No more running away.

"She must have a soul pendant, right?" Jarrod matched Huron's horse

"I hope so." Huron loosened his swords in the scabbards. "Only way to send her back, otherwise…"

"What?"

"Should the Ruin prophesy takes hold for good, we lose everything." Huron stopped, and climbed off his horse. "Go back to Agni. Tell him there is a problem at the Palace and he must return, to find Mother and protect her. I will seek him out after I take care of this situation."

"I'm not going to let you fight her alone," Jarrod said, drawing Ishmael's sword.

"You're not ready. Dandulain is far more skilled with her daggers. She would cut you to ribbons before you got in one swing. Besides, she would be the warrior god, or goddess," Huron said. "That's if I hadn't killed her."

"If she wins, sends you back, or kills you, I'm as good as dead," Jarrod said. "Might as well not wait around for her to murder me in my sleep."

Huron considered his words and laughed.

"What's so funny?" Jarrod asked.

"You are as stubborn as she was," he said. "Fine, you may come. Don't engage her in direct combat. We don't have to kill her, just remove the pendant from around her neck and smash it. Once it is gone, she can no longer remain here in a physical form. Don't forget, Jarrod, should you be slain while I am here in the physical form, you do not ascend or go to Gehanna or Anu."

The dream right after Hannah's death, dancing with her in the green fields of Gehanna, he knew she must be waiting.

"You defeated her once," Jarrod said. "This shouldn't be so difficult."

"You underestimate me." A figure dressed in black stood at the base of a hill. She pulled back her hood allowing raven black hair to stream down her shoulders. Her skin was pale and she gave Jarrod a devious grin. Her words carried up the hill as easily as theirs must've carried down to her. "This is your Champion, Huron. I can see why Mother hid him. He is merely a boy. A pity, he must die before he can grow a full beard. Is he so naïve to believe the story of how you killed me? Did you tell him the real story of how you defeated me when last we met in mortal combat?"

"I spun no tales," the Blades Man said.

"Never the one with fancy words." Dandulain grinned. "Think, farm boy, would I be a goddess now if he killed me while he wore the skin of the created?"

Both of them would have fallen if she didn't Ascend. The Blades Man wouldn't be with Jarrod, nor would the Mistress of Shadows threaten their very existence, unless he was in his godly form the moment she died.

"You didn't kill her," Jarrod said, feeling like he was punched in the gut. "Another lie."

"My sword stuck the mortal blow," Huron said. "My only error was selfishness."

Dandulain laughed. "It wasn't your cut that started my metamorphosis. I suffered worse by hedge bandits. No, I feigned my death just to see what you do. You proved me right. Nothing more than a coward who fled back to mommy instead of finishing what he started. All you gods are the same. That's why I'm going to purge everything you have done and restart fresh."

Huron drew both his blades.

"I will atone for my grievous errors."

The Mistress of Shadows raised her right arm, palm towards them as though trying to halt their actions. A bright blue light extended towards them, growing to encompass Jarrod's entire vision. He closed his eyes as a concussive force struck him and he was lifted off his horse and flew backwards, hitting the ground, air rushing from his lungs.

Snout saw the bright streak in the sky. He didn't need his nose to smell out trouble. The hairs stood on end as the entire air seemed to crackle. He reigned in, wanting to turn around and go the opposite direction. *Mistress Johanne will string me up by my guts if I arrive empty handed.* He was tasked with tracking Bernal and Thramel to find the girl. Only place he could think of going was back to Shadow Manor and he was for damn certain not passing through the Black Marsh. He'd lead the strikers south of the Keep before riding north, hoping to pick up a trail.

Why do things always have to be complicated?

"What is that?" Captain Lethers asked beside Snout.

"Nothing to worry about," Snout said. "We'll head north of the Keep and pick up the Sands Road."

The Keep itself was less than a day's ride away. They could resupply there and continue on with fresh horses. A large ball of blue light careened up a hillside and exploded in a bright flash that left sparks in Snout's eyes. The ground rumbled and quaked even though the impact point was quarter a league away.

"We should investigate what caused that and report back to her Highness," Captain Lethers said. "She needs to be aware of this new potential danger."

"No way," Snout said. "Our duty is to find the woman and escort her back to camp."

"You can tuck your tail and run if you like," Captain Lethers gave him a disgusted look. "I will make certain she hears of your actions."

"Then send a couple of men and if they don't return, you can report the danger."

"A very good idea." Captain Lethers grinned. "You go, since you are a scout."

"I'm a tracker," Snout said.

"Good enough. Go track the cause of that light," Captain Lethers said. "I'll send the silent wolf with you. That way you don't risk any noise."

"I would've been better off sticking with Thramel," Snout muttered.

"What was that?"

"Nothing, sir." Snout wrinkled is nose. "Figuring out the best path to take so as not to end up killed."

"Snout, I wouldn't plan on running off, either. Take a quick look and report back to me immediately."

"If I die?"

"Make sure you don't."

Jarrod's ears rang as he looked up at the grey sky. He sat up, a fiery ache in his tailbone. *I fell,* he thought. *No, I was thrown by a blue*— He clamored to his feet, working Ishmael's sword from the scabbard. He wasn't sure how much good it would do against a force like a goddess. A few yards away his horse screamed, legs thrashing as it tried to stand up. Its front leg wouldn't support him and he tumbled back over, big eyes pleading with Jarrod. *Nothing I can do for you.* Jarrod shook his head, counting himself lucky the horse didn't land on him, crushing him beneath its weight.

Off to his left, the Blades Man knelt on one knee, pushing himself up. He held one long sword in his right hand. A broken hilt lay on the ground, the shattered blade jammed into the dirt.

"Run," he said, looking at Jarrod. "Go, quickly."

Where?

The Mistress of Shadows approached. Her eyes lit up with power and she looked to raise her hand again, a flicker of blue light glowing in her palm. The Blades Man threw himself forward, pressing against the ground as a smaller ball of light rushed over him. The hairs stood up on Jarrod's arms and back of his neck, the air grew warmer and crackled, smelling of sulfur. The blue ball of light continued on, picking up speed as it dissipated over the empty plains.

Mother, it's a wonder we're alive!

The Mistress of Shadows laughed.

"You weren't expecting this, Huron," she said. "While you were off piddling around with these weak creatures, I learned a few more tricks."

"Stole them," Huron replied, shoving off the ground and to his feet. "How did you get the star of creation? That power belongs to Mother. She alone knows how to properly yield it."

"Mother no longer requires it."

"Foolish girl, what have you done now?" Huron growled, scrambling to his feet.

"Set things in motion that can't be undone," she laughed. "Might as well accept your fate."

"I accept nothing from you."

The Blades Man rushed at her, *Reaping Sorrows* slicing the air as the blade cut upward. The Mistress of Shadows crouched under the slice, dropping into *Spider in the Grass*. A dagger in each hand, she racked the sides of his armor missing the vital gap as he spun past. She thrust a dagger at his throat. *Broken Lattice* deflected the knife off the sword hilt and he kicked her in the side. She rolled away, escaping *Thrashing the Wheat*.

A black cloud rose up from the ground around her, slowly consuming her. The Blades Man thrust *Wrathful Thorns* into the cloud and whirled as the blade was batted away.

"I am the darkness that lingers in the light," she said, fully enveloped by the black cloud. Three small bursts of blue light burnt threw and struck the Blades Man in the side, exploding against his armor and shoving him back. He grunted as each blast hit, leaving behind white scorch marks on the black armor. "I am shadow in the light." The Blades Man retreated, falling into *Ox Guard*. The black mist closed in on him. Dagger points blurred like cat's claws. He batted one away, but the second racked across his exposed thigh. Blood seeped from the gash and he retreated again.

Jarrod watched the black mist flow towards the Blades Man, the frenzy of desperate sword strokes and red droplets flicking off in the mist. Rooted to the ground, Ishmael's sword nothing more than a twig in his hands, Jarrod watched helplessly. *How does a mortal fight in a battle between gods?*

If I don't help, he's going to die. If he dies, I die.

Listening to the Blades Man's grunts, the battle wouldn't last much longer.

Jarrod squeezed the leather grip and let out a squeak. He ran towards the battle. Lacking a true target, his blade arched down cutting into the black mist, hoping to make contact with something inside. The blind stroke passed through as though cutting smoke. A sharp blow sent him staggering away. He grabbed his ribs and felt ice shards in his side. He ducked, covering his head as something struck out of the mist, swishing overhead close enough to feel the breeze on his knuckles.

The Blades Man took advantage of the distraction to thrust into the mist. A pain filled shriek came from it. The black mist melted away and the Mistress of Shadows clutched her side. Blood seeped from around her black gloves. She grimaced and then began laughing. Blue light emanated across her side. She straightened and removed her hand, revealing a hole in her leather armor, but the skin was knitted together.

"Something else I learned from Mother," she said.

The Blades Man growled and resumed his assault. Precise, agile strokes that would kill an ordinary man were turned aside as though he was a child holding a stick. He kept her on the defensive, preventing her from using other powers. Despite his efforts, she found the weakness in his armor until red smattered on black. Jarrod attempted a few swipes at her, catching her black cloak on the blade, the cloth tearing as she stepped lithely away in a dance he was too slow to follow. Her blade nicked his hand and he dropped the sword, leaping away from a slice that nearly gut him.

"Get away!" the Blades Man shouted. Sweat poured off his determined face, a gash weeping red below his left eye. He charged her again. A blue ball caught him in the chest and he flew backwards. She pounced on him, driving the dagger points into his sides. The Blades Man growled, arching his body to push her away. She held on, squeezing with her knees as she yanked the daggers out, splattering more blood.

She's going to kill him.

He remembered what the Blades Man said. They didn't need to kill her, but send her back to the Palace. All he needed to do was break....

"The pendant," Jarrod said. He dropped the sword and leapt on her back.

At first his weight bent her over, knives no longer plunging in the prostrate warrior god. He groped for the pendant around her throat. An elbow caught him in the gut and he nearly tumbled off. Fingers wrapped around several chain and he tugged. They didn't move. She twisted, and he went over her shoulder, landed on his side, and rolled across the grassy knoll. Everything was upside down. He saw an object streak towards his face and quickly rolled over to see the dagger stick hilt deep into the dirt. The Mistress of Shadows stood, searching her throat. Jarrod's hand ached and he looked down. Threads of blood dripped from his closed fist. He opened his fingers to find three objects in his palm. One had a crystal swirling with a purple smoke, another a blue light shown and the third was a black disc.

Which is the soul pendant?

"Give those back," she said, pressing the knife point under the Blades Man's chin.

"You'll just kill him anyway," Jarrod said. He slipped the chain with the black disc over his head. "All I have to do is break these and you go back."

"He dies and you don't ascend," she said. "You die and go into nothing. No eternal paradise with the girl you loved. What was her name?"

Jarrod fought the rage overpowering his thought. She wanted him to react, to strike out blindly. Instead, he set both crystals on the ground, placing his boot heel on them. "You really think I care about you or him, or even about where I go? You gods don't know a thing about those you created. The more shame on you, because you were mortal like us once and knew the pains of living."

"You are nothing, an insignificant speck of dust."

Her arm wiped towards him and he felt a hard thump in his chest, driving him back a step. Jarrod stared dumbly at the dagger hilt protruding from him. The blade cracked bone under his right clavicle.

I'm going to die, but at least I'll send her back. Jarrod stomped on the crystals. The heel of his smashing against them.

He smiled at the small victory. Only it didn't last. Instead of a satisfying snapping, he felt them sink into the ground. Jarrod wavered, pain flaring in his chest and blood spread across the front of his jerkin. *The wet ground.* He stared at both crystals partially immersed in the dark dirt. He dropped to his knees and reached for the chains. His fingers closed over them when he felt needles digging into his flesh.

He lifted his eyes and stared into the dark holes of what may have once been beautiful. Beauty was replaced by anger, hatred, twisted into a dark unforgiving creature. Unrecognizable as human.

"I was wrong." Jarrod gasped against the pain, his vison blurring. "You were never human."

"Let go," she responded, tearing flesh from the back of his hand. With the other hand, she shoved a palm under his chin, cracking his teeth together. "These are mine."

He squeezed the crystal as she gripped the dagger's hilt. Metal grated against bone as she twisted the blade. Jarrod screamed, feeling a sharp snap and a pinch in his palm. The dagger ripped from his chest and the color drained from the world. The dark image of the woman greyed then winked out. Fingernails prying at his flesh disappeared, leaving red gouges from the wrist the meaty part of his thumb.

She's gone. Sudden pain and disorientation hit him as he dropped to his knees. *I'm going to faint. Darkness. Nothing but darkness. I will fade away into nothing.* Smoke rose from his right hand. He opened it, looking at the shattered crystal shards poking into his flesh among tiny red pools. Wispy smoke came from the broken remains and he breathed it in. He coughed, turning his head away, but the sour smell filled his nose. A renewed vigor filled him limbs and the color returned to the gray surroundings. Warmth spread across his chest and hand. He could feel as well as see the wounds closing. Tiny shards popped out of his skin.

Jarrod slipped the solid blue crystal over his head where it clanked against the dark disc. He stood up, strength flowing through his limbs. He looked around and saw no trace of the Mistress of Shadows. *She's gone.* He smiled. His smile faltered as he noticed the Blades Man lying motionless in the grass. *Not him, too!* A thin squeal came from his throat. *Don't be dead. Please, don't die.*

Jarrod ran towards him. The Blades Man clutched his throat, blood seeping through his fingers. He looked pale, each breath shallow and red, wispy froth foamed from the corners of his mouth, painting his lips red. Red rimmed eyes stared at Jarrod seeming to cloud over.

Without explanation, Jarrod understood what must be done. He leaned down and saw the blue crystal streaked red with the Blades Man's blood sticking partially out of his breast plate. He couldn't pull it from around the god's neck, at least not without endangering his life anymore. He searched around and found one of his longswords in the grass. He slid the blade between the crystal and chain. As he was doing so, he felt a tug on his arm. The Blades Man pointed at the disk and crystal around Jarrod's neck.

The message was clear: he wanted to take them back to their original keepers. He wanted to take them back to Mother and Father.

Don't give them to him, a small, yet powerful voice spoke up.

Jarrod flicked the blade, separating the chain and pulled the crystal from the loop. He looked from it to the dying god whose hand beckoned for that which belonged to them.

Jarrod stepped back and held the crystal in his palm.

Huron made a gurgling noise, sounding like, "Please."

Jarrod crushed the crystal between his fingers and watched as the Blades Man faded, eyes narrowed as he slipped from the land of the created, bloody hand still outstretched as though Jarrod might reconsider in the last moments.

Wispy smoke rose up from his hand and he breathed it in, smelling strong citrus. Jarrod felt a surge of power overtake him and he began to laugh.

Snout watched it all from the base of the hill. The blue light flashing, dark fog attacking the black armored man and farm boy. He wanted to turn his horse around and ride back to camp. *Only fool interrupts a battle between the gods.* The farm boy was a great example of a fool. He leapt onto the back of a goddess. Not any goddess, but the bloody Shadow herself. He was impressed that the boy could find her, from the way she slipped into dark fog, back and thought it didn't surprise him how she shrugged off like a blowfly on a horse's rump. For his trouble, he got a knife in his chest.

Yet, somehow the boy didn't die. Instead, the Mistress of Shadows disappeared. The boy acted as though nothing had happened. He knelt next to his fallen companion, another god, perhaps, and took something of his. Then that god slipped away as well. Snout rubbed his eyes in disbelief.

"That boy jumped into a battle between two gods, like a mouse coming between two cats, and he walks away unscathed," Snout said to the *Mors Faunis* at his side. The Death Howler began to dismount. "I wouldn't do that if I were you. Now's not the time to finish off old grudges."

The *Mors Faunis* stalked up the hillside, leaving Snout behind. Snout gathered up the horse's reign, ready to ride. *After I watch the wolf fight the mouse.* Only the farm boy wasn't a mouse anymore, nor was he a boy.

"God touched," Snout said, and spat between forked fingers. Only fools fought one of those.

Snout was no fool.

The hole in his jerkin was stiff with blood. Jarrod pocked a finger inside, anticipating a sharp pain as he probed the gaping wound. Instead, he touched solid skin. He ripped open the hole and stared at skin knitted together. Red stained hair gave the only sign he was wounded at all. The scratches on his hands had closed up as well. The only pain he felt was a minor headache. *Probably from breathing it whatever dust the crystals held.* He touched the one crystal and disc around his neck, reassuring himself they were still there.

They don't belong to you. A voice spoke up in his head. He felt a little guilt over not returning them to the Blades Man.

"They're not his either," Jarrod muttered. "I'll keep them safe, better than he ever could."

Mine now, another voice said and laughed in his head.

Jarrod felt a little dizzy. He sat on the ground where the Blades Man laid. Some of his blood still speckled the green grass. Drowsiness competed against a wild energy flowing through his limbs. Sleep competed against the urge to run.

Someone approached and looked up. A man wearing a snarling wolf's head crested the hill, sword drawn.

"You came to finish what you started?" Jarrod asked. He looked around for the second. They always came in pairs. Jarrod couldn't defeat one, let alone two of Joanne's wolves. They would tear him up in a matter of moments. That didn't mean he wouldn't try. Jarrod got to his feet and held the Blades Man's blade in *Ox Guard*. "Where's your partner?"

The *Mors Faunis* didn't reply, but kept moving closer. Jarrod glanced to the sides and took a step to the right to check his rear. It appeared this was a lone wolf.

He didn't wait to strike.

Half-moon sliced towards Jarrod and he countered with *Wind-Break-Through-the-Willows*. His arm moved on its own, effortless course. He didn't think, but reacted feeling his body under the control of some other, like the time in the Tower. The *Mors Faunis* made two sweeping attacks, forcing Jarrod to retreat several steps. He turned aside the blows, steel clashing against steel. He crouched into *Shy-Lily* sweeping low at the Death Howler's legs. Cloth tore as the blade bit home, slicing flesh, The *Mors Faunis* limped, striking at Jarrod's left flank. A quick *Falling Star* caught the blade on his and Jarrod pressed forward, swirling the guard so the point struck the ground. A sweep of the blade caught the Death Howler in the neck, severing the metal wolf's head from his shoulders.

Jarrod glanced around for another attacker. He was alone on the hill. Alone with the corpse of the Death Howler.

"Were you the one holding the sword as she fell on it?" He kicked the corpse.

No response came and he noticed movement below the hill. A lone horse rider took off, holding the reins of a second horse. The man on the horse looked familiar. *Too short to be Thramel. The sniveling hound, then. He'll know where to find Thramel.*

Jarrod wiped the sword on the Death Howler's trousers. It was too big for the sheath meant for Ishmael's sword, so he tucked it into his belt. He then ran down the hill. The horse was fast and would out distance a normal human.

I'm something not normal, *yet not a god.* He laughed as his legs carried him on a new found vigor. *I'm coming for you little doggy. I won't stop until I have you.*

Jarrod ran.

CHAPTER TWENTY

The only thing separating the Gods from the Created is that we should know better. We were the wise ones seeking to enlighten the dark. Now I realize that we asked the wrong question: Not can we do this, but should it be done at all? In the end, or, in an end since each end is another beginning, we failed to live up to sour established standards, denying responsibility. As a result, we lost everything. Or perhaps we gained something much more precious.
          —From "Tome of Essence"

Huron gripped the pool's stone edge and gasped as his head breached the surface. Fingers slipped on the slick stone and his head disappeared under water, heavy black armor dragging him down. Bracing against the stone floor, he shoved upward. Water cascaded over his face. He tore off his helm, tossing it over the wall. He clutched at his throat. No gash. No blood. With the flesh discarded, so went the leaden weight of dying.

The boy took them! His hands trembled. Fingers curled into an empty fist. He had reached out for the disc of darkness and star of creation. Instead of handing them over, the boy crushed the soul pendant, returning Huron to the Palace. *He* stole *them!* The repercussions for leaving such power in the greedy hands of the created were unimaginable. *I need another pendant! I'll kill the boy myself, crush his insignificant life and take back what belongs to us!*

A whimper sounded off in the corner. Huron reached for his swords, but the scabbards were empty. Double shame, he'd left both swords behind. Sloshing through the pool, he climbed over the edge. A small form curled up against the far wall. Silver hair rolled over her back as she shivered, knees drawn up to her bosom. Sin glared at Huron; fresh tears stained her cheeks.

"Why?" she asked, the word coming out in a whisper.

"I don't understand."

The palace trembled and Huron stumbled, bracing an arm against the wall to keep from falling on her. He noticed the cracks in the stone walls for the first time and the debris scattered over the floor. The Pool of Reflection, however, remained intact.

"You allowed *her* to kill my children in Elysium and Blackwood." Sin's vehemence drew his attention back. She scrubbed her red eyes. "You made *her* and she took everyone from me."

Elysium! The children Joanne's soldiers tried to kidnap were Sin's progeny.

"Dandulain wanted them," Huron said. F*or what reason?*

"They're all dead." Sin snarled

"No, they're not," Huron said.

Sin eyed him suspiciously.

"Look here." Huron touched the pool and it bubbled, water parting to the sides. A group of children sat around campfires eating roasted meat, talking, and laughing. The image closed in on the face of one girl. A yellow glimmer flickered in the corner of her eyes. Sin put a hand over her mouth to stifle a sob. "I rescued six of them. She killed the adults, but wanted these children for some reason.

"Also, a woman and child travelled with the farm boy. They were stolen away before I arrived."

Sin let out a low moan and nearly staggered, would have fallen into the water if he hadn't caught her. She wrapped her arms around his waist. Her thin body felt frail, not at all god-like.

"She wants them for her own," Sin whispered. "She wants to twist them to her ways."

A shudder ran through the stone.

"What's happening here? Where is Mother?"

"We were tricked!" Sin made a high-pitched moan. "We were made into fools."

"Where is she?" He grabbed her thin shoulders, resisting the urge to shake her.

"Gone. Forced into the Shadow throne." Her anger gone, Sin looked deflated. The Palace shook again. "It triggered this."

Ruin Prophesy.

Mother tried to warn him.

"Where is Menrva?"

Sin shrugged.

Huron pulled his hand from the pool, the image closing in a froth of bubbles. He broke into a run from the room.

"Where are you going?" Sin asked.

He needed to track down Dandulain, to force answers from her, but he had no way of knowing where she slunk off to hide now that her powers were diminished. One other god, he could think of, who kept more secrets than the rest. He may be the key to understanding how to stop all of this destruction before their world and that of the Created perished.

Giant cracks formed in the floor and the walls along the hallways. The Palace seemed to lean, like a battle wary soldier about to fall over adding to the pile of corpses. Chunks of stone littered the path way, blocking of entire sections of hallway that forcing them to take a different route. Patches of light shone from giant gaps in the ceiling, some places the holes were big enough to crawl through.

Sin pattered behind. "Slow down," she'd say occasionally, but Huron kept the same steady pace. He had to get to the lowest regions before whole place crumbled apart, burying his one lead. Half the stairway had broken off and the remaining stone shifted under Huron's boots. He leapt the final four stairs and landed among scattered debris.

"Are you just going to leave me?" Sin whined, leaning against the wall as though the stairs could disappear from right under her feet.

Huron did consider leaving her. After all, she was part of the reason the place was falling apart. He held out his arms and said, "Jump."

Sin shook her head.

"I'll catch you."

The Palace gave another hard shake. Sin squeaked and shoved off the wall, silver hair trailing like moonlight. Sin landed hard, Huron's large hands enfolding around her waist, holding her up as her knees buckled. For a moment the fear passed and color bloomed high in her cheeks. Huron set her back on her feet.

"Where is the door that leads to the Seat of Judgment?" he asked.

"This way." Sin took the lead. They rounded a bend and he nearly ran over Sin. She stopped, hand to her mouth.

The hall was in ruin. Stones scattered along the listing walls. Holes gapped wide enough to swallow the entire palace from one side of the wall to the next. A chilling breeze emitted from the gaps. Huron moved to the edge, staring over at... nothing. There was no end to emptiness. He nudged a stone over and it fell, disappearing into the darkness.

"Where does it go?" Sin asked.

"Oblivion," Huron said, unsure of what that meant. "Be careful not fall in."

Hugging the wall, they shuffled along the ledge half as wide as his feet. Huron didn't look down, concentrating on moving his toes. A large stone blocked his path, and he nudged it with his toe. It teetered and fell soundlessly into the oblivion.

They reached the other side and followed the hall. It widened into a chamber where Sin put a hand on his arm.

"It's somewhere in here." Sin said furrowed her brow. The ceiling had mostly collapsed, giant chunks shattered on the floor. Among them Huron noticed two forms slumped among the rubble, a fine grey dust covering them.

"Mother's blessing." Sin knelt beside Moko, sprawled out like a broken mountain.

Huron turned Hacawit over onto his back. Glazed eyes stared up at the crumbling ceiling. Hacawit's chest rose slowly and fell, a faint pulse in his neck.

"How is he?"

"I can't tell" Sin grunted. "Help me clear away the stone."

They cleared away the debris trapping Moko's legs. It a great heave, they had him over on his back. Spittle shone on the side of his mouth.

"Who could have done this?" Sin asked.

"Dandulain," Huron said. "She tried to kill me when I was with the Created."

Sin frowned, cupping her elbows.

"She can't kill us," Sin said, "at least not in the Ascended form, right? She hasn't gained that much power, has she?"

"Not anymore."

Sin raised her brows.

Huron turned away, not wanting to answer her question. Especially since he needed answers himself.

Whatever she did to these two, they deserve it for choosing the wrong side of the battle. He regretted the thought as soon as it came. *What about you? Don't you deserve a worse fate because you were first the fool?*

He found another, smaller hole in the floor. This one wasn't a leap into oblivion, but had stairs. They spiraled down into darkness. Soft weeping echoed and he followed the sound. Donn sat with a comforting arm around Qetesh's shoulders. A blanket draped over her as she sobbed uncontrollably. She sucked in a deep breath, her body tensing.

"Who's here?" she asked, her voice high and teetering on hysteria.

"Only our brother, Huron," Donn said and patted her shoulder. Qetesh relaxed.

Huron noticed the thin film over her eyes and realized it wasn't from her tears.

"What happened?" he demanded.

"She was blinded by our sister of Shadows," Donn said. "It seems many of us were."

"We have a greater problem," Huron said. The palace shuddered overhead. "We need to find a way to save Mother. Otherwise, the Palace will collapse around us and we will fall like flaming stars down on the Created."

"'Shadow will rise up and take its place over light'," Donn said, quoting the Ruin prophesy.

Huron shook his head.

"No. Everything will return to that state it was before Mother and Father changed it...except there will be one true god." He took the note from his belt pouch and handed it to Donn. Donn scanned it. "There will no longer be Ascended, there will no longer be any of us. Just one. One Transcended being."

"What will become of us?" Sin asked.

"If we survive the fall, we become mortal," Huron said. "I have delayed—"

Movement from the far corner caught his attention and he reached for the sword no longer in its scabbard. His hand froze.

Mother's blessing! Could it be her?

A young woman stepped out from the shadows. Her hair had a golden hue and her green eyes blazed. Her small, pink mouth frowned.

"Where is Jarrod?"

No one responded. Huron stared at Hannah, stunned. Everything seemed to be spiraling out of control. She glanced at each of them, a strange power glowing around her. "I want to go home."

EPILOUGE

*C*hains snapped like ice smashed with a hammer, freeing his chaffed wrists. Flesh, metal, and stone merged in stasis for so long, time ceased to matter. Time was beyond him. An invented concept to measure mortality. For a captive immortal, it served to preoccupy his mind so insanity couldn't seep inside and rot it. He counted to a million and started over. He began changing it up, skipping the odd numbers, then counting by tens.

Nine hundred thousand nine hundred and ten, nine hundred thousand nine hundred and twenty, nine hundred thousand—Click! The dark metal shattered, freeing his wrists. Weightless, his arms flopped to his sides, forgotten limbs shedding from the trunk. His legs forgot how to hold his bulk. Groaning, he collapsed onto his hands and knees. Muscles trembled as he forced them to stretch. They felt shriveled, useless, a rusty coil trying to bend. Nerves tingled and after some coaxing, he found he was able to stand. Too long trapped alone in the dark. Too long forced into idle despair.

He groped along the wall, feet shuffling. The floor was smooth stone, hard to tell where it rose and fell. He came to a joint corner and turned, following its length. His palm pressed against one stone and it shifted. He stopped, testing the loose stone, prying it with his fingers. It fell, making a loud clatter in the chamber. He stuck his hand inside the wall and felt a wooden handle. He pulled up it, but it wouldn't budge. Then he yanked it down, the lever dropped with a metallic grating. A spring clicked. The sound of pulleys gyrating, stone vibrating under his palm. Light appeared in a crack. It burned his eye and he closed them.

Water streamed over his feet, cold and shocking a gasp from him. The wall had opened to reveal another room. Sloshing through the cold water, he moved into a space very much like his own. Against the far wall, a vague form leaned. Light and water poured down from a grate overhead. A head lifted.

"Father." The word came out as a statement in disbelief.

"Yes, child." The sound of is voice echoing in the chamber sounded old, tired. He made his way carefully to her, the strength returning to his legs. Menrva held her arms out to him. He lifted her and she wept.

"I've slept for too long. Now I'm awake," he said, clutching Menrva close to him. "Let's go home."

Appendices

Retribution

In 476 BLW (Blood Line Wars), Lord Desmond lost the third War of Ascension. His sons, Alfred and Thomas were spared. In 489 Thomas usurped the throne with Alfred's assistance and began the fourth War of Ascension. Neither survived long. Thomas was defeated in 492 at the Battle of Twin Rivers, Heartwood Pines. The people rose up and slayed Alfred in his Keep, killing everyone, man, woman, and child, ending the BLW permanently.

—from "Blood Lines and Battle Fronts"
Mathius, scribe to Samson the Wise, 5th Season of the Council

The torch blazed a dragon tongue, lapping wood to ignite the thatch roof. Fire devoured dry straw and pitch. It roared into life, puffing up dark smoke, working its way down to the wooden walls. Startled cries came from within. The front door opened and a man stood in the frame of smoke and fire. An arrow struck him in the chest and he crumpled onto his stoop.

That man, Dinel, had a wife and how many daughters? Jarrod chewed his lip, watching the devastation. He had agreed to this night raid, but only to put a scare into the man. Killing people was not what he expected. Three harvests had passed since he'd last seen anyone killed and that'd been during the invasion of Heartwood Pines.

Except now we are the invaders.

"This is wrong," Jarrod said, standing in the thicket beside the bonfire that was once a home. Red embers floated in the sky like the souls of those dying in the fire.

"Shut your mouth," Kris said, punching him in the arm. Kris was taller, and a cruel grin on his twisted face, his nose mashed and his right cheek broken in the war. "You don't want to be heard saying things like that. They'll think you're a sympathizer, or worse. A supporter."

How crazy has the world become when sympathy is looked on as near treason?

"Look." Kris pointed at the back of the house. A small shape dropped outside a window. Jarrod heard harsh coughing and sobbing. Another shape fell out beside the first. Then a third. "We have some chickens trying to fly the coop. Time to round them up and put them back inside."

Jarrod's stomach sank at the thought of putting the children, innocent young girls back into the house to burn alive. They had nothing to do with the war or those who deserted it.

"Come on, Jerky," Kris said. "This is our part of the job."

"They're just…." Jarrod tried to swallow. The thickening black cloud made it difficult. His eyes began to burn and tear up. "They're k…" He coughed, clearing his throat. "…kids."

"That's what they said about Lord Desmond's brats," Kris said. "And you know what they grew up to do."

Jarrod nodded; they all knew what happened when the princes came back for retribution. Hesitant, he moved towards the girls as they crawled away from their burning home. As he approached, they stopped and one by one looked up at him with red rimmed, wet eyes. He had no idea what to do. Those innocent faces, marred with soot and tears, stared blankly at him. A high-pitched screech sounded from the window. "No! Leave my babies alone!"

Dinel's wife, Kera, straddled the sill, ignoring the flames that crackled behind her. "Not my babies!" She shouted, and tumbled from the window. Kris caught her under the arms and held her while she pounded on him with her fists, kicking her legs in a frantic struggle to get away. Her night shift tore down her right shoulder, exposing a white breast. Kris laughed, and pinched the breast.

"Look at this dug ripe for milking!"

"My babies," Kera repeated, tracks marking her cheeks. "Let my babies go, please!"

"Beg all you want," Kris said, gripping her by the hair and pulling her head back, "but those chicks are going to roast like you, momma hen."

Kris pulled a dagger from his belt. The blade moved swiftly across the woman's throat and her cries turned into gurgles. Blood, dark red in the fire light, gushed over her white shift, splashed down her breast and covered Kris's arm as he held her weak, struggling body. Her arms reached out for her children and she stared at them until life left her eyes dark and empty. She sagged in Kris's grip.

"Hush little mommy say no more words," Kris sang and chuckled. He lifted the limp body up and stuffed it back through the window.

Jarrod watched, horrified. His stomach tried to empty his supper, but he held it back, hiccupping up bile. One of the younger girls screamed, a sharp ear-splitting noise. The eldest held her sister as she tried to crawl towards her mother's killer. The smallest sat there in a stupor, eyes wide and mouth gaping.

"What are you waiting for? Grab the little bitches by the scruff and toss them into the fire," Kris said, grinning, and laughed a strange, high-pitched sound. "Their momma's waiting for them."

"No," Jarrod said, barely audible. He repeated the word stronger, wrinkling his nose in disgust. "No!"

"Fine, I'll do it myself. You know Fraster's going to hear about this cowardly breach," Kris said.

He bent down for the small one and scooped her up.

She did not struggle any more than a sack of potatoes.

He took a couple of steps towards the house.

"Don't, Kris. They're children," Jarrod said, grabbing him by the shoulder.

"There are no children in war," Kris said, shrugging him off. He hefted the girl overhead and stopped. The girl slipped from his hands, tumbling to the ground.

Jarrod pulled his sword from Kris's back, tipping him sideways so his body would not crush the child. Arms trembling, he sheathed his sword. *Oh gods, what have I done?* Silence responded, broken only by the snapping of the fire. The heat was so hot, sweat poured off his forehead, though he felt cold and icy. The two older girls stared at him, eyes wide in terror. The littlest one lay on her side, and Jarrod feared she was dead—the shock and horror of these events stopping her innocent heart.

"Jerky! Kris!" cried Fraster from the other side of the house.

Jarrod jumped and moved forward on stilted legs. He knelt, testing for life and the girl's eyes fluttered as he brushed past them. Jarrod gently lifted her up, cradling her to his shoulder and walked quickly in the opposite direction of Fraster and the three other men he had with him. The two sisters remained still, so he stopped next to the oldest, and whispered, "Come on. They'll kill you if you stay."

The girl helped her sister up and they huddled together, following Jarrod like two wary mongrels. They had reached the edge of the thicket just before the line of weepers and creepers, when Jarrod heard the first curse.

"Jerky! You damn fool!" Fraster shouted. "You better run fast, because death is going to catch you."

A whistle sounded a few yards behind. "I see them. Over there!"

"Run girls!" Jarrod clutched his bundle close to his chest and ran into the dark.

Large, twisted trees called weepers, because they had the appearance of a grieving person, loomed in the darkness, waiting for him to smash into their trunks. The weepers grew far enough apart for them to pass, but the creepers—long, thick vines that hung snake-like from the limbs—could lynch someone from their feet. Jarrod ducked under a creeper just before it caught around his neck. Unexpected holes, roots and hundreds of other obstacles tried to twist their ankles, catch their toes and trip them up. They ran, jumping over roots, breaking off branches that dug at their faces, and stumbled over unseen objects hidden by the night. Jarrod glanced over his shoulder to make certain the other two girls kept pace. Each time he saw his pursuers gaining ground. His arms ached, his legs cramped, his chest heaved and his throat burned like he had swallowed cinders, but he kept running.

There's got to be a house. Gabriel's farm is somewhere close by. Or was that in the other direction? Panic gnawed at him. *We are running blind!*

A root caught his left foot, sending his shoulder smashing into a trunk. He spun in a circle, fighting for balance, and nearly dropped the girl. After shuffling her weight to his right side, he continued at a quick walk. His legs refused to do anymore.

"Why are you slowing down?" the eldest girl asked.

"I can't... I can't..." Jarrod heaved for breath, his chest heavy. "...go anymore."

Their pursuers had not given up. He heard their feet crashing through the brush.

"Take... take sister," Jarrod said, gulping in air. A stitch formed in his side, feeling like someone jabbed a knife into him. He handed the eldest the little one, now heavy as a rock in his trembling arms, and bent over, breathing heavily. "I'll hold them... I'll hold'em off."

The girl waited a moment. "Thank you," she said.

"For what?"

"For not being like them," the girl said. She carried the youngest, while holding the hand of the other, leading them into the dark woods.

Jarrod drew his sword and leaned back against a weeper. When it came to fighting, he was outmatched. They would slice him open like a ripe melon. He just had to hold them up, delay them so the girls might have a chance at escape. Escape to where? Three young girls, alone in the woods, lost without food or water or even shoes. Maybe they were better off burning with their parents. Slitting their throats may have been a mercy to what they might face.

No, Jarrod shook the thoughts away. They were alive and if the gods be good, they will find help.

Footsteps approached in the dark. Another whistle went out.

"I found one. It's Jerky!"

"Grist? Is that you?" Jarrod got his breathing under control, though his heart pounded and the sword felt really heavy in his hands. "Just go on home. Leave me be and… and you might live."

"You really are an ass, aren't you Jerky?" Grist said, stepping out from between two weepers. He was of equal height to Jarrod, tall and thin but with stronger arms from chopping wood and working the grinder at the mill. "The only way you killed Kris was because his back was to you, you coward."

"No one spoke of hurting children. Hurting children is coward's duty."

"How about you tell me where the girls went, and I will just let you walk away," Grist said in a friendly tone, as though asking Jarrod to get a pint of ale at the White Mule. "No one else needs to be hurt this night."

"You won't be hurting those girls, Grist. I'll run you through first."

"We both know that's not possible. Your scrawny arms can hardly hold that sword, farm boy. Besides, it's not like we get to make the decisions. We just follow orders like in the war," Grist said matter-of-factly. "Fraster will find them with or without you. Once he does, they are joining their parents in the Gods' Circle. That's what happens to traitors."

"Those girls are too young to be traitors."

"Their father was," Fraster said, appearing on the other side with, Arrny and Belthoy, both flanking Jarrod. Fraster was much older, closing in on fifty name-days. He sneered at Jarrod like he stepped in something nasty and had to scrape his boot. "And we learned our lessons about not striking down the saplings with the parent tree. Enough talking. Belthoy, kill this big bag of fertilizer and let's continue with the search. They couldn't have gone far."

"I'll put him down," Grist said.

"Fine. Catch up afterwards." They slipped past, each giving Jarrod a hard stare.

"It didn't have to end like this." Grist drew his sword and frowned. "Sometimes life's not fair. You just do as you're told and you try to sleep at night."

"No way was I going to kill those girls." Jarrod replied, holding up his sword. Silently he prayed, *Blade's Man, just let me put up a good fight and die well.*

Grist jabbed at him. Jarrod deflected the blade, metal ringing in the night. He stepped away from the weeper, knowing he was trapped and would have a better chance on open ground. Another quick jab to his thigh that he easily pushed away. Grist was testing him, though he usually beat Jarrod soundly in the sparring circle. The next came in a series of three quick strokes. Jarrod stopped two, but was too slow. The third cut him down his left forearm.

"Should have paid more attention to your sword practice and less on fertilizing plants, farm boy." Grist swung hard at Jarrod's head. Jarrod caught it, the blow vibrating down the hilt and he lost his grip. The sword dropped and he threw himself to the left in time to miss a fatal thrust at his chest. He struck the ground, trying to cushion his fall with his left arm. Strings of fire blazed up and down the arm. He rolled over onto his back, biting back his scream of pain. Grist stood over him.

"Farewell, my friend." Grist raised his sword arm.

Jarrod crossed both of his arms in a feeble warding attempt. Turning his head away, he squeezed his eyes shut and gritted his teeth, awaiting the killing blow. *I tried.* He thought about the farm where he lived and raised crops, the war where he killed and razed camps. *Gods don't judge me too harsh, I tried. Let it be swift. Let it not hurt too much. Let it-* He heard a grunt. Something warm and wet splashed on his hands.

Peeking between his crossed hands, he saw Grist standing over him, a pain-filled, confused expression on his face. The sword tumbled from his hands. He coughed up dark blood and sagged forward. Jarrod saw the sword point jutting from Grist's broad chest before it slipped away. Grist fell sideways, revealing a large man with graying hair standing in his place.

"Gabriel?" Jarrod asked in disbelief. "What are you doing out here at night?"

"Saw the fire and I thought there might be trouble." Gabriel spat on the fallen body. "Guess I was right."

Jarrod sat up quickly, wincing at the burning cut on his forearm. "There are three girls out there, Dinel's daughters. Did you see them?"

"I did," Gabriel said, wiping his blade on Grist's trousers.

"Were they… are they… they weren't—"

"Dead," Gabriel finished, letting the word hang in the air as he stared down at Jarrod.

Jarrod winced. All that running and holding Fraster and the others off, served for nothing. The gods were not kind. They were cruel, sparing him and taking the three innocents. Life wasn't fair, just as Grist said.

"No," Gabriel continued. "They are safe."

Jarrod breathed out a sigh of relief.

"What about the men? Fraster, Belthoy and Arrny chased after them."

"Belthoy and Arrny won't be running after anyone no more. Now," Gabriel said, bending down and placing his sword point against Jarrod's chest, "you are going to tell me what happened out at Dinel's and why you are running around with his girls in the middle of the night."

"I wanted no part of the killings," Jarrod said, easing away from the sword point. Gabriel just pushed it harder, drawing a pin prick of blood to trickle down and wet his shirt. "I swear by the Mother, I wanted nothing to do with it. Oh gods! Kris was going to burn them up and I killed him because he wouldn't stop. They wouldn't stop. They just won't stop."

Gabriel studied him, searching his eyes. The sword point lifted.

"Hannah told me you saved them. I just had to be certain for myself." He offered Jarrod a hand. "Come with me, we got more talking to do."

The root cellar was cool and damp. It had the earthy smell of canned fruits and mushrooms stored by hard working hands. Hands that knew how to tend a field. Jarrod missed the sweet taste of the soil, the sweltering heat and sweet rains. He held his cup of tea, huddling in a chair in the corner as Mira, Gabriel's wife brought another blanket to cover the sleeping girls. She was young looking, with the care folds around her eyes and mouth, like she smiled or laughed a lot in her blossoming days. She was pretty, in a simple way, full-bodied, not scrawny or overly ripe. Grey shimmered in her blond hair, tied back with a blue ribbon, and she wore a tight brown dress that showed her curves without revealing skin.

The poultice itched on his forearm. Mira said he had to wear it for the next day or so to keep it from going green and pus-filled. Fortunately for him, the cut wasn't deep enough to sever muscle. He could flex his left hand with some great pain, but that was all. He wore a clean shirt from Ishmael, Gabriel's eldest son. His own had been cut up to staunch the blood on the way to Gabriel's home.

Gabriel filled him in on the details of the girls' flight. He had seen the fire and roused his three boys. They each went armed with bows and spears left over from the war. Gabriel was the only one with a sword. From the scars on his hands and face, he had seen extensive action in battle during the Heartwood Pines invasion. They had found the girls running in from the direction of their home. Hannah, the eldest Dinel child of eleven name-days, gave a brief, tearful account of what happened. He had his youngest escort the girls to the house, to lock them in the cellar with his own sister and mother, and to let no one in but Gabriel. With bows strung, arrows notched, they waited for Fraster and the others to blunder into them.

"That one was never a good woodsman. I could hear him breaking brush and snapping twigs well before their ugly faces showed up," Gabriel said, shaking his head in disgust.

They had aimed true, killing Belthoy and Arrny with a single shot each, but Fraster spun away in time for the arrow to graze his shoulder. He had taken off running with Gabriel in pursuit.

"I heard the clash of your swords and that's when I found you," Gabriel said. "I remembered Hannah mentioning a rescuer and when I saw you, I was surprised. I knew you were no good with a sword. I swear, the Blade's Man must have blessed, or pitied, you to keep you alive for so long. I had to save you."

Watching the girls resting in blankets on the cellar floor, Jarrod couldn't understand how they could sleep after such a horrific event. He was bone tired, but his eyes refused to close. Every time they did, he kept seeing Dinel's wife's throat being slashed and the blood flooding out in a dark, red river to drown him. *Kera. Her name was Kera.* Jarrod would hold her name in his memory for the rest of his days. He felt responsible for her death. Even if he hadn't drawn the blade, he did nothing to stop it. All that blood. A rain bloated river of blood would haunt him until the end of his days.

"Poor babies," Mira whispered, stroking the hair of the youngest. "So much sorrow."

"How did you get them to pass out?" Jarrod asked

"Chamomile and weep bark," she replied. "The same is in your tea."

That explained his drowsiness.

"Then why am I not asleep?"

Mira smiled. It was a very pretty smile, one that could swallow his heart whole. It made his head fuzzy and his face feel hot, or maybe it was his head hot and his face all fuzzy. Ideas swam before him and his mind grasped at them like a child chasing butterflies. They fluttered just out of his reach. Mira unlatched the cellar door and disappeared up the stairs. Gabriel came down next with Ishmael. Ishmael was the same age as Jarrod and had the strong jaw and sharp nose that Jarrod lacked. The girls would swoon for Ishmael, pushing past Jarrod just to gaze on Ishmael. *If I were a girl, I'd do the same*—the thought swam up from the surface of goo. They both had trained during the war at the Fox Den. Unlike Jarrod, Ishmael proved himself to be skilled with a sword, spear, and bow. Jarrod only found his usefulness the same as he was brought up; a simple farm boy who knew his way around racks, hoes, and shovels. Those were his tools and they had him tending the camp garden when he was not soldiering out in the yard.

"Ah, I see you are feeling lucid, like your thoughts are swimming through a bowl of warm milk," Gabriel said. He pulled up a stool and sat in front of Jarrod and Ishmael stood behind, arms folded. "I apologize for this deception, but we need to be certain that what you tell us is the full-truth. No inconvenient omissions of information."

"You didn't need to poison me," Jarrod said. He set his cup down before he threw it. Anger wanted to surface, but it slipped under waves of drowsiness. "I would have told you all I know."

"It's not poison, just a sedative. A kind of truth serum we used in the war for enemy spies," Gabriel explained. "Three snippets of weeping bark put you in a deep, dreamless sleep. One snippet made you sleepy, and more cooperative. The only side effect you will have is nightmares. After what you went through, that is to be expected."

"To be expected," Jarrod agreed. The room faded in and out as his eyes drooped, then flashed open. *No more blood!* He wanted to scream, but only nodded. "Yes."

"Good boy." Gabriel patted his leg. "What foolishness did you get yourself involved with tonight? Why did Fraster want Dinel dead?"

"We were given a list of names," Jarrod said. The words came from a distance. His mouth just worked on its own. "Names of those who fought against us in the war, but… but got pardoned. And those who did not fight us directly, they were on there, too. Those lot gave aid or information to the enemy. I think." He scratched his chin, fighting for control of his words. "Fraster told us. Fraster was very clear that they were all traitors. They had to be punished for their crimes."

"Is that what you believe?"

"Yes." Jarrod looked at Gabriel, trying to see if he was serious. All he saw was a blurry face that cleared and went blurry again. "My father died fighting Desmond's spoiled princes. Anyone who helped the enemy has to be a traitor."

Gabriel frowned, that Jarrod saw plainly. His hands wrung together and he spoke in a measured tone. "In the waning days of the war, Dinel found a boy, a little younger than you. He was bleeding from a side wound and half-dead from starvation. Dinel bandaged his wounds, fed him and sent him on his way. It was only later he discovered the boy was a scout for Thomas's main force—after the boy was captured and then strung up. Dinel said to me before the execution, 'Enemy or not, he was a boy who needed help. Was I to let him die on my stoop because he served a different cause?'"

Gabriel leaned forward and the furrowed lines on his forehead matched his frown. "Dinel's crime was human decency."

"I didn't know," Jarrod spoke in a hushed voice. "I… I didn't know."

"Of course, you didn't," Gabriel said. "Else you wouldn't have gone along. Then those girls sleeping there would be dead. Sometimes divine luck is required to stop evil from fulfilling its goal."

Divine luck? Jarrod's eyes burned and he squinted to keep the tears back. *Just another tool, again.*

"Do you know who else is on the list?" Gabriel asked.

"Just one other name. The one below Dinel was Jonial and his family." Jarrod stopped and closed his eyes trying to remember what Fraster said. Again, he saw Kera's throat slashed and a great flood of dark red rushed at him in a roar of pain. When he opened his eyes, he noticed Gabriel and Ishmael looking at him with concern. Then he realized the roar was a scream he had let out. He looked at the girls, hoping he had not awakened them. They were sound asleep.

"I think that is enough for one night," Gabriel said. "Get your mother and bring him a cup of full weeper bark."

Ishmael left them alone.

"One more question," Gabriel said. "Who gave you the list?"

"Captain Thramel. He formed us up and named us the Manus Poena. I don't know what it means."

"The hand of retribution," Gabriel said. "Thramel hasn't accepted that the war is over."

Ishmael brought him the tea. Jarrod drank it down. Within moments he was fast asleep in the chair.

Gentle rocking slowly dragged Jarrod from the depth of sleep. His eyes opened; a small, blurry face filled his vision. He blinked several times and he saw the youngest Dinel daughter. Her sad expression looked out of place for one so young. Jarrod guessed she had four name-days at most. The girl climbed up onto his lap and nestled into him, resting her head on his good arm. He was careful not to move his left arm, fearing that the numbness would give way to the embers of pain. Listening to the easy, smooth sounds of the girl sleeping, Jarrod drifted off.

The next time he woke it was to the sound of Gabriel clomping down the cellar stairs. "Up, up, up," he said in a loud, deep voice, "everyone up."

Jarrod recognized the soldier's urgency.

"Is't an attack?" He tried to stand, but there was a weight on his legs. The Dinel girl was still there in his lap. She yawned and stretched like a cat before sliding down to the floor.

"Would I be the one down here waking you up?" Gabriel asked. The answer was obvious to Jarrod, it would most likely be Mira or their daughter. "You get upstairs while the children get ready to travel."

The cellar door opened into a small kitchen. The smell of kettle cakes and frits was so strong it made his stomach ache with hunger. The light coming in from the window was a warm white chasing away the gray residuals of night. Jarrod moved a little slowly, still under the effects of the tea. His arm throbbed beneath the poultice and he collapsed into a chair beside the table.

"Once these frits are done, I'll take a look at your arm," Mira said, sparing him a quick glance. She stirred a metal skillet atop an iron wood burner stove.

"Thank you," Jarrod replied.

"Elly, set the plates around the table," Mira said to a girl about the age of Hannah. She had long blonde hair like her mother, but done up in a braid.

"Yes, ma," she said, eyeing Jarrod curiously.

"I can help," Jarrod said, rising groggily from the chair.

"No, sir. You are a guest," Elly said. "Besides, I don't think you can do much with your left arm."

The cellar door opened again as Gabriel entered. He kissed Mira on the back of her neck, grabbed a cake and spooned some frits onto it. "Make sure they get ready fast," he said to Mira. "I'm going to relieve Ishmael."

"Be careful out there," Mira said, and smacked him lightly with the rag she'd used to move the iron skillet off the stove. "Next time, wash your paws before grabbing food."

"I'll make sure Ishmael washes before he comes in." He stuffed the cake and frit in his mouth, chewing a little as he went out the door.

"Men are never civilized without a woman. You would eat off the ground like dogs if we didn't make you sit at a table," Mira said. She smiled, but it seemed strained. Under the circumstances, Jarrod sympathized. If it weren't for me, they might be having a nice family breakfast, sitting around the table and planning for the day. Instead, they have four extra mouths to feed and to keep watch for an attack. He slouched in his chair, wanting to slip away into the dirt between the floorboards.

Mira set aside her pans and knelt beside Jarrod. She gently peeled the poultice back. It felt like a scab being lifted. The wound was red and puckered. No sign of green, or worse, red spider webbing up his arm that meant blood poisoning.

"You seem to be doing just fine," Mira said, placing the old poultice on a metal tray. She opened a jar of something that smelled bitter, stuck a stick into it and stirred it around until it thickened like butter. Elly watched over her shoulder. "I worked at the healing stations during the war. Saw hundreds of cuts, bruises, scrapes. Had to help take off a few legs and arms, too." She talked as she spread the bitter butter on his arm. It was cold at first, a cold that burned deep to the bone. Jarrod bit his lip to keep from crying out. The burning faded, leaving him more awake. "Never thought I'd have to treat another sword wound again in this life."

She wrapped his arm up in a bandage.

"All you men want is to kill each other. We women just have to patch you back up again so you can do more fighting." She packed her supplies into a satchel. "It just isn't right."

"Thank you... I'm sorry," Jarrod said, uncertain of what else to say.

The cellar door opened again. Hannah helped her younger sisters up the stairs. They mirrored each other with broken innocence on somber faces. The middle one's eyes were still red and puffy. She rubbed them as though she could squeeze the tears out without having them reach her cheeks. They wore simple dresses, a bit loose on them, and it looked as though Hannah had tried to brush her sisters' hair with a half-hearted attempt. They all reminded him of refugees from the war. Their bare, dirty feet added to the pitiful picture.

"Elly, get them the shoes," Mira said. "They may not be an exact fit, girls, but it's the best we have on short notice. Come on up to the table. Breakfast is ready."

"Thank you, ma'am," the girls said in hushed voices. Heads down, they moved to the empty chairs. The youngest sat in Hannah's lap, refusing to move.

"Lily, stop fidgeting," Hannah said in a quiet, stern voice.

Lily settled in and was still.

All three of them picked at the breakfast, eating more out of politeness than hunger. Jarrod's appetite was not as strong as it was earlier. He chewed and swallowed because chewing and swallowing gave him something to do other than think about the girls and the situation he helped cause.

Ishmael came in, wearily setting his strung bow at the door with the quiver of arrows. He nodded at those sitting at the table, and then took the plate his mother offered.

"Still quiet out there," he said to her inquisitive look.

Mira smiled at him and left the kitchen.

"Do you think…" Jarrod began, but stopped because the girls were in hearing. Jarrod stood up and walked towards the window. Ishmael followed. "Do you think Thramel will come today?"

"I don't know," Ishmael said. "He was an unpredictable one when it came to tactical maneuvers. I remember sitting all day and night on a hill as the enemy set up pickets below. I thought we would strike as soon as the prince's men dropped gear, but Thramel stayed us. As the enemy slept comfortably, we kept watch all night until day. While they went about preparing for a morning excursion, a separate company of our unit struck them from behind. In the confusion, Thramel had us attack. It's hard to say what Thramel has planned. If we knew more of those on the list, we could better prepare."

"Did he ask you to be a part of Manus Poena?"

"Never heard of it until last night."

"By the Blade's Man! Why did he want me?"

"My guess is he wanted people who'd lost family during the war. People who wouldn't mind a little retribution."

This made sense. Arrny had lost a brother, Desmond had lost cousins and a nephew, Grist's father was killed, and Fraster… well Fraster had a bad case of blood lust. Jarrod's entire family was murdered at a night raid on his farm, while his father and himself had been out at a war camp. His father died shortly after in the battle of Twin Rivers. The only reason Jarrod was alive was the fact that he'd been training at the Fox Den.

Loud thumping came from the front porch just before the door burst open. Gabriel stumbled in, half dragging, half carrying a bloody Jonial into the house. Blood caked the right side of his head where an ear used to be and his shirt was cut open in several places along the sides and sleeves. Those too were stiff with dried blood. Ishmael went to Jonial's other side and helped his father carry the man into another room.

Soft weeping was heard at the table.

"Shhh, little Buttercup," Hannah said, holding and stroking the middle child's hair. Lily sat on the floor, hiding her face in Hannah's dress.

Elly entered, holding three pairs of shoes. She looked to Jarrod, who was flabbergasted by what was happening. The world seemed to be bending in on itself, crushing anyone with whom he made any contact. Madness. Everything was madness. He noticed a trail of red left by Jonial across the floor. Jarrod closed his eyes, trying to shut everything out. A red curtain closed behind the eyes. He took a deep gulp of air and released it.

"Here now, let me help you," Elly said to Hannah who was drowning in her own form of misery with two others clinging to her. Elly took the middle girl by the hand, leading her gently off her older sister. "Hey there Buttercup, that is a sweet name."

"It's what my sister calls me. My name is Kellen."

"See here what I have for you, Kellen, and Lily." She held out the shoes. Kellen wiped her face and sat next to Elly on the floor. Lily refused to move, shaking her head still buried in her sister's dress.

Exasperation read on Hannah's face. She tried cajoling her out, but Lily remained stubborn, crawling under her sister's dress. Hannah just sat back in her chair, folding her arms, and blowing a string of hair that covered her face. "You cannot stay there forever, Lily-pad."

"Yes," came her muffled reply.

"You don't want to try on the shoes?" Elly asked.

"No."

"May I see the shoes?" Jarrod asked.

Elly handed them to him. Jarrod sat on the floor, bent his right leg in so he could take his boot off. It was awkward using only one arm, but he managed to pull it off. He held the small shoe up—he could fit a thumb and finger in it. He held it over his big toe and said, "I don't know, Elly. They don't fit me at all."

Lily peeked from under her sister's dress. She giggled, watching Jarrod set the shoe on his toe where it dangled.

"Do you have nine more so I can walk around in them?" He wiggled his toes. "This isn't working so well."

Lily crawled towards Jarrod and stole the shoe from his toe.

"Not for you. It's for me," she said and slid her bare foot into the shoe. The fit was loose, but it stayed on as Lily held her foot up and waggled it at Jarrod. "See."

"Yes. It looks great on you." He handed her the second shoe and she put it on.

Hannah gave him a relieved expression.

"She likes you," Elly said.

"Only because I'm silly," Jarrod said, struggling with his own boot. Putting it on one-handed proved more difficult than taking it off. Elly helped him.

A sharp cry came from the other room where they others had taken Jonial.

"I'm going to see if they need help," Jarrod said. "You are all right with the rest of this?"

"Yes," Elly replied.

A wall divided the sitting room from the kitchen space. Jonial sat in a chair, shirt off and half-dazed. Mira probed the wounds. Lots of cuts opened in mouths to tell the tale of a bloody fight. Gabriel and Ishmael stood out of Mira's way as she examined each cut thoroughly. Jonial moaned, crying out and hissing as Mira pulled back scabbed flesh.

Mira moved away to get her satchel.

"I'm going to run out of bandages at this rate," she grumbled, passing Jarrod.

"Thramel?" Jarrod asked. Guilt sank in his belly like a stone.

"Aye, the bastard came in the early morning," Jonial said, bent over, looking at his feet, eyes squinted closed. A strange gurgle came from his throat. Jarrod recognized it as agony. Jonial clenched his fists and opened his mouth. The gurgle became a screech and a sharp intake of air.

"He burned them all. All! I was in the privy when I smelled the smoke and heard his men shouting, laughing like they was at a bonfire celebrating All Shadow's Eve. I found one of 'em and bashed his head in with a rock. Others came and started cutting me up. I ran, oh gods, I ran! My children, my wife, my home all burned while I ran." Jonial heaved a wet cry. "I should'a died with 'em."

Gabriel looked up at Jarrod.

"Jonial found one of our soldiers trying to rape his daughter during the war. He killed the boy and was acquitted in front of a tribunal."

"Damn right, I killed him! I would do it again ten thousand times!" Jonial said. "The boy's father was there with that wretched lot, holding a torch to my house. When I catch 'em, I'm going to hold one to his balls!"

"Manus Poena," Jarrod said.

"The hand never stops, but keeps on destroying everything until nothing is left," Gabriel said. "We need to cut the hand off at the wrist."

Dinel, Kera, Hannah, Kellen, Lily, Jonial and his family. Gods! He didn't know all their names. It was more to add to an increasing list of misery. How many before it all stopped?

"He's got dozens of men, all former soldiers," Jarrod said. "They don't have a base of operation either. They just move around from place to place."

"What's he nannering on about?" Jonial asked.

Gods strike me, I am a fool. Chattering on and on without thinking that he knows nothing of my involvement. Jonial will kill me now.

"Jarrod infiltrated Thramel's group of thieves and murderers," Gabriel said, covering Jarrod's mistake. "You weren't the only ones attacked. Dinel and Kera are dead. The girls would be too, if Jarrod hadn't saved them."

"Shadeslayer! Not Dinel and Kera, too!" Jonial shook his head. Pain crumpled his face, withering it into old, hard leather, cracked by the harsh sun. "Such good people. It doesn't make any sense."

"He's on some sort of campaign to wipe out war criminals," Gabriel said.

"War criminals?" Jonial asked. "My Bessy wasn't even born until after the war was over. He should hang himself. I've seen what Thramel done in the war. I turned a blind eye because we needed his leadership to win. Now I see that was a mistake."

Mira returned with a warm kettle of water and her satchel of salves. She washed the bloody wounds, placed the bitter butter on them and wrapped his head and torso. Gabriel gave Jonial an old shirt. The house had a somber silence, one of waiting and expectation. Jarrod realized no one was watching for an attack. He started for the front, when a sweaty, out of breath boy entered the room.

"Da, Thramel is moving," Michael said, excitement and fear on his face.

"Where?"

"Here!"

Smoke rose to the south. Jarrod observed how Mira made a concerted effort not to look back. Determination masked the sadness visible in her slumped shoulders. The family home was gone. Their little band of walking wounded and children marched west with the sun high overhead and arching down. They had two pack horses among them. Jonial rode the one and Elly the other, holding Lily in the saddle with her. Ishmael took point while Michael, Gabriel's middle boy, scouted ahead. Jarrod walked beside Hannah and Kellen. Mira and her youngest boy, Azriel, were ahead of them. Jonial rode behind with Gabriel covering their rear.

"We have a quarter day's lead, thanks to Michael," Gabriel told Jarrod and Ishmael as the others readied to leave. Michael was sent to watch Jonial's house at dusk. He was the one who had instructed the wounded Jonial to go to their home. Then Michael trailed Thramel, and overhead their plans for the next attack. "It's not enough, I don't think, unless we push hard to the Barracks." He laid a hand on his eldest's shoulder. "Ishmael, when we get to the Twin River's ford, you will head east and get Harmen, his brothers, and their boys. Tell them Thramel's gone rogue and we require his assistance at the Barracks."

"Yes, Da," Ishmael said. "Why don't we send Michael now?"

"Because I am sending him with Azriel and the girls off to the Yellow Valley," Gabriel said.

"That leaves three of you against a dozen," Ishmael said. "Honestly, only you are capable of defending. I don't like that, Da. With me we can hold longer—"

"You will do as I say, boy," Gabriel said. "Without Harmen's assistance we will all be as good as dead. Then who will stop Thramel from slaughtering innocent families?"

Ishmael tightened his jaw, displaying his dismay with the arraignment.

They walked in relative silence, listening for the sounds of pursuit. Thramel preferred moving on foot, and kept to that preference. Jarrod figured if Thramel had horses, they would have known by midday. Shadows lengthened and warm midday light thinned by the needled branches of Pine Groves. Jarrod heard the first sounds of water as the Twin Rivers rushed away from the crossroads ford to join the Sapphire Sea. Soon their little party would break up into smaller groups hoping for survival.

The pine trees thinned into clearings of sandy rock. The Twin Rivers intersected at this point and moved off east and west. Signs of the war were prevalent. Rusty helmets, broken spears, swords and odd pieces of armor scattered the ground. Where the swelling of the river did not carry them away, they could be seen sticking out of the shoal—the lingering bones, after the flesh of war melted away. They had to step carefully to avoid being cut or tripping over the battle refuse. The water was hardly ankle deep and they could travel across easily. In three or four moons the rains would come and swell it so the only passable points were the bridges a league apart.

It was here that Jarrod's father had died. Any of the debris could have belonged to him— the hilt of the sword or the tattered leather grieves. At the rivers' twining, they had successfully halted Thomas's excursion and turned the tide of the war in their favor. Tales were told of the water turning red for half a season, as though the rivers themselves bled.

Ishmael stopped the party at the edge of the water.

"Where is Michael?" he asked. "Wasn't he supposed to meet us here?"

"Maybe he crossed over?" Jarrod asked.

The strain on Gabriel's face as he stared across the ford told that he believed a different story. The crossing was less than twenty yards and the pine forest picked back up on the other side. Dark shadows permeated through the trees.

"What do we do now?" Ishmael asked.

"You go east," Gabriel said. "We will wait for Michael."

"Da, they'll be on you soon."

"Do as you are told. We won't wait long," Gabriel said. "Your mother knows the way. She could lead them and Michael will catch up later."

"Da—"

"Go on, boy," Gabriel said, embracing his son. "Don't turn back without their help."

"I won't," Ishmael said, "Even if I have to drag them kicking and screaming."

"You're a good son." Gabriel patted him on the cheek.

Ishmael hugged his siblings and mother.

"Godspeed," Mira said, kissing him on the forehead.

"Take the horse," Jonial said. "I can walk the rest of the way."

Ishmael tried to protest, but Jonial had already climbed off. He handed Ishmael the reins. "Make sure to tell Harmen he owes me nothing for the field work this past spring if he takes the bastard's head off."

Jarrod watched Ishmael ride down the river, climbing out once the bank rose. He was out of sight in a matter of moments.

"Where do you think Michael went?"

Gabriel shrugged and moved away. "Mira. I need you to take Azriel and the girls to the place we had set our hearts on when we were younger. When I find him, Michael will follow."

"I will not," Mira said. "Send Jarrod. I refuse to leave you alone with none but the walking wounded."

"Stubborn woman, "Gabriel griped. "There's no time to explain. Jarrod has no idea where to go and neither Elly nor Azriel know the area."

Jarrod moved away from the argument. Once more he felt helpless, like a rake when a hoe was needed. He saw movement up at the pines beyond the crossing. A single person walked down the path. It was Michael.

"There he is," Jarrod pointed.

Gabriel and Mira quit bickering and looked up hopefully at their boy. Jonial stood up and started towards the river ford. Elly waved her left arm over her head excitedly while holding onto Lily. The figure waved back with his right hand.

"That's not him," Gabriel said. He quickly strung his bow. "Mira. Take the girls and Azriel, now! Go!"

"How do you know?" Jarrod asked.

"Michael waves with his left. He is left-handed."

Behind the waving figure, six other men came rushing out.

"Ride to Ishmael, Elly," Mira said, grabbing a bow and quiver from the saddle. "Hannah, take Kellen and Azriel. Find somewhere to hide in the woods."

The first arrow struck the ground near the horse. The horse reared back, whinnying and Elly gripped the saddle tightly. Another arrow flew over their heads. Just as she settled the horse, a last arrow struck him in the haunch. Elly grabbed hold of Lily, as their horse bolted in the opposite direction. Jarrod heard the girls scream as they were swept away in a panic. Gabriel cursed and let loose an arrow. It came up short of his target. The men sprinted across the ground, closing the range. Two broke off to give chase to the horse.

Hannah took Kellen's and Azriel's hands and hurried back into the pines. Azriel pulled away just as she reached the tree line, running back to his mother. He clung to her leg as she worked to string a small bow.

"Azriel, come here!" Hannah cried.

He shook his head and held tighter onto his mother's leg.

"Run, child," Mira said, trying to pry him loose.

A second arrow thrummed over Mira's head. She ducked, knocking Azriel to the ground. Jarrod picked him up in his right arm and the boy started to wail.

"Hide with Hannah," Jarrod said, setting him down. "You'll be safe."

Azriel stood for a moment, looked at his mother, who nodded at him, and back to Jarrod. Then he ran to Hannah. They slipped away into the woods.

Jonial stood at the water's edge, spear in hand. "Come on! Try and finish what you started!"

Gabriel stood at his side, sighting one of the runners. His arrow took the man in the chest, knocking him off his feet. Mira shot at the flank and missed.

"Jarrod," Gabriel said, loosening another arrow. "Go after Elly. Make sure they don't get her."

Jarrod started running. He heard a scream and turned to see Mira hunched over, gripping a shaft that jutted from her side. A second one struck her chest with a thump. Mira crumpled to the ground. Gabriel struck one assailant in the head with his shot. Two of the men crossed the ford, followed by the third who had a shaft sticking out of his shoulder.

Jonial met them, spearing the lead man through the gut. The man gave a grunt and slackened. Jonial kicked the body off the spear and looked up. The one impersonating Michael sliced at him with a long sword. Jonial lifted his spear and the blade shattered the wood. Then the man swung his blade around, slicing Jonial's head off his shoulders. Jarrod watched it spin and fall into the water leaving a spray of blood in its wake. Gabriel dropped his bow and met Jonial's killer in the water. Their swords collided with a loud, metallic clang. The wounded man joined the other in attacking Gabriel.

Unable to watch the results of the combat, Jarrod turned and ran. He could not help his friends at the ford anymore. *Blade's Man, bless me with your luck once more to aid Elly and Lily.*

They were specks in the distance. With the sun sinking towards the horizon, Jarrod saw shadows trailing the inclined embankment. The horse with Elly and Lily left the river and rode up the western bank, slowing as it climbed uphill along a thicket of pines. The soldiers appeared to be gaining ground. Jarrod ran as fast as he could, knowing that he might be too late. They had a long lead on him.

An idea occurred to him. He stopped running, took in a deep breath, cupped his hands over his mouth and shouted. It echoed up the river bank.

"Hola you… you cowardly bastards! Stop chasing children and come for me!"

The soldiers both glanced back. There was a moment of hesitation.

"That's right, I killed Kris and… and Gris. I helped the Dinel children escape, too."

It's working.

"Gods-blasted-slink," one shouted back. Jarrod recognized the voice immediately. It was Fraster. "Jerky, I'm coming to kill you myself."

"Oh Gods, not again," Jarrod said, as Fraster started down the bank followed by the second soldier, a man he did not know. Shuffling backwards, Jarrod drew his sword. *I am going to die.* He saw Elly and Lily dismount the horse and sneak off into the pines.

"Don't run off like the dog you are," Fraster said. "I don't want to stab you in the back like you did to Kris."

"Two against one is not even odds," Jarrod yelled. He took a couple steps back, preparing to run away, allowing the girls more time to hide in the woods. "I guess you don't mind, since you like picking on little girls and killing defenseless people."

The distance between them was close to two hundred yards, and closing. Jarrod glanced over his shoulder, taking another step back. The Twin Rivers were too wide to cross here, not without being swept up in the current and bashed against rocks. He would have to retrace his steps. Looking back, he gave a surprised cry at how quickly Fraster ran. They were nearly a hundred yards away. Heart beating rapidly, he spun around and started to run. He took a few steps and stopped. Run? Where? Thramel and his men? Jonial was dead, Mira was down and Gabriel was probably dead as well.

There's nowhere left to go. The weight of impending doom grew heavy on his shoulders. *No one left to help me. I am alone and must help myself.*

Jarrod turned, and drew his sword.

"I guess you don't want to die with a sword in your back after all," Fraster said. The other soldier approached Jarrod, grinning eagerly, but Fraster grabbed him by the collar and yanked him back.

"I'm going to finish what I should have last night." Fraster unsheathed a long sword strapped to his back and planted it point down into the river sand. "Shadeslayer! I am going to even the odds and make it fair." He lifted the chainmail over his head, and handed it to the soldier. Then he laughed. "I guess I would have to tie my arm behind my back to really make it fair. I'm surprised you even know how to hold a sword, and not just scratch at dirt with it."

"I guess I surprised Gris as well," Jarrod said, brandishing his sword in one hand.

"You are not deceiving anyone, but yourself. Gabriel killed Gris. Otherwise, you wouldn't be a thorn in my foot today." Fraster took up his long sword. "Too bad we had to kill his son. They were such a nice family."

Michael! Another name for the list. It has to stop here. Jarrod lunged at Fraster. Fraster turned him aside with a flick of his wrist.

"I don't understand," Jarrod said. "Why do you have to kill children?"

"Aren't we all somebody's child?" Fraster laughed and sliced at Jarrod's sword arm. Jarrod deflected the blade, and stumbled to the side. "Killing the parent does no good if the child lives. Retribution. Revenge. It's a vicious circle that we prevent by killing the entire family. These people you want to protect all committed treasonous acts that harmed us in the war."

Two quick slashes and Jarrod stopped one. His left thigh burned. The first trickles of blood dripped down his leg.

"I thought you, of all our people, understood, Jarrod," Fraster said, circling around to his left side. "Did your father die in vain, like his son? We will not let these crimes go unpunished." Fraster swiped at Jarrod, who flailed at it, barely knocking the blade away. "I am disappointed in you. That you allow more of our people to die because you sympathize with these traitors."

"You are wrong, Fraster," Jarrod said, limping as his leg burned under his weight. "You can justify murder all you want. Taking a life, the life of an innocent, is worse than murder. It's a massacre. The gods damn you for it!"

"Thank you for that clarification," Fraster said. "I will be certain to write it on your statue."

The long sword cut down at his left shoulder. Jarrod parried, swung around to deflect a second blow and brought the sword up to push off a third attack aimed at his head. Overwhelmed, Jarrod stepped back on his injured leg and it bent under the pain. Fraster cut down again, knocking Jarrod off balance. It was like he was reliving his experience from the prior night. Fraster raised his sword—no long speech, no words of regret. Just death coming from above. Jarrod found a fist sized rock and threw it at Fraster. It struck him square in the forehead, gashing the skin and releasing a trickle of blood. Fraster's swing went wide cutting through Jarrod's baggy shirt, leaving him an opening. *For all the people you hurt!* Jarrod jabbed low with his sword, cutting through boot and tendon. Fraster let out a cry of anger and pain. He dropped to one knee, grabbing at his severed ankle. Jarrod kicked back out of sword reach and had just gotten to his feet when a large body collided with him, sending him skidding across the rocky shoal.

"Kill him! Kill him! Kill him!" Fraster yelled.

Jarod got to his hands and knees. Viewing from between his legs, he watched the soldier come at him with his sword drawn. Jarrod's own weapon was nowhere around. Just as the man got within striking range, an arrow sprouted out of his chest. He stopped, and looked at it, dumbfounded. Another arrow took him in the throat.

Gabriel, bow raised, arrow notched, limped along the water's edge.

"That's two I owe you," Jarrod said. He got up and went to help Gabriel. Gabriel pushed past him, his arrow trained on Fraster, who held up both hands.

"I yield!" He tried to crawl away. Gabriel released and the arrow pierced Fraster's hand. As he dropped it, Gabriel loosened another, shattering his forearm. Fraster screamed.

"Where is Thramel's striking point?" Gabriel's last arrow aimed at Fraster's face.

"Nowhere. He moves about!"

"Where is it?"

"I will tell you if you let me live," Fraster said.

"Done. Tell me where it is."

"Watch Tower Hill."

Gabriel lowered the bow, and released the last arrow into Fraster's groin. Fraster grunted and doubled over.

"That's for Michael," Gabriel said. "The Mother grant you never have children."

They left Fraster screaming on the river bank and moved up the slope. Jarrod stopped Gabriel. "Is there anyone else? Mira? Is Mira...?"

Gabriel just shook his head.

At the Fox Den they had laughed and called him Jerky. Unlike the other boys who had learned to use swords and spears swiftly, Jarrod found himself hesitating. His swings were unsure as he thought through every little movement. Fraster was the one who gave him the name, saying he looked like a corpse spasming in its death throes.

"And you will be a corpse if you keep jerking that sword around," Fraster would say, and then send Jarrod back to the vegetable garden. Jarrod saw battle once. After his father was killed, he volunteered to join the cleanup forces to push the Prince's army out of Heartwood Pines. He killed for the first time there, not thinking about his movements, just seeking revenge for his father's death. He found a soldier hiding in a thicket. Without thinking, Jarrod hacked the man up as he screamed until only blood bubbled from his mouth. The brutal act did not bring him solace, his father was still dead—it only brought him misery at the idea the he could do that to a person

Jarrod thought about that as he and Gabriel searched for Elly and Lily. When he asked about Hannah, Kellen and Azriel, he just tossed him a shoe, covered in dirt with pine needles stuck to the bottom. Jarrod did not know who it belonged to, but from Gabriel's reaction to Fraster, the children were alive.

Thramel had them.

Heavy orange light darkened the pines before they discovered the girls' hiding place. A small white shoe lay on its side, caught in spider webs and wispy thickets, just outside a dark, damp hole leading beneath a great pine over a hundred hands tall. The girls refused to come out. Jarrod finally convinced them, saying, "The shoe I found out here doesn't fit me. Do you have nine more, Elly?"

The girls climbed out, dirt covered and scraped up knees. Elly wrapped her arms around Gabriel, and cried into his neck. Lily clung onto Jarrod, burying her face into his shirt. She whimpered a couple times, her little fists balled up around his arm. He had to carry her out of the woods because she would not let go. They found the horse cropping flower tops. Elly and Lily were still able to ride her, making the next part of their journey less painful.

Stars occupied the sky, twinkling around a horn-shaped moon as they made their way to the Barracks. Their wounds forced them to move slowly. Jarrod had the cut on his thigh and Gabriel was covered in bloody, ragged bandages. They arrived to find several campfires burning. Dozens of shadows flickered in the lights. Ishmael ran out to meet them. "Where is everyone?" Ishmael asked.

"Take your sister," Gabriel said, lifting Elly off the horse.

"Da, where is Ma, Michael, and Azriel?" Ishmael asked again, holding Elly who was nearly too large to be carried. She was in a stupor and refused to move on her own. "What happened?"

"We were ambushed," Jarrod said, taking Lily from the saddle and holding her against his shoulder. "Thramel took Hannah, Kellen, and... and Azriel."

The worry on Ishmael's face turned into grief.

"So Ma and Michael?" his lip trembled like a little boy's.

"We will mourn them after we get the children back," Gabriel said, mounting the horse.

"Where are you going?" Ishmael asked.

"I'll be back before first light." Then he was gone. Lost in the darkness with only the sound of dissipating hooves to mark his existence.

Harmen and about thirty of his relatives and neighbors joined the resistance against Thramel. Many were war veterans, bearing their swords, spears and makeshift armor. They sat around the fires, solemn after the ill-tidings that night. A few voiced that they should strike the Watch Tower Hill, tonight, before Thramel knew what was coming.

"Not until my father returns," Ishmael said.

"How do we know he is returning and not seeking his death?" Leven asked. He was a short man, balding and missing a tooth in a row of crooked ones. "We don't know if Thramel is really at Watch Tower, or out raiding another home."

"He took my brother for a reason," Ishmael said.

"It's to lure your father out," Harmen said. He reminded Jarrod of a bear. Large, tall, and had brown hair that covered his head and chin. He also smelled of wet fur and horses. "I know Gabriel is not a fool to go get himself killed for reasons of revenge, but rescuing his child, he would risk much. I would do the same for any of my children. Throwing his life away heedlessly does not help his boy."

"Grief does a strange thing to a man," Leven said. "Clouds his thoughts."

"We wait until his return," Ishmael said, ending the conversation.

"From what I learned these past two nights," Jarrod said, "that man will turn up. I don't think anything can kill him."

He left the men silent in wonderment at his words.

Jarrod found an empty room with a row of straw beds in the Barracks. The straw didn't smell too moldy, and there were a few old sheets he shook out. Lily clung to Jarrod until he sat down with her on the bed.

"I need to help find your sisters," he said. "So, I need you to be strong and brave, to stay here where you are safe. Elly will help you."

Lily kissed him on the cheek and said, "Bring back 'annah. Bring back Buttercup."

"We will, Sweetie," Jarrod said. He lingered a moment longer, watching Lily curl up next to Elly.

Elly gazed up at him with eyes glassy with tears.

"Azriel, too," she said in a hushed voice. "Keep… keep my Da safe."

Jarrod nodded and left them in the room alone.

Gabriel returned in the gray haze of dawn. Jarrod was on watch with one of Harmen's sons, Carmen, when the horse clomped slowly up the hill to the Barracks with Gabriel swaying on its back.

Thank you, Father, for watching over him, Jarrod prayed.

He smiled and hailed Gabriel.

Gabriel did not return the friendly gesture. Behind him were tied two neatly wrapped bodies. He rode silently through the pickets into the Barracks. Inside, he dismounted, and removed each body with care, refusing assistance.

"Wake everyone up," he said.

"Gabriel," Jarrod said. "You need to rest. You haven't slept and the fighting—"

"They have my son," Gabriel said, turning sharply on Jarrod. "I will not allow them to hurt him anymore."

Jarrod shrank back, feeling the guilt rise once more. Mira and Michael added to an ever-growing list of dead. More weight for him to shoulder. He promised Elly he would watch out for her father. He did as he was instructed, going to each room and waking those who slept. Elly and Lily looked at him, expectantly.

"Soon we will get them," he said. Their disappointment was like salt in his wound.

In the courtyard of the Barracks, Gabriel was giving instructions.

"Two of us will need to scout the Watch Tower. Make certain they are where Fraster said they would be. One reports back while the other follows their movement. Our main force will split. I will lead four of us into the Watch Tower to rescue the children. Harmen will lead the rest on a front assault to distract Thramel."

"I will go inside with you," Ishmael said. Gabriel shook his head.

"You will take Elly and Lily down to the Yellow Valley as planned."

"I am more than an errand boy, Father," Ishmael said, "Let me fight!"

Gabriel continued, ignoring his son.

"Who are my scouts?"

"If I had been at the ford when you were attacked, instead of playing messenger boy," Ishmael said, interrupting. "The children may not be lost and Ma may still be alive."

Harmen turned and grabbed Ishmael by the ear.

"Now you listen up, boy. I will not stand here listening to you disrespect your father—"

"It's alright," Gabriel said. Pain crumpled his face. "Let him go."

Ishmael stalked off into the Barracks.

"Who are my scouts?"

"Me," Jarrod said. When the fighting began, he knew he would not be of much use.

Gabriel studied him for a moment. Jarrod saw him gauge his trust.

"Fine, you take Nell. Stay outside the perimeter. Observe their movements and report back. Both of you come back if Thramel is not there. At midday we approach the tower. Nell will remain to observe movement." Gabriel clenched his fists. "Do not draw attention. I want the children back unharmed."

Watch Tower Hill was the tallest point in Heart Wood. Prince Thomas' invasion of the west was observed from that tower. The diligence of the handful of soldiers alerted Thramel of the invasion, allowing for a hasty defense that prevented Thomas from conquering Heartwood in one day. Although Thomas had burned it after three days of tough battle, the stone foundation remained and it had been re-built at the request of the High Scribe.

Thramel must have influenced that decision, Jarrod marveled at the forethought of the man, plotting revenge before the last bodies cooled from the war.

Half a league from the tower they dismounted and proceeded on foot. The pines thinned south of Watch Tower Hill, giving way to more weepers and creepers. Nell, a short, pudgy fellow with long shaggy hair moved deftly through the terrain. Jarrod tried desperately not to make a sound, but every twig he stepped on seemed loud enough to echo off Watch Tower. Nell stopped often and hissed, grumbling about Jarrod being like bears and pottery shops. Jarrod would apologize quietly. That seemed to set the man off worse.

Weepers and creepers dissipated, becoming tall grass that they crept through, crouched so low that Jarrod's lower back ached. His left arm joined his lower back with burning and itching complaints of its own. Nell held up his hand, motioning for a halt. They had reached the edge of the road. Nell remained still for a long time, head cocked and ear turned to the east.

"What is it?" Jarrod asked, quietly.

Nell glared at him.

After a moment, Jarrod heard the crunch of boots on the dirt road. Nell held up all five fingers, and then added a closed fist with his thumb pointing down. Five soldiers. One scout. How the man knew without being able to see baffled Jarrod. Nell lowered slowly to the ground, until his belly was flat. Jarrod copied him. As soon as he settled down, he heard the footsteps of one person moving along at a deliberate pace. The footfalls stopped right in front of them. Jarrod still couldn't see anyone.

Please let that mean he cannot see us.

The sound of grass rustling told him the man left the road. Then that ceased. It was silent, except for the crunch of approaching boots further away. Jarrod squeezed his eyes shut and willed his heart to beat slower, it sounded loud enough to alert the scout. He imagined his body sinking into the ground so only dirt and grass covered the mound where he lay. Certain that they had been discovered, Jarrod resisted reaching for his sword a moment longer, letting heart beats pass in long stretches. Grass rustled again, the footfalls moving back onto the road. They retreated, sound dissipating up Watch Tower Hill.

Nell climbed onto his hands and knees, peeking over the tall grass. Jarrod crawled towards him, and Nell motioned for him to move to the left. They sat down in the grass. Nell cupped his hand and held it to Jarrod's ear.

"Good news. Someone is home," Nell said, mouth pressed to his cupped hands. "Bad news is there's no way in, except for the front door. Report to Gabriel. Tell him that he needs to reconsider his secondary plan on infiltrating Watch Tower."

Jarrod pressed his own cupped hands to Nell's ear.

"What about the other side?"

Nell shook his head.

Hannah, Kellen, and Azriel were in there. Jarrod considered the spiraling stone structure. It had to be thirty or forty spans up, with at least four floors.

"What can we do?"

Nell moved Jarrod's hand away and repeated the precaution.

"On the other side of the road everything is cleared. No place to hide an attack. They will pick us apart with bows if we try mounting an assault up the hill. During the war, it took an entire army three days to dig the defenders out. We are only a handful in comparison. There won't be anyone left to rescue the children. It's the perfect honey pot to kill a charging bear."

No one can get in. The idea made his heart sink. Gabriel won't stop until they kill him or he gets his son back. Keep my Da safe, Elly had pleaded last night. There was no way he could stop him. None he could think of, except to-

"No way would he listen to me," Jarrod said into cupped hands against Nell's ear. "You need to tell him. Convince him that he needs a new plan. I will watch the army. If they move, I will follow and report back to the Barracks once I know their new destination."

Nell squinted one eye and his mouth puckered in distaste of the idea.

"I know, it's not a part of the plan. The plan has changed, don't you agree?"

Nell thought for a moment. He nodded. Jabbing a finger in Jarrod's chest, he then pointed to the very spot he sat. The message was clear. Stay put. Jarrod nodded, watching Nell slip away as silent as a breeze.

Jarrod plucked at a loose piece of grass and looked at the sky. Gabriel said the assault would begin at midday. He wrapped the blade of grass around his finger. The sun was a quarter of the way to its zenith. He doubted Nell or anyone could convince Gabriel to abandon the attack. In the blackened stone rising from the hilltop, the children awaited their fate. They had to be in there to lure Gabriel here. Some of the blame was on Jarrod. He could have done something to prevent it, if he hadn't been blinded by hate and sorrow.

I can do something now, he dropped the grass and stood up, dusting the dirt from his trousers.

"Manus Poena," he said, and began walking up the hill. No challenge was given, no arrow struck him down. He reached the front gate before being stopped.

"Look at who we got here," Yarl said, prodding Jarrod with the shaft of his spear. "Jerky's come home to roost."

Most of Yarl's teeth were missing or broken: a result of taking a mace to the chin. Scars puckered up and down his jaw line, leaving trails where a beard refused to grow. When he smiled at Jarrod, the cruelty and disgust were emphasized by the scars the way big teeth made a dog's snarl more frightening. Jarrod refused to back down. He shoved the spear shaft out of the way.

"I'm not some trapped hare you got to poke to see if it still lives," Jarrod said. "I have a report for Thramel."

"Oh, do you now?" Yarl asked. "You mean to tell him why you turned traitor on us? To beg for a swift ax to the neck? Why don't you confess to me and I'll go get Stump with his ax."

"You were never a smart one, were you Yarl?" Jarrod said. "I have a report on Gabriel."

"Hey, you watch your tongue before I make it wag on both ends, dirty worm," Yarl said, bringing his spear point up for emphasis. "You ain't getting in without a good reason. If I was you, I would run afore he gets whiff of your smell. You're not on his good list, exactly."

"I made a mistake," Jarrod said. "I'm here to correct it. Whatever punishment he wants to deal out to me, I'll take it."

Yarl hesitated, considered Jarrod and lowered the spear. He retreated back inside the tower's entryway and shouted, "Marly, I got something important down here. I need your orders."

Heavy footfalls approached with the clinking of metal.

"What do you want?" A heavy-set man in an oversized mail shirt asked, lumbering behind Yarl. He stopped upon seeing Jarrod, his mouth dropping open in a stupor. Marly recovered from his surprise and smacked the back of Yarl's head. "Is your head full of dough? Take him in."

"Shouldn't we remove his weapons?"

Marly rolled his eyes, hands clenched to strike again. Yarl cringed. Marly used his thick arm to push Yarl out of the way.

"Hand over your sword belt," Marly said.

Jarrod unbuckled it and gave it to Marly, who tossed it at Yarl. Yarl dropped his spear, catching the sword, but not before the scabbard thumped him on the forehead. He glared at Marly. Marly proceeded to pat Jarrod down. Jarrod cringed as Marly squeezed his injured thigh.

"Hold your hands out," Marly said. He tied a thick twine around Jarrod's wrists. The fibers scratched against his skin. "Now follow Yarl. Careful he don't trip you with his stupidity. Gods' own luck he hasn't run himself through on that spear he carries."

They climbed a spiraling staircase, Yarl in the lead and Marly taking up the rear. On the second floor, Yarl walked into a small room with a square table and three chairs. The walls were bare except for steel plates with hinges that opened up murder holes, places for archers to launch arrows, drop stones, or other projectiles in relative safety. A half-eaten meal of bread and pine nut paste sat in a wooden bowl on the table. Jarrod's stomach rumbled at the sight of it. To make matters worse, Marly sat Jarrod down on the opposite side of the bowl.

"You two get comfortable, while I report to the General," Marly said, lumbering up the spiral staircase.

"General?" Jarrod asked.

"Thramel got promoted," Yarl said.

"From who? He was the highest-ranking officer left alive," Jarrod said. "Did he self-promote his title?"

Yarl sneered. "Why are you really here?"

"I told you already."

"Yeah, but you know what I think." Yarl's sneer became a twisted smile, more horrific than the sneer. "I think you are here for the sweet, pretty flesh we took away. I can see why. Thramel promised us a turn with her, or the younger girl… even the boy."

Jarrod gave him a disgusted look, hoping it hid the relief he felt. *At least I know they are here.*

"Desires of the flesh," Yarl said and laughed. "You're no different. Why else would you throw away what you had with us, if not for the girl? I don't blame you. Ripe flesh ready for plucking." He leaned in close so Jarrod could smell the rot off his teeth.

"How did she feel? All smooth and tight, I say."

Jarrod turned his face away.

Yarl's mouth formed into an O and his eyes widened in a comical expression of surprise. "Oooo, oh ho ho, you didn't. Did you? They say I'm stupid. You, my friend, have showed me up with your sympathizer's soft heart. Soft heart, soft head."

Marly reappeared, wheezing as he climbed off the last step. "Officer on Deck," he said, and then stood at attention.

Yarl jumped up from his chair, snapping off a salute.

Thramel entered the room. Black armor bearing the arms of a hand crushing a serpent on his broad chest made him larger than last Jarrod remembered. A red cape hung off his right shoulder, and a gold emblazoned sword pommel stuck out on his left hip. Thramel had a long, sharp nose and solid blue eyes the color of a sky after a storm. Black gauntlets covered both hands and glistening black boots covered his feet as he stood, filling the room with his greatness.

Jarrod rose. "I would salute, but…" he held up his tied hands.

Yarl hissed. "Show some respect."

"It's fine, Worm. I wouldn't expect anything less from this one," Thramel said. His voice was the deep, rumble of thunder. He moved closer to Jarrod. "Sympathizer, Traitor, why have you returned back to the Manus? Speak wisely your last words, or so they may be as I deem."

"I… I have come to make amends for a mistake I made," Jarrod said. He couldn't keep the tremble out of his voice. He felt the awe of this man to his very core.

Thramel studied him. Jarrod felt sweat drip down the back of his neck. The man's gaze could melt iron.

"Continue," Thramel said.

"I should have… have never strayed from your designs," Jarrod said. "I was wrong in helping the brats escape. I am to blame for our brothers-in-arms losing their lives. It's my fault your plans have been disrupted. As part of my penance, I have information for you."

Jarrod paused, trying to gauge Thramel's expression. He could glean more emotion from a stone.

"What information?"

"Gabriel intends an attack in the early hours of the morning. He believes his son is here and he has the assistance of Harmen to aid in retrieving the boy."

"I have deduced as much. Your information is worthless to me, as are you," Thramel said and began to turn away.

"I will make whatever amends you require to return to the Manus," Jarrod said. Desperation flooded him. He had to keep delaying the inevitability of his death. That was the only way to keep the children alive.

Thramel turned. "You truly desire to return to the Manus?"

"Yes."

"As verification of this, I declare you complete the mission you failed," Thramel said. He signaled to Marly. Marly stood up and disappeared down the stairs. "Upon completion, your reinstatement will be provisionary. You will be assigned a Master soldier, whom you will serve for six full moon tides. After that, your actions during this tenure will be reevaluated based on your performance of service. If performed at a satisfactory level, you will be a full member of the Manus and rewarded according to your rank. Agreed?"

"Agreed," Jarrod said. Resentment rose and he bit it back.

Marly returned, hauling someone behind him. As he stepped aside, Hannah stood there, angrily fighting her bonds. Upon seeing Jarrod, she stopped, and looked questioningly at him.

"You failed once to kill this girl," Thramel said, he pulled his dagger and cut Jarrod's bonds. Taking Jarrod's sword from the scabbard Yarl held, he gave it to Jarrod, hilt first. If Jarrod had been quick and strong like other men, he would have jammed the sword point straight through Thramel's armor. "Finish the task you were assigned."

Jarrod took the sword hilt. He looked at Hannah who realized that Thramel assigned her an executioner. She began to whimper, "No," over and over and "Please" in a child's voice.

"Strike the heart," Thramel said over his shoulder, speaking directly in his ear. "Death is easiest there."

The sword felt like an immovable weight in his hands. The tip pointed at the floor as he watched the tears course down Hannah's checks. Marly had a difficult time holding her in place, until he gripped the girl around her midsection and held her head clamped to his chest, leaving a perfect opening where Jarrod could slide the sword into her heart, ending her struggles and misery. If Gabriel failed in the attack, she was dead anyways. From what Yarl told him, her death would not be easy, her body and spirit tortured. Jarrod held the power to end it quickly, almost painlessly. At least she would not be raped by dozens of men.

"Finish what you started," Thramel urged. "She will die, eventually. Release her from the pains of worry, despair, and torment."

Why not sacrifice her? Maybe I could save Kellen and Azriel.

What about my promise to Lily?

"Do it!" Thramel said, sharply. "Or die with her!"

Jarrod lifted the sword. It was a great, heavy, and encumbering weight. An immovable object. The point touched Hannah's right breast, slicing the fabric where it made contact. She closed her eyes, head shaking, still mouthing no. Jarrod's arm tensed, a simple thrust and it would be over. She would be released.

A horn bleated from the top of the Tower.

Gabriel! His arm relaxed.

Thramel glared at Jarrod.

"Make certain he kills her," Thramel said to Yarl, "If he doesn't, kill them both."

Marly gave Hannah over to Yarl, who grinned, squeezing her young body and grinding his hips into her backside. "Consider it done," he said.

Thramel and Marly hurried down the spiraling stairs. More men followed, metal clanking, curses shouting. Overhead, men began shouting orders. The horn bleated twice more and then stopped. Jarrod wanted desperately to open a murder hole to watch the events unfolding. Hannah whimpered and squirmed.

"Hurry up and stick your sword into this sweet piece of flesh," Yarl said. "There are men out there needing killing."

Jarrod lifted the sword from her chest, looking directly into Hannah's fright filled eyes. She shook her head and moaned "No." Jarrod lined the blade with her chest. Yarl watched eagerly, smiling with hungry delight.

"Forgive me," he said and thrust the sword forward. Hannah screamed. Blood ran down his blade. Yarl gurgled, bloody frothing from his mouth as he stared stupidly at Jared.

Jarrod grabbed Hannah as Yarl's body slumped backwards, sword embedded in his throat. She hugged him, crying against his chest. "Thank you, thank you, thank you."

"Where are your sister and Azriel?"

"Below, in some dark room."

Jarrod took Hannah's hand and led her down the stairs, moving quickly, but alert for soldiers. Before they reached the bottom, Marly came back through the door. He looked at Jarrod and opened his mouth to speak. Then he saw Hannah behind him.

"Should have killed you the moment I laid eyes on you," he said.

"Back up the stairs," Jarrod told Hannah.

Marly lunged at Jarrod, using his bulk to drive his sword. Jarrod blocked him. He retreated up the steps, fending off each powerful blow. The ring of metal echoed off the stone. Finally, Jarrod pinned Marly's sword against the wall and used his right leg to kick the large man, who tumbled down five steps. Jarrod's injured thigh caused him to slip on the stair, striking his tail bone and clicking his teeth together. He stood up just as Marley regained his feet. Jarrod hurried up the stairs, a fire spreading across his leg and hip. They passed men shooting out of murder holes on the third floor. None paid them any attention, engaged in the task at hand.

"In here," Hannah said on the fourth floor. She had entered a small room with a door that opened inward. After Jarrod entered, she shut it.

"There's no way to lock it!" Jarrod searched the room and noticed a desk at the back window. It was made of dense heartwood. He dragged one corner free, digging his heels in as it scraped on the stone. Hannah shoved the other end to help position it faster. Jarrod's back, thigh and tailbone ached and his eyes stung with the salt of his sweat dripping from his forehead by the time it was in place. He saw a fresh bloody bloom on the bandage around his forearm.

Marly bounced off the door, causing the desk to shift. Jarrod braced it with his body, gritting his teeth with each jolt. One of the drawers had opened in the move, and it crashed to the floor next to him. Two parchments bearing broken wax seals slipped to the floor. One seal had part of a snake crushed in a hand—Thramel's arms. The other seal looked to be a halfmoon, or a sun, not one Jarrod recognized. He snatched both parchments up and slipped them into his boot.

The desk jumped again and the door gave a tell-tale groan. It wouldn't hold up much longer.

"Hannah," Jarrod said, "pick up that drawer. I have to move because the door will splinter in half. Step over there, clear of the desk and door. Throw it with all your strength at the first person you see coming in through the door."

Jarrod gritted his teeth against another jolt.

Hannah had the drawer in her hands, standing in the center of the room. She raised it over her head.

"Ready?" She nodded.

Jarrod rolled away from the desk, gathering his feet just as the Malty hit the door again. The frame splintered, driving the door inward, desk and all, until it thudded against the side wall. Red faced and sweaty, Malty righted himself, weapon in hand. The drawer struck him a glancing blow on the right side of his face. Malty had no time to react before Jarrod thrust his blade into the fat man's body, through the joint in the armor under his arm.

"We did it," Hannah said, near tears with fright. Then her eyes widened and she groaned, grasping at an arrow shaft in her side. She collapsed, whimpering.

No! The word screamed inside Jarrod's head. He jumped over Marly's body. At the top of the stairs, a second man was drawing his bow for another shot just as Jarrod, jammed his blade up to the hilt into the man's chest. He yanked the dead body out of the stairwell, hoping not to be noticed. He looked down the stairs for more of Thramel's soldiers to kill. No one else came.

Jarrod stepped over Marly again. Blood spread across the dirty white dress Hannah wore. She sat, holding the arrow shaft and cried. Jarrod knelt beside her.

"Let me see," he said, taking her hands gently off the shaft. It had missed her heart and from the length of the shaft it didn't look deep. She would still bleed out unless he took care of the wound. He needed a knife or something to cut around the arrow "Press here. I know it hurts, but we need to taper the blood flow."

Hannah whimpered, pressing her hands around the wound.

Jarrod found a dagger in Marly's boot. He used it to cut a ragged circle around the arrow shaft.

The tip of the arrow broke the skin on her side.

Another finger length up and it would have hit a lung. Jarrod cut the bottom off her dress up to the knee and sliced it into four strips, creating makeshift bandages.

"This is going to hurt," Jarrod said. He handed a piece of wood he found on the floor. "Bite down on this. Put all the pain here."

As he pushed the arrow into her, Hannah gave a shriek, her jaw clamping down on the wood. Her eyes rolled up. Jarrod got the head of the arrow out enough and cut it off the shaft with the dagger. Carefully he pulled the shaft out from her body. Hannah slumped against his shoulder. Her breathing was shallow. Jarrod lifted the remains of her dress to bunch under her arms. He wrapped her with the strips of bandages, layering and tying them off as tightly as he dared to without cracking her ribs. Then he resettled her dress over her thighs. Blood seeped through the first few layers and continued to expand from a tiny spot to almost the size of his fist.

I need to close these wounds or she'll bleed to death. A large metal sconce stood by a window, but the tapers were unlit.

Jarrod moved to the window, to watch the progress of the battle below. Bodies scattered the ground below, many pierced with multiple arrows. Still objects projected from the murder holes a floor beneath him, striking Harmen's kin and neighbors. Dozens of skirmishes were spread out closer to the tower's base. Gabriel fought below, killing his man just before an arrow struck him in the shoulder. Harmen battled Thramel closer to the Keep's door.

They need my help. Those archers below are picking them apart. Once more he came to a difficult decision. He may not be much of a warrior, but he was all they had. *Blade's Man bless us that I am good enough.*

He checked on Hannah before he left. She was unconscious, but yet breathed. The red blossom grew slower on her bandages. Taking the bow from the dead body in the stairwell, he tested its draw. He pulled the string back to his shoulder, letting it thrum. It would work for him. Shouldering the quiver, he notched an arrow and crept down the stairs.

Six men worked three murder holes. One shot while the other reloaded. Each station had a wooden box with half a dozen full quivers to draw from. They were spaced twenty hands from each other. Jarrod had one shot before they knew he was there. One shot and no one to rescue him this time. Steadying his aim at the center group, he took in a deep breath. The bow shook slightly in his hand. As he released, he knew it was too high. Unexpectedly, the man moved directly into death's path. The arrow struck the base of his skull and he dropped forward with no more than a grunt. His partner turned with surprise. Jarrod had dropped the bow and was running at the soldier.

"Behind—" the man said, his words cut short along with his life. Blood sprayed off the edge of Jarrod's sword as the soldier's body crashed beside his partner's.

The same killer's calm came over him as it had after his father's death. In his mind he was striking down the weeds with his hoe, ripping them up by the roots. His body seemed possessed by someone, or something else. He did not fight it. *Relinquish control,* an inner voice said to him and so he did.

Jarrod swiveled, moving towards the team on his left. His sword knocked the first man's bow aside, causing the shot to go wild. Swinging his sword back around, he caught the man under the chin, driving the sword point through his skull. It stuck. Jarrod released the hilt and reached for the weapon at the man's hip. As he bent down, an arrow thrummed over his head from behind. He drew the sword and went after the soldier in front of him.

The soldier had abandoned his bow and held a dagger in his hand. Jarrod lunged at him and the man side-stepped, dragging the blade across Jarrod's exposed ribs. Jarrod felt a distant burn in his mind, but ignored it. He feigned his next attack and waited for the man to sidestep again. As he did, Jarrod's weapon took the man's hand off at the wrist. The man screamed, holding his bleeding stump.

A sharp pain bit into his right calf. Jarrod stumbled, knocking the wounded man over. Jarrod tried to get up, but the arrow in his calf stopped him from rising. Another thud and fire exploded into his left thigh. Jarrod pulled Marly's dagger. He threw it at the soldier in front, hitting him in the chest. He fell to the side, knocking his partner's aim. The arrow went stray, embedding into the corpse of the second man Jarrod had killed.

Jarrod forced himself to his feet, once more shoving the pain to the back of his mind. He hobbled towards the last of Thramel's soldiers standing in the room. The man swung at Jarrod with the bow. Jarrod cut the wood with his sword. Before he could draw another weapon, Jarrod fell on top of him.

"Blade's Man's fury! What are you?" The man's eyes were wide in awe.

"Manus Poena," Jarrod said, bringing his blade down into the man's chest.

He struggled to get up, and felt something thump into his back. Once more there was pain and a distant weight on his shoulders. A blade yanked free and Jarrod twisted away. He saw the one-handed man holding a blade ready to plunge it back into him.

"I got you now," the man said, laughing hysterically.

Jarrod took his sword from the corpse next to him, and as the one-handed man came down at him, the soldier drove himself onto the sharp point. Hot blood gushed out of the man's mouth, splashing Jarrod's face.

Before the room went dark, Jarrod thought, this was a good death.

"Death? You long for death now?" A strange voice asked, sounding close to mocking.

Jarrod squinted his eyes against a bright, white light. He saw a blurry shape of a man outlined by the light. The man approached, wearing black scaled armor emblazoned with two swords crossed at the midriff. A black helm covered his face, the visor closed. The hilts of two long swords stuck out from his left hip.

"N…no," Jarrod said. "I long for peace."

"I guess death is a long-term peace, unless you are called on to be my servant," the man said.

"Who are you?" Jarrod asked, although he had a good idea who this figure represented. "Why would I serve you?"

"Ingratitude is not good payment for one's assistance."

The white light faded, revealing a dark green glade in the middle of seven large stones. This was the Circle of Gods. This was where men or women sat in judgment once the spirit left the body. Jarrod noticed he sat in the Defendant's stone chair. It felt like a vivid dream, lucid as though he drank weeping bark. He could smell the sweet taint of death-bell blossoms and hear the buzz of carrion beetles flying outside the circle. The stone chair was hard against his flesh. Jarrod tried to stand up, but his body refused to obey his commands.

"Assistance?" Jarrod asked. He almost said, *I feel more like a prisoner.* He doubted it would aid his cause.

"How else do you think a gardener killed six armed men?"

"Desperation."

"Desperation." The man weighed the word, considering its value. "Yes, desperation does open the door for us to walk through."

"Once more I was only a tool," Jarrod said, unable to disguise his disgust.

"We are all tools. Some are better honed for specific tasks than others."

"Now my value is over, am I to be discarded?"

"No." The man laughed. "No more than a sword should be thrown away because a war ends. It can be reforged to suit the nature of the time. Besides, why assume your value is over?"

"I am here."

"Yes, you are here, but for a different reason than most," the man said. "Foremost, I must inform you that your decision to defend innocence is the reason I do not forsake you. You are not here to have your guilt judged. Nor are you released from the responsibility you shouldered."

"What do you mean?"

"You are yoked to your duty," the man said. "As am I. Hilt to blade."

"I don't understand."

"You shall," the man said. The bright, white light returned, enveloping the Circle of Gods. The man turned and walked towards the light. "Rest, Jarrod. Every warrior must heal before the waves of war crash upon him again."

"I am no warrior," Jarrod said, anger rising. *A tool, nothing more than a tool for gods and men.* "I am just a gardener."

No reply came.

"I'm no warrior!" He shouted to white light, helplessly restrained in the stone chair. "I'm a gardener!"

Jarrod woke up in a place much different than he remembered. He had expected hard stone and green grass, or at least the stone walls of the Watch Tower. Instead, soft light shone through the canvas of a tent. He felt warm. Fur blankets covered him and he was nude beneath, except for the bandages that wrapped his body. He tried to move, but his body ached all over. Pain was the body's way of reminding you that you still lived, his father often said before the war. What about misery? Was that the soul telling him he was still around, that his usefulness had yet expired?

Did I do any good at all?

Jarrod laid there in a heap, wallowing in sorrow.

"You're awake?" Gabriel asked.

"Either that or we are dead," Jarrod said. The dull ache in his back told him otherwise.

"Last time I thought you were awake, you screamed in my face and tried to claw my eyes out," Gabriel said, and laughed. "I learned my lesson."

"What about Hannah?" Jarrod asked. He remembered the red blossom spreading on her bandages and held little hope.

"She lives," Gabriel said. "Once again, because of you. Azriel and Kellen were found, too."

"So if I am here, alive, I guess Thramel was defeated."

"No."

"Where is he?"

"He ran off as soon as the battle turned against him. Whatever you did in Watch Tower, killing nine men on your own, it helped us outside. Once the arrows stopped falling, we overran Thramel's defenses. He took off running."

"I found some writings in the Tower. I think they were his."

.ey were. We took them from your boot. Thramel was being paid by
ɔ sow dissent in Heartwood Pines."

no is Joanna?"

Half-sister of Alfred and Thomas. She has an army ready to march on us
.d take our lands."

Jarrod closed his eyes. Another war. More fighting, more death.

Yoked, hilt to blade.

"What are the plans?" Jarrod tried to sit up.

Again, his body refused.

"No, my friend. Your part in this fight is over," Gabriel said, placing a cool
hand on his chest to keep him from struggling. "Harmen is raising the cry for
arms now. We will have plenty of defenders to beat back her assault. Even the
pine bends in the fierce winds."

Jarrod wanted to tell him what he saw. Tell him all about the Blade's Man
and his proclamation that Jarrod was not yet released from his duty. It sounded
like a fever dream, but it was real, wasn't it?

"What am I to do?"

"You will join Ishmael with the children in Yellow Valley. We must
persevere as a people."

A full moon passed as Jarrod and Hannah healed. Gabriel gave Jarrod a
map and three horses. No protests, no more delays. Jarrod led the children in
an exodus to Yellow Valley. The journey wasn't long and after four sun turns,
they arrived at the place Gabriel had marked just as the sun was rising on the
green grass and flowers.

"Jarwed! Jarwed!" Lily cried upon seeing him. She was outside playing in a
field of yellow poppies, and white lilies. She ran to him, throwing her arms
around his neck and kissing him on the cheek. "You brought them! Annah and
Buttercup!"

Her laughter and smiles lightened his heart so much he hadn't realized how
the impending clouds of war darkened it.

"As promised," Jarrod said, hugging her back. Elly hugged him after Lily left
to clamp onto Hannah and Kellen.

"Da?" she asked, trepidation in her voice and hope in her eyes.

"He is well," Jarrod said.

"Thank you," Elly replied, hugging him again.

Ishmael came out of the small house cut into the eaves of stone, a smile o his face.

"What news from my father?" he asked.

"We are to stay here," Jarrod said. He looked over the Yellow Valley, hidden between the Mountains of Dawn and Dusk. "We will persevere."

About the Author

Matthew Johnson is a graduate of the MFA Creative Writing program at University of Riverside Palm Desert. He has published fantasy short stories in "The Blackest Knights," "Blackest Spells," and "Beyond the Shadows" anthologies, *Lazarus Rising* a zombie play, and is currently working on a Fantasy and Horror novel. His second play *Wooing the Dragon* is in production for Summer of 2023. He resides in Riverside California with his wife, director and actress Wendi Johnson, and his three lovable puppies. You can find more about his works at **www.professorgrimdark.com**.